SONS of THUNDER

The *Brothers in Arms* Collection

SONS of THUNDER

SUSAN MAY WARREN

The *Brothers in Arms* Collection

Summerside Press™
Minneapolis 55438
www.summersidepress.com
Sons of Thunder

ISBN 978-1-935416-67-8

Scripture references are from the following sources:
The Holy Bible, King James Version (KJV).

All characters are fictional. Any resemblances to actual people are purely coincidental.

Cover design by Müllerhaus Publishing Group | www.mullerhaus.net and by Steve Gardner | PixelsWorks Studios.

Interior design by Müllerhaus Publishing Group.

Summerside Press™ is an inspirational publisher offering fresh, irresistible books to uplift the heart and engage the mind.

Printed in USA.

EPIGRAPH

For Your glory, Lord

AUTHOR'S NOTE

It's every author's dream to have one of her favorite editors call and say, "Will you write me a story?" Uh, yes! And especially wonderful is when, months earlier, God has already dropped a story in that author's heart to simmer.

See, I was on a plane to Florida, and as I sat down, my seatmate was on his cell phone, speaking another language. I admit I was curious (some may call it nosy). So, I asked him what language he was speaking. Greek—and he was talking to his father who was an immigrant from Greece. And it got better—his grandfather was also an immigrant, and had fought in World War II, while his wife raised their children in Greece. But that wasn't all. There was an uncle involved, and family scandal and…hmm…interesting. This poor man graciously answered a thousand questions during our two-hour flight, and seeded in my heart a story about two Greek brothers who loved the same woman.

By the time I arrived at my friend Rachel's house, I had the entire plot worked out. Now, I just had to wait—until Susan Downs asked me to write it.

Thus, *Sons of Thunder* was born. I have long desired to write books set in the World War II era. Such a heroic, courageous time filled with heroes and epic romance, tales of hope and redemption. (Not to mention the amazing music and dress styles—oh, I was born in the wrong era!) More than that, as I've had the privilege of traveling the world and meeting amazing people from other countries, I've realized that many, many Christians fought in the war on both sides—British, Russians, Dutch, French, Americans—even Germans. Brothers united by a common lineage in Christ forced to pick up arms to fight in a war they may or may not have believed in, but because they were patriots for their country. My vision is to write stories from around the globe of heroes from all nationalities. I call it the Brothers in Arms collection.

As I searched for the theme for *Sons of Thunder*, Psalm 103:1–5 kept coming back to me—specifically this question: what does deliverance look like? I think, in our world, we want answers immediately. But the heroes from the Greatest Generation understood that sometimes deliverance doesn't happen overnight. Sometimes they had to fight for it, hold on to it, open their eyes to see it. I wanted to paint a picture of deliverance—forgiveness, healing, redemption, and mercy—and give it room to work out in the lives of my characters. I believe deliverance is something that happens over time, if we are willing to wait for it and hold on to it through the darkness.

I pray this story encourages you to see God's hand, delivering you through forgiveness, healing you of your diseases, and showing you His great compassion.

God delivered me through this book through the encouragement of so many friends. I'm deeply grateful to Carlton Garborg and the folks at Summerside for believing in me and this idea. And I'm so thrilled to work with Susan Downs, my editor. Her wisdom and friendship help me grow as a writer and a person, and I'm overjoyed to be able to continue to write books with her. I couldn't write a book without my writing partner, Rachel Hauck, who is on the other end of the telephone every day when I call and start with "what happens next?" And I'm deeply indebted to Ellen Tarver, long-time missionary buddy turned amazing editor (whom I call my secret weapon). Her tireless hours and attention to detail helped me get it as close to right as I could. Thank you also to Janelle Ashley, a ray of sunshine in my life, and her friend Dean, who stepped in and to help us on our journey to find the right cover.

Of course, I couldn't write a book without my family. A huge thank-you goes to my son David, who plotted this book in detail with me during a fun ride home from college. And hugs to Sarah and Peter and Noah for cheering me on. Finally, I'm the luckiest woman in the world to be married to my amazing husband, Andrew, who cooks dinner and sends me back to my office when I stare at him blankly (clearly still writing in my head) and helps me figure out how to winch wine casks from a cave, or "what a guy might feel when"...and is my biggest fan. I love him more every day.

Thank you, too, to my readers, who encourage me and who said, when I mentioned writing a World War II novel...do it! Thank you for your enthusiasm. And thank you for reading. May you see God's deliverance in your life.

In His grace,
Susan May Warren

PART ONE
Markos

CHAPTER 1

Markos Stavros would not go to war on the eve of his brother's wedding.

Even if he wanted to murder his best friend.

"Lucien! Come up!" Markos hung with one hand to the mast of his skiff, the pomegranate red hull of his fishing boat a sufficient buoy should Lucien need underwater navigation.

Of course, Lucien had to pick *now* to detour their trip back to their village on the crisp shore of Zante Island, just off the coast of Greece. And with a catch in their nets too. A glance at the bleeding horizon suggested his mother might be waiting for him with a sharpened tongue. *Markos, do you care nothing for your brother's nuptials?*

Apparently, the wind cared nothing for cooperation, either, dying to a trickle, leaving the skiff to barely list upon the smooth Ionian Sea. Perhaps it hadn't helped that the elusive yet delicious *barbouni* had played the sea nymph, unwilling to be captured in the heat of such a glorious day. The red-mulleted delicacy flopped, angry and zealous, in the live-well of the boat's stern, the mustard yellow nets in a tumble at the bow.

"Lucien!" Markos hung over the side, searching for his friend's porpoise body. He glanced at his brother, fourteen-year-old Dino, leaning over the edge of the boat, peering into depths so clear the algae-mopped rocks appeared within grasp, the sand, scurried up by sardines and shrimp, a puff of crystalline magic. "I swear he did this on purpose.

Theo was right. Lucien is a Pappos, and his big brother probably put him up to ruining the wedding dinner."

A wedding from which Markos and Dino just might be banned if they arrived home with rancid fish.

Dino shook his head. "No, Lucien wouldn't do that, even if Kostas asked him to. He loves Theo. He doesn't care about romance or Zoë Ramone and her father's olive groves."

"No, but he cares about his brother. And Kostas doesn't forgive easily. He'll not soon forget how Theo stole his bride—even after their betrothal. Not to mention the lost dowry that Zoë would have given the Pappos family. Yannis Pappos has his eye on a new fishing boat."

"Or a keg of *retsina*." Dino grinned, his teeth white against his bronzed skin. Under the wine-soaked sky, he appeared every inch the ruddy fisherman's son, a younger, reedy version of Markos, with his salt-slicked skin, a dark shank of hair tumbling over his eyes.

Maybe Dino was right. What did a fisherman's family want with an olive grove?

But Kostas—and nearly every other man in the village of Zante—certainly pined over brown-eyed Zoë, with her sun-dipped skin, her black-as-the-sultry-night hair. And Theo, in his drunken singing during last night's embarrassing party, only turned the knife in Kostas's open wound as he sang of his devotion (while emptying the family's supply of retsina and inviting all of the three hundred souls in Zante to the feast). It didn't help that his singing bore the edge of triumph, a conquest won.

No, Lucien probably hadn't given one errant thought to Theo Stavros's nuptials when he'd yelled, *I have to catch it!* and vanished over the side of the boat, slicing through the turquoise water after a dewy-eyed loggerhead turtle.

Lucien then disappeared, of course, into the maw of the white-washed caves that tumbled from the cliffs straight into the sea.

Indeed, the sea beckoned, the azure blue nearly hypnotic with its lure, and on a different day, Markos, too, might have surrendered to the chase. After all, he'd been bred for the taste of salt on his chapped lips.

Not today. "Lucien!"

Dino stepped up, a bare foot curled around the edge of the boat.

"Dino—you're not going after him. You're not strong enough—the waves will smash you against the opening."

"I'm not afraid, Markos."

Markos put warning into his eyes. "It's too dangerous."

How Markos hated Whistler's Drink.

Even if Dino managed to swim into the puckered lips of the cavern, the cave had already begun to fill and soon would engulf the escape, perhaps purge any air supply from the deep veins inside. Moreover, once inside, the cauldron could grab Dino's lanky body and thrash it against the rocks. Worse, legend spoke of tunnels that channelled inland, emerged into the lush olive groves overlooking the city, and enticed young divers to lose their lives in the twisted channels.

"I know he went into the caves—I'm going after him." Dino poised now on the boat's rim, one hand on the mast for balance, his eyes shining.

"No."

"I'll be right back!" As slick as a sardine, Dino sliced the water, a clean dive to the bottom of the sea.

"Dino!" But the boy was a fish, and slipped away, toward the over-hanging tongue of rock that lapped the water.

Why couldn't his brother see Lucien's fate? He worshiped the too-bold Pappos boy, tracking his footsteps through the golden sand, taunting crabs, swimming under the docks, despite Markos's warning. Didn't Dino see Lucien's reckless grin, the way he always teased danger, arms open in a dive, the wind in his face, a wildness in his dark-as-olive eyes? Someday Lucien would find himself in too deep to surface, maybe even drag one of the Stavros brothers down with him.

Not today.

Markos speared the water. The cool lick of it scooped his breath, slicked from his body the heat of the day.

He surfaced fast, gulped air, and dove back to the ocean floor, kicking toward the cave. A deep thrumming rumbled his bones even as he scrabbled over the slippery rock outside the entrance. The jaws raked his skin as he levered himself through a crevice just big enough for a boy of seventeen.

Just as his lungs begged to open, he surfaced hard and drank in the clammy air. Punctures of light from holes in the walls above illuminated enough of the cave to make out its yawning expanse. Of course, he'd been here before, too many times—most of them on the trail of Lucien, who explored these caves with too much abandon. Still, a shiver found his bones in the oily water, as the shadows pressed upon him. Here, in the gullet of the cave, creatures slithered along the bottom, sharks found hibernation, and an unprepared swimmer might be swallowed into the murky gullet of the mountain.

"Lucien! Dino! Are you here—"

A tentacle tightened around his ankle—yanked him under.

No! He thrashed, frenzied, and connected with flesh.

He broke free and surfaced so fast he slammed his head on the overhanging cave wall. Panic sent him back to the bottom. His head burned. This time his feet found purchase on the jagged wall and he shot out into the foamy whirlpool in the center of the cave. He surfaced again and accidentally inhaled the malt collected from the sea.

Laughter, sharp, high, ricocheted against the walls of his tomb. "You're a squid, Markos! I think you blackened my eye."

Markos pressed his hand to the hot spot on his head. His eyes hadn't yet adjusted, and his lunch of chilled *garides* slid up his throat. "Lucien!" He gulped back a curse. "You could have killed me."

"Aw, naw—I would have rescued you."

"I don't need your rescuing!" Markos lunged for Lucien's spiny outline, now pale in the darkness. His fist closed around water. "Where's Dino?"

"Dino?" Splashing. "Dino!" Lucien's singsong voice echoed in the cave. "Oh, Dino!"

"I'm here, brother!" Dino's adolescent voice reverberated close, laden with humor.

Then, again, hands clutched Markos's leg. Tugged him under.

He kicked out hard, clunked something solid. The grip released.

Treading water, Markos surfaced. "Dino?"

The waves rushed through the gap in the rock, slammed against the unseen epiglottis deep inside, thundered, then sprayed over him.

"Lucien?"

Nothing. "Dino! Lucien!"

He circled the cave—dove, scrabbling for a hand, a foot.

Nothing. He treaded water, listening, hearing only the thunderous gulp of the cave. Only felt the darkness pressing into his pores. Only tasted the brackish water that filled his lungs, pressing him to the bottom, unseen.

He dove again, hating his brother for the fear that burned through him.

How many times had he and Dino played hide and seek—certainly amidst the fishing boats in the bay in front of his family's taverna and, of course, around the ruins of the sunken ship caught in the white shoals, but—

"Dino, this isn't funny!"

He dove again, burned his lungs scouring the bottom of the cavern for his brother. Why wasn't Lucien here, helping, why?

He caught his hands on the side of the cave wall, hanging there, breathing hard. The sun had dwindled to a trickle of hope in the cave. "Dino!"

Maybe Dino had floated farther, back into the network of arteries. His little brother possessed a curiosity that frightened Markos, something in his eyes that told him someday Markos's sharp word wouldn't be enough to save him.

He let the current urge him toward the now-submerged opening to the tunnels. He hung on to the lip, letting his legs drift inside. Perhaps it opened into another escape hatch, maybe—

A wave slammed him against the rocks, sheering skin off his chest.

With a curse he dove toward the mouth of the cave, riding the current as it spilled back out to the sea. He gouged his leg as he kicked through the maw, fighting as the wave recoiled, clawing him back toward the cave.

Diving deeper, below the tug of the current, he kicked out, to the blue-skied sea.

The water had darkened, filled with shadow. Beyond the grip of the wave, he banked his feet on a ledge and launched to the surface. Air, quick and sharp, caught him. He sucked it in. Bobbing, breathing in hard.

"Markos! Where've you been?"

He wiped the water from his eyes, blinking fast against the amber sun.

Sitting astride the skiff, feet dabbling the water, Lucien lounged back on his hands, laughing, his dark hair long and sculled by the wind. "Did you find the turtle?"

Beside him, a towel around his neck, Dino grinned.

Markos clutched the edge of the boat, a roil of darkness choking off the hot relief.

Lucien pulled his legs in, stood, and hooked one hand on the mast, the sun in his smile, a sort of victory in his eyes. The other hand he held out to Markos. "We were just having some fun. Didn't mean to scare you."

Dino's eyes shone, an innocence in them that absolved him. Clearly, he hadn't yet caught on to the game.

The one between Lucien and Markos, with Dino as the prize.

The final blade of sun edged the horizon, turning the sea to blood. The wind had returned, adding chop to the waves.

The skiff bobbed, even as Markos dove for Lucien's hand, snagged it. For a moment, he braced his feet on the edge of the boat, his hand squeezing Lucien's. Lucien's knuckles folded inside it. His other hand whitened around the mast. His smile vanished. Almost imperceptibly he nodded, his olive black eyes darkening, acquiescing.

"Really, Markos, we're sorry. We were just having fun."

Of course they were. Because Lucien would do just about anything to escape the sorrow of his birth. The grief of an infant left to nourish upon his widower father's bereft anger. The terror of living under the scrutiny of a father who still fought the Turks, mostly in his sleep, except when it spilled out into the day, the taste of wine only riling his demons.

Yes, Markos understood that Lucien longed for someone—even a younger brother—to lure, to trick, to amaze.

Markos released his feet, bobbing in the water. Lucien hauled him aboard.

He tumbled into the bottom of the skiff. Lucien towered over him, his shadow pressing across Markos, cool to his already prickled skin. Now he cast upon him a smile, white teeth against his amber face, a hint of warmth nudging into his expression. Markos made out the foreshadow of a bruise on Lucien's face—probably his foot on Lucien's cheekbone. He winced at his own violence. How many times had Lucien shown up with the history of his father's fists imprinted on his body?

Markos cast a look at Dino dripping water onto the skiff's belly. His younger brother shivered, his eyes now absent their humor. "Sorry, Markos."

With each slowing breath, the anger uncoiled. Especially since Lucien held out his hand, seasoning the gesture with a look of chagrin. "Friends?"

Markos closed his eyes. Inside the caress of the Ionian Sea, with twilight skimming his face, his older brother poised on the eve of his marriage—today was not a day for war.

Friends?

"No, Lucien—brothers." Always.

CHAPTER 2

Sofia Frangos could save the world with her song. At least Markos's world, because that's what always seemed to occur whenever he happened upon her in time to catch the melodies issuing from her as she worked.

More of a humming than a song, really, and he longed for the words, feeling they'd be plucked from some garden inside her. Someday, perhaps.

Yes, he felt a voyeur, but he couldn't resist the lure of her voice. Probably, she knew her power—felt his hypnotized presence, although her blue eyes never appeared to notice him.

Someday, he hoped, she would see the ruddy fisherman's son.

The sun spilled into the sea by the time Markos moored his boat and retrieved his catch. He nodded to the other fishermen repairing their nets along the wharf, others simply smoking away the twilight.

"What is your catch?" Alexio Mizrahi, the Jewish doctor, sat with his son-in-law as he worked his nets.

"Barbouni—for Theo's wedding!" Markos lifted the lid to the metal canister of fish, noticed the smiles of older, more accomplished fishermen.

Surely he'd earned his father's toast at tomorrow's feast.

"Someday you will be a fisherman such as your father, Markos."

He let Alexio's words buoy his step, despite the late hour.

Sofia's song lured him as she stood, elbow deep in flour, kneading the dough for tomorrow's wedding bread. Her dark hair whisked back into a lanyard, tiny unheeded curls dripped around her face.

For a moment, he imagined that he wasn't the son of a fisherman, wasn't marked with the scratches from squid barbs, his hands coarse from tying the nets, his face darkened with the fury of the sun. No, he fancied himself a merchant, a man of means, who might be worthy of such a girl as Sofia.

Not that his mother would agree. After all, Sofia was little more than an orphan, thanks to the Turks, who'd felled her father on the shores of Sangarios, and to illness, which took her mother during those dark years. No family, no dowry, no *koumbaro* to stand beside her groom as a witness. Only her aging grandfather—and not even a real relation at that, being that he'd taken in her father when he was a child—to claim her. The village of Zante had predestined Sofia, even at fourteen, as their next midwife, or perhaps a taverna keeper.

Sofia's graceful fingers began to roll the dough into a long strip, ready to braid, to form the decorative flowers and stars. She'd already worked the aniseed, coriander, and fennel into the speckled dough. The piquant smells of roasting lamb, fresh onions, tomatoes, and baked figs awakened an animal in Markos's stomach. He sucked in his breath, willing himself invisible as he stood in his mother's taverna, the metal canister of barbouni slung over his shoulder, dripping seawater onto the stone floor.

"Markos, where have you been?"

He jerked, stepped back from the doorway, rounding as his mother, her black skirt gathered, stepped up from the portico of the taverna. Behind her, the wooden tables were arrayed in a sort of semi-circle, appropriate for the dance floor. Today, this moment, Ava Stavros appeared every bit the mother of the groom, lines of tradition worked into her brow, her long dark hair caught back in a black scarf, an apron around her sturdy form. She knew the sea, her men, and how to build a home on the golden sands. "I expected you hours ago."

"We got caught in the doldrums, Mama. I'm sorry. But I caught your barbouni." He slung the keg off his shoulder and plunked it down at her feet. The water dribbled from the holes, seawater darkening the white stones.

"That's my Markos." She caught his face in her hands, pressed a kiss to each cheek. "Just like your father. You are destined to be the best fisherman in the family." She opened the lid. The red-hooded fishes lay, some still flopping, in a sleek pile. "Brava! Carry it to the kitchen—Sofia will scale them."

Sofia barely looked up as he carried in the catch. The heat of the wood-fired ovens ripened his sea-dog odor, and he tried not to get too close as he set the kettle down near the table, wincing at his own oafish presence.

She moved to open the lid, and he collided with her as he stood up.

"Oh!" She held her nose, turning away.

"Are you okay?"

He only made out her blue eyes watering as she nodded.

"I'm sorry!"

She turned, shaking her head. "No, it's my fault." She offered him the smile that could sweep thoughts from his head. Indeed, he stood there like a fool, drinking in her eyes, the way the sun had tinted her nose, the beautiful sweep of her lips. And, as if he might already be inside his wildest dreams, she moved forward. "Actually, I need to talk to you. My grandfather is—"

"Out of my taverna, Markos." His mother lumbered into the kitchen.

Sofia cut off her words and turned away.

Mama shot her a dark look then turned to Markos. "This is not your place. Go—find your brothers. I'm sure Theo needs an airing out after last night's performance." She winked at him, grabbing up a towel and a knife.

But Markos's mind hung on Sofia's sentence—Her grandfather is…? Giving her hand away in marriage? Dying? Markos longed to scoop the words from her, hating how urgent they'd suddenly become.

But Sofia had already resumed her humming.

He chased his ego out, not looking back.

* * * *

Sofia's song twined through his thoughts—through the wedding preparations, down the street the next day during the groom's procession. Indeed, it seemed the entire village had accepted Theo's invitation—propelled, most likely, by curiosity, since Kostas, Zoë's spurned suitor, joined the groom's march.

Lucien lurked somewhere behind in the crowd—Markos caught occasional glimpses of him even as they tramped through the cobbled streets, past the white-washed stone homes, scattering the wandering goats with their tinkling bells, through to the town square with the fountain, the bird's-egg blue dome of the Orthodox church, right to the front steps where Kostas stopped to await his bride. Clad in his only clean shirt, a pair of wool pants, and a multi-colored vest, Markos sweltered in the sun beside Dino, Kostas, and their father, Galen, broad-chested and resplendent in his threadbare—and only—suit. "Do you think Father will allow me a glass of retsina?" Dino whispered, as the women appeared, beautiful Zoë flanked by her widower father in the bridal procession.

"Shh—no, of course not. It's for the guests."

"I'm a guest."

"You're annoying."

Dino made to stomp him on the foot, but Markos sidestepped him.

There—on the edge of the procession—Sofia. Like the rest of the unmarried women in the village, she wore a twined headpiece of ivy, ornamented with orange blossoms, little white stars. For a moment, his breath slicked out, remembering her face yesterday twisted in pain at his clumsiness. But today she shone, her blue eyes matching her simple dress, gathered at the waist. Then again, she would be beautiful in a kitchen apron, smudged with flour—

"There's Lucien!"

Dino's voice yanked Markos's attention from Sofia, to where Lucien sat on the cart attired to pull the couple from the church to the family taverna for the wedding feast. He wore the cap of the driver low over his face, but Markos made out a scandalous smile.

Not today, Lucien. Still, his friend struck a comical pose, standing on the seat of the carriage and dancing a mock *tsamiko.* A few of the women began to giggle.

"Fool," Galen muttered, his voice low. "Always playing the trouble-maker."

Theo only had eyes for Zoë. Radiant, with her waist-long hair down under a flowing red veil, a matching ornamented dress swishing along the cobblestone center square. Her father marched at her side, her hand tucked in the crook of his arm. A small man, with narrow shoulders and a tiny paunch, he might have looked younger had life not stolen his wife before she bore him more children. Thus, he guarded Zoë like a treasure, his surrender to Theo Stavros most likely won by Ava Stavros's attention, delivering meals from the taverna over the years.

Markos—and the rest of Zante—wasn't blind to the way Zoë's father eyed Markos's mother. Some even whispered that Ava Stavros, a foreigner from Athens and educated in literature at the university, might be more suited for a man of his station.

But Ava's devotion belonged to Galen. Now she smiled at him, dressed in her finest blue dress, a lacey white scarf bridling her dark hair. The Ionian blue topaz ring, the one she kept hidden behind her bed in a notch in the wall, sparkled in the sunlight.

Today, indeed, was a special event.

Theo clutched Zoë's flowers—a bouquet from Mama's rose bushes. His forehead wept.

Markos pinned his eyes on Sofia and imagined the day when he would stand in the sun, holding roses, sweating.

The church should have been cool, with its soaring, frescoed ceilings, but the smell of incense stifled the air, and the heat of too many witnesses hastened the priest's recitation of the prayers, the biblical tale of the wedding feast at Cana, the presentation of the Stefanos crowns with the circle round the altar....

The grand pronouncement of Theo and Zoë's future.

They exited the church with a collective exhale. Thankfully, Lucien had abdicated his position to the hired driver. Markos searched for him, but he had vanished.

For their eldest son, the Stavroses laid out tables of *moussaka*, stuffed zucchini, and roasted potatoes. Giant red lobsters and grilled barbouni, fried *kalamarakia* and sardines baked in tomato sauce and oregano, boiled *hortas* with lemon, and green beans steamed from their plates, amidst fresh tomatoes, cucumbers, onions. Another table served honeydew melons, honey-soaked baklava, almond cookies, figs, and of course, sugared walnuts. Barrels of wines, unearthed, perhaps, from the cellars of the Ramone family—for the Stavros supply of retsina had gone to buy the favor of the village the night before—lay stacked on their sides, ready to be tapped.

A hired musician played the *bouzouki*, the strings of the small guitar sounding tinny against the stone floor, as Zoë and Theo stomped out their first dance. A *floyera* player stood up, his shepherd's whistle bobbing to time.

Still, no Lucien.

Kostas, however, sulked on the perimeter of the dance floor, his dark eyes fixed upon the couple, clutching a glass of wine, nursing his second, perhaps more—Markos didn't want to count. He wore a granite expression, although occasionally he raised his glass, shouted with the crowd.

Next to Markos, Dino had filled his plate with enough to feed a pack of wild jackals. "You know you will be sick."

Dino picked up a shrimp, dangled it towards Markos. Markos looked away and found Sofia, sitting with a knot of girls. She glanced over at him, gave him a whisper of a smile—

"Time to dance the *Kaslamantiano.*" Papa appeared at the table, whisking a hand across Markos's back. Whoops and clapping drove the musicians' beat, the tempo increasing. His father moved to the next table, urging his guests to the dance floor, to join in the hand-to-hand circle.

Markos timed his movements and caught his hand into Sofia's soft, yet strong hand. She tightened her hold on his, and for a blinding second, he again wished for merchant's hands instead of his—rough-cut, callused, and reeking of the sea. But she looked up at him, her smile in her eyes. Then the music started, and he fell into the dance.

Round and round, faster and faster. Slow step to the right, quick step right with the left foot, quickstep right with the right foot, repeat. Markos counted out the steps in his head, watching Theo lead them around the portico. Slow step backward with the right foot, quickstep backward with the left, quick weight shift—

Kostas broke into the crowd, grabbing a hand, the other balancing his glass. Something about his exuberance sent a ripple into the circle, the embarrassment of watching a man suffer.

Markos could even smell Sofia, something floral, the orange blossoms and the hot Ionian sun baked into her skin. Maybe he would ask her to take a walk with him across the moon-dappled sand to his boat. Maybe he would tell her that someday they would have their own Kaslamantiano dance, and he would hold her bouquet of Mama's roses—

With a shout, Kostas dove into the center of the floor, twisting and turning in an erratic solo as he danced—no, leered, Markos decided—at Zoë, then grinned like a shark at Theo.

Drunk. Of course. Like father, like son.

Zoë blanched. Some of the dancers stopped, although the music played on, tinny and quick.

"Kostas, go home," Theo said, still trying to reclaim the night, moving to shield Zoë. Despite his smile, a sharpness edged his tone, his eyes stony.

Kostas danced over to a table. "We're still celebrating." He picked up a plate, and with a flick, threw it to the floor. It smashed, a thousand white shards spraying the stones. Sofia jerked back, her hand over her face. The music stopped.

"Go home," Theo said again, advancing on the man, his hand around Kostas's wrist before Kostas could pick up another plate.

Kostas jerked his wrist from Theo's grasp, his face hard.

Go home, Kostas. Markos drew Sofia close.

For a moment, everyone stilled, as if drawing a breath. Beyond the taverna, the sea clawed at the shore, a storm in the wind, the chilly breath snaking into the party.

Kostas threw down his glass. It exploded against the stone floor. "You're a thief, Theo Stavros!" Kostas glared at Zoë. "And you're a harlot."

"That's enough, Kostas." Galen stepped across the floor, two giant steps, voice solemn, but enough to thunder. "You are not welcome here."

Hours later, Markos still fought to sort it out. He wanted to will it all into stone, something he could snatch and fling away into the night.

Perhaps if he'd been faster, slipped up beside his father, taken Kostas's blow on his own chest…

Heeded the impulse inside.

Because, in the sliver of time between Galen's words and Kostas's attack, Markos knew. He heard it—a warning, or more of a moan, winding out behind him. Saw it, too, an omen written on the face of Lucien, who appeared at the edge of the portico, his mouth bloodied, his eyes wide with a warning that bespoke his mysterious absence from the party.

Markos even sensed it in a tremor through him, like the storm edging in on the shore. A cold, slick turning of the tide—"No!"

But he hesitated, afraid of the thunder inside.

Kostas outgirded Galen, and wine made him bold. He slammed his fist into the center of the older man's chest, the full weight of his sodden fury behind his blow.

Galen stumbled back, his mouth open, without a breath.

He fell with a deadened thud.

Mama screamed as Theo erupted.

He tackled Kostas, knocked over tables, drawing blood, brawling at the feet of the musicians. In the chaos, a man roared and charged into the brawl—Yannis Pappos, bully drunk, dangerous. He pushed aside Kostas to beat Theo.

Sofia had let go of Markos's hand. Which was better anyway, because Markos might have hurt her as he threw himself at Yannis.

Kostas turned to the first man who tried to intervene, threw him down, and broke his jaw with a kick. He then caught Markos off the top of Yannis's back and threw him with the force of a mule across the room.

Markos landed, stunned, the breath whisked out of him. He gulped like a fish to live.

At once, Lucien appeared. His hands closed around Markos's wrists, pulling him up. "Run!"

But Markos had no sight to recognize his friend's warning. He shoved Lucien away and turned back to the fight.

Dino had his skinny legs clamped around Yannis's beefy back, a crab even as Kostas closed his hands around Dino's scrawny neck.

Theo, on the floor, had gone limp, his face white, his eyes unseeing.

"Dino!" Markos lost himself to his rage, unable even to sort through his movements as he snapped.

Kostas unhanded Dino, whirled around, yet not fast enough to catch Markos. He tackled Kostas with the speed of a wild boar, slamming him with a bone-jarring crash into the wall.

Kostas screamed, writhing on the floor, hands to his neck.

The ugly shard of a broken plate protruded from his neck. Blood poured onto the stones.

"Markos!"

His mother bent over Galen, her hands on his chest, her twined hair undone. "Help me!"

His father's eyes had swiveled back into his head, leaving only the eerie white of a fish's underbelly. Markos skidded to his knees, put his ear to his father's mouth. No breath. He grabbed his shoulders, shook. "Papa!"

Everything stopped moving then, a silence broken only by his mother's quiet pleading. "Galen, Galen…"

Markos looked up. Dino, white-faced, crawled to his father's feet. He bled from the mouth.

Theo lay in a widening pool of blood, his mouth slack, his skull crushed.

And Kostas's blood spilled freely, as he slumped against the wall, his eyes glassy.

No one moved to rescue him, even as Yannis pressed his hands against the wound. "Kostas!"

Markos looked away, a fist in his chest, crushing him, squeezing his breath.

"Kostas!"

Markos winced. Tightened his jaw. Because he'd seen the whites of Kostas's eyes too.

And then—"You—Stavros!"

Markos glanced up to see Yannis, blood dripping from his hands. He found his feet.

"Leave him be!" Mama threw herself at Yannis, intercepting his rage. "Leave him be!"

She held on, even as Yannis slapped her, held on as she screamed to her sons, "Run!"

Run.

Markos grabbed Dino's arm, yanked him to his feet, and, bile in his throat, fled from the wedding of his oldest brother.

In the distance, thunder shook the heavens, and it began to pour.

CHAPTER 3

"Please, Mama, don't make me do this."

Markos stood in the stone doorway of his bedroom where his mother thrust his clothing into a battered suitcase. Probably the one she'd carried from Athens.

This morning, with the storm clutter on the shore, the skies clear, the stench of death marinated their tiny stone house. No one came to visit, to stand vigil in the Stavroses' grief, as if fearing the family, by one passionate act, cursed themselves and all at the wedding. In Zante, death had never arrived so abruptly, with such violence or arrogance.

Theo. Kostas. Galen.

And, if Yannis made good on his threats, Markos and Dino.

"You *will* go." His mother walked over to the stack of books on the rough-hewn mantle, swept them off—classics he'd never read for himself, but the kind that would make his little brother, the one who actually listened to Mama's readings, wise. The writings of Homer, including his poetry, a book by Aristotle, which always seemed to Markos to be a textbook, a history of Greece, the binding frayed and gray, and finally her holy book, a Bible she'd brought with her into marriage.

"Mama, you're not listening to me. I'm not afraid of Yannis." Although, the memory of his scrabble through the dark sand, a mutinous Dino in tow, curdled Markos's words. Yes, last night, with the stench of Kostas's blood on his hands, Yannis's chilling threats chasing him into the storm, he'd been afraid. He had reacted on instinct, dragging Dino toward the safety of the docks and into the water, pinning him under the moorings of the fishing boats as a rabid Yannis searched for them, vowing his revenge until the storm drove him inside.

Hidden in the sea, Markos had gripped the legs of the pier, arms around Dino as the waves crashed into them. Lightning crackled against the pane of night, the thunder shaking his bones until, exhausted, he let the troughs sweep him to shore. There, they found shelter under an overturned skiff.

Morning burned him awake, and they'd skittered back to their house under the cover of dawn to find his mother packing their belongings.

"*You* may not be afraid—" His mother rounded on him, her eyes flashing, her face reddened with grief. "But I am. I—*am*." She shook her head then, as if freeing herself from the darkness he'd seen flash in her eyes. It hollowed him out to see her like this.

Mama wasn't fragile.

She dumped the books into the suitcase, grabbed the knitted blanket from his bed, wadded it, and threw it in on top.

"I don't need a blanket—"

She turned and caught him, her strong, village-woman's arms around his neck, bowing his head down to her bosom. Her chest heaved, as if she might be weeping, but she remained strangely silent. He closed his eyes, wrapped his arms around her waist.

She always smelled of olives and feta cheese, of cucumbers and roast lamb. He savored it.

Then, abruptly, she pushed him away. Found his eyes with hers, a power he'd never escaped. "You will go. You will take Dino, and you will be away from here and this place of grief. You will find my brother in America and you will start a new life—"

"What about you?"

She turned, closing the suitcase, shaking her head. "I will live with Zoë…on Ramone land."

With Zoë's widowed father? Markos said nothing about the strange taste in his mouth as he lifted the bag, followed his mother down the stairs.

Dino perched on a chair in the living room, his legs knotted to his chest. He'd said nothing—not a word—since Markos dunked him under the frothing black water. Since Yannis had marched down the pier shouting their name. *Stavros! You will die, I swear it.*

The worst part was the lingering fear that the village might agree with Yannis's vengeance. After all, Theo had stolen Kostas's bride.

And Markos had killed Kostas.

Markos pushed the thought away, fearing the swell of dark, rabid satisfaction.

Killed. He'd *killed* a man.

And death, in the crisp light of a summer morning, was not pretty.

Even when laid out on the kitchen tables in wedding clothes, faces cleaned, boots oiled. Theo's head bore a clean white bandage, covering the debris of his wounds. Whoever said a dead man appeared as sleeping should take a closer look at the sagging cheeks, the sunken stomach, the whitened skin.

Markos looked away before he became sick. Again.

He had stumbled up the seaweed- and shell-strewn beach, past the taverna, past the blood on the stone floor, now dried nearly black, past the shattered plates and rancid lamb. Past the redolent casks of wine, and through the kitchen, to his home.

Stepping down into the main room, he had spotted Theo, still in his wedding clothes, his mouth open, as if in a silent scream, his body tossed onto the floor, disposed of by one of the village men. Zoë bent over him, shaking with grief, her moans almost guttural.

It was then Markos emptied his stomach for the first time onto the stones.

Now Markos glanced over at Dino, at his gaunt expression, and knew that to escape might be the only way to survive.

Either that, or allow the rage to pour into his empty spaces, to nourish. To rule.

His mother picked up a bag of food from her stone counter, shoved it into his hands. "This should keep you until you get to the ship. Your passage money is there—"

"Where did you get the money—"

She tightened her lips, gave a shake of her head, and he knew. Ramone. Still, he buried his words, seeing the pain furrowed into his mother's face. Her cheek bore the blush of a bruise from Yannis's hand.

Markos took the bag.

"Gaius Frangos will meet you at the pier. He is there now, waiting. And God bless him for his generosity."

Gaius— "Sofia's grandfather? Why?"

"He will go with you—he and Sofia had already arranged passage. He will stay with you until America and help you find the train to Chicago." She turned and shoved an envelope into his hands. Stained, yellowed, the edges fraying. "This is from my brother, Dmitri. Find him, and he will take you in. I will try to send a telegram but…"

She shoved the envelope into his shirt pocket. Then she cupped her hand to his chin. "You will return, one day, Markos. I promise."

She held his gaze, again, as if daring him to argue. He nodded, albeit caught on her words—*Sofia had already arranged passage.*

So, that was Sofia's message—that she would leave him. He refused to recall her soft hand in his.

"Dino." His mother's tone softened. Dino looked at her, unwinding himself from the chair, moving toward them as if ill. He didn't even look at their father, at Theo. Or, indeed. Markos, as he came to stand, lifeless, beside his older brother.

Mama swept him into an embrace. "You will listen to Markos. And you will read." She let him go, wrapped her hands around his shoulders. He stood eye to eye with her, but even Markos felt tiny under Mama's gaze. "You will become something—a doctor, or lawyer. A judge. You will be someone great, and leave your mark on the world." She kissed him hard on his forehead.

He barely blinked.

She stepped back, nodding, her eyes back on Markos. "You are the eldest Stavros now, and it's up to you to take care of him. Don't let me down." Her gaze turned fierce. "And learn how to write so you can send me a letter. I want to know you're safe."

"Yes, Mama." His voice emerged as if from far away, and like Dino, he couldn't move.

"And—oh, I nearly forgot. Wait—" She left him and disappeared into her room.

Wait. The word boiled inside him. Wait. *Wait!* Stop—he couldn't leave, not with his brother's body hardening on the table, his father's fishing nets empty, his mother forced to leave her—

"Take this." She shoved a coat into his hands. His father's coat, worn on the cuffs, with the hand-carved buttons and salt dried into the wool. "He'd want you to have it."

"Ma—"

"Please, Markos." Only now did her voice break, just a crack, and perhaps it was this that made him take it. Then, her fingers still dug into the cloth, she stepped close. "Keep it, as if it were your life."

He nodded, shot a glance at Dino. He hadn't moved.

"Now go. Before Yannis sobers up." She pressed her hand to his cheek, tears flush in her eyes. "Go, Markos. God will deliver you."

She swept another kiss across Dino's cheek.

Markos pulled the boy out after him.

The sand seeped into his shoes, hot and gritty as he plowed toward the pier, the suitcase banging against his knees. Dino stumbled beside him as if on a tether. Markos's chest boiled, tears clogging his throat. He would not cry, would not turn back. Nor would he spare a glance to the sea, calm now after spending itself on their village.

No, he looked ahead, to the long wooden pier, jutting out like a gang-plank into the sea. A seagull dove, chiding him, or perhaps he heard the cry that he longed to release.

The air smelled of a thorough scouring, raw and empty.

Beside him, Dino tripped. Markos grabbed him around the shoulders.

Sofia stood on the pier, her hair untied, the wind molding her dress to her body. Her blue eyes stayed expressionless as she watched them approach. He wanted to look away, to hate her for her omissions.

She had planned to leave him.

She held his gaze all the way up the dock to the very end, where the ferry to the mainland warned of its departure. He approached her silently until he thunked his case down next to hers. Only then did she look away. "I was going to tell you."

He nodded, but nothing would emerge from his raw, stripped throat.

He'd never ridden the ferry to the mainland, always watched it motor up to the long Zante dock, park at the end. Two decks, with tall dark masts that speared the sky, the ferry resembled a great shoe, like a rhyme Markos had once heard. Travelers huddled on long open-air benches, or hung over the rails, their faces to the wind.

Gaius Frangos, gaunt, white-haired against his black wool fishing cap, his face saggy with years, approached him. "You won't make any trouble."

It wasn't a question so much as a promise. Or an agreement. Markos nodded. But Gaius's dark eyes darted to Sofia, then back.

Markos nodded again, swallowed.

He carried all their cases aboard then settled Dino on the top deck. Dino again drew his legs up, a fetal gesture.

The ferry whistled again, and only then did Markos surrender to the urge to look back.

Zante, with its blue-painted roofs, its whitened nest of buildings climbing a rocky slope to the Ramone olive grove above the town, glistening black and silver in the sun. The tinkling of goats, meandering out to the hills. The sea, now again quiet, having deposited the froth of its anger on the shore. The fishing boats, red, yellow, blue, listless at their berths as if in repose and grateful for a day to exhale, sails strapped against masts. Orange buoys floated in the bay. His gaze went to his bedroom window, the tiny one overlooking the sea, next to the taverna. For a moment, he thought he saw a hand. He lifted his own—

"Markos!"

His gaze jerked from his farewell to find the voice.

Lucien. Markos pulled his hand back, everything inside him seizing. Lucien ran down the pier, both hands above his head. Not the cheerful, *Markos, take me with you* lopsided grin on his gaunt face. No, this *Markos!* reeked of desperation, his eyes wild. "Don't go!"

The ferry whistled a final time, the engines churning up water as the ferrymen loosened the riggings from the pier.

Lucien stopped at the end. His eyes finally found Markos. "Please—Markos!"

Markos gripped the slick, cold rail of the ferry. Stared at his friend, at the bruises darkening his eyes, the body that could slip through the water like a mackerel, the hands that had rescued him from the stone floor. *Run!*

Run, because Lucien had known his brother's, his father's intentions. Run, because Lucien was a Pappos.

Something inside Markos ripped free, and he released himself to the dark boil inside. He clenched his teeth. Narrowed his eyes.

Lucien lowered his hands.

Markos turned his back to him, his shadow long in the morning light across the deck as he returned to his brother. He draped Dino in his father's coat and let the ferry steal them away.

CHAPTER 4

Markos had become a foreigner in his own skin. As if he'd left himself back on the dock or perhaps sitting in his square, white-washed window, the shutters wide, watching the sun's blush on the waves creeping over the fishing boats and charming him to sea.

But not this sea. This sea he didn't know, with its endless caldron of jagged valleys, edged with spittle, and at night, so black, the wind over it an endless lament. At night, the sky appeared so immense, yet miraculously intimate, it seemed he could pull the stars from their moorings. And, he'd never been so cold. A kind of chill that he couldn't flee pressed into his bones, turning him brittle. The wind from this black, sometimes green sea—never his Ionian blue—moaned in his ears, burned his throat.

Most days, he wrapped himself into his blanket—the knitted wool a mockery against the shearing wind—and traced the mischief of the seabirds. Markos watched as the birds dipped into the troughs between the waves and let themselves be lured to the stern of the boat by children offering biscuits and smoked herring smuggled from the breakfast table. Once he'd spied an albatross, and something about the great span of its wings, riding the gales without effort, lodged a stone in his throat.

Three times he'd seen a whale, once with a calf. He'd watched them in anonymity for a full ten minutes before someone—one of the nearby bull-board players—happened to the rail in time for the spray of water from the blowhole.

He lost the view then, as the crowd pushed to watch, most of them also attired in their long-coats and rented steamer rugs. Only then did he notice Dino, swallowed in his father's woolen jacket, expressionless, perched on a barrel near the slanted, marked board of the bull-board gamers.

Dino lifted his eyes to him, held for a moment, turned away.

Around him, the foreign syllables gnawed at his ears. At first, he had strained to make out anything familiar from the cacophony that rose from the dining room, but his brain burned with the effort and, after downing his porridge or milk scones, he escaped to his third-class berth, or better, to the steel-edged winds of the promenade deck.

His berth smelled too much of mildew, a prison that muddied his lungs, snarled him into his thoughts—Lucien, begging at the end of the pier. His father's body, bloating in the morning sun. Mama, her chapped hands grasping her apron to draw it over her head as he'd left.

And Sofia. Standing at the rail as the ferry puttered away from shore, her face a stone. He'd found her there, braced against the wind as they'd neared the port in Peloponnesus.

Somehow, the eight-hour trip to the main peninsula had boiled his anger down, and although it remained a hot coal in the center of his chest, he'd found he could finally breathe around it by the time the sun nudged the dark waters.

Sofia had stiffened as he'd slipped up beside her on the way to Peloponnesus. He wanted to take her hand then, to find if it might be as warm as the night before. Instead, he clutched the rail, his hand inches from hers.

"Why did you not tell me that you were leaving?"

She didn't look at him, and he found her just as beautiful in the outline of twilight, the sun a pink halo at her back, her blue eyes unblinking as the lights of the port town winked at them from shore.

"My grandfather decided only a week ago. He received a letter from his brother's son, with tickets for our passage. And—I didn't know—how to tell you."

She shot him a quick look—fast, as though she feared him.

And for a second, he saw himself launching at Kostas. He may have even heard his own feral scream in the wind.

She drew away, wrapped her knobby wool sweater around her. A strong gust just might toss her into the churning waves. "Grandfather is feeling ill. I should check on him."

They'd found passage to London on a ship through the Mediterranean—the SS *Adriatic*—and he thought perhaps Sofia would come to him, sit with him on the deck. But she hid herself away in her cabin, leaving him to roam the ship as the coastline slid by.

He longed for her song.

When they'd reached London, Sofia appeared drawn, her grandfather fragile, as they'd disembarked. Markos had purchased the passage for America on an American shipping line.

He bought tickets in third-class steerage, hoping he had enough for the train to Chicago.

During the journey to London, he'd sounded out his uncle's letter then managed to find a map of America. Such a large country, and Chicago seemed so far to travel.

Not until he reached London and stood in the shipyard did he understand his mother's instructions. Around him, families camped out upon their worldly belongings, fatigue scrawled in the eyes of the women, the children chasing seagulls or playing games between the crates and coiled ropes, fishing gear, and oil slicks. Everyone seemed skittish, unsettled. Clinging to their own.

Yes. He would go to Chicago, to be with his uncle's family. Because they spoke Greek.

Markos stared at the foreign letters over the ticket counters, the same ball of heat in his chest that he felt every time his mother pulled Dino to her lap and they read aloud together. The fluency in their tones made him turn away, slam through the house, and out to the sea. It cooled him like nothing else could.

To live in America, he'd need family.

Just like in Zante.

* * * *

The whistle for lunch blew, a high shrill that never failed to make him wince. He debated his hunger, then unwound himself from the deck chair. Dino had dug into their luggage and unpacked his mother's books and now claimed a space in the shadow of an overturned lifeboat, *The History of Greece* in the nook of his up-drawn legs, the collar turned up on his coat. Markos nudged him with his foot. "Lunch."

Dino shook his head.

Markos grabbed his collar. "Mama will kill me if you starve to death."

Dino shrugged out of his grip and shot him a glare, but stood up. Markos considered it a victory, of sorts.

In the dining room on the saloon deck, the stewards had already begun lunch service—green soup—probably pea—and a meat pie, biscuits smothered in brown gravy. How he longed for lamb, or perhaps a tilapia, grilled with lemon and basil.

Markos stood over his food, made the sign of the cross.

Dino sat down, lifted his spoon, and dug into his food.

"Dino—we've not lost everything of ourselves, have we?"

Dino ignored him. Markos tucked himself into the deck chair affixed to the floor.

"Markos, I need you."

Sofia's hand skimmed his shoulder, enough to turn him. Wrapped in her sweater, with her hair tucked into a black scarf, she appeared almost wan, weaker than he'd last seen her—although with her cabin situated what seemed an entire village away from his on the middle deck, he hadn't sought her out. Indeed, she seemed to be avoiding him.

Murderer. He shook the word free. "What is it?"

"My grandfather. He has a terrible fever; he's saying things, and...I think he needs a doctor."

Markos longed to reach for her hand. "Doesn't the ship have a doctor?"

She nodded. "But...Grandfather is stubborn. He wants someone Greek."

"Dr. Scarpelli can speak Greek." Dino wiped his mouth. "I will fetch him."

Markos followed his brother down the aisle. "Who is this doctor?"

"He taught me how to play bull-board."

He wove through the tables, away from Markos. Behind him, Sofia pressed her hand on Markos's back, urging him forward. Dino approached a well-dressed middle-aged man seated at one of the few round tables reserved for the first class. He leaned close to Dino as the boy whispered into his ear. Then he nodded and stood.

The woman with him looked up. Tall, with hair as yellow as a moonbeam, she wore it outrageously short and covered with what looked like a bucket, pulled down past her ears for an effect that only made her dark green eyes huge in her pale face. Her dress stopped him cold—green, and short, well, shorter than many he'd seen—surely shorter than what Sofia would ever wear—with a deep neckline furred in white, the same that encircled her wrists. A long strand of pearls, knotted nearly at her waistline, swayed as she rose and took her husband's arm.

"Who is she?" Sofia asked, but Markos had no words to answer as the woman glided toward them like a mermaid, mesmerizing, beautiful, mysterious.

The doctor, his dark hair oiled back, his mouth pinched, had picked up his coat. He seemed older than the woman, despite his full head of black hair, his handlebar moustache. Although shorter than she—nearly boxy—he had such a walk of confidence.

Dino beamed up at the man.

"This is my brother, Markos."

Markos hadn't a clue how to react to this strange Dino. "Markos—this is Dr. Scarpelli."

"Nice to meet you," the doctor said, his Greek nearly impeccable.

Markos met the doctor's hand, aware of his calluses. "Thank you for your help, sir."

"Where is your grandfather, young lady?" Dr. Scarpelli said.

Sofia's gaze affixed to the woman, who smiled at her gently. "We'll be glad to help, if you'll take us to him."

"We're down on D-deck, sir."

"Well, that's half his problem," Mrs. Scarpelli said.

If Markos thought his cabin emitted mildew, the cabins in the deck below smelled of algae, the kind trapped in rocky creases after a storm. He coughed as he passed an open cabin. Six berths—four of them occupied by small children.

"Poles," Dr. Scarpelli said as he walked by. "All sea-sick."

Markos pressed a hand to his mouth. In this aft compartment, the thunder of the waves on the hull reverberated to his bones, and a deep rumble shook his feet.

"The screws. That's what you feel, boy. There are three of them on the *Minnekahda*."

"Screws?"

"Propellers," Dino said, cutting in front of him, edging up to the doctor.

So Dino *had* decided to speak to him.

Gaius Frangos lay under a sheet in his berth; a bed that Markos had determined precariously narrow in his own accommodations seemed to swallow Gaius. The elderly man had sunk into himself, bloody spittle in a bowl on the floor next to him. He seemed asleep but emitted a long moan, a sound that turned Markos's empty stomach. Mrs. Scarpelli drew out a handkerchief from her tiny purse, put it to her mouth.

The doctor pulled up a chair next to the bed, took the old man's pulse. "I need my bag, Dino. Run and fetch it?"

Dino nearly shoved Markos aside. Markos watched him go, wordless.

"How long has he been like this?" Dr. Scarpelli asked.

Sofia slid into the compartment. "Since we left Zante. I thought he might be seasick—he was a shoemaker, never a fisherman. He didn't like the sea."

How could someone not *like*, not live for, not breathe in, the sea?

"But he never recovered. He hasn't eaten since we left port in London, and for two days now, he hasn't taken even a sip of water."

The doctor laid a hand on Gaius's forehead. Gaius didn't even open his eyes. "Sea sickness might be the cause, although…" He pressed his hand on the elderly man's abdomen. Gaius emitted a slow moan. Again, when the doctor moved his arm.

"Gabriella, please take the girl, and Markos. Tell Dino to leave my bag at the door—"

"What is it?"

Everything inside Markos had clenched at the doctor's tone.

He turned. "Take the girl to the women's bathing rooms. Make sure she washes herself well. You should give her something to wear, also."

"I'm not leaving my grandfather. I'm not—"

The doctor shot Markos a look; the words in it made Markos reach for her. "Come Sofia—"

"No!" She slapped at his hand. "No, I'm not going anywhere."

Dr. Scarpelli had found his feet. Now he took her by the shoulders, his voice low. "Sofia, if you want to go to America, then you must listen to me. Your grandfather is very sick. He needs to be quarantined so this entire compartment doesn't get sick. And, if I'm not mistaken, you too have a fever, no?"

She ducked her head. Looked away.

What? Sofia had a fever? Oh, why hadn't Markos checked on her? He'd let her wounded eyes—the ones that made him remember his sins—silence him. Drive him away.

Never again.

The doctor pitched his voice low. "I am not sure, but I fear that your grandfather may have influenza."

Sofia went pale, pressed her hand to her mouth, and Markos saw in the gesture his own mother as they stood over the graves of the fallen of Zante in the influenza pandemic that swept their island along with the rest of the world. He'd been five, or maybe six, and could still remember the heat thrashing him in his bed, feel the ocean clawing the fever from his hot body as his mother and Dr. Alexio tried to cool him.

Oh. Sofia's mother counted among the fallen.

Sofia put out her hand, as if to push away the doctor's words. "No—no. he's just seasick. All he needs is medicine—just something to make him better. He doesn't have—"

"I'll kindly ask you to keep your voice down, Miss. We don't need—"

"You need to make him better! He can't—"

Markos reached out for her. He didn't flinch when she jerked away from him, nor when she slapped his hand as he pulled her from the compartment. "No, Markos! Make him make grandfather well!"

He pulled her against himself. "Shh."

She slammed her fist into his chest.

"It's going to be okay."

Dino appeared, running down the hallway, the doctor's bag thumping against his leg. Markos didn't ask how he knew where the doctor berthed.

He stopped at the sight of Sofia in Markos's arms.

Dropped the bag.

"Let me go!" Sofia leaned back, slapped Markos across the face.

"No, Sofia." He caught her hand before she could hit him again, this time drawing her hands together, pressing his forehead to hers. "I'm never letting you go."

* * * *

"I have nothing to bury him in." Sofia's whitened hands gripped the rail, as if for balance. The wind took her hair, whipped it into her mouth. She shook, although when Markos had tried to touch her, she edged away. Not that he blamed her for her disgust. Not when he'd stood guard outside the women's bath in case her shouts alerted concerned passengers. Not when he'd agreed with the doctor to bar her from her grandfather's deathbed.

The waves today pitched the ship. Even the pellet gray sky conspired with eternity to press despair into the hour. After five days, the old man had slipped into the hands of heaven sometime before the night lifted.

Sofia sounded strangely calm. "We don't even have a priest. The captain says I have to bury him at sea, so the infection doesn't spread." She wove her hands together, as if in prayer. Had it only been three weeks ago that he'd seen these same hands kneading Theo's wedding bread?

"He can have my blanket."

Sofia frowned at him.

"For his...burial. The blanket."

She shook her head. "You need your blanket."

"I don't. We will be in harbor in a few days. And then I will go to my family in Chicago. I have no need for it." He longed to clear her hair from the way it netted her face.

She stared at him, her jaw tightening, her breaths long, deep. Finally, "Thank you, Markos."

Turning away, she tugged her sweater against herself, walked to a deck chair, and sat at the edge.

In the stern, Dino had joined a troupe of men playing bull-board. The last four days had seen a transformation in his demeanor—at least when with Dr. Scarpelli. He trailed after Dr. and Mrs. Scarpelli as though they might be royalty. Indeed, they possessed some sort of imperial powers, because they had arranged for Gaius to be moved from his squalid berth to one on the B deck, in the middle of the ship where the churning of the waves couldn't increase his pain. Dr. Scarpelli had barely left the man's side, wearing a handkerchief over his face as he mopped Gaius's brow and attempted, in vain, to ladle beef-broth down the old man's parched throat.

Dino stationed himself in the hallway outside the room, attuned to the doctor's every movement. Occasionally, he let himself be led away by Mrs. Scarpelli, who read to him in English—Markos had caught them twice on the promenade deck, the way she turned out the syllables sharp in his memory.

Sofia tucked her hands inside her sweater. Markos noted how the sleeves frayed, the wool balled and dangling on the edges. "He's not really my grandfather, you know."

The sun had begun to fade from her face; they were all losing Zante faster than he would have imagined. Her blue eyes darkened. "He took me in after the influenza took Mama. I can't remember my father—he went to war long before my memory. Grandfather said I reminded him of his own daughter."

She was so beautiful it made Markos ache. How he longed to put his arms around her.

"I never wanted to leave Zante, but I couldn't abandon Grandfather. He so wanted to see his family again before…" She closed her eyes. Drew in a breath. Covered her face with her arms.

Oh, Sofia.

"I'm cursed, Markos. I am…cursed. Everyone I love…leaves me. Dies."

Never.

"I am poison."

He flinched, even more from her tone than from her words.

"You are not poison, Sofia Frangos!" he said, surprised at his anger. But she'd gotten up, walked away from him, and when he followed, she slammed herself into her room.

He sat outside her door and tried not to weep.

The sea had calmed, nearly to the doldrums, as it swallowed Gaius Frangos to the depths. A Catholic priest said the appropriate prayers, although Markos couldn't understand a word. Afterward, Markos stood vigil beside Sofia as she stared at the foam churned up in the wake.

He slipped his hand into hers. "We'll go back to Zante someday, Sofia. I promise."

"It's such a wretched trail the ship leaves. Why do the porpoises love it?"

The sun rimmed the horizon, red gold, the waters turning to amber. *Red sky at night, sailor's delight.* His father's voice thrummed inside. "All I wanted to be was a fisherman."

She sighed. "You would have been a great fisherman."

He sensed more than heard Dr. Scarpelli edge up next to him. "Markos, I'd like to speak to you."

If wine could take on melody, it might sound like the music spilling from the saloon into the crisp air. Lamps pressed through portholes, dots on the inky water. A few passengers, wrapped in their long coats and wool hats, lingered on the promenade deck.

Markos turned to the doctor. Next to him, Sofia didn't move.

For the first time since Markos had met him, Dr. Scarpelli seemed… unsettled. He cleared his throat, took a breath, and peered past him into the night.

"It hasn't escaped us the precarious position Gaius's passing has left you."

Precarious—"I'm not sure I understand you."

"I know that you were under his charge."

"I wasn't—"

Dr. Scarpelli held up his hand. "I am not assuming, of course,

Markos, that you needed any assistance from Gaius. In fact, I rather suspect he, and his…family, may have been under your care." His eyes flickered to Sofia, then back.

Markos didn't move.

"However, with the elderly man gone, I am wondering at your intentions once we reach America."

Markos opened his mouth, closed it. Swallowed.

Next to him, Sofia had raised her head.

He hadn't…yes, he had *intentions*. But—

"Don't misunderstand me. I am sure that you are capable of taking care of yourself. You seem an industrious boy. I've seen you watch your brother, and am not ignorant of the way you care for Miss Sofia here. But America is not a place to begin a life unprepared. A boy needs time to find his footing. To grow up."

He was grown up. Had grown up the night he watched his brother murdered.

The night he'd taken a life.

He'd grown up every single day he'd watched his homeland fade from his skin.

However… "I'm not sure I understand."

"I'll speak plainly." Dr. Scarpelli took off his gloves, wound them into his hands. "A few years ago we had a son. Jovanni."

He took a breath. "Unfortunately, his constitution wasn't healthy and he passed, far too early."

"I'm sorry—"

"There is nothing harder than losing a child." As he said it, his hands closed on the rail. "There is a place inside my wife that refuses to heal." He sighed. "I fear it may never heal. Unless…" He looked at Markos. "She is very fond of your little brother."

Inside Markos, a trickle of heat stirred.

"And he is fond of her, I believe."

Sofia slipped her hand onto Markos's forearm.

"I have a proposition—"

"No." Markos said it fast, the word cutting into the night. "No—"

"Hear me out."

Markos tightened his jaw, his chest webbed.

"We won't adopt him, of course. But we can provide for him. Give him an education. He already loves to read—you've seen it. And—"

"No."

"You can come and visit anytime you'd like—we'll even send you money to travel. Chicago. That isn't so far from Minneapolis. I have a job at a hospital there—"

"No."

"And see, we'll even take Sofia if she'd like to go." He looked at Sofia. "Would you like that, Sofia? You can learn English, and perhaps become a—"

"No!" Markos roared. He grabbed Sofia's hand, probably crushed it, but the burning had turned to a full-out boil, and he couldn't breathe. No. No— "I—" He thumped his chest hard and it seemed to dislodge his words. "I can take care of them. And I will. We are a family, and we won't be separated. Never!"

He yanked Sofia away from the rail, away from the trail of her grandfather's body. "Markos—"

Tears scorched his eyes, and he stifled a curse, whisking them away before Sofia could see them. He pushed open the door to the saloon deck, pulled her down the hallway.

"Markos!"

He stopped, rounded on her, pushed her against the wall.

Her eyes went wide. He put a finger into her face. "I will not leave you. Never. Do you hear me? *Never.* We will stay together. *All of us.* I swear it."

Her mouth opened, something in her eyes he couldn't name. Not fear, maybe—hope?

Yes, hope, gulping in his words as if they meant something. As if they could nourish her.

Oh...he couldn't stop himself. He pressed his lips to hers—so fast he wasn't even sure later he did it—just leaned in and kissed her, something he'd longed to do for so long—

Sofia.

But he tasted her tears, her body shaking against his. He jerked away.

She brought a trembling hand to her mouth.

Oh no. He braced one hand above her shoulder, hung his head, winced. What was his problem that he didn't think, he just—let his emotions ride him. "Oh, Sofia, I'm—sorry."

Tears ran over her fingers, into the cuffs of her ratty sweater. Then, oddly, she curled her hand into his collar. "You won't leave me, right?"

He shook his head. "Never. *I promise.*"

She ran her hand down his face. "I believe you, Markos, I believe you."

And then, softly, she kissed him back.

CHAPTER 5

"Dino—put that back!"

Markos snatched the apple from his brother's hand, shooting a glance at the vendor, who had his back turned, tending to a mother and her two waif-looking children. He replaced the apple on the stack outside the store and snagged his brother by the arm of his leather jacket—a gift from Dr. Scarpelli right before they'd disembarked the ship in New York.

Of course, the good doctor had chased Markos down a final time with an offer to take Markos with him. Markos didn't bother to censor his response.

If his mother had known what kind of America she had sent her boys to, she might have let Markos take his chances with Yannis. Markos didn't have to understand English—although yes, during the past week he'd made attempts to learn at least the alphabet, thanks to Sofia's prodding—to comprehend the state of the people queuing up for bread or jobs on the streets of Chicago.

They bore the empty-eyed expressions of the soldiers who'd returned to Zante after the Greek-Turk war. Saggy-limbed, dressed in long-coats, dog-earred fedoras, or low-brimmed fisherman's caps, curled newspapers sticking out of their pockets like clubs, they loitered outside what looked like employment offices with ripped notices posted on windows. Others hunkered down in the doorways of abandoned buildings, playing dice, their eyes tracking Markos and Dino as they'd carried Sofia's trunk between them down the street. Markos balanced their suitcase in the other hand.

"I'm hungry!" Dino yanked his arm from Markos's grip, sulked away to where Sofia sat on the trunk, her arms clamping her sweater against her body. Too bad they'd burned Gaius's clothing. She could have used his overcoat.

Markos took off his father's jacket and settled it over her shoulders. It swallowed her whole, and in the black scarf, the black coat, her skin seemed even more ashen, her eyes that much hungrier. She may have said thank you, but he couldn't hear what issued from her lips.

"We'll eat later." *Please, please let Uncle Dmitri still be in Chicago. Please let him have received Mama's telegram.*

Although, with no greeting at the train station, Markos's hopes had settled into his empty gullet.

"It's okay, son, he can have it." The sound of his native language stopped Markos, and he stared at the shopkeeper wearing a cloth apron, a black wool fisherman's hat, and a smile vacant more than a few teeth. "I won't stand for stealin', but I can't very well let a fellow Greek go hungry." He handed over the apple.

Dino reached out, hesitated, then took it. Slipped it into his pocket. "Thank you."

The man nodded. "Name's Peter Kazalos. From Sanatorini."

Markos held out his hand. "Markos and Dino Stavros. And our friend Sofia. From Zante."

"Where you headed?" Mr. Kazalos shook it.

"North side. Our uncle's place."

"Is your father with you?"

Markos swallowed, not sure if his grief showed on his face. He'd managed to bite it back for so long, when it roared to life, it could almost consume him in a gulp. He shook his head.

"I see. If you boys need anything, you come to me. Okay?"

Markos hated the sudden burning in his eyes. "Yes sir."

The day had given their arrival in Chicago dour greeting—a smoke grey sky spit down on them, into his jacket collar, down his spine. He'd long since ceased to remember real warmth, the cold having metastasized to his bones by the time they disembarked at Ellis Island.

The humiliation of being led like goats through the processing center, examined, queried, and spit out into America like he might be a fish on the dock didn't stir any warmth, either.

Markos did have to admit to a begrudging gratitude to Dr. Scarpelli for the quarantine on Sofia's grandfather. The American health department cleared Dino, Sofia, and Markos for entry—while the Polish family who'd survived the trip ended up in the dentition cells for further scrutiny.

Markos had bought their ferry tickets to New York City and didn't bother stopping for a night in the city. He bunked them down in Grand Central Station and purchased, with nearly his last monies, train tickets to Chicago.

Dino barely acknowledged Markos after he left a sobbing Mrs. Scarpelli on the deck of the *Minnekahda*. Markos had taken the doctor's proffered address in Minneapolis. Pocketed it. Accepted the man's handshake.

The look in the doctor's dark eyes haunted him the entire overnight trip to Chicago, while Sofia and Dino slept in the open berths across the aisle.

"I'm tired, Markos," Dino said, lifting Sofia's trunk. It bumped against his legs as he walked, his eyes away from Markos. Like Sofia, the sun had left him—or it could be the effect of the sour day, the chaos of the street.

Train cars on wires spit sparks as they plowed through traffic, scattering muddy automobiles, the occasional horse-drawn deliveries filled with fruit, burlap bags of potatoes, or metal canisters of milk. The earthy smell of animals, the acrid grit of coal smoke and unwashed bodies burned into his nose. Buildings loomed over them—four and five stories high, and he tugged Dino toward one, huddling under a green awning as it began to drizzle. A uniformed footman by the gold-embossed door narrowed his eyes at them.

Sofia huddled in behind Markos.

"It's not much farther."

"How do you know?" Dino dropped his end of the trunk with a thud, nearly jerking Markos's arm from its socket.

"I showed someone in the train station Uncle Jimmy's address. They drew me a map." He held out the now fraying envelope that showed the penciled drawing.

"Let me see it." Dino swiped the letter from Markos.

Markos held his hands up in surrender and glared at him as Dino turned and walked up to the footman. He tucked his arm around Sofia as he listened to Dino fumble with English, sufficient to elicit further directions.

Markos memorized the footman's gesticulations. Down the street, take a left…keep going…

He bit back a remark as Dino picked up his end of the trunk, both hands behind his back, trundling his end of Sofia's belongings as he led the way.

They dodged street vendors—Dino's eyes lingering on a stand of hot meat sandwiches an elderly woman was selling on the corner of an alley-way. The smell, something that reminded Markos of his mother's roast lamb, nearly turned him inside out.

Cars honked, and above the din, a policeman's shrill whistle pierced the air. Storefronts displayed exotic clothing, mannequins in slinky furs, and lacey green and red dresses—the kind Mrs. Scarpelli wore—shiny, pointed shoes with thin, raised heels. And all manner of hats—bowls, and wide-brimmed felt hats, and hats with no brims at all.

For a moment, he tried to imagine Sofia in such a hat, her dark hair trailing down her back. He pushed the thought away.

Dino led them down another street then stopped, nearly ramming the trunk into Markos's knees.

"Zante's." Dino pointed to a sign hanging vertically amidst a long row of buildings. He yanked Markos forward.

Markos stopped outside the door. "Wait here, Dino—"

But Dino had already dropped his end and begun climbing the steps. Markos lunged after him. Grabbed his arm. "Wait *here*."

Dino glared at him. Markos glared back.

"I'll watch our bags," Sofia said softly, touching his arm.

"Are you sure?"

"I just need to sit." She collapsed onto the trunk, ducking her head into the collar of his father's coat. He turned back to Dino. "Be a gentleman."

Dino tightened his mouth and stepped down to stand over her.

The smell of Greece nearly brought tears to Markos's eyes as he entered the restaurant. It resembled a galley-style café with tables down the middle, wooden booths along one wall, a long counter flanking the other, behind which a Greek man—he had to be Greek with his dark eyes, dark hair, the tooled mustache—watched Markos enter.

Markos stepped up to the counter. "I'm looking for Dmitri Stavros. He's—my uncle."

Two men, dressed in suits and perched on the round stools, glanced at him. Markos hadn't considered his appearance, his three-day body odor, the fact that sometime between his escape from Zante and now, he'd grown the beginnings of a beard. He swiped off his fisherman's hat and tried to smooth his hair.

"Jimmy's in the back," the man at the counter said, pointing with a jerk of his chin.

Markos trekked through to the back room, passing what looked like the kitchen. The smells of home leaked out—roasted lamb, onions. His stomach fairly leaped with joy. He knocked on the closed door.

The face that met him didn't in the least bear a Stavros resemblance. Short brown hair, green eyes—a body built like a keg. "What?"

So, maybe he'd thank Sofia for the rudimentary English lessons. Not that he had resisted spending time with her, her soft voice blending with his as they sounded out words together.

He crushed his hat in his hands. "I'm here for…Dmitri Stavros."

"Jimmy? Whadaya want with him?"

"He's—my uncle." Oh, he sounded about three years old. But he sucked in a breath, met the man's gaze. Greek men didn't run. Or, rather, he wouldn't run again.

And, Dmitri was family—

The door closed in his face.

Markos took a breath, waited. He glanced toward the front of the café, spotted Dino's face pressed up against the glass. Why couldn't the kid listen to him just once?

The door opened. Markos stared into the eyes of a hairy, oily-eyed man that, if he squinted hard, had his mother's nose. "Theo? Is that you?"

Markos swallowed, grabbing at his voice, which had decided to desert him. At least he spoke Greek. "Uh—no. It's Markos."

"Markos?"

"I'm Theo's—younger brother."

The man stepped forward, caught Markos's face with both hands, looking him over. "Yes! Of course." Then he flung his arms around Markos, pounding him hard on the back. "Markos Stavros, at my doorstep!" He leaned back, kissed Markos on both cheeks, loudly, with Greek flourish. "My nephew is here, in America!"

Markos fought the boyish urge to fall into his uncle's embrace, maybe cling to the man's girth. Instead, he nodded, glancing to Dino and back again.

"Did I miss a letter from my sister?" He grabbed Markos's arm. "Come, sit down. Are you hungry?"

"Yes, but—"

"Moussaka for my nephew!" Dmitri yelled, ushering him into the seating area. "Sit, I will feed you. And you will tell me everything." He grabbed Markos's hat, treed it by the door.

"Uncle—"

He shoved Markos into a seat. "Some coffee?" He switched to English, barking at the man behind the counter.

"Uncle—listen—I'm not alone. My brother, Dino, is here—and—"

Dmitri rounded, his eyes going to the door. "Dino?" He crossed the room, but Dino had already beat him to the entrance. "Little Dino!" Dmitri kissed him, again, both cheeks, then caught the boy into his bearish arms.

Dino looked over his uncle's shoulder, his wide eyes connecting with Markos's.

"Markos?"

Sofia edged up behind Dino, her gaze flashing back to their belongings on the street.

Dmitri set Dino away from him, looked at Markos. Raised an eyebrow. "Is this your wife, Markos?"

Wife? "No, Uncle—she's—she's from Zante. Her grandfather died on the journey over. We thought, perhaps, maybe..."

"Of course, Markos! Of course."

Sofia didn't move as Dmitri took her hands, kissed each one. "Of course, such a lovely young lady as yourself is welcome here, at Zante's!"

Sofia looked to the floor. Was that a blush? Markos moved past them, out the door. He grabbed up his suitcase and carried it inside.

Uncle Dmitri had ordered more coffee. "I don't have much room, but..." He turned to the patrons in the café. "My family has come from Greece!" He clapped above his head. "Tonight we celebrate!"

Markos let Dino and Uncle Dmitri retrieve Sofia's trunk from the street as he cupped his hands around the coffee, drank it in slowly, letting the dark pungency seep into his bones. From the kitchen, the smells of supper stirred the feelings of home, of watching his mother knead bread, bake the fish.

He closed his eyes, putting his forehead on his hands. Listened to the Greek—albeit choppy and oddly foreign—around him. The coil inside him began to unwind.

See, he didn't need Dr. Scarpelli's charity. Markos Stavros knew how to take care of his family.

* * * *

Never did Markos think he'd despise the smell of fish. But, locked inside his uncle's sweltering kitchen, surrounded by potatoes, onions, garlic, tomatoes, and piles of herring in need of cleaning, everything about him reeked of the sea. It embedded his skin, his hair, his pores. The bloody entrails chapped his skin, his hands shredded from the scales, slicking tears into his eyes when he moved on to peeling and chopping onions.

Or, perhaps it's wasn't so much the smell he minded as the reminder of his losses. Theo, Papa, Mama. Roast lamb on the spit. Baklava. Fresh figs…

"Markos! Are you finished with the fish? Because the potatoes need skinning."

While Dino swept the restaurant after close and served as a busboy during the days, Sofia rose early, her strong hands again turning chapped as they worked the dough and transformed the restaurant into a bakery.

However, she still refused to sing, and, although Markos ached for it, he didn't ask.

Even at night. In the darkness, in their tiny room overlooking the café, he longed for anything that might stir his memory of home, anything to yank his thoughts from the raucous music that spilled out into the streets, the dogs barking, cats howling, the chill that found him as he huddled under a flimsy blanket. He slept on a mat on the floor, Dino in a cot next to him. To Sofia, they'd offered the narrow metal bed, hanging a curtain down the center of the room to cordon off some privacy for her.

He tried to be thankful, especially with the soup lines he passed when his uncle sent him out on errands.

Sofia managed to bring some life to their room, finding a dresser and covering it with a piece of lace she'd brought with her, filling a pitcher with flowers discarded from a street vendor.

He would have been happy with just her singing.

Markos winced as the knife accidently slid through the soft flesh of his thumb.

"Where's Sofia?" Uncle Jimmy stuck his head into the kitchen. He'd insisted on them using his American name, and had begun barking at Markos only in English. Thankfully, Markos understood more than he spoke.

"She went to the movies. With Dino." Markos didn't look up, wrapping a towel around his cut, stifling the anger that stirred inside. Dino had figured out a way to sneak him and Sofia into the back entrance of the Cinema Palace. The kid had turned into a regular street urchin, bringing home filched apples, peanuts, even an occasional carnation for Sofia's flower vase.

At least, Markos assumed he'd filched them. Although, on occasion, Dino had mentioned Peter Kazolas's name.

Markos wanted to throttle the kid, all the same. He couldn't afford flowers. Couldn't even afford to buy Sofia a winter coat instead of that ratty wool sweater. She tromped around in the brisk November air in her black scarf, her thin summer shoes. Not that she'd complained.

But once when she worked as hostess, he'd seen her in the coatroom, running her fingers through the softness of a patron's fur coat.

How he longed to buy her such a coat. But he barely had time to sleep; how could he take on another job?

The blood had stopped. Markos wiped his forehead with the back of his arm, tossed the filet into a bucket of salty water.

Uncle Jimmy picked up a piece of peeled garlic, gnawed on it. "Listen, I got a little treat for you tonight." He slapped him on the back. "After you get done, take a bath and meet me after the restaurant closes. It's time you figured out how to live in America."

The crisp night gathered the stars overhead as Markos slipped out the back of Zante's. His uncle sat at the wheel of a shiny Model T coupe, the motor coughing out exhaust, the headlights like eyes on Markos as he gawked.

"I didn't know you had an automobile." Markos ran his hand over the plush seat then slipped in beside Uncle Jimmy.

"There's a lot of things you don't know, my boy," Jimmy said with a wink. He'd cleaned up, wearing a suit, his black hair oiled back. For a moment, he reminded Markos of Dr. Scarpelli. But Uncle Jimmy didn't want to steal his family. Uncle Jimmy *was* his family.

Markos pulled his father's coat around him, suddenly conscious of his own threadbare wool pants and shirt.

The automobile gears growled as they rolled out into the cobblestone street. "You can't tell Dino, or even Sofia, what you see tonight, okay, boy?" Uncle Jimmy reached over, patted him on the shoulder. "It's for men only."

Men. His mind whisked back to his father, hauling him up to do the Kaslamantiano. Markos nodded.

Uncle Jimmy parked his car in a lonely alleyway between two brownstones. They got out and Markos followed him down a stairwell blocked by garbage cans. Uncle Jimmy stopped at a blackened door, knocked.

A panel in the door slid out, and eyes peered through.

"Hornsby," Jimmy said, quietly.

The panel closed. Silence. Jimmy had removed his driving gloves and now slapped them in his hand.

A lock slid back with a click and the massive door opened.

Music spilled out as Uncle Jimmy hooked Markos's arm and pulled him inside the basement room. "Welcome to America, boy."

Green draperies covered the walls, tiny gaslights flickered at each round table inhabited by women with rouged lips, painted eyes, low-cut frameless dresses, some long, others fringed at the knee. They wore the brimless hats and high-heeled shoes he'd seen in storefronts. A blond by the door, with hair cut to her chin, settled her eyes on him, a cigarette in a long black holder balanced between her fingers. She blew out a smoke ring as he passed by, her eyes trailing him.

Men in crisp suits and wide ties drank glasses of amber liquid.

Uncle Jimmy practically pushed him to the long bar.

"What is this place?"

"Tony's."

Tony's—gin room? He'd heard the term, hadn't really known…

At a stage at the far end of the room, a blond sat on a stool, her low-cut red dress a siren in the dark club, crooning out a song with a husky tone that roused to life something inside him. His eyes fixed on her, the feeling growing at the way her gaze latched on him, the smile that crept up her blood-red lips. She turned and began to sing to him.

His entire body glued in place.

Behind her, a musician with man-sized bouzouki plunked out low tones, another played a shiny flute—stepping forward to solo as the woman finished, her final notes hanging in the blue haze of smoke, caressing the crowd.

"That's a saxophone," Uncle Jimmy said, handing him a glass of something dark. "And this is what we call coffin varnish. Go easy, kid." Jimmy lifted his glass. Then, with one quick movement, downed it. "*Oopa*!"

Markos put the glass to his lips, sipped it. His eyes watered. Even retsina, which burned his throat the few times he'd finished off his father's drink, seemed as milk to this. He swallowed fast, regretted it, and coughed, ready to retch. "What is it?"

"Homemade liquor, son."

"Like wine?" His father had made their own wine—

"Not exactly." Jimmy signaled the barkeep.

The woman on stage began to sing again, and this time her eyes landed on Uncle Jimmy, another luring smile on her lips. Jimmy swayed to her song. "She's some kind of songbird, ain't she, kid?"

Markos nodded.

"Name's Hedy Brooks. She's sweet on me."

Indeed, at the end, she blew a kiss to the audience, then hung up her microphone and floated off stage in a way that dried Markos's mouth.

She stopped before Uncle Jimmy and ran her finger down his lapel. "Buy a girl a refreshment, Jimmy?"

He slipped his hand around her waist. Snapped his fingers at the barkeep.

She turned in his arms, leaned back against him. "So, who's this?"

"My nephew. All the way from Zante Island."

"Greece? Hmm." She accepted the drink, sipped it. Markos noticed she didn't even blink, not a hint of flinch. "He's a young one. But… sturdy." She ran her finger along his jaw. "Such pretty blue eyes."

"Hedy—"

"They're Stavros eyes, Jimmy." She glanced at his uncle. Pressed a kiss to his chin. Jimmy grinned, downed another drink.

"So, what does Markos do?"

"He works at the restaurant. But I was thinking about your little problem." His eyes latched on Markos. "I thought Markos could help you."

She raised a thin eyebrow. It seemed as if she ran her hands down him with her eyes. Something hot scurried through his belly.

She looked up at Jimmy. "I thought it was *your* little problem."

Jimmy lifted one shoulder, winked at Markos.

She gave Markos another perusal, this time quick. "He looks like he can handle himself." She took another sip of her drink. "I'll give him a try, but no promises." She reached out and patted Markos on the cheek, her perfume thick, curling through him. "What do you say, kid? Wanna work for me? I'll make this chiseler pay you twice what you're getting at the restaurant."

Markos glanced at Jimmy.

Jimmy wore an indulgent smile and shrugged again. "Anything for you, Hedypie."

She rose up on her toes, gave Jimmy a kiss on the mouth.

"But what about the restaurant?" Markos asked, that heat in his stomach now filling his chest.

Hedy finished her drink. "Aw, I just need you after the joint closes. Get me home safely when Jimmy here is tied up." She turned, slipped her arms around his neck. "Which is too often for me."

"Doll, I got things to do. Markos will keep you safe."

His words slipped into Markos, touched something fragile. Markos felt himself nodding even as his thoughts caught up to him. Twice the pay. Enough to get Sofia her own room. Maybe buy her a coat. Shoes.

Take her out, maybe not to a joint like this one, but a real first-class restaurant.

C'mon, Markos, you know you can't take care of them.

The band kicked up another song. Jimmy put down his glass, grabbed Hedy's hand, tugged her out to the dance floor. Began to sway with her, his body molded close. Not a dance the likes Markos had ever seen.

Markos lifted his glass, studied the amber liquid, and then, with a jerk, downed the entire drink. He braced his hand to his chest, his eyes watering, but held back a cough.

"Another one, barkeep," he said, lifting the glass as warmth touched his toes for the first time in two months. See, he could do just fine on his own.

The barkeep filled his glass. He drank down the next shot.

Yes indeed, welcome to America, Markos Stavros.

CHAPTER 6

Hedy found the perfect coat for Sofia's Christmas gift in the gilded archways of Marshall Fields on State Street. Markos felt the vagabond in his father's coat the moment he stepped inside, swiping off his fedora. He followed Hedy as she sashayed down the main aisle, under magnificent chandeliers dripping light, past ornamented, rounded glass counters that displayed all manner of jewelry, pots of rouge, bejeweled containers of inebriating perfume. For the holiday season, great wreaths adorned the balconies that soared four stories. A pianist at a grand piano plunked out holiday songs—a few he recognized from Hedy's song-list.

Hedy greeted clerks by name, stopping to kiss a few. She eventually marched him to a room filled with coats. "Gretchen, we need something special for my friend's Jane." She plunked herself into a leather chair while Markos tried to blend into the racks of furs.

Usually, when Hedy asked him to drive her to Marshall Fields to spend the day lunching and partaking in an afternoon fashion show, he passed the time out in the car, sounding out the many English primers she'd purchased for him.

He'd begun to understand even the clandestine conversations in the back of the speakeasies. Like the fact that Jimmy the Greek, aka Uncle Jimmy, actually worked for someone named Joe Aiello, offering "protection" for his neighborhood on the north side of town.

"Protection from whom?" he'd asked Hedy later, as she unwound herself in the backseat of the Model T, pulling off her sequined headband.

"Oh, you know. Big Al and the outfit. They're trying to take over his part of town."

Markos equated it to the Turks and Greek War, and vowed silent allegiance.

"Here we go." Gretchen returned with a box, opened it, and pulled out a wool coat in the finest shade of amber, like the beaches of Zante at sundown. It buttoned on the side and bore thick fur at the lapel and wrists, striped in black and gray. He ran his fingers through the fur, could almost hear Sofia in it, humming her delight.

"It's perfect."

"It's raccoon—all the rage."

He found the price tag of the coat, and his mouth dried.

"Oh, darling, don't worry." Hedy tweaked him on the cheek. "It'll be worth it when she flings herself into your arms."

In his wildest dreams. Ever since he'd rented her a single room over Uncle Jimmy's restaurant, he'd barely seen her. He missed listening to her breath on the other side of the curtain.

He couldn't bear to remember her singing.

"Oh, what is this face? Is she still not talking to you?"

"She spends all her free time with Dino, going to the penny movies and learning English."

"You should bring her with you some night. I wouldn't mind." Hedy winked at Markos and he blew out a breath, trying to pinpoint why that idea rattled him.

"Naw. She's..."

Hedy raised a thinly plucked eyebrow, pursed her red lips, waited.

"Not you."

She smiled. "Well, of course she's not, darlin'. But you said she likes to sing. Maybe she could favor us with a little ditty."

The idea of Sofia on stage, in a dress cut above her knees, pearls swaying as she cooed into some microphone…

"I can't afford the coat, Hedy."

"Oh, horse feathers. We'll put it on my account. And I'll tell Jimmy to give you an advance in pay in time for Christmas. But she needs a hat to go with it." Hedy nodded to Gretchen, who boxed the coat up as Hedy led him to a room dedicated to hats—wide-brimmed felt hats with veils and the shell-like cloche hats that Hedy wore so well.

Markos picked up a skullcap with a wide, lacey trim around the outside.

"Of course, she'll have to cut her hair if she wants it to fit," Hedy said.

Markos handed her back the hat. "I'll just take the coat."

Hedy led the way to a cashier while Markos fumbled with the math. He'd owe Uncle Jimmy a year of pay at the rate Hedy had him spending money. But it took cash to be a dandy, as Hedy put it. She'd already redressed him in a pair of oxford bags and saddle shoes, an early Christmas gift. *Can't have my companion dressed like a ragamuffin.*

And Uncle Jimmy seemed to want him to squire his girl around town. He had practically handed over his Model T after taking Markos into the country to teach him to drive, although his true test of faith in Markos came in handing over Hedy to Markos's arm. Markos couldn't deny the power that coursed through him, motoring through the traffic of Chicago, beautiful Hedy Brooks reclining behind him, puffing out circles of cigarette smoke. And, she hummed. Low and raw edged, tunes that made him watch her in the rearview mirror, even as she powdered her knees or rouged her lips with her pinky finger in her signature Ox-blood red hue.

A part of him that he didn't recognize loved Chicago. The city had an avant-garde, almost adolescent feel, with the dapper dons, the flat-chested girls swinging their pearls, the hot jazz, and underground gin-rooms secreted in basements and behind slotted doors of candy stores and groceries and shoemaker's shops. Life buzzed below the crust of the city, accessible with passwords that he memorized daily.

He'd learned to blend into the crowd, watching Hedy woo her audience at Tony's—or even some of the other gin-mills; the Green Door, Lottie's, the Rainbo Club. When she crawled onto a baby grand to perform, he appeared to lift her back to the floor; when one or two of the sheiks who wanted her favors forgot she belonged to Jimmy the Greek, he gave them a gentle reminder. Just Jimmy's name seemed enough.

She made Markos feel twenty-eight rather than eighteen.

"Let's get *you* a coat too," Hedy said, fingering the collar of his father's wool coat. "This is so…old."

He caught her soft hand. "No thanks." But he did allow her to choose a white silk scarf and drape it over his neck.

Winter cast a dismal pallor over the city as he hiked out to the car then collected Hedy from under the awning, where the footman held her bags and his coat box.

She climbed in. "I'm serious—bring Sofia to Tony's tonight. I'd love to hear her sing."

Markos pulled away from the curb, the car splashing through blackened pools of icy water. Yes, he'd love to hear her sing too. But not at Tony's.

No, Sofia wasn't a canary. Never would be.

Sofia wasn't in her room when he returned to the restaurant. She'd shown up for her regular hostess duties during the restaurant's dinner hour, but vanished by the time he finished taking out the trash. Markos paused outside her room, his hand formed to knock, when he heard laughter inside. Then, Dino's voice, teasing, something in English. Markos couldn't make it out. He palmed his hand on the door a moment before hustling to the bathroom to clean up for Hedy.

Just wait until Sofia saw the coat. Then she'd see that, while Dino was still a child…Markos had become a man.

The night had turned crisp as he walked home late under the lamp-lights. He'd retired the coupe in Uncle Jimmy's garage two blocks away and carried the coat box under his arm, his collar turned up. Snow, soft, almost ethereal, drifted from the sky, turning to diamonds under the streetlights. He hummed one of Hedy's tunes, tried out a step he'd seen from the hoofers tonight. Someday he'd ask Hedy to dance—she always tried to hide the longing in her eyes, but he sensed it as she watched the fellas sway with their ladies.

Probably Uncle Jimmy wouldn't mind if he took her for a twirl around the floor.

The restaurant's fluorescent sign had flickered out; Zante's finally silent after the day's chaos. He used his key to open the front door then slipped inside.

Streetlight glimmered on the slick wood floor, across the glass countertop. The smell of lamb and onions embedded the walls. He ran his hand along the smooth counter as he moved toward the back.

A captured breath from one of the wooden booths stopped him.

He turned, froze.

Sofia sat in the shadows, her hair down long, her blue eyes watching him.

"Sof—what are you doing here?"

She looked at her hands palming the table. "Just sitting. Waiting."

"Waiting?"

She lifted a shoulder. "For you. I do, sometimes. You always walk right by, without seeing me."

He did? He stepped to the booth, set the box on the table. "I didn't know that."

"Now that you're home, I'm going to bed." She moved to rise.

He put a hand on her shoulder. She recoiled as if he'd burned her.

Oh. He pulled his hand away. "Listen—I was going to wait until Christmas, but..." He found a smile and pushed the box toward her.

She looked up at him. "What's this?"

"Your Christmas gift."

"But—I don't have anything for..." She shook her head. "It's not Christmas yet, Markos. Let's wait."

He sat down opposite her. "Please, open it." How he longed to see her face, but the shadows hid her expression from him.

Finally, "Okay." She lifted the lid. He turned on the lamp in time to see her mouth open.

"Oh." She ran her hand over the coat, held it up. "Oh." But her tone sounded more pain than joy.

She let the coat drop and covered her mouth with both hands. Shook her head. The bubble of happiness turned to bile inside him. "What's the matter?"

"It's not—I can't accept this. It's too expensive."

"No it's not. Hedy is getting me— Aw, never mind. It's perfect. C'mon, try it on."

She didn't move. "No."

"What are you talking about?" The anger in his voice surprised him. "But—but— You *need* a coat. You're practically freezing to death in your old sweater..."

"It was my mother's sweater."

"It's ragged. It makes you look like a—a village girl."

"I *am* a village girl. I'm not one of your fancy shebas—"

"How do you know that word?"

"I know a lot of things, Markos. Like that woman you're always with. She's a—a—floozy. They call her a *charity girl*."

He hated the swirl of anger, how he wanted to yank her words from her mouth. "Hedy's *not* a charity girl. She's a singer. And Uncle Jimmy's girlfriend."

"Not only Uncle Jimmy's."

"What are you talking about?"

"I think you know." She stood up. "Is that what you want, Markos? A flapper? Someone who runs around with her knees naked, swinging pearls, her hair so short it looks like a man's?"

He just stared at her, trying to get a fix on her words.

She shook her head, her jaw tight. "This was a mistake. Thank you for the gift, but I don't want it. Give it to—Hedy Brooks."

"It's not for Hedy Brooks! She has plenty of fancy things."

"That's right, she does. She shouldn't have you too!"

"She doesn't." He stood, touched her shoulder. "What are you talking about?"

"I'm talking about the fact that you're in love with her." She'd let her voice drop low, trembling, but she could have been shouting at the top of her lungs for the way it hit him.

He stepped back, staring at her, the shimmer of anger in her blue eyes, her dark hair long and over her face. She breathed in hard, as if waiting for his response.

He had no words, only a roaring in his head.

She slid away from him. "I shouldn't have waited for you. I don't know what I was thinking— Maybe— Just, good night, Markos."

He grabbed her arm. "It's not true, Sofia. I'm just her driver."

She seemed thinner than he'd remembered. In fact, standing next to her—closer than he'd been, really, in weeks, she seemed almost fragile. "Let me go, Markos." She pried his fingers away.

"No—I told you, I'm not leaving you. I mean that."

"The Markos I know already left."

"I don't understand you! What are you saying?" Now his voice hissed, and he heard in it something unfamiliar, something even dark.

"Nothing—I just wish—I miss the Markos I knew."

The Markos she knew? "I haven't changed. I'm just trying to make a life for us."

"You're not the same. Ever since you started working for Hedy. Something inside you feels...different. Dark. It's in your eyes. You don't look at me the way you used to. And now, you...you smell like...*her*." She curled her nose up. "Perfume and cigarette smoke, and...hooch."

Another word. He wasn't sure he liked any of them coming from Sofia's pretty lips. "It's my job, Sofia. I have to carry Hedy's coat, drive her around, keep her safe." He stalked back over to the table. "At least I'm not going to movies every day and stealing from apple carts."

She drew in a quick breath.

He tightened his jaw, picked up the box. Turned. She had her arms wrapped around herself, tiny and stiff in the blade of streetlight. "Is that what you think I'm doing every day?"

He stood there, the box between them, hating himself for the words boiling inside, for wanting to splash them on Sofia. Why was he the only one who had to hurt? "I don't know what you're doing. But I know you seem to prefer Dino's company to mine." He winced at how petulant the words sounded and shoved the box at her.

Her eyes darkened. "Dino and I've been attending classes. English classes at the Greek Orthodox Church. He wants to go to school. Make something of himself. He's even been working for Mr. Kazalos at his apple stand."

Oh.

She took the box, set it on the counter, ran her hand over the lid. "I know you're trying to take care of us, Markos, but I'm afraid I'm losing you. Every day you sink into a place I can't see. I'm screaming, but you don't hear me."

Her blue eyes sheened with tears as she looked up at him. "Please, Markos, quit this job. I don't need a coat. I don't even need my own room. I miss being with you and Dino. I—"

The picture window exploded.

Markos threw his arm around Sofia, flattened her to the ground.

Shots peppered the room, shattering the canisters of candy on the counter, splintering the mahogany counter, shredding the padded stools. Markos scooted Sofia to the bank of booths, curled with her under a table.

Then bullets destroyed the cigar box display, chipped at the chandelier until it crashed to the floor. Glass splashed across the polished wood. Sofia screamed, and Markos slapped his hand over her mouth. "Shh. They'll hear you."

Then, just as abruptly as it began, the shooting stopped. Motors revved on the street, peeling away.

Markos didn't move. Just held Sofia's shaking body to himself, pinching his own fear back. He closed his eyes, listening to glass drop from the front window, the sounds of feet thundering down the hallway above, Sofia's soft sobs. "Shh, don't cry. I'll protect you."

But behind his words, he heard hers—*something inside you feels—dark*. Indeed. Even now darkness filled his chest. Bracing, hot, like a batch of strong hooch. It seeped through him, calming, as if he'd surrendered to a darkness he'd been fighting too long.

Probably even since he left Zante.

He held her close. Drew in the smell of her hair, the softness of her skin, so painfully familiar, as Jimmy's men burst into the room.

"It'll be okay, Sofia. I promise." The words tumbled out, soft at first, gathering heat, power. "I promise."

She rolled in his arms, staring up at him, her eyes wide. Then without a word, she untangled herself from his arms, climbed out from under the table, and left him lying in the destruction of Zante's.

* * * *

Dino!

He kicked through the thin jaws of the cave's mouth, surfaced fast. Gulped a breath. Dino!

Markos's own voice echoed through the dark chamber, even as he thrashed in the water. He clawed for the surface.

The cool waters of the tunnel tugged at his feet. A wave rushed in, threw him against the rocks. Light exploded in his head, even as he went under again, gulped water.

Markos! His name sliced through the darkness, someone at the other end. *Markos!*

The current tugged, sucking him in even as he fought it.

Markos!

He opened his eyes, breathing hard, sweating, despite the chill of the room. He listened for the voice.

Nothing, except Dino's even breathing from the cot near the wall. Markos turned in his bed, the springs squeaking, his body quivering with the freshness of the dream, the sound of his name, as if being called from a distance, echoing through the darkness of the cave.

He stared at the fingers of moonlight tearing at his ceiling.

When he woke again, morning spilled into the room from the small, grimy window over the bed. Dino had vanished, his bedclothes and blanket in a tumble on his cot.

Markos expected to hear the sounds of delivery trucks, maybe the aroma of coffee, frying eggs on the griddle.

Pulling on his pants, he snapped his suspenders onto his shoulders, slipped his feet into his saddle shoes, and headed downstairs.

The chaos in the restaurant seemed even more damning in the daylight—shards of glass glittering on the floor like knives, tables pocked and splintered, chairs overturned, the glass countertop shattered.

The coat box sat on the counter, drilled with holes. He couldn't bear to look inside.

Uncle Jimmy sat in a back booth, nursing a cup of coffee with a man Markos didn't know. He motioned him over. "Markos, I want you to meet my friend Joe."

Tall and thin, with a short crew cut, Joe looked Markos over with a pinched look, earthy eyes. He drummed his fingers on the table, as if tapping out words to himself like the rat-a-tat of the Tommy guns that had leveled Zante's. Finally, in broken Greek, "You see the outfit who did this, kiddo?"

Markos shook his head. Joe fingered the fedora that lay on the table, tightening his lips into a knot. Then he met Jimmy's eyes with a look Markos couldn't decipher and slid out of the booth. He slapped Markos on the back before replacing his hat.

Markos slid in opposite his uncle. "Who was that?"

"Someone who's watching out for us." He gave Markos a grim look. "Listen, from now on, I don't want you to leave Hedy's side. You're on her like some sort of glue, you understand me?"

"What about the restaurant?"

"What restaurant?" Jimmy held out his hands. "Naw, Scarface just started a war." He hooked his hand around Markos's neck. "This is time for family to stick together, boy. Don't let me down."

CHAPTER 7

"Hedy, how long have you known Jimmy?"

Markos sat facing the door, inside the cramped quarters of her private dressing room at the Blue Moon. The place swam with her perfume, the cloying smell of a woman's clothing. He'd wanted to park himself outside, in the hallway, but Jimmy had come by that first night, seen him loitering on the wrong side of her door, and nearly took off his head.

Now he just tried not to glance in the mirror, where the bright bulbs illuminated her array of make-up pots, jewelry, and discarded headdresses. Or the hosiery that hung over the top of the dressing screen.

"I've known him about two years." Hedy's voice emerged from behind the screen. Thankfully, she'd learned to slow her words, to enunciate. He understood her most of the time. "He picked me out of a chorus line at the Rainbo Gardens, sent a message back to the dressing room, and was waiting for me when I came out. That was that."

"You fell in love with him?"

"Love? What's love, anyway? He's handsome and rich. And he made me feel beautiful."

You are beautiful. Markos clamped down on the words before they escaped.

"Can I ask you a question, Hedy?"

"Shoot, doll."

"Who is this Scarface?"

"You mean big Al Capone. I told you about him already. He runs the outfit on the other side of town. He's been trying to take over the business in Chicago for a couple years now."

"The business?"

"The racket, you know? It's like a war. Big Al's guys go into a joint like Tony's, put the bite on him for protection money. You know, from the fuzz, although plenty of them's on the dole. Or maybe the business is legit, and it's just a smoke-and-cards game. But see, say Jimmy's guys have already been there, and they don't like Al's men cutting in on their profits. So, they attack Big Al's outfit. They hit him, only, he hits them back, harder. Like last year—a gang from Al's outfit, armed with a bunch of violins, rubbed out Bugs Moran's entire gang, and on Valentine's Day too. Bugs, of course, got away. They always do. But that's what it's about. Dough."

Really, sometimes Markos could make out the words, but he had absolutely no idea of their meaning.

"But Jimmy's really in it now. Aiello's threatening all-out war on Scarface." She slipped out from behind the screen. "So, what do you think?"

He turned, and his breath caught in the cotton of his chest. Low-cut black sequined dress, high cut at the knees, white patterned stockings, a feathered headband, and a boa.

"Do I look shiny enough for the New Year?"

He must have managed a nod.

"Not bad for a girl from Ames, Iowa. And to think only three years ago, I'd run away from home, headed to the big city."

Her words were a blur, but he nodded again.

She came close, played a tune on his face with her fingers. "You're such a gentleman, Markos. That's what I'm going to call you. The Gent." She lifted his chin. "You know, if you wanted to kiss me, you could."

This, he understood. Heat rushed to his face.

She laughed. "It's the New Year, kiddo. You get one kiss."

"You're Uncle Jimmy's girl."

Her smile fell, just for a second, then she laughed. "Aw, you're the smart one, aren't you?"

Smart? Sometimes he felt like an idiot next to Hedy.

She sat at the dressing table. He knew he should turn away, but he couldn't quite find it in him. Instead, he watched as she curled her hair tight to her face with her fingers, held it there for a moment. She rouged her cheeks, her earlobes. Lined dark kohl on her green eyes. Used her pinky to apply her blood-red lipstick.

Her gaze flickered over to him. "You like watching me get ready?"

He turned away, burying his face in his hands. Her laughter trickled high. "Oh, Markos, you're such fun!"

His chest burned. "I'll wait for you out in the hall." Finding his feet, he pushed away the chair, reaching for the door. But she had crossed the room and now planted her hand over his. He turned even as she slid close, her hand on his chest. He hadn't noticed how small she was, really, without her costumes, or wrapped in her vamp persona. Now, she seemed almost petite, even…needy. Especially since the tease had left her eyes. Her fragrance wound around him, tugging at him.

"He won't want me forever, you know."

Markos stared at her, his hands at his sides, fighting the urge to run them down her skinny arms…

Her voice turned low, bore a huskiness she usually reserved for her songs. "I know Jimmy has other girls."

"Hedy, he loves you." Markos's voice sounded thirteen, with a hitch in it.

"Aw, he loves himself. Loves having a dame on his arm." She ran her finger down Markos's cheek, eliciting a trail of fire.

He caught her hand. Her eyes. "Do you love him?"

Her voice turned flat. "Does it matter?"

"If you don't, why don't you leave him?"

Her laugh came out harsh, and he winced, startled. "Nobody leaves Jimmy the Greek. Unless it's in a coffin." She shook her head, patting his chest. "You haven't figured that out yet?"

"I—"

"He's using you, Markos. Just like the rest of us. He's got a plan for you, and you're not going to escape it."

"He's family. He'd never do anything to hurt me." The strange panic had died, swallowed by the familiar simmer inside. He closed his hands on her arms to move her away.

She gave a little huff, raised one of those sleek brown eyebrows. "We'll see." But she resisted his push, lifting her face, those red lips just inches from his. So close that— "But we can have a little fun all the same, can't we?"

Markos sucked in a breath, held his hands up in a sort of surrender, as if she might be a pineapple—a mafia bomb. Oh…yes, he wanted to kiss her. Wanted to taste those lips, wanted to know what it might feel like to pull her curves into his arms. A coy smile tipped her mouth even as he breathed in her intoxicating, sweet smell.

He leaned toward her.

"Besides, you know he's already found his next sheba," she whispered, her lips parting.

His gaze went to her mouth, so red, like a Zante pomegranate, and probably as…sweet….

So close—

Oh. He closed his eyes, leaned his head against the door. "Please, Hedy...don't."

"Oh, Markos." She pulled away, tease in her smile, tucking her fingers into the lapel of his father's coat. "I don't know why you wear this. You know it's not you anymore. I would happily buy you a raccoon coat."

He'd been lit on fire. He curled his hands around her wrists, noted that they shook, pulled her grip from his coat. Finally heard her words. "What do you mean, he's found his next sheba?"

She gave a chuckle, winding her fingers into her pearls. "Don't think for a second that you can dangle a pretty girl under Jimmy's smeller and not attract his attention. He's had his gaze on Sofia since the second you dragged her into Zante's."

Markos stiffened. "Sofia?"

She laughed. "She's the same age I was when Jimmy found me. And look at me now." She smiled, but it quivered, just a little.

Nineteen? Hedy was nineteen? His shock must have whisked through his eyes. Her smile vanished.

"What?"

"Nothing...it's just...let's go. We don't want to be late."

"You don't believe me, do you?"

He blinked at her.

"Tell me this...do you really think that Jimmy wanted you to protect me...or just keep you away from his new girl?"

"Sofia is *not* his new girl." His voice, however, shook.

"She will be."

"He's family."

"He's a man. And he's not *her* family."

Markos just might be ill—he needed to leave this too-seasoned room, and fast. "She's...a village girl."

Hedy sighed, patted him again on the chest. "So was I." But her smile wavered.

An image of her rattled through him then—her blond hair long and braided, her face clean, tanned by the sun, wearing a simple dress....

It scared him, just a little too. He put his hands on her shoulders, so tiny beneath his grip. "Hedy, why don't you...just leave? Can't you go home?"

She sniffed—it sounded more like a smirk. "Home? How do you go home after you've become a girl like me?" A tear at the edge of her eye slurred her makeup. He ran a thumb under it.

She caught his hand, drew it to her lips. "Yes, you're the Gent."

He stood there, suddenly not fooled for a moment by her dark, dangerous eyes. "Not really, Hedy. Not really."

She pursed her lips, nodding. "Yeah. Well, more than most."

She turned her back to him, picking up her purse. "My mama sent this to me last week. Of all things, a Bible verse." She pulled out a crumpled letter. "Like it would matter."

"What does it say?" He could hear his own mother's voice, reading from her frayed book. He hadn't thought of that for...well, it seemed as if that life had never really existed.

She lifted a shoulder. "Second Timothy 2:13. I remember it from the tent meetings." She transformed then, right before his eyes, into the vamp he knew, playing a part, her voice rising as if she were behind a pulpit. "'If we believe not, yet he abideth faithful: he cannot deny himself.'"

Again, he wished he understood her words.

She dropped the letter in the trash bucket at her feet and swished past him from the room.

* * * *

Zante's contained a chill conjured more from the destroyed silhouette of the restaurant than the wind hissing through the cracks between the boards of the front window. Markos let himself in through the back, climbing the narrow stairs to his room. As usual, he looked for a light on in Sofia's quarters, some puddle of life leaking from under the door. But why would she be up at 3 a.m.? He let himself into his darkened, frigid room.

Dino huddled in a ball under his blanket on the cot. Markos shed his father's coat and laid it over his brother's form. Then, shucking off his shoes, he pulled off his clothes, folded them on the dresser, and moved toward the bed.

Hedy's husky voice twined through his thoughts. And not just the songs she'd sung tonight, but her warning over a month ago—*Nobody leaves Jimmy the Greek.*

He would. The thought kept turning in his mind, as if on a spit. He would save up his money, get train tickets for all three of them, and go…somewhere. Start over.

Maybe in Minneapolis. Wasn't that where Dr. Scarpelli said he was headed?

They wouldn't live with the Scarpellis. But Dino could borrow some books, learn to be a doctor. And Markos and Sofia could get married.

Most of all, they'd be safe. From Scarface Al.

From Uncle Jimmy.

He's had his gaze on Sofia since the second you dragged her into Zante's.

He didn't want to believe it. But a coldness settled deep into his bones, in the well of his stomach, tightening every time Hedy climbed on stage.

Yes, they had to leave.

Someone had left a package on his bed. Bound in dark paper and twine. He picked it up.

"It's from Sofia," Dino said, behind him. He leaned up on one elbow. "She said it was a late Christmas gift."

Markos closed his eyes, wincing at the memory of her beautiful coat in tatters, although she'd taken a needle and thread to it and tried to repair it. He hated that she wore it, scarred. He longed to buy her a new one, but he still owed Jimmy too much, saw his paycheck shrinking every week, thanks to the interest Jimmy tacked on.

"Look what she gave me." Dino pulled back the covers. "Socks! Three pair!"

Markos pulled the twine to release the package. The paper fell open. He snapped on the lamplight and it pooled over a knit brown blanket. He ran his fingers into it. "It's so soft."

"I saw her working on it. She said you didn't have one."

He picked it up, and the length of it fell to the floor. He imagined her hands working the needles, row by row, brought it to his face, and inhaled. It smelled like her, orange blossoms…the scent of home. Crazy tears whisked into his eyes. "No, I don't have one."

He wrapped it around himself, turned off the light, and climbed onto the bed. The springs squeaked under his weight.

"Do you ever think about home, Markos?" Dino's voice emerged soft and quiet.

Markos watched the moonlight trickle over the worn floor, Dino's discarded dark shoes. "All the time."

"I miss the sea. The taste of it on my lips, and chasing sea turtles." He looked over at Markos. "You remember that last night, right before Theo's wedding? How Lucien and I chased that turtle into Whistler's Drink—"

"I don't want to talk about Lucien." Although the mention of his friend dredged up his expression as he'd stood on the pier. *Markos, don't go!*

Markos curled his fists tight into the blanket.

"He made me laugh," Dino said.

"He was foolish. And someday you would have figured that out."

"He was my friend."

Markos closed his eyes.

Silence. Finally, "I'm sorry for that trick I played on you, Markos. It was Lucien's idea, even before he jumped off the boat. He knew you'd chase me into the cave. Knew you'd panic if you thought I'd drowned. He knew how afraid you were of the cave."

Markos glanced at him in the wan light. Were Dino's cheeks shiny?

"It's okay."

Dino shook his head. "No, it's not. I should have never forced you to come in after me."

"Maybe I wouldn't have."

"No. You always came after me. You wouldn't leave me there." Dino reached up, wiped his face with the meat of his hand. Markos looked away.

"Sofia says you're learning English at the Orthodox Church."

Dino stared at the ceiling. "Papa Minos caught me trying to steal the communion wafers."

"Dino!"

"I'm sorry. I saw them, and I was hungry. Now I sit in his office and read to him, in English."

Markos would have to thank Papa Minos. Although probably a guy like himself shouldn't be setting foot in a church. He hadn't crossed himself for so long, God would probably cringe if he tried.

"Sofia said you've been working for Peter Kazalos. He's nice to you?"

"Yeah. He goes to church sometimes. I like him. He reminds me of Papa." Dino fell silent. Then, "Markos...do you think we'll ever go back?"

Markos's throat burned. "I don't know."

Dino's breath shuddered, as if he might be trying not to cry. "I miss Papa and Theo. And I'm starting to forget Mama's voice. Do you remember it?"

You are the eldest Stavros now, and it's up to you to take care of him. Don't let me down. "I try to."

"I sometimes imagine her, standing at the end of the pier, her arms open wide as we get off the ferry. Just like that time when we went out and the storm came up and we had to camp on the north side of the island. When we returned, she was standing on the shore worrying her prayer beads—remember that?"

He remembered her tears. Remembered the tremor of her voice as she scolded him for not making it home earlier, right before pulling him into a clench.

Remembered the softly breathed prayers of gratitude. *Go, Markos. God will deliver you.*

Really, Mama? He closed his eyes. Because it surely felt as if God had stayed behind, in Zante, His feet glued in the soft sand of the shore.

* * * *

"I gotta surprise for you tonight, kiddo." Hedy held out her gloved hand for him to take as he helped her from the car. He'd parked away from the road, in the alley, aware of the drive-by shootings at gin joints habited by friends of Jimmy.

"Consider it a Valentine's Day gift."

"What is Valentine's Day?" Markos held out his arm for her as he led her down the steps to Tony's. He rapped on the door, the little slot slid open. "Wrigley," he said.

The door swung open and music curled out around him, tugging him inside.

"It's the day of love," Hedy said, hooking one skinny arm around his neck, turning to smile at him. He winced at the bite of alcohol on her breath.

Disentangling her arm, he ushered her into the room. He helped her off with her jacket, hung it on a rack next to the door. Men nodded to her as she swept by them, their eyes hanging on longer than Jimmy would have liked. A few women lined up at the bar, smoking cigarettes. Another stood in the front of the room, mourning out a jazz tune.

"I thought Jimmy would be here." Hedy leaned against the bar, her red lips in a pout.

He hadn't seen Jimmy for days—but the newspapers detailed the bloodbaths from the night before, like the scores of a baseball game. Grainy black and white photographs of the fallen from both sides of Chicagoland.

Worse was when the innocent died—children, a mother walking home from market. Between the despair of the soup kitchens and the blood on the streets, Chicago had become a war zone.

Markos scanned the room for familiar faces, nodded to a few of Jimmy's lackeys. If they were here—yes. "Jimmy's sitting up in front. C'mon, I'll bring you up—"

"No—" She yanked her hand from his grip. "Let's stay here." What looked like panic flashed through her eyes, but she smoothed it with a milky smile. "Just—wait."

Markos ordered her a drink, nothing for himself. She smiled over the brim of her glass at him as the announcer got up and introduced the next singer.

Only the name stuck with him. *Fifi.*

She emerged from the side, a slender gal wearing a short white sequined dress, her stockings rolled down below her knees, high heels, skinny arms. And short bobbed, wavy black hair. She turned her back to the audience, letting the light splash over her as the piano trickled out the first notes.

She turned, stepped up to the mic, head down. Her hair fell over her face.

There's a saying going 'round and I begin to think it's true

His breath caught. He knew the tone, had imagined the voice, but had never heard actual words—

It's awful hard to love someone, when they don't care 'bout you

Tangy and intoxicating, the song trickled across the audience, as the singer raised her head.

Once I had a lovin' man, as good as many in this town

"I told you you'd be surprised."

Sofia. Her voice tremored even as she sang out, now meeting the eyes of her audience, one by one by—one.

But now I'm sad and lonely, for he's gone and turned me down, now.

I ain't got nobody and nobody cares for me.

Markos couldn't move, despite the hot roaring inside. *Singing.* Sofia's words tore through him. He clutched the side of the bar, watching Jimmy, his hand on his drink, smiling up at her.

He knew that smile. Seen it before, for Hedy.

I got the blues, the weary blues...

Hedy turned to look at him. "You okay, kiddo?"

"I'm not a kiddo," Markos said, his hand wrapping around her upper arm. "I'm only a year younger than you." His gaze stayed, however, on Sofia, burned to the sight of her swaying side to side, her beautiful hair shorn, her eyes darkened, her lips blood red. The transformation only made her look younger, as if Jimmy had plucked her right out of some mother's arms.

His arms.

"Ow, you're hurtin' me, Markos."

Hedy's eyes betrayed real pain. "Sorry." He loosened his grip as he pulled her toward the door.

And I'm sad and lonely, won't somebody come and take a chance with me?

Her mouth tipped up into a smile as it landed on Uncle Jimmy.

I'll sing sweet love songs honey, all the time...

"Where we goin'? I don't wanna leave—Markos!" Hedy's voice lifted as she tore away from him. A fella near the door rose from his table.

"He giving you trouble, lady?"

If you'll come and be my sweet baby mine...

Markos stepped back, breathing hard, his chest knotted. He shot another look at Sofia.

She'd seen him, and for a moment, recognition registered in the flutter of her voice. *'Cause I ain't got nobody, and nobody cares for me.*

"C'mon back, Markos." Hedy grabbed his hand.

Sofia stared at him hard as Hedy dragged him back to the bar. *Won't somebody go and find my man and bring him back to me...*

Then she flashed her beautiful smile once more on her benefactor. Jimmy blew out a long breath of cigarette smoke.

It's awful hard to be alone and without sympathy... Once I was a loving gal, as good as any in this town but since my daddy left me, I'm a gal with her heart bowed down....

Her last notes trickled out, and she ended with a blush, a coy smile that only Hedy could have taught her.

Markos shot her an accusing look, and Hedy shrugged. "A gal's gotta have a protégé."

But Hedy swallowed, too fast for her own good, and looked away.

Uncle Jimmy leaped to his feet, clapping even as he reached out for Sofia. She sashayed toward him, took his hand.

A fist had Markos by the chest, squeezing out his heart, his lungs. Especially as Sofia leaned forward and kissed Jimmy's fat cheek.

"I gotta get outta here. Stay if you want," he growled to Hedy. Even her hand on his arm couldn't stop him as he banged through the crowd.

He brushed by two men in overcoats, just entering. Something sharp clipped his leg, as if—

No.

He turned, spotted the bulky outline of a Tommy gun against the second man's flowing coat.

"Jimmy, look out!" Markos launched himself at the shooter as he brought the gun up to his hip. The other had already begun to spray the room.

Screams, the pepper of shots, shattered glass, shredded tables—people dove to the floor.

Hedy clung to the counter, eyes wide in shock. Markos scrambled to his feet just as the gunman turned his aim on her. He heard her screams—or maybe his own—as the bullets tore through her body. "Hedy!"

She twisted and fell in heap.

One of Jimmy's men launched himself toward the gunner Markos had taken down, and dispatched him with his handgun. Another took aim, took the other shooter down.

Thirty seconds, tops. Hedy lay bloodied, her body chewed with bullets, eyes unseeing. Women screamed, stepping over bodies as they ran toward the door. Markos pushed against the crowd toward the stage. "Sofia!"

Please, oh, please, God—

Jimmy lay on his side, cursing. A bullet had nicked him—blood poured down his arm.

Under the piano, Sofia curled in a ball, shaking. "Sofia!" Markos crawled under it, pulled her free. "Are you okay?"

She shook, her eyes in his, and he didn't get an answer. He ran his hands down her arms. "Are you bleeding?"

She grabbed his jacket, buried her face into his chest. "No…no, I don't think so."

He touched her hair, tangled it in his hands. "You could have been killed. What are you doing here?"

Behind her, Jimmy had pushed himself up. Someone helped him to his feet, and he staggered over to Markos. Held out his hand. "You saved my life, boy. I always knew you'd come through for the family."

Markos stared at the hand, fingers like frankfurters, slick with blood, and didn't think—couldn't. Every thought emptied from his mind. Before he could even make out words, he found himself on his feet, his voice roaring, everything boiling out in a rush. He slammed his hands into Jimmy's chest once. Twice. Again. And then, as Jimmy backed up against a table, he made a fist and threw everything he had into it.

His hand exploded in pain as it connected with Jimmy's face.

Jimmy howled, his nose destroyed, blood spurting into his eyes.

Yeah, that's right. For the *family.*

Jimmy tumbled to his knees just as Markos felt the first blow, from behind, deep in his kidneys.

CHAPTER 8

"I'm gonna let you live, Markos, because you're family, and I know you're real sorry. Besides, your mama would want me to give you another chance."

Markos said nothing, his mouth too swollen to form words. He didn't even attempt to muster the energy—or perhaps the courage to glare at Uncle Jimmy, who'd taken it upon himself to give Markos his beating.

After, of course, Jimmy had spent a couple hours getting stitched up at the hospital.

"Uncle Jimmy! Let me in. Please!" Dino's voice outside the door bore a ragged edge.

At least Sofia had stopped screaming. Markos didn't know what was worse—the steel edge of Jimmy's fists or Sofia's endless pleading.

Markos had never been in the basement of Zante's—a cellar off the alley that smelled of mildew and the tinny pinch of blood. He'd be okay if he never returned to the restaurant's bowels. Actually, the pain in his arms laced above him, hanging from a pipe, turned him almost blind. He'd already retched out parts of his stomach, probably even pieces of his kidneys. He couldn't take a breath without his ribs shearing through him.

Jimmy plunked down on a chair, working off the brass knuckles from his hand, wiping his brow. "I know you love her, kid, but she's got a voice for the clubs and frankly, I need her." He stood up, grabbed Markos's face in his mitt. "I promise, I'll treat her right."

"Like you did Hedy?" The words emerged slurred, and due to Jimmy's flinch, intelligible.

"She got the best from me, didn't she?" He threw Markos's face away from him. "She was sweet on you the minute she laid eyes on you. And don't tell me you didn't enjoy every minute." He put his lips next to Markos's ear. "Did you love her?"

Markos closed his eyes. Hedy's smile, sometimes too bright, always tinged with a hue of sadness, swept into his mind. Her husky voice, that fragrance that tangled his thoughts. Yes, maybe he'd loved her. He tightened his jaw, relishing now the pain.

"Cut him down," Jimmy said.

He wanted to howl when the bonds on his arms dropped and he collapsed to the floor.

"Let them in." Jimmy stood back, eyes on Markos as the lock slid open. He heard Sofia's cry.

And then, she was there, her hands cradling his head. "You're a monster!" she hissed at Jimmy, but she flinched as he took a step toward her. Markos wanted to lift his hand, maybe spit something threatening out of his mouth, but he couldn't move, his body turning to slurry on the cold dirt floor.

"I didn't kill him," Jimmy said, leaning close to her, his voice low. "You owe me for that." He slid a hand under her chin, gave her a kiss on the cheek. She jerked away.

Jimmy laughed and stepped around them out of the room.

"Let's get him up to our room." Dino, his voice stretched taut. Markos tried to bite back a groan as Dino slung his useless arm around his skinny shoulders. He wore a grim expression as he hauled Markos up.

Sofia braced him on the other side.

He had legs. He knew it. But they didn't seem to want to work. "I'm sorry—" he rasped, even as they dragged him from the basement, wrestled him up the stairs. He just wanted to cave in to the pain, let it drag him under.

Make him forget.

Forget that he'd killed Kostas Pappos.

Forget that he'd left his widowed mother and run away from his crime.

Forget that he'd turned his back on Dr. Scarpelli's kindness.

Forget that he'd practically run into the arms of Hedy Brooks and her speakeasy life.

Forget that he didn't have a hope of protecting Sofia and Dino from Uncle Jimmy and whatever plans he had for them.

Forget that he hadn't the strength to keep his promises.

Sofia tripped on the top step and pitched into the grimy snow; Markos landed beside her in an explosion of agony. Dino caught himself on his hands.

"Just leave me here."

"Shut your yap," Dino said, climbing to his feet, wiping his filthy hands on his pants. "Just—shut it, Markos." He slammed the palm of his hand against his cheek, as if wiping a tear.

"I got us into this—"

"Theo got us into this! He's the one who started it, by stealing Kostas's girl. Why couldn't he just stay away from her? He betrayed us all!" His eyes bore a craziness, his voice shaking. "And now—now we're here, and I—I'm scared, Markos." He ground his jaw shut, looked away. Shook his head. "It doesn't matter. Let's just get inside." He grabbed Markos's arm and again wrapped it around his shoulders. He seemed stronger when he clutched Markos's waist. "Help me. I can't do this on my own."

Markos stared at his little brother, straining to lift him from the dirt, his face flushed, his cheeks wet, almost—yes, angry as he hauled Markos to his feet. The anger gave him power. Focus. A place to put his fear.

Markos knew it too well.

Anger had fueled every step he'd taken from the island, a darkness seeded the night Theo and Papa had died. It twined through his heart, his body, his thoughts, strengthening him, blinding him.

Anger gave him courage. Strength. Power.

It buried his fear.

God will deliver you.

Not a chance, Mama. He'd stood over Kostas's body, had his blood embedded in the creases of his hands. He knew the truth.

No, God wasn't on his side. Couldn't be.

Markos balanced himself on the edge of the doorframe as Sofia found her feet, and for a moment lifted his face to the cool air, drying the blood, scouring the dank basement smell from his lungs. He drank it in, not caring that it bit his skin, burned his throat.

"I'm going to get us out of here," Markos said to Dino. Although, honestly, he hadn't a clue how they might break free, escape the life he'd trenched them in.

"I know," Dino said softly as he carried him into Zante's.

Markos couldn't remember shuffling up the stairs, or even Dino removing his shirt, his pants. He wished he could dredge up the memory of Sofia washing his wounds, mopping his brow as he spiked a fever. Wished he knew whether Uncle Jimmy had dragged her away to sing for him at Tony's.

But he fell into a bruised, painful place, nursed by the tenor of his own whimpers, a heat that turned him inside out, a cold that rattled him through to his teeth. Every movement raked up pain.

He may have cried out, but as he finally sank into darkness, he heard a voice—his, only broken in a way he'd never before heard.

Please.

* * * *

Markos would know the song anywhere, but especially the way it lifted above the rush of the waves, more like a feeling than a tune, seasoned with the tang of the sea, the jangle of goats' bells in the far-off hills. The setting sun poured over him, hot, soothing. On shore's edge, the wind glued her long linen dress to her body and teased her long hair as her voice beckoned him down the hills of Zante.

"Sofia!"

He raised his arm, but she didn't turn. Her song wound out on the breeze. *"Sofia!"*

She turned. Her eyes drifted past him, and she smiled. Then she crouched, holding out her arms. Markos stopped, the rust sand mortaring him in place, as a little boy, dark-haired, his feet bare, ran across the beach and leaped into Sofia's arms. She twirled him, his feet flinging out, his head back.

Markos paused, caught in the embrace of their joy, especially when she began dancing with the child.

Then, abruptly she stopped and looked back at Markos.

He lifted his hand.

She grabbed the boy's hand and, with one final glance at Markos, turned and began to run up the beach.

"Sofia!"

"Shh, Markos, I'm here. I'm right here." A cool, soft touch on his forehead, and he rose out of the clutches of the dream with a shout.

"Sofia!"

She stood over him—not the Sofia of his dreams, but the one caught in his nightmare. Her short hair, curls pasted into place, her amazing blue eyes bigger than he'd remembered, ever. Her perfect lips rouged. Into his mind flashed the memory of her on stage, hips swaying, that voice twanging out a song that intoxicated every man in the joint.

Including himself. "Sofia."

She gently pushed him back into the pillow. He couldn't help it—he reached up and fingered her bobbed hair.

She caught his hand, her thumb moving over his wrist. A soft sadness filled her eyes. "I'm sorry I cut it."

He shook his head. "It's beautiful. Makes your eyes so much more blue. Reminds me of the sea."

She thumbed away a tear and managed a smile. "I think your fever broke." She brushed his sweaty hair away from his face. "You're looking better."

He winced when she caressed his left eye, still swollen shut, not needing a mirror to assess the damage. He must look like he'd been dragged under a train to elicit Sofia's expression.

"Where's Dino?"

"He wanted to be here, but Jimmy has him doing errands."

Errands? "I know what kind of errands Jimmy sends people on."

"He delivered a package yesterday. A—pineapple, you know?"

Markos wanted to sink back into the darkness. Jimmy's idea of a "delivery" was a case of so-called gin bottles with a bomb inside. "Was he hurt?"

"No. He got out before it went off. But the front of the gin-joint was a candy store—"

"Please tell me no kids died."

"Just the owner. But Jimmy's been breaking the glass on the fuse, setting the bomb ticking before Dino leaves, so he knows Dino will do the job. One of these days—"

"Dino might not be so lucky."

"This is all my fault." She kneaded her hands together. "Jimmy said I could make him some money, and Hedy told me that if I sang for him, he'd give me more gigs. She was the one who cut my hair, dressed me up."

"Hedy did this?"

I have a surprise for you; consider it a Valentine's Day gift. Hedy stepped into his thoughts, that dangerous red smile, those eyes that had the power to turn him inside out. *I think I'll call you the Gent.*

"She taught me how to sing too."

He came back to Sofia, to the shame in her eyes as she looked down at him. *Oh, Sof.* "You already knew how to sing. Just—not like that."

"You didn't like it."

He blanketed her hands with his. "I—love hearing you sing. Just—I don't want you caught up in Hedy's world."

"You liked it when Hedy sang."

Her voice emerged so soft he might not have heard it if she hadn't widened her eyes, as if also surprised the words had escaped.

Yes, he had liked it when Hedy sang. And for that, yes, he probably deserved Uncle Jimmy's fists. "I'm sorry, Sofia. I..." He didn't know where to start. Sorry for loving Hedy Brooks? Perhaps. Sorry for letting her inside his head, his heart? Sometimes. Sorry for letting her pull him into a current that hurt Sofia? Definitely. "I miss your songs from Zante."

"I have no songs left in me."

"I should have let you and Dino go with Dr. Scarpelli. I just—I just wanted to keep us together."

"You were keeping your promise. But—it nearly killed you." Her face crumpled just a bit then. *I'm poison.* He saw her words, felt them. For the first time he understood—*poison.*

"No. *I* nearly killed me. You were right, Sofia. I do have blackness inside me. I let it in, feasted on it, thinking it would make me strong, but it's only—it's only confused me."

She stared at him, something new in her eyes. Not fear, not anger…

"I don't know what to do, Sof. We're trapped, and I don't know how to get us out of here."

She leaned close, clamped her hand over his mouth, put her mouth to his ear. "I do." Her eyes darted to the door. "I know where Jimmy keeps his protection money."

He almost didn't recognize her, the way she morphed into a moll right before his eyes.

"Sofia—no. If he caught us—"

"I can't watch him kill you, Markos. I have some money saved, but it's not enough to get us away."

And he had none. In fact, Jimmy owned him further out into the future than he could see.

"He has a compartment in his desk where he hides his money. I saw it once, when I delivered his lunch to him. He didn't know I saw him—I came in without knocking, then ducked back out. But he keeps his stash there before he puts it in his safe. We could sneak in, take it, be away before—"

"Shh. Listen to yourself. We can't steal from Uncle Jimmy—"

"Markos—he's been stealing from us since the day we arrived here! You work every day in his kitchen, every night you drove for his floozy." She cut her voice again low. "Dino's scrubbed every surface of the restaurant day in and day out, and..."

"And—what?" He pushed himself up on his elbows, gasping at the claw of pain, not caring. "Sofia, what has Uncle Jimmy done to you?"

"Nothing—nothing, Markos." She pushed on his shoulders. "Lay back. I'm fine. I just don't think that taking what's due us is stealing."

"He'll kill us if he catches us."

"He'll probably get us killed if we stay here."

Markos collapsed into the pillow, hitching his breath.

"He'll find us. You don't understand, Sof. He's got long arms. It's not just Jimmy's gang, it's Joe's—he'll put the entire Ghenna family after us. And then there are the cops. Half of the Chicago fuzz is on the dole. We won't be able to hide."

"So, we'll leave. We'll run. You're smart, Markos. You'll keep us safe."

He stared at the ceiling. Judging by the shadows that reached into the room, he guessed he'd spent another full day in bed. "I can't, Sofia. I'm in way over my head—I feel like I'm drowning."

Sofia hitched a hip onto the side of his bed, touching his hair. "I like it without the Brylcreem in it. Reminds me of when you'd return from fishing, your hair tangled by the wind." She ran her finger under his chin. "I miss your tan, though. And the way you would stand at the rudder, guiding in your boat. You loved the sea—I saw it on your face."

"You were watching?"

"I was always watching. When you were at sea, you weren't afraid. You had a strength about you, an energy. You were invincible."

"That's because I knew the sea, Sofia. I knew the currents and the beauties. I could read its moods, and even its fury. I felt at home in the sea."

He let the memory of it pour over him, the peace that soaked through him when he surrendered to the waves. "I'm lost here."

"Then ask for help." She leaned forward, and sweetly, probably so as not to hurt him, brushed her lips across his. He slipped his hand around her neck, drew her closer, kissed her like he'd longed to, not caring about his bruised lips. She tasted sweet, and smelled so good—fresh and clean, and the way she caught her breath and moved into his kiss made him want to weep. *Sofia.*

He pulled away, held her face in his hands, kissed her cheeks, her forehead, finally met her eyes. "You're so beautiful, you know that? I can't even remember when I started to love you. You've always been there, inside of me." He ran his thumb over her soft lips.

A tentative smile tipped under his touch. "You're still the Markos I know."

Her words sent a wash of heat in his eyes. "I don't feel like it."

"I'm still watching you, Markos Stavros. I see that you're a good man."

And of course, then he was crying. No longer twenty-eight, not even eighteen, but probably eight, as he gulped in her words. Her hand touched his cheek, soft, thumbing away his tears.

She touched her forehead to his. "You don't have to do this alone. Let us help, Markos." She cut her voice to a whisper. "Dino and me—we've got a plan. It'll work, Markos. But you gotta trust us."

The look in her eyes had the power to reach through him, untangle the clog in his chest. "I don't know—are you sure we won't get caught?" His voice hitched. "I can't watch him beat you, Sofia."

A knock at the door jerked her away.

Uncle Jimmy stood in the doorway. "Fifi. It's time to go."

Sofia ducked her head, moving away from him—*No, Sofia, don't go!*—even as Jimmy walked over, patted Markos on the cheek. "Feeling better, boy?"

Pain speared through Markos's skull. "I'm glad to see you're on the mend. The family needs your help, kiddo." He smiled, like a shark.

No one leaves Jimmy the Greek.

Jimmy tugged Sofia from the room. But at the door, she looked back at Markos and winked.

And that's what scared him most of all.

CHAPTER 9

The last time Markos had stood on the steps of a Greek Orthodox Church, it had been the day of Theo's wedding, the hot sun winking off the cobblestones of the courtyard, Sofia walking toward him, glowing as if she might be the bride.

How he missed the sun. The March wind still contained the lick of winter, slicking under the neck of his father's coat. He shivered, thankful it no longer scoured up a wince. Apparently his bones had healed, although in the crisp mornings, sometimes the frost still pressed him into his bed, aging him a century. Today, cold pressed clear through him, rattling his teeth, his bones, made worse by the fog that slinked in from Lake Michigan. It seemed that even the skies mourned Hedy's death—it had poured down sorrow nearly every day for two weeks since Markos finally pried himself out of bed and back into the life Jimmy required of him.

Namely, guarding Sofia. Perhaps Jimmy thought that he'd beaten enough fear into Markos to keep him from stealing Sofia away into the night.

Or maybe he just meant to grind defeat into his bones, because Uncle Jimmy barely left Sofia's side, his hand always on her arm, the small of her back, breathing his stench into her neck. Markos watched from the front seat, his hands white on the steering wheel, trying not to retch. He spent most nights—and days—chauffeuring Jimmy through the streets of Chicago in his new Model A town car, shadowed by a group of Jimmy's boys in his old Model T.

Parishioners began to trickle out of the church into the wet twilight, dragging with them the smell of incense, the mourn of the organ. Markos gripped the umbrella, watching the rain dribble off the sides, averting his eyes from the faces that passed. Probably they could see his guilt—even if he'd managed to justify it with Sofia's words. *It's not stealing.*

It felt like stealing. The way he and Sofia slunk into Uncle Jimmy's office—she'd actually picked it with a lock pick set she'd purchased—another skill he regretted Chicago teaching her. Inside the desk lay the stash of dough from Uncle Jimmy's daily racket earnings. He felt like a criminal the way he'd shoved the cash into a paper bag, hidden it in his coat, left in its place a Michigan bankroll—a wad of paper wrapped in a hundred-dollar bill. He kept glancing at the coupe, flinching when he heard Jimmy's voice greet the priest.

Markos caught Dino's gaze on him. *Did you get it?*

Markos gave barely a nod.

He already hates me, Dino. If he catches someone—it's going to be me. Yes, he'd won their argument, in hushed, angry tones, waged over the past two weeks. No need to bloody Dino's hands too. If Markos wanted God to deliver them, he needed to ensure at least one merited the Divine's protection.

Dino flashed a quick smile, handed Uncle Jimmy his fedora. Sofia emerged behind them both, waif-thin in a black dress and raccoon wrap coat, nicer than the one Markos had purchased for her. Of course.

Markos moved in beside Uncle Jimmy, angled the umbrella over his head. "On to Tony's, Uncle?"

"I need to stop by Zante's first, Markos. Pick up a package." He held out his elbow for Sofia, who slipped her gloved hand into it. She glanced at Markos, fear in her pursed lips. Markos gave a tiny shake of his head.

Probably he'd lose himself right there.

If Jimmy returned to the office to get his *package*, well, he'd find it missing. Mostly because it was currently wrapped inside Markos's blanket in the trunk of the coupe.

"Are you sure you don't wanna go straight to Tony's, Uncle Jimmy? I gotta practice." Sofia cozied up to Jimmy as Markos ground his molars to a fine powder.

Since when did Jimmy go home after mass? Of course, in the past Markos had usually delivered him to Hedy's, probably for a different kind of nourishment, while Markos sat outside on the street, trying to sound out the newspaper, blocking from his mind the silhouettes in Hedy's window.

So far, Uncle Jimmy hadn't turned his more intimate charms on Sofia. So far…

"Well, that's a tempting offer, doll." Jimmy slung his arm around her, pulled her tight to himself.

Dino shot him a look. Markos took a breath.

"But I gotta do some work. You wait for me, I'll make it up to you."

Sofia giggled, and Markos thought he might be ill.

Markos opened the door for them, and Sofia climbed in without meeting his eyes. Dino slid into the front seat while Markos stowed the umbrella in the trunk.

Jimmy appeared behind him. "It's cold today. Hand me that blanket for Sofia."

Markos froze. "Uh—okay." He barely stilled his hands as he reached in, tried to shake out the package from the blanket before he handed it over. But he'd wrapped it too tight. Uncle Jimmy took it, slid in beside

Sofia. Markos held his breath even as he crossed to the driver's side, waiting to hear Uncle Jimmy roar, to feel the press of a gun's barrel to the base of his head.

"There you go, doll. Nice and warm." Jimmy had spread the blanket over her lap.

As Markos got in, Sofia gave him cool, unfazed eyes.

He barely drew a breath as he drove them through the north side of town back to Zante's. He stopped in the alleyway, got out to open Jimmy's door.

Jimmy pressed him back with two fingers to his sternum. "You stay here, wait for your brother." He jerked his head at Dino. "Hurry up."

Sofia climbed out of the car, leaned into Markos. "I don't know what's going on, but I'll be there. I promise."

There. At Union Station in Chicago. The 10:40 p.m. train, Burlington to Minneapolis. Markos touched her hand as she slipped past him. She gestured with her chin behind her, directing Markos's gaze inside the passenger compartment. On the floor, under the blanket, where she'd hidden it with her feet, lay Uncle Jimmy's roll of cash.

When the back door of Zante's clicked shut, he swiped up the money and pocketed it.

He could taste his heartbeat.

He stood for a long moment, letting the rain run down his collar, cooling him. Then he got in and braced his hands on the steering wheel.

Blew out a breath.

Oh, God, please deliver—

"Move it, Markos." Dino slammed into the car, his face white, holding a suitcase. *Markos's* suitcase, the one he'd packed and slid under his bed.

"What are you doing? Did he see you—"

"He knows." Dino shook his head, his voice odd, high-pitched. "He put a bomb in here."

Markos stared at the suitcase. "Is it..."

"Yes. He broke the glass, the fuse is already burning. We—we have an address. It's Kazolas, Markos. Peter Kazolas."

Heat, what little he had, drained from Markos. He stared at the suitcase. At Dino.

"How much time do we have?"

Dino stared at the case. "I don't know. Maybe twenty minutes."

Markos slammed his hand into the steering wheel. "He knew this—knew we wouldn't let him hurt old man Kazalos."

Dino stared at him. "We can't stay here. Uncle Jimmy's waiting for us to leave...if it goes off, Sofia will be killed."

"Give me the case."

"What are you doing?"

"Get out, Dino. Get out and go to the train station."

"What are you going to do?"

"Get out and run, Dino. *Now*!" *For once, please, Dino, listen—*

Dino's jaw tightened. Pulsed. "You'd better be there. You'd better *be there*!" He put the case on the floorboard and got out.

"Run, Dino. *Run*."

Dino disappeared down the alleyway.

Why would Uncle Jimmy want to kill Peter Kazalos?

To hurt Dino? Or force Markos to choose?

Markos grabbed the suitcase, got out. Stood in the alleyway. The rain bulleted him as his heart thundered. *Please God, deliver us.*

Walking over to Jimmy's basement entrance, he heaved open the door and stumbled down the steps. Then, without turning on the light—he didn't need light to trace every inch of the dark folds of the room—he took the pineapple and wedged it behind the gas line to the building.

****

Please, Sofia, please.

Why hadn't he waited for her? Markos paced the hallway of Union Station, his saddle shoes squeaking on the marble floor. Although his father's coat shed most of the water, the wool retaining its warmth, he shivered.

Dino hid in a shadow of one of the tall Corinthian columns, watching the south entrance.

Markos leaned into an alcove, glancing at the clock hanging from the archway. Ten minutes to the train. Ten minutes to freedom. Already they had announced the boarding.

Please, Sofia, please.

He longed to jump back in the coupe, race back to Zante's, but probably half the city—Jimmy's men, as well as the fuzz on his payroll, scoured the city for him—thanks to the explosion that leveled the restaurant. Thankfully, it hadn't lit up any other houses on the street. More than that, his plan had worked—or maybe his crazy, desperate prayers had worked, because for the first time in months something went *right.* He'd driven away, toward Kazalos, and Uncle Jimmy bought the hustle. Markos had watched, his breath leaking out in an agonizing gush when Sofia and Uncle Jimmy paraded out the front door and into the waiting Model T.

They were long gone to Tony's by the time the bomb exploded. Markos longed to chase after them, to slam the coupe into the side of the Model T, rescue Sofia, motor them both to safety. But with the heat carried by Jimmy's crew, they would be mowed down before they turned the corner.

Instead, he drove straight to Union Station. To wait.

Markos ran his hands through his rain-slicked hair. What if Uncle Jimmy thought she helped plan—

"Markos!"

Her voice stopped his heart. He stepped out of the shadows just as Sofia flung herself at him, her arms hooking his neck. She shook, soaked through, her hair plastered to her head, her arms bare. "Where is your jacket?"

"I had to leave it at Tony's. We got there, and then Jimmy's crew ran in and said that Zante's blew up—and in the chaos, I just…I just ran away. I didn't look back." She pulled away, stared up at him. "You set Uncle Jimmy's place on fire."

He tightened his lips, trying to scrub the sound of the explosion from his mind.

She bracketed his face with her hands. "I knew it—and worse, I think he knows it too. He roared out of there, saying, 'That kid!'—and you're the only kid I know who could make your uncle that angry."

The train whistle blew, and somehow Dino appeared at their side. "We gotta go, Markos. Now."

And behind them, at the end of the corridor—two policemen entered the station.

Markos shucked off his coat, settled it on Sofia's shoulders. "You go. I'll catch up."

Sofia's blue eyes widened. "Markos—you're coming with us."

The two cops had him in view.

"Listen—I'll catch up. I have the coupe—I'll drive to the next station. Dino, give me my ticket."

Dino handed it over, made to follow with the cash.

"No—you keep that. Just…in case."

Dino's face whitened. "Markos?"

"Listen to me, both of you. Jimmy knows I did it—they want me, not you. Go—now. Get on that train. You have Dr. Scarpelli's address—he'll take care of you."

"I don't want him to take care of us. I want you!" Dino said, his voice angry, dark.

"I can't anymore—don't you see? If I go with you, the danger will follow. The fact is—it's followed us all the way from Zante."

"What are you talking about?"

Markos closed his eyes, the truth distilling through him. "It's my fault we're in this mess. I was so angry, and I held on to that. But really, I was holding on to my pride. I didn't want to think I needed help. That…"

He met Sofia's eyes. "I wanted to be the one that took care of you. I thought that maybe—well, that God wouldn't really want to help someone like me, and I didn't want to take the chance that I was wrong. But—I only destroyed our lives."

He shot a glance at the cops. They'd stopped, now looked him over.

"I'm sure that Jimmy's people are looking for me all over the city. If we wait, he'll follow us all the way to Minneapolis. We'll never get away from him. But if you go without me, I can lead them away." The words burned in his throat even as he said them. "I'll find you, I…" No, he wouldn't promise.

Dino voice snapped, high, stricken. "I can't go without you. I don't know what to do…"

Markos hooked his brother around the neck, touched his forehead to Dino's. "You take care of her. Promise me you'll do a better job than I did."

You don't have to do this alone. Sofia's words thundered into his mind. No, he didn't. Not anymore.

If we believe not, yet he abideth faithful: he cannot deny himself.

Hedy's voice, shimmering with hurt, swept into his brain. Faithful. God couldn't turn his back on him—because he was God.

And just like that, for the first time since leaving Zante, Markos could breathe. The coil of hot anger simply…drained away from him.

The cops made a beeline toward Markos. The train whistled again.

Dino pulled at her. "It's going to leave, Sofia. We gotta go!"

"No—Markos. Please." She had him by the lapels.

She stood there, her eyes flush with tears, both hands fisting his coat, and with everything inside him, he wanted to flee. To scoop her and Dino up and race to the train and…run.

Just run.

"No. I'm not going. This is the right thing to do. You have to go. I have to stay. God *will* deliver us."

Dino gave him a strange look. "You sound like Mama."

Finally.

"Markos—" Sofia said, her voice wrecked.

"I can't run anymore." He shackled her wrists, pulled them away from his lapels.

Sofia shook out of his grip. Stepped away from him, his betrayal on her face. "You…promised." Her voice emerged raw, full of barb. "You… *promised* you wouldn't leave me."

"Sofia—"

"You! Stop!" The cops broke out into a run.

He caught Dino's eyes and put everything there, hoping Dino could still read him. Still trusted him. *Take care of Sofia.*

Dino nodded, his Adam's apple thick in his neck. He grabbed Sofia's arm.

"No." Her voice tore at the end. "No!"

"C'mon, Sofia."

She shook her head, held up her hands, her face turning away as if she couldn't bear the sight of Markos.

Dino gave him one last broken look. "I promise."

Markos flashed him a smile, a grin not unlike something Lucien would have given, turned, and ran from the station.

CHAPTER 10

A hazy, watery breath filled the air, the night turning steely gray, the hint of dawn. Markos flattened himself behind an applecart, watching, listening.

Praying. Because as he'd raced out of Union Station, as he'd heard the train pull away, he'd lifted his face to the rain and let it pour over him.

Cleanse him.

Wash him of the anger…at Theo, at Kostas, at Uncle Jimmy. At himself. The rain seemed to clear the fog that had been around his mind over the past six months, and for the first time he saw clearly not only his mistakes, but the hovering hand of God.

He abideth faithful.

In the form of Dr. Scarpelli. Of Peter Kazalos. Even…Hedy.

In fact, Hedy's attention had probably kept him from becoming one of Jimmy's rodmen, his assassins. He certainly had possessed enough anger for it.

A police car splashed by, littering icy, black street water into the alleyway. He'd made it out of Union Station and spent most of the night on the north side "L," hopping on and off, weaving through alleyways, finally looping back around to where the coupe parked in the shelter of an alleyway off Canal Street.

He'd conjured up two plans. One included hijacking the coupe and heading north. The second seemed simpler—get on a train headed the opposite direction as Dino and Sofia. Maybe to Kansas City, or even New York.

He'd have to believe that with God's help, he would find them again.

Uncle Jimmy had Union Station under patrol. Which meant that either way he'd have to hijack the coupe. Preferably before the dawn peeled away his hiding place.

Indeed, the street had begun to stir to life. The bakery churned out a smell that made his stomach roar. A newspaper truck tossed out the daily stack to a still-closed stand. Dogs watched him with sharp eyes from behind a pile of broken crates and barrels.

Markos turned up the collar on his suit coat, ducked his head, and stalked down the street, crossing it, then passing the bakery, until finally tucking into the alleyway. He pulled away the debris he used to hide the coupe then slid into the smooth, cool seat and fired it up.

He inched the coupe out of the alleyway.

Bullets raked the storefront beside him, shattering the glass of the bakery. Markos slammed the accelerator, tore out of the alleyway, fish-tailed onto the street, and gunned it.

Typewriter shots took out the back window. Markos ducked his head, mashed the pedal, glancing behind him.

Spotted a Model T hot on his tail, with Jimmy's triggermen hanging off the running boards.

He barely touched the brakes as he screwed the wheel left, skidding onto Monroe. Silent gray buildings loomed above him. He passed a cop car and it pulled out behind him, sirens wailing.

The wheels bumped against the cobblestones. Ahead, the skyline opened up.

And, between the buildings, the sun pushed out of the pocket of night, fingers of orange gold beckoning across the murky darkness of Lake Michigan.

The sea.

Bullets strafed the car. He hunkered down, reaching for the ticket in his pocket. Taking it out, he crumpled it with his fist and tossed it out the window. "Sorry, Dino."

Pushing the pedal to the floor, he swerved to miss horse carts, a reckless Packard. The coupe had power—more than the Model T, even more than the Model A's of the local police force. He swerved, terrorizing a dog that ran out in front of him, and clipped an apple cart. The fruit exploded like a bomb, meaty shrapnel littering his wake.

Ahead of him, at the end of Monroe Avenue, stretched the pier.

And, blocking the entrance, Uncle Jimmy, flanked by a squadron of Tommy-toting rodmen, ready to unload on Markos.

Markos slowed the car twenty feet away, kept the motor running.

Uncle Jimmy shook his head as he walked forward, his arms out. "Markos. Nephew. What are you doin'?"

Markos gripped the wheel.

"Okay, so we're even. I get it. I'll even forgive you, again. The truth is, I got insurance on the place, and compassion. I know you loved the girl. I even let her run away—how's that?" He held out his sausage hands, as if in penance. "Just get outta the car, kid."

Markos drew in a breath.

"You know you like it. The cars. The money. The power. I can make you strong. I can make you a Stavros. You and me, together. Family."

Markos closed his eyes, drew in a shaky breath.

"C'mon, kid. Stop the games." Uncle Jimmy gestured toward his men. They lowered their guns. Markos didn't look at the pile-up behind him.

"We're gonna win this war, and someday everything I have will be yours."

Inside, a too familiar darkness stirred.

The wind caught the tang of the lake, drifted it into the car. For a second, the smell swept him back to the clammy cave, to the swells pounding him against the rock, to the cool pull of the currents into the tunnels...into the darkness.

No. He wouldn't give in to himself again. "You're not my family! I don't belong to you!" The words issued from him without thought, more of an impulse, almost a scream.

Uncle Jimmy stopped. His smile vanished.

No one leaves Jimmy the Greek.

Yes, they did. Markos slammed his foot into the accelerator.

Uncle Jimmy dove out of the way, as his men opened fire.

But Jimmy had ordered for himself an armor-plated coupe. Markos ducked, letting the car take the bullets as he aimed for the entrance to the pier.

No, Markos, don't go! Lucien stood at the end of the pier, waving his arms, the sun in his dark eyes, shining, hoping.

Markos saw himself this time, lifting his arms above his head. Waving. *I'll be back, Lucien!*

He thumped over the curb as another spray of bullets took out one of his tires. The rim ground into the dirt as he muscled the car toward the water. He clipped the edge of a Model T, slammed past it onto the dirt lot.

He tharrumphed the car over the edge of the walkway, the clear lake before him, the sun now carpeting it with a bath of gold.

"Friends?" Lucien held his hand out to him.

The coupe broke through the wooden railing.

And then, for a second, he was flying. Weightless, as the car sailed out into space. Like a giant albatross, soaring above the troughs and ridges. Above the darkness and into the gilded morning. O God, deliver me....

No, Lucien. Brothers. Always.

PART TWO
Dino

CHAPTER 11

He had fooled them all.

Because Dino Stavros, a fisherman's son, would never be welcome in the home of Dr. Lionel Spenser, with the gilded ceilings, the gold wallpaper, the dark mahogany columns, the embroidered draperies. The three-story mansion emanated wealth, even from the street, the snow piled on each side of the cobblestone walk like the walls of a fortress, the electric lamppost sentries splashing light upon the cobblestone path as he'd forayed to the door for the annual Fairview Hospital Thanksgiving party.

But he wasn't Dino Stavros, penniless immigrant who should, by all rights, be huddled over some open fire in a snow-banked alley off Minneapolis's Hennepin Avenue, homeless, starving, his body riddled with worms: living a life of crime and deceit.

No, he'd left that life behind in Chicago. It hadn't a hope of finding him anymore.

He'd even scoured out of his diction his Greek accent, waxed his long hair back with Brylcreem, and tonight, dressed like a man of means in his pressed khakis, a pair of loafers, a white shirt, and a tie. Thanks to his roommate's tweed jacket, he'd turned into a regular Dapper Dan.

Dapper Dr. Daniel Scarpelli.

A rising surgeon who had not only scored an invitation…but after tonight, if he played it right, just might be a member of the family.

Yes, he'd left Dino Stavros, penniless, vagrant immigrant, a lifetime behind.

"Quite the digs, huh, Danny?" Reg St. John lifted a martini glass as he eased up beside Dino where he stood in the library, trying to make sense of one of Dr. Spenser's oil paintings.

From the radio in the next room, Glenn Miller's band belted out "Somewhere Over the Rainbow." The song filtered into the hallway, ribboning against the soaring two-story ceiling and along the corridor toward the library. A few feet away, the chief of pediatrics lounged in a cigar chair, flirting with one of the charge nurses from the TB ward. A klatch of other nurses perched on the wide stairs leading to the second floor of the mansion, chattering about the doctors and perhaps the interns too.

How strange to see them out of uniform—in holiday dresses, their hair dolled up.

A few even moved their feet to the beat.

He should probably ask Lizzy to dance. Dino searched for her and found Dr. Spenser's daughter leaning against the open French doors to the living room, her beautiful lips parting to laugh at a joke from a fellow nursing student. For a moment, he traced the shape of her neck, her blond hair knotted at the nape of her neck, usually fitted with a nurse's cap. She appeared anything but a nurse tonight in a calf-length black party dress that nearly bared her shoulders. He had the urge to find her mink stole, put it around her.

That or simply settle his arm around her.

"Did you hear that Spenser even hired extra wait staff? And somewhere around here is a cigarette girl that will make your eyes pop out of your head." Reg lifted an unlit cigar, rolled it between his fingers.

"I saw her." Or at least the back of her. Fishnet stockings, a short, scandalous dress, a pillbox cap. Dino shook his head. "My eyes belong to Lizzy."

Reg laughed, turned to survey the piece of so-called artwork that Dino had been trying to figure out for the better part of ten minutes.

Well, to be accurate, he'd been trying to figure out exactly how to ask Lizzy's father for her hand in marriage and trying to keep the voices of his past from talking him into bolting.

"Have you figured out what you're going to say to the old man?" Reg asked, his eyes darting to Dr. Spenser as he worked the crowd. Not a big man, he wore the salt-and-pepper of wisdom around his temples, a sternness in his eyes that made even the best intern's hand tremble when he hovered over him in the operating theater.

Whatever made Dino think…

No. For all Reg and the rest of his fellow interns knew, Dino was the son of the chief-of-staff, Dr. Antonio Scarpelli. After all, a poor immigrant—one without citizen status—would hardly attend university. Hardly become a doctor.

Hardly dare to ask for the hand of Elizabeth Elaine Spenser in marriage.

Run. The little voice in his head had nearly stopped him cold on the sidewalk outside the house. Had nearly frozen his hand on the brass knocker.

What had made him think he could pull this off—showing up at Dr. Spenser's home, slicked up, like he belonged in a place with velvet drapes, crystal vases filled with poinsettias, and the smell of roast turkey roaming the halls and stirring his stomach?

Reg clapped him on the shoulder with his delicate surgeon-to-be hand. "What do you think he's gonna say, champ? No? To Dr. Antonio Scarpelli's kid? C'mon. He'll be dancing for joy."

Dino sucked in a breath and stared at a bold, somewhat grotesque painting of what seemed to be a woman dressed in a toga sitting on a beach. A deformed woman, huge shoulders, tiny head, black flowing hair. "I've been trying to figure out if this is a real painting or a joke."

Reg laughed, sipping his martini. "*Femme au bord de la mer. The Woman by the Sea.* It's a Picasso. Cubism. Supposedly set in Greece."

"It's ugly." And certainly not the shadowy Greece that sometimes found him. The one with the wind that reaped the tang of the olive groves and filled his memory with the heat of golden sand mortared between his toes, the taste of the cool, salty blue sea, the smells of roasted lamb on a spit inside the taverna. In it, he might even hear his mother's stern voice, the echo of a song embedded in his memory.

And, if he stopped long enough, Markos… "*I'll find you.*"

Oh, how he hoped not.

"It's art. It doesn't have to be pretty," Reg said.

"Are you sure it's supposed to be Greece?" Dino asked.

Reg lifted a shoulder. He finished his martini and set it on the tray of a servant who passed by, taking a second to rearrange his cuff inside his tux. Of course, Reg had a tux. And a Mercury Sport sedan. And his own apartment on Franklin Avenue instead of a boardinghouse room downtown shared by a fellow intern. But the boardinghouse had been Dino's choice. He had to stop living off the Scarpellis sometime.

But not tonight, when everything he wanted ranged just beyond his fingertips.

"I think so. I'd like to go there sometime. You know, just for a vacation. Maybe after my residency." Reg gave Dino a wink. "I hear they have beautiful women."

"I…wouldn't know."

Reg picked up an envelope opener from the credenza. Ivory-tipped, it looked like a keepsake from one of Dr. Spenser's travels—something that accompanied the gazelle head mounted to the wall. He picked his fingernails with it. "I know you only have eyes for Lizzy. But it wouldn't hurt you to look around, mate." Reg nudged him. "You don't have the old ball-and-chain yet." He put his hand out to stop another waiter, a dark-haired chap dressed in the white jacket of a hired servant.

"I'll take one of those." He lifted another martini from the tray. "I 'spose old Scarpelli is at the polio clinic again?" Reg's gaze travelled past him, landing on a fresh crop of nurses from the Swedish Nursing School.

Lizzy had wandered into the foyer and now stood staring at the fifteen-foot Christmas tree. She swayed to "In the Mood." The memory of her twirling in his arms, her scent—lavender and rose water—twined suddenly in Dino's head. That, and the press of her lips on his, soft and surrendering as they'd stood on her back step, the cold brisk wind around their ankles, their noses brushing like Eskimos.

"Danny?" Reg brought him, reluctantly, back.

"Yeah. He and Mother do their annual Thanksgiving day rounds."

"Figgers. They're a couple of do-gooders."

Dino shot him a look.

Reg held up a hand. "No offense. Your folks are okay. It's just that, if anyone should be here, it's the chief-of-staff."

Yes, Dino could have used the old man's affirmation that he, indeed, belonged in the room with the rest of the blue bloods.

And sometimes Doctor and the Missus actually made him believe it. Especially when Mrs. Scarpelli greeted him as if he might really be her son, filling his skin-and-bones with homemade gnocchi. Her adoring smile could beguile him into forgetting the moment he'd stood on their doorstep, exhausted, hungry, and yes, not a little scared.

Dr. Lionel Spencer walked by them, nodding to Reg, smiling. "Good to see you here, Daniel. My regards to your folks tonight."

Now. He should ask now, but his words pasted to his throat. He may have managed a nod back, but he couldn't remember even that as the man moved away.

The ring in his breast pocket hung like a boulder on his chest, so heavy he thought he might be having some form of coronary attack.

"So, are you really going to ask him?" Reg did a poor job of hiding a smirk as he threw a glance at Lizzy, now rearranging ornaments on the tree.

"Yes…of course. I just need to find the right moment…." Oh, even he could hear the tinny pitch of his fear. Swell. Yes, he was a fool for even allowing himself to think that a girl like Lizzy might want…

She turned then, and for a second the world stopped as her amber eyes landed on him, as her lips curled up in a smile.

"Oh, you've got it bad, kid." Reg shook his head as he handed him his martini. "I think you need a little more courage."

Dino reached for the drink, but his hand shook. Reg saw it, laughed. "You'll have to do better than that in surgery, Danny boy." He turned one last time to the picture. "Yes, I sure would like to find me one of those island beauties."

Lizzy glided toward him, wearing a smile that had become like music to him since the day he'd seen her in the halls of Fairview, carrying in a food tray to one of his patients. Three months—had it only been that long since he'd started breathing in her cheer, her smile?

"Hey there, Dr. Scarpelli." She took the martini from him, shooting a frown, and set it on the credenza. "Reg, I thought I told you. Danny doesn't drink."

Reg grinned that all-American-boy smile that usually acquitted him of trouble. "Tonight he does, honey." He winked and clapped Dino again on the back as he moved away toward the giggling nurses.

Lizzy traced the lapel of his jacket. Cocked her head. "What did he mean by that?"

Dino shot a look at the martini. He hadn't had a drink since—well, probably never. He remembered tasting retsina back in Zante, but that life didn't exactly count. And Dr. Scarpelli hadn't allowed alcohol in the house.

He could probably use a beverage, anything that might loosen his lips. Instead, he took Lizzy's elbow, moved her away from the living room, looking for an alcove where they could talk.

Oh, he wanted to ask her. Especially when she shot him a half-smile, half-frown. "You're acting strangely." Only, her giggle suggested she didn't mind. Especially when he backed her down the hallway and into the back room near the alleyway door. Wool coats hung three deep on hooks, piled on a side table. Light from the hallway spilled into the room, backlighting her face.

"What are you doing?"

He wove his fingers into her hands. "Kissing my girl." He leaned forward, brushed her lips with his. She tasted of cherry Coke, sweet and very, very tempting. She held still for a moment, then untangled her hand from his and pressed on his chest.

"Not here, Danny."

He traced her face with his fingers. "Maybe later we can take a walk—"

"It's cold out. And Daddy's afraid of another blizzard." A smile chased her words, however.

Yes. A blizzard. Like the one that had trapped him and Lizzy for four days at the hospital two weeks ago. Four days to decide that, yes, he wanted to marry the kind of woman who thawed the feet of homeless war veterans in tubs of cool water, and ladled broth down the gullets of hungry, frozen street urchins who needed shelter. Watching her rock the newborn baby of a mother from the TB ward had convinced him. Lizzy Spencer would be his wife.

Please.

"Maybe I could help clean up—"

"Daddy has servants for that. And besides, Senator Shipstead and his family are staying. I have to be here to help Daddy. Mother will undoubtedly go to bed with a headache."

He tucked his finger under her chin. "Of course you do. Maybe instead you would come out with me this weekend..."

Her smile fell. "Actually, Danny, I meant to tell you..." She caught his hand, took it from her face. "My family is leaving on Saturday. We're spending Christmas with Jerry, on base with him."

"In Hawaii?"

"I know. We were going to wait another week, but Daddy is afraid of more snow, so we're taking a train to the coast, then—we're taking a real live airplane! The Pan American Airlines." She grinned up at him. "Imagine, flying over all that water. It gives me a sort of funny tingle."

He didn't mention the two weeks he'd spent on a boat, crossing an ocean. Never, in fact, would. As far as Lizzy knew, he'd been born in America. He managed something that felt like a smile. "Maybe I could... or we could..."

Those beautiful amber eyes caught him, her smile crooked. "What?"

"Oh...I just thought maybe we'd spend Christmas together." Engaged. He longed to say the word.

"Oh, I'll be back by the New Year. Reg already told me your fraternity is having a party." She rose on her tiptoes, kissed him on the cheek.

He fought a ridiculous spark of jealousy. To his knowledge, no, Phi Chi didn't have a party on the calendar, but he'd put in grueling hours lately...

She turned to go, but he caught her hand. What if he just—asked her now? What if he didn't wait for her father? What if—?

She patted him on the cheek. "We'll spend New Year's together, I promise."

Of course they would. And maybe time away would be good for them, allow her to miss him a little. He leaned down, kissed her cheek. "I'll miss you."

She giggled. "Oh, Danny, sometimes you are so sweet."

He didn't feel sweet as he followed her into the hall.

Where was that drink Reg had left him? Only, really, he didn't feel much like a drink, or even a party, as Duke Ellington's robust tones wheedled through the crowd. Yes, he needed to leave before he started saying stupid things, making mistakes that could cost him his future. His appetite had vanished, anyway.

He returned to the back room, retrieved his coat, and heard a voice outside, muffled by the darkness.

"No! I told you, I'm not that kind of girl."

He stilled. Something about the tone, high, shrill—Dino moved to the window, found it cracked.

"Please, I don't want—" The woman's voice cut off with a muffled cry.

He dropped his coat, moved to the door, flinging it open. There, near the back porch leading to the kitchen, away from the lights, a man pressed a woman against the snowy bank, her leg kicking against him.

A fishnet leg. Her hands fisted in his tuxedo and—

Reg?

Dino froze, watching as Reg swept his hand up her leg, catching it. “C’mon, honey, you know you were eyeing me in there.”

“Reg, buddy, uh, everything okay out here?”

He wasn’t sure where the words came from, just issued from him, quietly, but with the sharp edge out.

Reg turned, and a smile slicked up one side of his face. “Hey, Danny Boy. Leaving already?” He curled his arm around the woman’s shoulders, pulled her up tight to him, like they might be out for a Sunday walk. “What, the old man turn you down?”

But Dino had no words for him, his eyes fixed on the woman. On her black hair, down in tangles around her shoulders. On the heart-shaped face, on the blue eyes that latched on him, twined through him, clung to him.

Sofia.

Her gaze held him.

He opened his mouth, but nothing emerged even as his promise hammered against him. *Yes, I’ll take care of her.*

Was it his fault she refused to come with him to Dr. Scarpelli’s door? That she’d insisted on waiting at the train station for Markos?

That when he’d gone back to check on her, she’d vanished?

Reg’s smile dimmed. “Hey, it can’t be that bad, pal. He’ll come around.”

Oh, Sofia. What was she doing here?

And if she opened her mouth, well, his entire life would shatter at his feet. So much for Dr. Spenser coming around.

Yeah, like he’d let his daughter marry an illegal immigrant, long past his seven-year grace period.

Still— “What are you doing, Reg?”

Reg's expression changed so suddenly, it scared Dino a little. For a moment, he stared into his past, watching Kostas as he pounced to his feet, threw a plate to the ground.

"Nothing. Go home, Danny."

Sofia made to move away from Reg, but he tightened his grasp on her. She winced.

"Let her be, Reg."

"Leave, and I won't tell Lizzy what I heard in the trauma ward that night those two drunks wandered in."

Dino frowned.

"You know—the ones who spoke Italian."

Greek, actually. They'd spoken *Greek.* And no, he hadn't known Reg had been prowling around, or maybe he wouldn't have tried to separate them when they'd begun a brawl on the ward floor, throwing in a few Greek commands to get their attention.

"You said you were born here, that you didn't know Italian. *Really.*" He raised an eyebrow. "I think maybe Danny Scarpelli has a few secrets."

"Danny?" Sofia said softly.

Reg glanced at Sofia, back to Dino. "You know this dame, Danny?"

Dino's mouth tightened, his eyes flicking to her and back. "No, of course not." But the lie emerged high-pitched, unwieldy. He schooled his voice. "Let the girl go."

Reg stood just beyond the rim of light, as if measuring Dino. Everything inside Dino tightened, a burning, or perhaps more of an ache that poured into his bones. *Please, Reg—*

Reg tossed Sofia back, into the snow. "Too skinny for me, anyway." He pulled out a cigarette. "I'll keep Lizzy company for you." Then he winked and climbed the stairs, disappearing into the house.

Sofia sank in the snow, shaking, her coat—yes, he recognized it, the thick black wool, the worn cuffs. She tried to push herself to her heeled feet and slipped, falling back.

He caught her, lifted her out of the bank. She gripped his lapel as she righted herself, her eyes wide, beautiful. Hurt.

She unhanded him. "Sorry. I—"

"What are you doing here?" He pulled her coat tight, buttoned it. It seemed as if the life had been stripped from her face, hollowing her body to nearly a stick. But those blue eyes—they always had the power to stop him cold.

No wonder Markos had loved her.

"I—I needed the money. My former roommate works here—in the Spenser home…and she got me the gig."

He turned up her collar. "Are you a maid?"

"I work at the theater. The Orpheum."

He wasn't sure why, but this gave him a jolt. "Are you still singing?"

She went nearly as white as the snow still caught in her collar. "No. I—I don't sing. I check the coats. And I clean the place."

He stood a half-foot taller than she did, and it occurred to him that now he wouldn't have to fight her so hard to pull her away from Markos, to force her onto the train.

She might even fit into his arms…. "Are you okay? Do you need a lift home?"

She ran her finger under her eyes, her makeup smearing. "Do you have a car?"

"No, but I could find us a cab or—"

"No." She pulled away from him. "I don't need your help, Dino—er, *Danny*."

He winced a little, although he wasn't sure why her tone should sting him. He'd been the one to make something of his life.

"Sofia, let me see you home."

"You must be cold. Go back inside." She shot a look at the house. "It looks like you're a big shot now." She managed a wan smile. "A doctor?"

"An intern. But yes. I hope to be a doctor soon."

"What did that guy mean, about her father turning you down?"

He lifted a shoulder. "Nothing. He's just drunk. C'mon, let me take you home."

She wound her arms around herself. "No—I'm fine. Thank you, though."

"Sof—"

She held up a hand, her smile watery. "We each made our choices. It's okay…um, Danny."

He closed his eyes against a flash of pain in his chest. *They'd made their choices.* "How's Markos? Did he ever—" He closed his mouth, too late to stop the boy inside.

"Markos never showed." Sofia's eyes gentled, and then slowly she shook her head. "I stayed at the station for three days. I met every train. But I know he'd be very proud of you…Doctor." Then she turned and limped down the alley.

He stood there, the shadow of the big house chilling him through as the wind licked down the alleyway, moaning in her wake.

He didn't move, didn't run after her.

Didn't return inside, either.

It came to him then that maybe the only person he'd fooled all these years had been himself.

CHAPTER 12

He'd be very proud of you....

Dino lay on his back in the empty bed of the general ward, fatigue pressing him into the starched cotton sheets, listening to the breathing of the patient next to him. The man's leg, up in a sling, cast eerie shadows across the long room, the tile ceiling, the curtained windows.

He'd be very proud of you....

Sofia's voice whispered in his brain, chasing away sleep, although his body felt as if it had been dragged through the snowy streets behind a streetcar. Twelve hours mopping up the slop of Saturday night drunks, his mind on the fact that, right now, Lizzy probably lay in the sun on some sandy beach in Hawaii.

Her ring finger bare.

Sofia had looked so thin, her hair snarled in the wind. She hadn't worn a hat, her feet probably frozen in those high heels.

He'd wanted to go to the station to see Lizzy off, had even called her home to wish her good-bye. Of course, she'd already left.

Why hadn't he asked her to marry him right off?

No! I told you I'm not that kind of girl!

What kind of girl had Sofia become? A coat-check girl? Or was that shame talking?

Her leg—flung out in fishnet, turned his stomach...

He'd be very proud of you.

Dino threw his arm over his eyes. Sleep. Oh, he longed for sleep.

I'll be back by the New Year. Reg already told me your fraternity is having a party.

Reg. The way he'd looked at Dino as he'd flung Sofia into the snow—he hadn't seen such a cold look since the night Theo died.

No. Uncle Jimmy had looked at Markos that way.

Or perhaps the way Dino had looked at Markos on the boat to America. But he'd been grieving. And afraid. And so very angry. He still hadn't laid hold of why, but thankfully, the anger had long ago died to a cool ember inside.

Until, of course, Sofia reappeared to stir it to life.

Dino pulled the cotton blanket to his ear, rolled over on one side. Someone pushed a gurney filled with surgical utensils past the door; it rattled like a china service.

He'd become so accustomed to the odors of antiseptic he barely smelled them anymore—that and cotton and rubbing alcohol.

Now however a new smell brushed through his memory—not Lizzy's sweet lilac aroma, but something exotic, foreign.

Orange blossoms.

We're going to be okay, Sofia. His voice filtered back to him, young and broken. He sat next to her on the red vinyl seat of the train, his hand on her back as she turned away from him, stared out the window, silent tears cutting into her chapped cheeks.

And Markos?

He'd had no words, and wanted to throw up.

Not a little of it came from the sheer relief of being away from Uncle Jimmy. And…Markos. Markos scared him—always had. Just a look from Markos turned Dino into a child.

His throat swelled, scratchy.

He'd always believed—or hoped—that Markos had made it to Minneapolis.

Married Sofia.

He rolled onto his back, listening to the springs protest.

The man next to him groaned. "Can't sleep either?"

Dino stared at the ceiling.

He'd be very proud of you.

"No, he wouldn't!" He sat up, closing his eyes, rubbing the sweat from his forehead.

"Wouldn't what?"

Oh no, he had spoken aloud. "Nothin'. Just a dream."

"Sounds more like a nightmare." A chuckle that sounded nothing like humor emitted from the lump in the bed. "I'll tell you what a nightmare is—going out in the morning to collect the milk and landing on your backside, only to have your leg broken in two places. At least, if I was going to break my leg, you'd think I might have a better story for the dames."

Dino managed a half smile. "It'll be our secret."

"As long as you're up, whadaya say you help a guy out. I got a little nourishment in my jacket pocket."

"I don't think the nurses would much like that." Dino slipped out of bed, however, tiptoed over in the darkness, and lifted the water pitcher on the table. He poured a glass and padded over to the bed. "Here you go."

The man pushed up on one arm. "Thanks, but I was actually talking about my Bible. I'm feeling a bit parched."

Dino raised an eyebrow but fished through the man's belongings piled on the metal table next to the bed until he came upon a pocket Bible. He handed it over as the man used his triangle to hoist himself to a sitting position. "I don't suppose you'd turn on my light? There's no one here but us, I think."

Dino flicked on the bedside lamp. Light haloed over a younger man—maybe eighteen. Skinny, with striking blue eyes, oiled blond hair, a crooked smile. A real Bible-thumper type, the kind Dino had seen on the street during the Minneapolis summer crusades when the do-gooders hit the corners for sidewalk evangelism. A few had even made it onto the university campus.

Dino shuffled back to his bed, grabbed the pillow off it. Maybe he could find a place in the doctors' lounge—

"'Blessed is the man unto whom the Lord imputeth not iniquity, and in whose spirit there is no guile. When I kept silence, my bones waxed old through my roaring all the day long. For day and night thy hand was heavy upon me: my moisture is turned into the drought of summer.'"

"What are you doing?" Dino stood at the foot of the bed, hands tight in the pillow.

"Reading aloud. Would you rather I sing it? It *is* a psalm."

"Please, no."

"Tomorrow's church. I figure, since I'm going to miss it, I should probably fill up now." He cleared his voice.

Dino didn't move.

"'I acknowledge my sin unto thee, and mine iniquity have I not hid. I said, I will confess my transgressions unto the Lord; and thou forgavest the iniquity of my sin—'"

"I haven't sinned, if that's what you're driving at."

The man looked up at him. "I didn't say you did."

Dino stared at the pillow.

"But you did sit up in bed and scream."

"That wasn't a scream."

The man smiled. "Name's Billy. And let's just call it a nightmare."

"I wasn't even asleep."

"Then that's a pretty powerful regret."

"I have to get some sleep."

"Fat chance, with that kind of guilt."

"Listen, if you weren't already laid up—"

"What? You'd lay me out?" Billy closed the Bible, handed it over to Dino, who stared at it as if it might be one of Uncle Jimmy's pineapples. "You're fighting the wrong person, Doc."

"I think you belong in the crazy ward." Dino set the Bible on the table, held his hands up, backing away.

Billy smiled. "Maybe I'm not the only one. Turn off the light on your way out, will you?"

Dino left the room, leaving the light on, stalked down the hall. Margie Neider raised her head at the nurses' desk. "Are you okay, Doctor?"

He stopped at the desk. No. Maybe. *He'd be very proud of you.*

Of whom? Dino? Or Danny Scarpelli?

For day and night thy hand was heavy upon me.

He saw Sofia shuffling away as the darkness closed around her. *We each made our choices. It's okay…um, Danny.*

"Okay, fine."

The nurse looked up at him, startled. So maybe he should check *himself* into the crazy floor.

"Do you have paper and a pen?"

She nodded, pulling a blank sheet from the drawer, handing it over with a pen.

He carried it to the doctors' lounge, flicked on the light, poured a cup of coffee, and sat at the table.

Dear Lizzy,

I know you didn't expect to hear from me until New Year's, but I can't seem to get you out of my mind. ~~What's more, I have to tell you something~~... I want to ask you something, but before I do, I guess I need to tell you the truth about me. You see, I wasn't always Danny Scarpelli. In fact, I'm not legally the son of the Scarpellis at all. I'm from Greece. My real name is Dino. I had a brother, Markos, and together we came over about ten years ago. I met the Scarpellis on a ship, and they adopted me.

Well, not legally. In fact, I'm technically not yet a citizen. But I will be. I should have told you long ago, and I'm sorry.

I love you, and I wanted to put things right between us before you came back. I pray you will have me, still.

Yours,

~~Danny~~

—Dino Stavros

No. What was he trying to do? Destroy his life? Just because he'd run face-first into his past didn't mean it had to derail him. He wasn't Markos—or Theo. He wasn't going to let one decision made in the throes of emotion destroy his life. He'd worked too hard to get to this place. To become Danny Scarpelli.

He crumpled the letter and tossed it in the trash.

* * * *

"Is there a radio in here?"

The voice roused him as he lay on his side, wedged into the short length of the spongy lounge davenport. His neck screamed when he pushed to a sitting position, the hot seams of the vinyl drawn into his face. His mouth tasted as if he'd chewed on cotton batting.

The sun fanned through the flimsy curtains at the window, dust particles swimming through a high beam of light. Outside, the sun allowed a blue-skied day. No blizzard today.

"Turn it on." He recognized Phyllis's sharp tones as she leaned against the wall, her face wan. She closed her arms over her white uniform.

"What's going on?" He tried to smooth down his hair, suck the cotton from his teeth.

"Shh!" Phyllis barked at him.

Static filled the room while his intern roommate—Beanie McPhearson—fiddled with the radio in the corner.

"What time is it?"

"After noon," another voice said, and Dino caught Reg's dark expression as he entered the room, leaned against the wall. "Planning to sleep the day away?"

"No—"

"We're at war, okay? So shut your yap." Reg exploded off the wall, pulled a cigarette from his pocket, shot Dino a glare as he walked to the window.

War? Dino tried to sort through his words even as the voice of a newscaster finally cleared the static.

"...7:55 a.m. this morning, the first of the Japanese airborne attacks hit the Pacific fleet, lined up at Battleship Row, at the base in Pearl Harbor."

Pearl Harbor.

Dino stilled. Jerry Spenser was stationed in Pearl, right? On a ship—the *California*?

Or…was it the *Arizona*?

"The second attack came an hour later, but by that time the great Arizona had already sunk, taking 1300 souls with her."

No… He tightened his hand on the back of the sofa. Certainly Lizzy wasn't near the damage. Certainly she lay in the sun on some resort beach…

We're going to stay with him on base—

"Even now, rescue is underway in the greasy, burning harbor, and the smoke from Hickam Field fills the countryside…"

Hickam Air Field—that wasn't near the naval yard, was it?

Beanie turned the volume down. "That's it. I'm going down to the recruiter's right now. I'm going to sign up."

Reg let smoke unfurl from his mouth. "Just calm down, Beanie. The draft board will come after you soon enough." His gaze flicked to Dino. "At least some of us."

Dino frowned at him, got up. "Turn the volume back up."

Beanie adjusted the volume, even as Phyllis covered her mouth with her hand. A few other nurses had filtered into the lounge. One wiped her glistening cheeks.

Dino moved over to the radio, placed both hands on the table, leaned close.

"President Roosevelt and his cabinet are convening to form a response to this sudden and vicious attack—"

"What about the naval base?" Dino yelled at the radio.

"Geez, Danny, calm down—"

Dino rounded on Reg, nearly grabbed the cigarette from his mouth, nearly—

He stalked out of the room, down the hall, stopping at the desk where Margie sat, tears running down her face. Another radio ticked off the news.

"Locals are being asked to give blood, and the hospitals are overrun with soldiers, many suffering terrible burns."

He slammed his hand on the desk. Blew out a breath. Combed his fingers through his hair. Turning to Margie, "I need to make a call."

She stared up at him, unseeing.

He grabbed the phone and dialed Lizzy's home. The butler answered, a needle-nosed man who'd never seemed to like him. "It's—Danny. Scarpelli. I need to know where Lizzy and her family were staying."

"Mr. Scarpelli—"

"Doctor."

"They are staying at the Pearl Harbor Naval Base, by special request of Captain Spenser—"

"I need a number."

Silence.

"Please." He closed his eyes, hating how his voice trembled.

Silence. Finally, "Just a moment, sir." He heard shuffling, then he came back on. "I have an address. You can send a telegram."

He took the address down on his palm, unable to find paper.

A line a half-block long snaked out of the downtown post office. Dino formed the telegram a thousand times in his head before he reached the counter.

He had it half-recited before the woman could transcribe it. She seemed to be shaking, even…crying.

He took a breath, started over. "Send it to the naval base at Pearl Harbor."

The woman pinched her mouth, swallowed hard, didn't look at him. Nodded.

"To Elizabeth Elaine Spenser. Stop. Please update me on your status. Stop. Crazy with worry. Stop."

To this, the woman raised her head. Her eyes watered. She pulled a handkerchief from her sleeve, pressed it to her eyes, kept writing.

He tightened his jaw, his throat hot. "Please reply asap. Stop. Doctor Daniel Scarpelli. When will that go out?"

She glanced at the telegraph operators, each with a pile of telegrams, and raised a shoulder. Shook her head.

Right. Well.

Darkness had already begun to seep through the alleys, dust the city with a palpable doom. He read the faces of the people, grim, jaws tight, huddled against a biting northern wind, dodging the streetlights, the glow of the downtown bars. Tonight, they seemed louder than usual. He turned on Hennepin Avenue, trekked with his head down toward the trolley. Papers skittered down the gutters, smoke from the fires of alleyway vagabonds bit at his eyes.

Across the street, the Orpheum, with the poster for *Citizen Kane* in the window, remained dark. He passed another bar, heard voices, loud and angry.

He opted to walk instead of taking the trolley back to his boardinghouse.

Someone had swept the snow from the stairs. The tang of Elsie's *Hansenpfeffer*—some sort of German stew, probably thick with carrots and potatoes, onions and garlic—twisted his stomach, but he'd probably lose it anyway. He climbed the stairs and found Beanie in their room.

Packing.

The skinny intern had taken out a leather case, begun emptying his bureau drawers.

Admittedly, Dino didn't know him well—he reminded him, sometimes, of Lucien, tall, thin, dark, but without the charismatic smile. Beanie—Jim, Dino thought, might be his real name—was a mess of desperation and angst, the youngest of a line of brothers, the first to go to college. Dino had heard the entire story three months ago, when he'd moved in for the new academic year. And the occasional nights that Beanie stumbled in, whiskey on his breath.

Dino tossed his jacket on the bed, topped it with his fedora. "What are you doing?"

"I'm going home. I'm going to join up in my hometown—it'll give me a chance to say good-bye to my folks."

"Beanie—calm down. You don't know—"

"They bombed us, Danny. Doesn't that mean nothin' to you? They killed a thousand of our boys, while they were sleeping." He grabbed his lab coat and tossed it at Dino. "What are we doing, anyway? I'm already a doctor—now maybe it'll be put to good use."

"Just because we've spent the last month thawing feet and nursing drunks—" Dino shot his lab coat back at him. "You're not going to do anyone any good getting killed. You have a perfectly good life here. Don't wreck it."

"What do you know, Scarpelli? You've never had to fight for anything in your life. You don't know what it's like to be Irish and poor."

"I do know about regret. Don't rush into this, Beanie."

"What's wrong with you, Scarpelli? Don't you want to be a hero?"

You will be someone great, and leave your mark on the world. Oh, his mother's epitaph found him at the oddest moments. "Maybe I just have a different definition of hero."

"I think a hero is doing what's right, no matter what the cost."

"Yeah, well, I think a hero thinks through the cost. I have a plan, and this isn't it."

Beanie picked up his lab coat, tossed it into the trash. "I certainly hope your plan turns out the way you hope."

Dino stared at the address written on his palm and closed his fist over it.

CHAPTER 13

Tommy Dorsey, with his new lead singer, Frank somebody, was crooning out "This Love of Mine," and with everything inside Dino, he wanted to put his fist through the tall Zenith radio in Elsie's dining room.

He wasn't sure what might be worse—the silky tones of a man who clearly had never been in love or he wouldn't sound so unbroken—or the too-happy tones of Elsie and the brigade of boarders in the next room singing and pounding out "Auld Lang Syne" on the upright piano in the parlor.

At least that's what he thought the song might be. With Elsie's guttural German, the nasal accents of the two Swedish interns, and the two Scots who insisted on singing it in their native brogue, it sounded more like the inside of the general ward at midnight.

Outside, a blizzard was in the making, with the wind at least in league with him as it moaned against the glass. Twinkles from the Christmas tree burned against the window, a blur of red, blue, and white. The tree showed more patriotic fervor than he could muster, despite half his fellow classmates heading off to be slaughtered by the Japs—and now Germany and Italy, thanks to Hitler's declaration of war on America. The daily reports of war preparations—not to mention the cleanup of Pearl Harbor—only made him want to hide in his room.

Not that he didn't care about America and her battles. But, well, he wasn't a citizen, was he? A fact the draft board would notice the minute he signed his name. Besides, he wasn't going anywhere. Not until he found out what happened to Lizzy.

Twenty-four days and nine hours since he'd heard the news about Pearl, and not one word.

He tried not to imagine the worst. Really. Tried to dislodge the image of her burned body, perhaps buried under the debris in the shipping yard, from his thoughts. Tried to batter from his mind her bloated and decaying corpse, pinned under a sunken battleship.

Thirteen telegrams. To the naval base. To the nearby hospitals. Even to local hotels. No one had seen Lizzy.

Missing. Like she'd been misplaced.

It didn't mean she was dead.

Even though they'd found and identified her mother and father. He'd read their names among the obituaries listed in last week's Tribune. Apparently they'd been visiting their son aboard the USS *Arizona* when it went down. Captain Jerry Spenser had also perished in the attack.

But apparently, no sign of sister Elizabeth.

Please, she couldn't be trapped inside the ship, one of the 1300 who went down…

He stared out the dark window, his chin in his folded arms balanced atop the back of a straight-backed chair. His stomach pushed against his spine, and for a moment he longed for his mother's—no, he meant *Mrs. Scarpelli's,* turkey. Of course, she never cooked it herself, but he thought of it as hers since she did the carving, Dr. Scarpelli looking on, a beam on his face.

They'd forgone a New Year's celebration this year to visit children in a local orphanage. Of course, they'd invited Dino.

He'd never done well at the orphanage, the desperate eyes of the children reaching too deep inside.

He blew on the window, watched a mist form.

"Come and join us, Danny." Elsie touched his shoulder. A rounded woman with hair so white he thought it might be spun from cotton batting, she wore her shoes sensible, her dresses long, her collars to her chin. She had a list of rules that a nun might find a challenge to keep, and he usually heard about his infractions in her native German tongue. Still, he'd do just about anything for her beef stew, sauerkraut, and *brötchen*.

Usually.

"No thank you, Miss Elsie." He continued to stare into the blackness.

She gave his shoulder a squeeze. "If you change your mind, we're having *weihnachtsstollen* in the dining room."

He nodded. He loved her Christmas loaf, could smell the lemon and the rum from here.

The festiveness made him ache. Laughter drifted in from the next room, and it choked him, the air suddenly stale.

He got up, turned the chair back to the round table, and strode through the house to the entry where he slipped on his coat, grabbed his hat.

Elsie's voice trailed him out. He closed the door on it.

The frigid air closed his lungs for a moment, even as he stamped down the stairs. The stars above the cloudless night sprinkled across the blackness, pinpricks of light so close he felt he could reach out and grasp one if he wanted.

He shoved his hands into his pockets, tucked his chin into his collar, and followed his breath into the night.

The ruckus from the other boardinghouses and the few corner bars chased him as he dragged out of his neighborhood and kept walking. Down the trolley line, through the park, and along Hennepin Avenue.

He didn't have a destination, not really. Just anywhere to break free of the quiet that fisted him the moment he closed the door of his boarding room.

High, tinkling laughter preceded a couple spilling out of an establishment with frosted windows. The dame looped her hand through her escort's arm, tipping on her heels. Music—

Benny Goodman, he thought, trailed them out and he watched them pass, the woman staring at her man with shiny eyes.

The door began to close and he caught the handle, stepped inside.

The heat of too many bodies, gin, and cheap perfume sucked him in. A group of already lacquered collegiate-types bumped him off his feet, and he grabbed at the bar, sloshing the drink of a patron with glassy eyes and the arms of a steel-worker.

"Watch it!"

"Sorry." He wove into the crowd, wheedling through to the back, past men dressed in zoot suits, women in swing skirts, some even in trousers—many of them jitterbugging on the tiny wooden dance floor as a couple of saxophones and a drummer cranked out a fast swing beat.

He squeezed onto a stool. Next to him, a kid held up his empty draught glass for another. Although his jeans and collegiate sweater marked him as a student at the local university, he appeared no older than the evangelist he'd met a month ago—or less? It seemed a decade since the night he nearly confessed all to Lizzy.

The bartender, a bully of a man who reminded him of too many of Uncle Jimmy's thugs, his dark hair Brylcreemed straight back and wearing only an undershirt, grabbed the glass. Beer spilled over his hand as he filled it from the tap, slid it back to the too-eager student.

"What ya drinking?" he asked Dino.

Dino opened his mouth, nothing escaped. He glanced at the kid's beer, and something inside him seized.

He shouldn't be here—

A second later the bartender delivered a tall draft, foam lapping over the edge, pooling in an ocher puddle beneath his glass.

Dino picked it up. Smelled it. Gave a sip. It burned, the taste sharp, bitter.

The co-ed lifted his glass. "Happy New Year!"

Indeed. Dino took another sip. It reminded him of Elsie's brown bread, the kind with molasses that she served with her potato soup.

He drank the rest of the beer without stopping. Held out the glass to the bartender.

The next went down easier, and after the third one, he switched to whiskey.

That burned, at first. Then it heated him through to his marrow. For the first time, Lizzy drifted from his brain—

"Are you here all by yourself?"

Certainly the voice couldn't be directed at him—but yes, he turned, following the nudge on his arm, right into the smile of a doll-faced co-ed, her hair parted to one side and curled down to her shoulder. She wore a pretty black dress, something shiny, and she grinned up at him with bright brown eyes. "It's the New Year, and you look glum."

He pulled his arm from her hand. "I'm fine—"

"Aw, c'mon. Let's dance." She turned her mouth down and gripped him again.

"No—I said no."

It came out sharper than he intended, that and the force with which he pulled his arm away.

It didn't help that probably she'd already packed in too much celebration. She cried out as his gesture swept her off balance, and she grabbed at the arm of the university student next to him.

Who caught her as she slipped, pulling him with her.

They landed on the ground with a shout.

Oh—Dino stood up, held out his hand. "Sorry—I—"

The kid launched off the floor swinging. He caught Dino on the chin. Pain exploded in his head, quick, hot, and he plowed into the row of thirsties behind him. One caught him, shoved him back into the fist of University Boy.

Dino spun around at the blow, something loosing inside him. His fist had already found a home by the time he'd cleared his mind—University sprawled on the deck, holding his nose.

The bar erupted. A blow to his kidneys and Dino crashed to his knees. He rolled, kicking, hit his feet, and dished it back out.

For the first time in a month, he could breathe, feel himself move, roar without wanting to crumple. His body came alive, adrenaline hot inside him. He slammed his fist into cheekbones, sucked breath as knuckles found his ribs, lashed out with a kick, and howled. Around him, brawlers turned on each other. Glasses crashed. Women screamed.

Dino soared. He swung his fists, tasting blood in his mouth. He slammed his fist into the soft mass of a doughy patron, head-butted a man as he wrapped burly arms around him, dropping him hard. He rolled off him, found his feet, and grabbed another body around the waist. They crashed together onto a tabletop.

The music stopped as Dino beat his way through the room.

Yes. The violence consumed him, he drank it in even as two men plucked him up by the arms. He kicked out his legs, raging, feasting on the heat that coursed through him.

He jerked his knuckles back, connected with the face of one captor. Pounded his foot into the ankle of the other. The man howled.

Then, the bouncer-slash-bartender—and yes, he'd probably done time with some northside Minneapolis gang—grabbed him by the lapels, and suddenly Dino crashed through the front doors, winging into the street.

He skidded across the sidewalk, rolled, and landed on his face in the blackened snow. Shards of ice cut his skin even as he lay there, breathing in blades of air.

Blood ran into his mouth, his lip split. His eye burned, and he couldn't see out of it. And when he breathed in, his body turned to flame.

He rolled over, sprawling on the sidewalk, his pulse slowing enough now to taste his broken parts.

Overhead the stars still winked at him, as if saying, yes, Dino, we see you. He raised his arm, his fingers slowly closing over one, the brightest, until finally, he snuffed it out.

* * * *

"I should have guessed the hobo on the sidewalk was you."

The voice raked over him like a storm wave, gritty, cold, even violent as it turned him. It dragged him across the gravel of the beach, filled his mouth with sand, turned out a moan. He flayed his arm out and it caught in seaweed, trapped him. He thrashed against it—

"Dino—stop. I'm just trying to help. Give me your arm."

He tried to pry his eyes open, but one of them didn't work. A frost bore through him, so cold he couldn't feel his toes, and his fingers had turned fat. His lips wouldn't move. "Hel…"

Someone moved his arm, and he nearly cried when his ribs rubbed against each other. "Ahh—" Was that *his* voice? It sounded far away.

The second moan, however, he knew came from him as his rescuer dragged him to a sitting position. "No—just leave me…"

"You'll freeze."

He recognized the tone now, short, angry.

Sofia. He rolled his head back—it seemed as if on marbles. Opened his good eye. Sofia, indeed. Her hair pulled back in a bun, her blue eyes darkened with mascara, her lips rouged. "Sofia."

"Use your legs, Dino. I can't lift you."

Behind her, the stars still sprinkled across the sky, the music still pulsed as it dribbled from the bar. He gritted his teeth, trying to push from the sidewalk.

With a cry, she fell as he collapsed, hard. He caught her—or rather cushioned her with a mind-numbing burst of pain. "Oh—"

"Sorry—but you're not helping. Get up!" She scrambled off him, brushing herself off. She wore a dress under Markos's coat, her feet in a pair of high heels.

"Howdchya fine me?"

She wrapped her arms around his chest. "C'mon, Dino. Give a girl a break."

He shook her off. Leaned back on his hands, his head again swiveling back. "Were ya celbratin' the newyr?"

She made a face. "Are you *drunk*, too?"

"No…I donthinso." Although the way she split into two, spun, well… "Just lemme sleef."

"I should. I should leave you right here. I can't believe I'm walking home only to find you crumpled on the sidewalk, looking like you riled a fleet of navy men." She glared at him. "What would Markos say?"

"I don' care! He's gone….it don' matter anymore." He knew his words probably squirrelled out into an incomprehensible knot, but what could he do? He hung his head, let the tears dribble out. "Is all gone. It's all…"

He stood above his father, watching his mother moan.

A gentle touch on his cheek. "Come home with me, Dino. It'll be okay."

He hated how he leaned into her soft hand. How he let her wrestle him from the sidewalk, how he draped over her shoulders as she shuffled him across the street, through an alleyway, and up the back steps of a nearby rooming house. How he swallowed her down—the entire lovely form of her, from her delicate neck to her beautifully knotted lips as she fumbled with her lock. Or that he flopped into the only bed—a single bed—shoved into the corner of the room.

He lay there, watching her ease off his shoes, his coat. Closed his eyes as she sponged off his face, put snow on his swollen eye.

What would Markos say?

He didn't care. He'd left Markos and his empty promises long behind. Especially when he sandwiched her hand in his, tucking it into the pillow under his head as he drifted off to sleep in her comfortable, sweet-smelling bed.

CHAPTER 14

He couldn't place the smell. Rich and earthy, only with a tang that made his stomach growl. Dino breathed in, winced, his breath webbed inside a fist of pain.

"Oh…"

"Shh…don't move. I think you should go to the hospital."

He opened his eyes—only one worked. Light stabbed into the room between the shuttered curtains, fanning out as it hit the tiny bureau kitchen, the one-burner stove, the porcelain sink. A faded green chair pushed against a round table in the corner, a stack of books piled on a side table. In the other corner, paper cutout ornaments hung from a frail pine tree in a silver tin bucket.

Sofia turning away from him, wearing a bulky green bathrobe, cooking something on the stove. Her black hair brushed her shoulders. He remembered when she'd cut it off, how delicate she looked then, almost breakable.

Dino also remembered how Markos had nearly lost his mind.

"What are you making?"

"Fig bread. I thought you needed a taste of home."

He edged himself up on one elbow. A familiarity syrupped through him, something sweet and warm as he watched her hands move the dough on the small counter. "With cloves and coriander?"

"Cinnamon. It's the best I could do. And I wouldn't have had the figs if it weren't for Zoë Petros downstairs. She has a friend who runs a Greek restaurant." She still didn't turn around.

He lay back on the pillow, now running his fingers over his body. He felt his ribs, decided that nothing was broken, although his eighth and ninth seemed swollen. He could be bleeding internally, but, although he winced at his own touch, none of his organs seemed distended or hardened. His face, however... He probed, and guessed that while his nose might be broken, his eye socket seemed intact—then again, the pain that nearly made him weep prevented too much examination.

He still had all his teeth.

"I can't believe I got into a bar fight." He stared at her paneled ceiling. "I've never even had a drink, let alone started a brawl."

Sofia said nothing as she formed the bread. He had a vague recollection of her cooking back in the taverna on Zante.

He lifted his hand, examined his torn knuckles. He'd always envied Markos's hands—chapped, calloused—he'd had working man's hands. Dino kept his soft, precise. Surgeon's hands.

Now they looked like someone had held them under a grinder.

"Would you like some tea? Or maybe coffee? I have a percolator." Sofia slipped the bread into the oven, her movements almost stiff. And in her profile, he saw her wince.

"Are you okay?"

She glanced at him—quick—and back again, nodding.

"I'm going into the bathroom to change. Make yourself at home."

Clearly, he already had. Still, he got up, noticing that she'd left him fully clothed. He hated that he'd soiled her sheets, and brushed off dirt piled in the center. She had a nice place—nicer than his boardinghouse. He clenched his teeth against a groan as he pushed himself off the bed, shuffled over to the table. A novel by F. Scott Fitzgerald—he'd read him in college—an abbreviated history of the United States. A dictionary. A Louisa May Alcott book.

The door opened, and Sofia emerged, wearing a pair of jeans and an oversized shirt. She looked about twenty, like she belonged on some college campus.

She kept her back to him as she opened the oven, checking on the bread. The fragrance of cinnamon and yeast nearly turned him inside out. The whiskey had snarled his stomach into a frothy mess. "Thank you, Sofia." He lowered himself to a chair.

"I couldn't let you lie on the street and freeze to death." She picked up a bowl, whisked her fork into it. "Would you like some eggs?"

"You could have. But you didn't." For a second, he was back at Uncle Jimmy's, watching her outline through the curtain as she climbed into bed. Or tracing the shape of her lips as they sounded out English in the basement of the Orthodox Church. "What were you doing out that late?"

"The Orpheum had a midnight encore showing of *Gone with the Wind*."

"Well, thank you."

"Stop saying that. We're family. Of course I brought you home."

Family. Maybe. Before, she had acted like a big sister to him. And yes, he'd always seen her as Markos's girl, her arm tucked into his, his dark eyes on her, studying her every move. He expected to hear him, any moment, tromp into the room, shuck off their father's jacket.

His gaze went to it, hanging from a hook by the door.

Markos never showed.

"Why didn't you come to Dr. Scarpelli's? We *agreed* you'd come. He would have taken you in."

She poured the eggs into a hot cast-iron skillet. They crackled as she pushed them through the pan. "I did."

Her long hair hung like a drape in front of her face. He expected her to look at him, to clarify. When she didn't, he pushed himself from the chair. "I don't understand."

She opened the oven, took out the bread. Set it on the counter. It was all he could do not to leap like a dog at it.

"I stood on the step, about to knock, but I knew I didn't belong with the Scarpellis. They were *your* life, *your* friends. I—saw that through the window, and decided to let you go."

Let you go.

The words should have brought him relief, perhaps a release from shame that could still find him late at night, suck him back into that moment at the train station when Markos reached out to him, extracted from him a promise he had no idea how to keep.

"You should have come in," he said quietly.

She scooped the eggs from the pan, piled them on a plate. "No. I… needed to start over too."

She set the plate in front of him, turned away.

"Sofia, why won't you look at me?" He caught her arm, and she stilled. When he moved to touch her chin, she turned away.

He took her shoulders then and moved her to face him.

Oh. For a sick, revolting second, he traced his own actions—please, God, don't let him have been the one to blacken her eye. Although, the bruise looked green around the edges, as if a few days old. "How did that happen?"

She snapped her chin out of his grip. "It doesn't matter."

"What are you talking about?" His voice thundered, and he didn't care. "Is someone hurting you?"

"It was an accident. He didn't mean it."

"He—didn't *mean* it? Who didn't mean it? He *didn't mean* to connect his fist to your face? What, he slipped, he accidently—"

"I fell, okay?" She tightened her jaw, turned away.

He watched her body posture as she moved away to cut the bread, and yes, she seemed stiff. As if maybe she *had* fallen.

Right.

"How?"

"I was coming home from work, and it was late, and he startled me."

"Who startled you?"

She shook her head. "Just eat, Dino. You need to balance out all the alcohol you have inside you."

"I'm not drunk, Sofia."

"Anymore."

He winced at that but sloughed it off. "I deserve that. But I want to know who startled you. Why? What is going on?"

"It's just—an admirer. He's been hanging around the theater."

"An *admirer*? You told me you weren't on stage."

Her eyes narrowed. "Does a girl have to be on stage to have a man think she's beautiful?"

Ouch. She should have just slapped him. "No—but—who is this guy?"

"Just a man I met. He—keeps showing up at the theater. Wants to walk me home, or take me out."

"And you keep turning him down." A picture had started to form in his mind, one that churned up a darkness he hadn't felt in over a decade.

The kind of feeling he had when Uncle Jimmy settled his sausage fingers on Sofia's shoulder.

He let his eggs go cold, caught her arm again. This time, she didn't pull away. "He didn't just startle you, did he?"

She didn't meet his gaze, those beautiful eyes cast down, and he ran his hand across her face, lifted it. When she raised her eyes to him, a jolt went through him. Yes, her eyes sparked with fierceness—but behind it he glimpsed something broken and even scared. Oh, Sofia. "We had a tussle. I fell down the stairs."

The ones he'd stumbled up last night? She didn't form the word, but he heard it. *Pushed.* Some fanatical jerk had pushed her down the stairs. The feelings that swept through him couldn't be called brotherly concern. No wonder Markos went berserk when she started singing for Uncle Jimmy.

"I want to know who this man is."

She gripped his wrist, pulled his hand away. Shook her head. "It's not your problem."

"Not my…it *is* my problem! I made Markos a promise—"

She shot him a look that, if he wasn't already bruised and beaten, might have leveled him on the spot. "I'm not your responsibility, Dino. I'm not your sister, or Markos's wife, or even a distant cousin that you have to watch over. In fact, trust me, you should probably stay far, far away from me."

"Are you kidding me? A distant cousin? Yes, fine, so you're not my sister, or even related to me. You're *Sofia*."

"I'm nobody."

She spoke without rancor, without heat. Still, the word could take him to his knees.

He'd be very proud of you. Oh yes. He wanted to put his fist through the wall. "I'm walking you home from now on. Every night."

"Don't be ridiculous."

"Ridiculous is me letting you stay at the train station, waiting for Markos to show up. Jimmy probably gunned him down, or worse, drowned him at the bottom of Lake Michigan."

Oh. His words flashed in her eyes, and he longed to grab them back, at least their tone. "I didn't mean—"

"Don't say that." She held up her hand, as if pushing his words away. "It's not true!"

"It—is. Sofia..."

She backed away from him, her hands up. "I am not listening to this—"

"I don't want it to be true! Oh, Sofia you have no idea how much I'd like to see him walk through that door."

Except. Even as he said it, his chest tightened, and bile backed up his throat.

No. He didn't. He didn't want Markos back. Not the Markos that stripped him of the man he wanted to be.

"I keep thinking that he got away, built a life somewhere. Maybe on the sea. I used to love to watch him sail on his boat, the wind slicking back his hair, the sun in his skin." She covered her mouth with her hand. Shook her head. "I should have sung for him."

Oh.

See, he hadn't been dreaming Sofia's love for his brother. He softened his voice. "He's gone, Sofia. Or he would have found us. He would have come back—at least for you."

She gave him a terrible look, one that made him want to weep. But he stared back, unblinking. "You need to face the truth."

Her jaw tightened, more control than fury. "I have. The day I showed up on the Scarpellis' doorstep and saw you in their dining room, bellying up to the table, hair slicked back, in clothes I didn't recognize, I realized that I didn't want to poison your life. Then… or now."

She turned her back to him. "I think you should leave, Dino."

"No. I'm not leaving until I find out who this guy is who's harassing you."

Stalking back to him, she picked up his plate. "Are you going to eat?"

"I'm not hungry."

"Fine." She tossed it into the sink. Swept up a towel and covered her eyes. Her shoulders shook and for a second, yes—he wanted to leave.

Flee to the boardinghouse. Sit by the Christmas tree and wait for a telegram from Lizzy. Clutch to his chest the fragments of his planned-out life.

Maybe he, too, had to face the truth.

Lizzy wasn't coming back. And that life he'd longed for had died with her.

But maybe…and it wasn't like he really believed in fate, or divine providence, but running into Sofia seemed like…a second chance to keep his promise to Markos. Maybe he *could* make him proud.

His voice gentled. "I should have stayed with you at the train station. I was so busy wanting to run from Chicago, I didn't look back." He touched her hair, surprised at how soft it was. "I'm not running now."

She sighed, and in her eyes, he saw a sadness that swept him back to the day they left Zante. He'd sat on the bench, knees drawn up, believing that if he could just wake up from the nightmare, he'd find himself in his own bed overlooking the sea. Or maybe in the bow of Markos's fishing boat, watching it part the foamy waters. But occasionally he'd emerge from himself and his gaze would land on Markos, caught in his own tragedy. And then Sofia.

As they'd drawn away from shore, she seemed—slapped.

Even, confused.

"You're scaring me a little." She touched his eye. "You—you remind me of Markos. He wouldn't listen to reason, he always thought he had to solve everything, even when he was in over his head. And—I can't live through that again." She flinched, and he was there with her, in the basement of Uncle Jimmy's restaurant, their voices scraped raw pleading for Markos's life. Dino had to run upstairs twice to retch into the snow before he emptied enough to feel rage instead of fear.

He'd forgotten the rage. Until now. Then, it had solidified into courage. Now, it could turn him numb, help him move past grief.

Move into a new life. He wove his fingers into Sofia's soft hair. "You won't have to. It's time I really did make my brother proud."

He met her eyes then and touched his forehead to hers. "I've missed you, Sofia."

And, for the first time since she'd picked him off the sidewalk, she smiled.

Yes, no wonder his brother had loved her.

* * * *

"You here again, stranger?" Sofia came out the back door of the theater, a streetlamp flooding down the alley to catch her weary smile. A dusting of January snow—crisp and bright—turned the sky above orange.

"We keep meeting," Dino said, then blew on his hands before reaching out to button her coat at the neck. How Dino hated the way it frayed at the collar, at the cuffs. She looked like a waif in it, not at all the elegant woman she'd become, her strong, capable hands that occasionally made him dinner, even at midnight, the hesitant, hard-earned smile that could stir him to life, even after a twenty-four-hour shift. He longed for the hour to tick to ten, for those moments when he'd wait in the alleyway, his hands tucked into the pockets of his leather coat, collar up, waiting for her to exit the theater. Sure, she only lived two blocks away. Fifteen minutes, if he dragged—and very often he did, devouring her words, her smile, the way she looked at him and saw both the boy he'd been and the man he'd become.

Or, the man he hoped to become.

He held out his elbow for her, and she wrapped her gloved hand through it.

"Someone is going to start talking." The words slipped out before he could stop them, yet he didn't yank them back, didn't soften them with a harsh chuckle. His old life, the one with Lizzy, had died that dusky morning when the Japs had decided to declare war on his country.

Or, well, not *his* country. Because if he joined up, they'd discover too quickly that he didn't belong here at all.

Sofia held a bouquet of carnations in her hand, and as they walked by a singed barrel, she dumped them inside.

He glanced at them. "From him?"

"He knows you're waiting here. He told me to get rid of my bodyguard."

Dino had made a point of arriving early, pacing under the lights of the theater, then in the alleyway, staking his territory.

Not unlike a dog, he supposed. Still, if it kept Sofia safe.

And on his arm…

They walked through the snow, her feet crunching lightly, even in her heels. The air nipped at his ears, his fedora poor insulation. She had turned her collar up, and her hat—a worn cloche probably from her days in Chicago—would hardly be warm.

He cupped his hand over hers. "Sometimes I think I can't get any colder, and then the wind will come in off the Mississippi and I'll feel my bones creak. Why couldn't the Scarpellis have moved to Florida?"

She laughed. "When we first came here, I shared a room with the other women at the Gold Medal Flour factory—"

"I didn't know you worked there."

"Oh, I worked anywhere I could. And I'd curl up in my boarding room, pull my feet under me, and dream of the hot Zante sand. Sometimes I could even smell it. That, and roast lamb, with mint. Your mother was an amazing cook."

He let his mother walk into his mind, felt her strong hands around him as she settled him on her lap, heard her low tones in his ear as she read aloud. She always smelled of the kitchen—onions and fried fish, dill and mint, and the sweet tang of orange juice. He'd never smelled the like of it since coming to America.

Except around Sofia. Maybe it was the coriander, the cinnamon, the way she kneaded love into her bread.

He might have put on a few pounds over the past three weeks.

"You mentioned you had a roommate—"

She glanced at him.

"The night at..." He lifted a shoulder. "At Lizzy's house. Thanksgiving. She got you the job there?"

"Helen. We roomed together at the factory until she started working for the Spensers. When they, uh...passed, she got a live-in position with a family in St. Paul."

They turned out into the street, walked under the puddle of streetlights, past O'Donnell's, the place where she'd picked him up, restarted his life. Tonight he recognized the sounds of Glenn Miller. He hadn't even asked her if she knew how to dance.

Because that, too, felt like a part of his old life.

"Do you ever think of going back to Greece?" She slipped and clamped her other hand on his arm. He caught her, righted her.

"Do you ever think of wearing boots? It *is* January."

"Women suffer for their beauty," she said, laughing.

Oh, the sound of it went right through his chest to his bones, settled there, set something ablaze.

Her voice turned solemn. "I sometimes imagine myself returning, stepping off the boat, taking off my shoes, and plowing my feet into the sand, or wading into the salty lick of the ocean. I even imagine the hot sun pouring over my face. It works on days like this when I can't feel my feet."

"I miss the ocean. I miss the currents and the power of it. It scared me too. I keep remembering one night—maybe a couple weeks before we left—Markos and I sat at our window peering out at the blackness. A storm was rolling in, we could hear it in the surf. It would slam against the rocks, huge booms. And then it started to thunder and lightning. It sounded as if the sky would collapse right on us. I remember shaking. Markos must have seen it because he told me—'Don't be afraid. God is in thunder. And the louder the thunder, the closer He is.' He most likely heard my mother say it, but from then on, I stopped being afraid. Started listening for the thunder. Waited for it."

She slipped again, and he leaned over, scooped her into his arms.

"Dino! What are you doing?"

"Keeping you from getting killed. It's part of my Hippocratic oath."

She put her hand on his chest. "Why did you decide to be a doctor?"

He turned down her street, cut through the alley, past a parked Packard, cold and dark.

"It seemed like the right thing. I made enough house calls with Dr. Scarpelli, saw how he cared for people—I wanted that. Everyone loves him."

"You love him."

"I admire him. And yes, probably I love him."

She twined her arms around his neck, and she fitted there, like she'd always belonged. He hated reaching her porch and putting her down.

Probably he held her too long as he righted her.

She looked up at him, sighed, a smile touching her lips. "Are you hungry?"

Yes. He put his hand to her face, traced her mouth with his thumb. "I have the four a.m. shift. I need some sleep."

Oh. Was he a jerk for liking how her face fell? He swallowed and for a second saw his arms around her, pulling her against him.

He wanted to know what those lips tasted like.

Lizzy.

The name slammed into him, and he stiffened. Had she meant so little to him that only six weeks after her death, his heart reeled out for another woman?

Not any woman. Sofia.

Markos's Sofia. He shook his head again. "Sorry, Sof. Maybe another night."

She patted his lapel, a softness in her blue eyes. They always seemed to follow him home, into his day, pull him back to the theater. "Thank you, Dino." She lifted herself to his cheek, kissed him. "You are a true gentleman."

Her words settled on him like a song even as he walked back down the empty alleyway home.

CHAPTER 15

If he didn't know better, Dino would believe that Reg had it in for him. Just because Reg might be a second-year resident didn't mean he owned him.

At least this was Dino's thought. Apparently Reg didn't agree.

Apparently he was on staff to fetch Reg coffee and a ham sandwich from the cafeteria.

He also took vitals on every one of Reg's patients, started two IVs, and did complete medical histories on two rummies that just needed a bed.

He shot a look at the clock. Already an hour past the end of his shift.

He also, apparently, was here to babysit Mr. Albert Phelps, passing a kidney stone in room 120. "Don't leave until he's out of pain," Reg said, as he shrugged on his coat, topped his head with a fur hat that he pulled over his ears. He eased on his leather gloves. "Two more years, pal. Then you can have a social life."

Dino turned away, glanced at the clock, imagining Sofia handing out the last of the coats, closing up the closet, cleaning out of the theater. In a half hour, she'd be waiting for him in the alley.

Or, walking home alone.

"C'mon, Mr. Phelps, if you could just try and drink more..."

"Listen, kid, the plumbing don't work like it used to." The doughy man took the drink from Dino's hand, his face a knot of pain. A tattoo on his forearm suggested time in the merchant marines. Still, twenty minutes later, the pain turned out his stomach onto Dino's lab coat.

And finally upset the bedpan onto his shoes.

Which of course, necessitated a scrutiny of the contents, wiping it up, pouring it all through a strainer in order to search for something the size of a pebble. The clock ticked past eleven. He just might hate Reg.

"Don't forget to finish filling out his chart," Margie said as he emerged from the locker room, wearing clean pants, hopefully smelling of soap.

The clock read midnight by the time Dino watched his words form in the air as he dug into his pocket and hailed a cab, pressing the driver to bend a couple laws as he hung on to the seat. *I'm sorry, Sofia.*

Darkness framed her boarding room window. He stood on the sidewalk, measuring his motives. Probably she'd gotten home without incident, had simply gone to bed. Her suitor had sent her nary a note for an entire week. Dino warred between hoping that he'd chased him off and the thought that, if so, she might not need him anymore.

He couldn't bear the thought of not walking her home. Especially with Valentine's Day a week away. He'd been entertaining thoughts of a candlelit dinner...

No. Sofia didn't belong to him. She considered him a *brother.* Sometimes he could still feel her kiss, burning his cheek.

The wind tossed paper down the street, into an alleyway, chapped his ears.

He'd just check to make sure she made it home. He climbed the porch steps, opened the door, and called himself a liar.

He missed her smile. The way she teased him when he told her about his crazy patients. She'd love the story of the kidney stone.

He tiptoed up the stairs, wincing at the creak, and stopped outside her door. Raised his hand. And that's when he heard it—the hiccoughed breath of captured sobs.

He stilled, held his breath.

Yes, most definitely crying. He knocked.

"Go away!"

The anger in her tone shook him. "Sofia, it's me, Dino…"

A pause, then steps to the door. He waited for the handle to turn, for her to open it. Even pressed his palm on the smooth oak.

Nothing. "Sofia?"

"Go away, Dino." Her voice shook, however. "Go…"

"Let me in." He found the tone he used for patients, for Mr. Phelps tonight. "Now."

Nothing.

He leaned his forehead on the door. "Please, Sofia. Please."

If he had held his breath, he might have perished. But finally, thank you, she slid the bolt back, and the door eased open.

Mascara bled down her face, even in the wan hall light. "Why are you in the dark?" She still wore her coat, although she'd discarded her hat. "How long have you been home?"

She turned away from the door, letting it hang open. He pushed through, hung his hat on the hook. Flicked on the light.

His breath seized inside him. Yes, she still wore the coat, but under it, the collar of her dress hung half-torn, a button missing from the top. And the heel had been shorn off her shoe. She stood, lopsided, her back to him, her arms curled around her body.

"Sofia—what—what happened to you?"

He touched her shoulders. The frailty of them—the way her bones moved under his hands—hollowed him out. And, she didn't even resist when he faced her.

He had no words for the rage that choked him. Angry finger marks striped her cheek, their imprint outlined in red from the force of the blow. "Someone hit you."

And guessing by the way she fisted her coat tight in front of her, maybe the abuse hadn't stopped there. "Please tell me that's all he did—not that it's not enough but…oh, Sofia." His brain nearly shut off as she covered her hands with her mouth. "Sofia!"

"No—no, I'm okay. I…hit him. I scratched him. He was so…*angry*." Her breath caught, her eyes so wide they seemed to swallow him. "I ran back here, locked the door." Her breath shuddered. "I was…so scared."

And then, she began to sob.

Sofia. Oh… "I am so sorry. I should have been here. I should have told Reg I couldn't—"

She looked up at that.

"Never mind." He moved close, cupped his hand on her cheek. "It won't happen again. Ever."

She shook her head. "You can't promise that, Dino. You have a career, something you worked for. You can't protect me—"

"I can!" The heat in his voice rattled him, and he held up his hands, walking away, to the window, blowing out a breath. "I will."

She came up behind him. "No. I'm going to quit my job. Move, maybe."

"You need to go to the police." But even as he said it, he winced. Yeah, sure. The Chicago police force had scoured from his mind any trust in the local police department.

He turned, caught her hand, icy in his hot grip. "Listen. Maybe there's something we can do…" He sucked a breath, the idea taking form, solidifying, turning to words— "Marry me."

"What?" She recoiled, but he held her hands, trapping her.

"Marry me, Sofia. I—I know that I'm not Markos, but, I care for you and—"

"I'm not charity, Dino! I've been on my own for ten years, and I don't need you to sweep in and save me. I can take care of myself—"

He kissed her. Sure, it surprised him, but he couldn't help it. Given that she'd just been attacked, probably his timing couldn't be worse. By all rights, he earned her palm on his face.

And he would have stepped back, begun a litany of apology, if she hadn't dug her hands into his lapels.

So, he kissed her again, a desperation in his touch. He didn't move toward, her, didn't curl his arms around her—although with everything inside him he longed to mold her to himself. Instead, he let her move into him, even as he softened his touch, deepening his kiss, needing her more with every moment. She tasted sweet, as if she'd sucked on a peppermint at work.

After a moment, she seemed to exhale.

Relax.

And although she'd kept him from moving away, she finally, *really* kissed him back. She made a soft little noise in the back of her throat, and it only made him reach up and run his hand behind her neck.

Sofia. He kissed her like he'd never kissed Lizzy, or any girl before her, her touch nourishing.

Delicious.

Right.

Sofia.

She finally caught her breath, backed away, not enough to twist out of his grip, but he saw everything he'd hoped for in her eyes. In her smile.

"Is that a yes? You'll marry me."

She touched her forehead to his chest. "I…"

He lifted her chin with his hand, made to kiss her again. But she untangled herself from his arms and moved away from him. She peeled her coat off and hung it in on the hook by the door. "Let me fix you something to eat."

What—? "Sofia."

"I'll bet you're hungry."

Very. But not so much for food.

"Sof—"

She pulled out a pan, a carton of eggs from the tiny fridge.

"I'm serious."

She cracked an egg, threw the shell into the sink. Cracked another. Threw that shell in. When she reached for a third, he caught her wrist. "You don't have to answer me now."

She turned and the force of her embrace around his neck shook him. He closed his arms around her. "What can I do?"

She said nothing.

He stroked her hair, weaving the softness through his fingers. "Please, tell me what to do."

She shook her head. "I am just so…tired. I'm tired."

He closed his eyes, rested his cheek on her head. "I'm staying tonight."

She lifted her eyes, fast, protest in her expression—

"No—Sofia, I mean on the floor. Or in the hall. I don't care. I just want to be here if that jerk comes knocking."

She closed her eyes, he thumbed away a tear, surprised when she lifted herself and kissed him again. He barely breathed. She had a smell, a way about her touch that turned his mind to liquid.

She pulled away, her eyes in his. "Why…are you so good to me?"

He frowned. "Why shouldn't I be?"

She ran her hand through the shadow on his chin. "Oh, Dino…I…" She looked away. "Yes, I want you to stay."

He nodded. "I'll make a bed on the floor—"

"No."

She lifted her face, and if he had any question about her intent, it was erased by the look in her eyes. "I don't want you to go."

Oh.

"Sofia—"

"Don't talk."

He opened his mouth, closed it, swallowed. "Are you—are you sure?"

She sighed. "I—I don't want to be alone." She smiled up at him, a smile that would make him fetch her the world.

"We don't have to—"

She slid her arms again around his neck. She smelled of perfume, and he saw himself in her eyes as she pressed her lips to his. Sweetly. Without pause.

He couldn't—or— He groaned, a sound that broke loose deep inside him even as he swept her up into his arms. She clung to him.

Oh, Sofia. "You're not alone, *kardia mou*. Not anymore."

* * * *

The sun had just begun to crest over the city, gilding the snow banks, syruping through the streets. He'd been standing at the window for far too long, his feet ice, his body shivering, shirtless. He'd found his pants in the dark and debated a long time about just slinking out.

That might make it worse, however. To slink away. Although he felt like a slug, leaving a trail of slime in his wake.

He tucked his hands under his arms. Stared at the sun bleeding into the sky. What had he done? He leaned his forehead against the window, hoping the shock would break him out of this moment, this glue that stuck him to his sin.

Nothing.

"Dino?"

He pressed his fingers against his eyes, wiping them. Yeah, that would be perfect. Let her see him crying. His soul leaking to the outside of his body.

What man cried after making love to the woman he adored?

The kind of man who saw himself becoming less and less the person he'd hoped to be. He took a breath, forced a smile. Turned. "Good morning."

She lay in the bed, covered in a sheet, her hair tousled, the smudges of her makeup under her eyes. She tried a smile, and it fell. "Are you okay?"

He nodded but didn't move toward her. Instead, he lowered himself into her straight-backed chair, leaning his body out from the wood, stiff, his body rattling in the cold.

"Come…come here."

He looked out the window, shook his head. "I think it's better if I stay over here."

She lay back on her pillow, stared at the ceiling.

Outside, the early morning milk trucks rumbled down the street. His stomach growled.

"It's guilt, isn't it?"

He closed his eyes, and oh no, the tears returned. He ran a thumb under his eye. Gritted his jaw. Nodded.

"Oh—Dino." She sat up, clutching the sheet to herself. "I—"

"Just—leave it, okay? Leave it."

He stood up, went to the icebox. Found a new voice. "How about I make you breakfast for a change?" The eggs, left from last night, lay in a congealed mass. He dumped them down the drain.

"Shouldn't we talk?"

He kept his back to her, braced his hands on the counter, hung his head. "About—what? What a terrible man I am?"

She turned silent behind him.

He waited for her to start crying, maybe, or to order him out. Oh, how he wanted her to hate him. Please—

"You're not a terrible man, Dino."

He sighed.

"But I understand. I'm not stupid. I know what that guy meant when he asked you if the old man turned you down. You're in love with Spenser's daughter."

What? She thought this was about Lizzy? He stiffened. Heard the rustle of sheets, her soft footfalls. He startled, a little gasp going through him when she touched his bare back. "We can forget this. It doesn't have to mean anything."

He spun around and stared down at her with what must have been a look of horror. He certainly wanted to pick up something—maybe the eggs—and hurl them across the room, watch them shatter and bleed down the wall. "Forget this? Are you serious? It *meant* something—"

She looked away, her face flushed. "I don't mean it meant *nothing.* But I understand that you don't love me. You're grieving."

Oh, Sofia. Now he wanted to throw *himself* at something. Or put his fist into her brick wall. Yeah, a real gentleman he turned out to be.

He touched her face. "I did love Lizzy. But she's gone, and I do care for you, Sofia. I asked you to marry me."

She leaned away from his touch. "Because you felt sorry for me."

Was that why? He wanted to pull her to himself, to smell her hair in his face, to wrap his arms around her and be lost in her touch. "No, I don't feel sorry for you."

She looked at him then, met his eyes. "Good. Don't. Because I don't feel sorry for me." She put her hand on his chest. Sighed. "Get dressed, Dino. And yes, you can make me breakfast if that will make you feel better."

It might. But, "No, you marrying me would feel a lot better."

She gave the smallest of smiles, her beautiful lips tipping up. "You don't always have to do the right thing, you know."

"Oh, I wish I did anything right, Sofia. Just one thing."

She reached up, cupped his face, and he leaned against it. "So like your brother."

She closed the bathroom door behind her as he retrieved his shirt. He pulled it on as the sun rose above the tops of the buildings and poured into the room.

Yes, so like his brother. And not just impulsive, angry Markos, but Theo too. The brother who'd stolen another man's woman.

Oh, yes, little brother Dino certainly embodied the Stavros legacy. Was really leaving his mark on the world.

But he would make it right. *Had* to make it right. He lifted his face to the rose gold of the morning and longed to believe in himself.

CHAPTER 16

After the past decade of slogging through crusty snow, thawing out his wool socks over the radiator in his room, and ducking his head against the cruel wind slithering down the frozen Mississippi, living in Minneapolis had taught Dino to appreciate spring. With pink buds on the maples and white flowers dotting the mountain ash around the university campus, the hint of life stirred the air.

And with it, Dino's spirit. Something had blossomed inside him since that night with Sofia—although he'd resisted the lure of her arms. He couldn't bear to face himself in the mirror until he convinced Sofia to marry him.

She would—he knew it. It would just take more time.

He shoved his hands into his coat pockets as he walked home from the trolley, the sun lazy as it fell into the horizon. Maybe this buoyant feeling came from freedom—Reg had taken his tyranny on leave for the past month. And with Sofia now living at his boardinghouse, Dino didn't have to pry himself from the grip of the hospital every night to know she was safe. With his first-year intern test behind him, two more years of residency in front of him, he could taste his future, like the breath of summer, just out of his reach.

He'd be very proud of you. Maybe. The thought swept him back to languid days on their fishing boat.

He'd spent more time in memory these days, his toe trailing in the tepid waters, watching Markos throw out the nets. Markos always looked seventeen, bronzed, strong, confidence in his dark blue eyes.

The Markos Dino saw in Sofia's eyes, probably. Dino tried not to read into her smile, believe himself a replacement.

Besides, Markos didn't teach her to dance or propose to her on a nightly basis over the past month.

One of these times, she might not laugh, might not wrinkle her nose at him, might not disentangle herself from his arms and bid him good night.

Maybe even tonight.

He climbed the stairs to the boardinghouse, the front porch cleared of snow after the last storm—March, in like a lion. The fragrance of Sofia's bread—he could nearly taste the cinnamon—beckoned him inside as he hung his coat on the tree by the door, toed off his goulashes.

One of the boarders sat at the piano, clunking out "Clare du Lune." Elsie plowed out between the swinging doors to the kitchen, holding a milk glass dish piled high with creamed corn. "Just in time, Danny. The *kuchen* is nearly out of the oven." She glanced back over her shoulder, said something in German. Over the last month, Sofia had received a crash course in "Elsie."

Sofia glanced up at him from where she stood at the sink, draining a pot of potatoes. Steam billowed up as she turned her face away. Still, it slicked sweat across her brow where she'd pulled her hair back into a black scarf.

For a second, he was back in Zante, in his mother's kitchen. Only this time, the boulder that normally lodged in his throat spread out in a warmth through his chest, seeping into his bones. "Hello."

She glanced over her shoulder. "Hello—Danny."

He'd taken a risk asking her to quit her job, convincing Elsie to hire her on as a domestic. Any day, Sofia could slip, refer to him as Dino. But it got her away from the theater, from late nights walking home, allowed him to focus on his studies.

And, frankly, maybe it was time for Dino Stavros to resurface.

He felt more like himself every day he spent with Sofia Frangos. Perhaps life had finally caught up with him.

He wound his arms around Sofia's waist, perching his chin on her shoulder, then pressed a kiss there, not allowing his lips to linger.

Not when temptation could so easily devour him.

She set the potato pot in the sink, turned in his arms. Her eyes, so blue he could lose himself in their warm waters, drew him in. "How was your day?"

"Good. But I switch shifts again tomorrow. I'll be under Reg's watch again. Expect me to come home smelling like a bedpan."

She wrinkled her nose at his joke, but he couldn't help but notice a shadow of something cool, even dark in her eyes. Something he might even name fear. "What is it?"

She shook it away. Smoothed her hands on his cotton shirt. "Nothing."

Oh. Perhaps the mention of the bedpans reminded her too much of the night. He kissed her on the forehead. "I'm going to change clothes. Dinner smells wonderful."

He walked back out to the living room—the piano player had left, and Billie Holiday played on the radio, her delicate, haunting voice following him up the stairs. He was surprised to find his room open.

Maybe Sofia had brought him fresh sheets. Sometimes she even made his bed—

A woman stood at his window, her back to him, a black trench coat cinched tight around her penny waist. Blond hair knotted at the nape of her neck. The wide ribbon from her black hat trailed down her back like a tail. "Hello? How did you get in here?"

"I wasn't sure when you'd get home." She turned, and in the movement, the breath left his body. He stood there, a shrill whooshing in his ears as his eyes focused on her face, hidden partially under the half netting of her hat. A face he could trace from memory. And her green eyes, solemn, even hurt, as she pinned them on him.

His gaze arrested on the scars that rumpled her smooth right cheek, as if someone had taken the skin and pinched, their finger marks still embedded.

"Lizzy."

She inhaled a breath. Glanced down at the bag clutched in her hands. "I'm sorry to surprise you like this, but I know you were worried, and I wanted to—"

"What happened? Are you okay?" In a moment, he returned to that day at the telegraph station, feeling as if someone had poured benzene through him, lit him afire. "I was—I thought you had—"

"Died? I wanted to." She held her gloved hand to her mouth, then covered her cheek with it, looked away. "We were on the dock when the Japs attacked. We tried to get away, but they were too fast. Daddy was onboard the *Arizona*. Mother and I…well…" She closed her eyes. "I don't remember anything after the explosions. They say they found me a day later, during the rescue efforts. I just remember waking up in the hospital."

The picture of it charred his mind, the screaming as the bombs fell, the boiling air as the battleship exploded, the noise and chaos. "Didn't they know it was you? I cabled the hospital, the naval base—I looked for you every day."

"I know. At first they couldn't identify me. But—after a couple weeks..." She sighed. "My face wasn't the only place burned..." She cupped her left hand over her right as she spoke.

He wanted to pull her into his arms, to kiss her face, to tell her that it didn't matter. But the way she bowed her shoulders, turned back to the window—he just stood there...

Burned.

The word lay on his chest like a boulder.

"Lizzy—it doesn't matter. I still..." Love you. He still *loved* her? Wait—

Her shoulders shook.

Oh no. He reached out then turned her. "Lizzy, please don't cry."

She looked up at him then and offered a smile, her lips as beautiful as he remembered. He leaned close, ready to brush them with his, then caught himself. Blew out a breath.

"Lizzy—I'm so grateful you're alive. I was so worried."

"I know...I'm sorry, Danny. I should have written to you. But I couldn't...I didn't want you to know until I was ready."

He held her chin, ran his thumb down her uninjured cheek. "You're still beautiful to me."

She looked away, a blush on her face.

"Uh—I don't mean to interrupt, uh, Danny. But dinner is on the table."

He froze, his throat hollow. Closed his eyes as Sofia's step padded down the hallway. He heard the stairs squeak.

Lizzy took his hand. "I'm starved."

Yeah, well, he might never eat again.

* * * *

"Of *course* you should marry her."

Sofia stood in the hall right outside the trauma ward, her arms tight around her body. A petite knot of frustration. From the nurse's desk, Margie raised her head.

Dino cupped Sofia's elbow, moved her outside, into the shelter of darkness. "Listen, I asked *you* to marry me. I'm not going back on that."

A remnant lick of winter wind cut through his lab coat. A fresh rain had scoured up the hope of spring, something that twenty-four hours ago revived in him a similar hope that, yes, he could be a man of honor.

Now he just wanted to run back inside, focus on cleaning and patching up the wounds of a couple of bar-brawlers.

Maybe even dive into the stack of reports he had to update.

Anything to drive from his brain Sofia's broken expression as he descended the living room stairs with Lizzy, his mouth turned to glue.

Thankfully, Lizzy didn't stay, her driver waiting for her outside the boardinghouse. Oddly, she didn't even try to lift herself into his arms as he bid her good bye.

Dino couldn't bear to look at Sofia, his eyes fixed on the stew, her handcrafted bread.

He hadn't even bid her good-bye this morning when he'd left for his shift. No wonder she'd tracked him down at the hospital, garbed in Markos's—no—his *father's* coat, the rain glistening in her olive-black hair. "I saw the way you looked at her. The way she looked at you. I understand, Dino."

"It doesn't matter—"

"It *does* matter. You love her—your feelings for me were just a reaction—"

He clutched her shoulders, twigs beneath his grip. "My feelings for you were—*are* real."

"I never said yes, you know."

"Sofia, you can be so frustrating! I know you didn't say yes. But—we belong together. I know it."

He should get down on one knee, perhaps even here, under the glare of the streetlamps. Except, Lizzy's eyes the way she looked up at him as if lifting to him her shattered hopes for him to mend, held him fast.

So shoot him, he hadn't become a physician without the desire to fix the broken.

Only, somehow he couldn't fix this. Couldn't seem to repair the betrayal on Sofia's face. Couldn't heal the scars on Lizzy's.

She must have seen his snarled thoughts, because her expression gentled, her hands catching his. "Listen, Dino. I know you loved her. You had a life planned with her—until I stumbled back into it and tangled it up."

"That's not the way I remember it."

"It's exactly what happened. We were never supposed to be together."

She didn't have to speak Greek for him to understand her meaning. Because she didn't belong to him. Not really. Even after what they'd done, even after how she'd given him so much of herself, in the end, her heart would always belong to Markos.

Which meant, here he was, begging a woman who couldn't truly love him, to marry him.

"But Sofia—I—we—we *need* to get married." He hated the tremor in his voice, the way his shame lay right there, in the soggy night.

She touched his cheek, her fingers soft. "We made a mistake. We don't have to make another one."

"It wasn't a mistake!" But his protest sounded just a bit too loud. Too raw. "I mean—it's not a mistake to love you, Sofia."

"There's where you're wrong, Dino. What you Stavros boys have never figured out. It is a mistake to love—"

"What are you doing out here, Danny?"

Even as the voice needled him, even as Dino made to turn, to shoot a retort back at Reg, he saw it.

Sofia flinched. More than that, she recoiled, her entire body moving into herself.

And just like that, time scrolled back, a gritty rewind. Sofia, pinned by Reg at the Thanksgiving party. Reg, ordering him to stay behind and work overtime at the hospital the night Sofia was attacked.

Dino turned and under the gummy lights saw the scars on Reg's cheek, fine lines, two of them, through his beard, down his jawline.

On his neck.

I scratched him.

"You," Dino said, almost under his breath.

"What?"

Dino launched at him. Reg's fist slammed into his chin even as Dino tackled him. They bounced off the entryway, stumbled, hit the ground under the glare of the hospital lights.

The first time Dino brawled, only a few months ago, he'd experienced a sort of release. This time the anger coiled inside, tightening, like a claw.

He hammered his fist into Reg's face, satisfaction sluicing through him when he grunted. "Get off me—"

"You animal!" Dino threw another punch—wanting to demolish that perfect, regal nose. Reg knocked him away.

Dino stumbled back.

"What is wrong with you, Scarpelli?"

"You were the one who went after her! You're the one who attacked her!"

Reg recoiled, his gaze snapping to Sofia. Then—and Dino couldn't be held accountable for what happened after that—he smiled.

Sofia gasped.

Dino sucked in a breath, so much fury inside it stopped him cold. Long enough for Reg to pounce. Dino landed with a breath-jarring slam, his spine nearly separating on one of the boulders along the pathway.

Reg followed with a fist. Dino took the hit on the jaw, saw the world explode, didn't care.

He brought his knee up, tossed Reg over his head.

Reg landed with a *whump* on his back on the pavement.

Behind the roar in his brain, he barely heard Sofia— "No, stop, Dino! Please!"

But he could no more stop the wind. He tackled Reg just as the man came to his knees. "You filthy—" They flew back onto the cement, the rocky edge of the path.

Then, just like that, Reg stopped moving.

Dino bounced to his knees, his fist recoiled.

Reg's eyes stared at him a second before they rolled back into his head. A pool of blood seeped out from under a jagged boulder jutting from the ground.

"Reg—?" Nothing. As Sofia whimpered behind him, Dino kneaded Reg's head for the trauma. Sure enough, under all that blood, above his brain stem, he found a mass of broken bone, the flesh soft and meaty.

He stared at the blood a moment—too long, seeing Theo, seeing Kostas.

Then it all rushed at him and he came to life. "No, no—" He whipped off his lab coat, put it to the wound, turned to Sofia. "Get help! I need a stretcher!"

She bolted toward the building.

He'd never felt so ill as he did when they scooped Reg up and carried him into trauma. Dino watched Reg's arm slip from the stretcher like some kind of doll.

And, as if his world couldn't implode more, the doors shut on Dr. Scarpelli, directing the trauma team.

For a quiet breath, Dino stood in the bright lights, staring at the stain of blood, his heart in his throat.

Run.

No.

He couldn't run, but he couldn't follow Reg, either.

Until Sofia grabbed him by the arm, fed her hand down to his. "I told you—I'm poison, Dino."

She gave his hand a squeeze, started to turn away. He grabbed her wrists. "What are you doing?"

"I'm leaving."

"Yes. Okay. Go back to the house. We'll talk there—I have to—I have to stay."

"No—I'm leaving—"

"Sofia. We'll figure this out."

She met his eyes then, a haunting look that reached in and took out his heart. Then she pressed a kiss on his cheek, turned, and folded into the night.

Everything inside him turned to ash as, God help him, he didn't stop her.

CHAPTER 17

Dino stood at the window, watching the rain weep against the pane, shivering. Fatigue had long since turned him raw, shredded his nerves as he paced the corridor.

Please, Reg. Live. *Live.*

His lungs burned with the scream, every muscle simmering. He closed his eyes, pressing his forehead to the glass.

He hoped Sofia had gone back to the boardinghouse.

And then, as he considered the dark specter of his reflection in the window, he didn't. Maybe neither of the Stavros boys deserved her.

"There you are."

He turned, and his father, or rather the man that *felt* like a father, entered the room, hands sunk deep in the pockets of his lab coat. "I don't suppose you got that cut looked at."

Dino's hand went to his cheek, where Reg's knuckles had separated the skin. Swollen. Raw. He winced, relishing, however, the sting.

"If you're wondering, yes, you're beating yourself up enough. You can stop now."

"I doubt that." He turned back to the window. "Please tell me he's going to live."

"He hasn't yet woken up."

Dino closed his eyes.

"His vitals are good, though. And his pupils are responsive."

The claws in the flesh around Dino's heart loosened, just a bit.

"Wanna tell me what that was about?"

In the silence, Dr. Scarpelli treaded up beside him, staring out onto the wet street. The rain pattered on the window, eroding the glow of lights on the pavement. It had long since washed away Reg's puddle of blood.

"I always liked your brother, you know."

Dino glanced at him. Dr. Scarpelli—he never got used to calling him Father, or Papa, or anything but—Doctor. Still, it seemed more a term of affection than a title. The elderly man wore his hair slicked back, not unlike the way he had on the boat. Now age grayed his temples, carved experience into his healer's eyes.

"It wasn't that I didn't think he could take care of you."

Outside, a trolley car splashed through a puddle, threw water against the curb.

"It was that he was so angry. He carried it inside him, like he needed it to survive."

Yes. Even Dino had seen that.

"But it wasn't so much his anger that bothered me. It was his fear. He tried so desperately to protect you, to protect Sofia. He bore it all on his own shoulders, unwilling to ask for help. It felt to me like he was raising his fist to God."

Dino sat on one of the stools, exhaustion tugging at him.

"I knew, because I too raised my fist to God, Dino. When we lost our son—I saw my wife die too. In spirit, if not in body. I let my grief turn me inside myself, let it stir my bitterness.

"Until you. I saw you on the ship, your hungry eyes watching us, and I realized I'd spent enough time feeding on my own pain. It was time to become a healer again."

He turned then and placed a hand on Dino's shoulder, kneaded it. "Son, you never really escaped Zante. Or what happened the night you left."

Dino glanced up at him, met his eyes, bounced away.

"Yes, Gabriella told me. I know about Kostas. I know about your part of the fight."

Dino flinched. Ground his jaw even as he looked away, seeing the nightmare afresh that had awakened him too many times in those early days.

Saw himself leaping onto Yannis's back. For a second, he could taste the old man's sweat, smell the wine on his breath, feel the rage ripping through him as Kostas tried to wrestle Dino from his back.

And then came Markos. Screaming—or maybe it had been his own terror, he wasn't sure. Just Markos, launching himself at Kostas. Dino couldn't remember being thrown off. Just the clear shout of pain as he crumpled into the corner, then clearing his vision just as Markos slammed Kostas against the wall.

He remembered—oh, how he remembered—the gut-wrenching tic of seconds as Kostas crumpled.

As if he might be again fourteen, bile flushed into his mouth, acrid, sour. He swallowed it down.

He'd spent years swallowing it down.

Trying to change the past, leave a different mark on the world.

He stared at the torn, scraped flesh on his knuckles.

Dr. Scarpelli's voice gentled. "Markos wasn't the only one holding on to anger, Dino. The guilt followed you from Zante. It's time to let it go, let God heal you."

Heal him of what?

He pressed the heel of his hands to his eyes. *When I kept silence, my bones waxed old through my roaring all the day long. For day and night thy hand was heavy upon me: my moisture is turned into the drought of summer...*

Yes. His bones had waxed away, his body dry, heavy.

Blessed is the man unto whom the Lord imputeth not iniquity, and in whose spirit there is no guile.

Oh, how he wanted to live without guile.

He expected his father to leave, to hear his footfalls echo.

Nothing. He opened his eyes, turned. The old man considered him. "I have to apologize to you, son." He held up a hand to Dino's protest. "I let you take my name, thinking it would help you start over. Maybe that was wrong. Because you will always be Dino Stavros."

"I know." The words twined out of him, almost like a groan.

"Oh, Dino." The kindness in his father's voice could break him in half. "Don't you know? That day you appeared on my doorstep, God reminded me that He does heal the brokenhearted. It's time to stop worrying about what you've lost, start to see what you've gained."

He smiled, in it so much affection Dino looked away. "You are not alone, son. And you are not lost—you just think you are. But I promise, you cannot find yourself by looking inside." He glanced at the window, where the rain splashed upon the pavement. "Greater love hath no man than this, that a man lay down his life for his friends."

He stood up, again squeezed Dino's shoulder. "That is how you will discover the man you want to be."

The man he wanted to be.

Not Danny Scarpelli, the image he saw in Lizzy's eyes.

But he didn't want to be Dino Stavros either—angry, arrogant, reckless.

However, if he looked closely—no, he hadn't seen that man in *Sofia's* eyes. No, she'd looked at him—*really* seen him, and kept smiling. And in her smile, he'd glimpsed the man he longed to be.

"Oh, God..." He covered his hand with his eyes, his shoulders shaking. "I am so foolish. As lost as I was the night I ran from Zante. Please—please forgive me. Make me into the man I should be."

The man he should be.

I'm leaving. He heard Sofia's words even as he shucked the moisture from his cheeks. No.

He washed his hands in the sink, scoured back his hair, cleaned the wound on his cheek. Please let him do one thing right.

Dino had nearly reached the exit when he saw her, curled in a chair, outside the trauma ward. She still wore her black trench coat, but this time had covered her head and part of her face with a silk scarf. "Lizzy? What are you doing here?"

The words *because I was worried about you* flitted through his mind, followed by a pinch of guilt. But even as he thought it, he knew.

He hadn't loved Lizzy. Not how he loved Sofia. The thought caught him full on, swept through him. He *loved* Sofia. He glanced out the doors, to the splash of rain, the puddles of light.

"What have you done?"

He'd expected worry, perhaps compassion, from Lizzy. Not the fury in her beautiful eyes as she rounded on him.

Huh? "What are you talking about?"

"Reggie!" Her voice broke, she covered her mouth, turned away. "Just because he loves me. Just because he came to Pearl when you didn't."

He stared at her, unable to comprehend her words. "I, uh—*what*?"

"For the past three weeks, he's been there, trying to persuade me to come home. He asked me to marry him. Reggie loves me, even after what—happened. And you—you—"

"You agreed to marry Reggie St. John? Then why were you in my room, waiting for me—*just last night*?"

She glanced through the waiting room, and he realized his voice reverberated.

She schooled her voice, her eyes hot. "I came to ask you for the truth. He told me about you. That you'd been lying to me. That your name was Dino or something like that. And he told me about the woman. I know she was the one at the door, Danny. I should have heard it from your mouth instead of through crude hospital gossip. But you kept lying—just looked right at me and lied."

"Lizzy, I can explain." But his brain tossed through memories, moments when Reg might have discovered his secret—all the way back to the day of the bombing.

To his letter, wadded in the wastebasket. To Reg, by the door, flicking his ashes into it. He must have seen the letter, not wanted to start a fire…

Except, of course, true to Reg St. John's form, he'd used it to flame an inferno.

"You can't marry Reggie." Dino tried, oh, he tried, to keep his voice low, but she recoiled anyway. Shook her head.

"Of course I can. If he *lives*." Her eyes filled and she backed away. "Get away from me, whoever you are."

Whoever you are.

He stared at her, a chill whisking through him.

"Dr. Scarpelli?" The charge nurse, a woman he didn't recognize, waved him over to the desk. "Your wife didn't keep her appointment. Can you ask her to reschedule?"

Wife? "Reschedule?"

"She said she was feeling ill. We ordered a TB test for her."

The words swept over him. Sofia had been feeling weak, looking pale. What if she had TB?

Now he realized why Sofia had appeared so shaken, almost afraid when he'd met her in the hallway. Why she looked at him with water in her blue eyes and nearly ran from him.

I told you...I'm poison, Dino.

Outside, the rain bulleted down, thrashing the earth, torrents forming rivers that furrowed the dirt on either side of the cement walk. He ran out into the deluge, past the watery lamplight—the water sluicing into his hair, down his shirt—and into the sodden darkness.

Sofia!

* * * *

The sun edged just over the cityscape as Dino finished making his bed. At least he should leave it the way Elsie hoped.

She'd served him a stew last night that should feed him for three weeks. But it still couldn't fill the hole gnawing in his stomach, the one that hollowed him more every day Sofia didn't return to the boarding-house, and every hour he sat in the train station those few days after she left, hoping she'd appear.

Dino shoved his sweater into his bag—he didn't need a big one, just enough for his kit, his shoes, a picture of Dr. and Mrs. Scarpelli. His mother's worn Greek Bible.

He stood for a moment at the end of the bed, staring out at the run of silky golden light into the city, pushing shadows across the lime green grass. Had it only been five months ago that Beanie'd collected his own belongings and shipped himself off to war?

To honor. At least that's the prize they advertised at the recruiter's when Dino had signed up. As Dino Stavros, future American citizen. A stint in the army would automate his citizenship.

Already he felt less of an enigma. Less of a vagabond.

A man with a mark to leave. Maybe a heroic legacy to pass on.

Dino tied the bag, threw it over his shoulder, closed the door behind him.

He stopped for a moment at Sofia's vacant room, palmed the paneled door. If only she'd left a note, something.

He ran his index finger along the bottom of his eye, wiped it on his dress pants.

Elsie waited for him by the door, wearing a buttoned smile.

"You didn't have to get up."

"Of course I did. I say good-bye to all my boys." She handed him a bag. "Hot brötchen. For the train." She leaned forward, kissed him quick on the cheek. He caught her and pulled her cottony body into a hug.

"Thank you." He whispered into her ear.

She patted his back. "I'll tell her you are a soldier if she ever comes back."

He closed his eyes, inhaling her words.

After a moment, she stepped back. "Okay then. Stay alive." She kissed him again on the cheek and shooed him out the door.

The lilac-rich breath of spring filled his lungs as he stepped off the porch, threw his bag once more over his shoulder. Stay alive. He intended to do more than that.

Much more.

CHAPTER 18

Dino had gone deaf with the pounding of the 105 Archie's anti-aircraft guns hammering the sky. Like thunder, only relentless, the rumble of them tunneled under his skin, turning his bones brittle. Right behind them followed the 88 barkers, those flak guns more like a punch deep inside his chest. They'd swept his breath clean out of him as he'd clung to the LST—Landing Ship Tank—plowing through the waves toward the Normandy shore.

He could barely hear the MG42s, the machine guns more like buzz saws or an annoying Minnesota mosquito behind the shouts and screams and explosions that obliterated Omaha Beach.

Thankfully, three days later, the odor of iodine and the tinny stench of fresh blood on the stone floor of his "operating theater" had cut away the stench of burning rubber, oil, wood—and the curdling odor of the animal carcasses.

"I need more blood over here and—"

A tray of utensils upended, forceps and surgical knives clattering to the stone floor.

Dino glanced behind him where Captain Stan "Flash" Gordon, a narrow-nosed Brit from the RMAC, bent over a patient, trying to insert a chest tube to relieve a tension pneumothorax. "Calm down, Flash. You're going to be fine. You just have to stabilize him to be evacuated—"

"I know—it's these bloody nurses! Where did they get them?"

Dino looked up at his own surgical nurse, a woman who had waded onto Omaha Beach through the bloody waters, pushing past soldiers bloating in the water or facedown in the russet sand, all so she could work non-stop delivering plasma, administering penicillin, and sending the bloodied through triage. "Sorry," Dino said softly.

Her name was Vivian. He remembered that now. Brown curly hair worn short; quick, sure hands. Not enough meat on her bones. She hadn't complained through eight hours of surgery, eighteen soldiers, four deaths on the table, and too many men going home in bags.

Overhead the lights of the cramped former boudoir burned the back of his neck. Then again, perhaps he should be thankful he wasn't stitching up this chest wound with bullets whizzing past his head. No, the Chateau Colombrière, an estate built some three hundred years earlier, with turrets and a beautiful courtyard, better suited for some exotic vacation than a makeshift hospital, had at least a decent water supply. And a line of Allied defenses.

And, thanks to the German's own recognition of an industrious location for a medical base, the U.S. medical corps had an instant working field hospital. Yes, Dino very much appreciated the use of the German's medical supplies, the iodine, the penicillin, and the sulpha they'd surrendered when the advance line of troopers who'd glided in behind enemy lines relieved the Germans of their hospital.

Occasionally he still heard the popping of a luger from the stables where, apparently, a crew of Jerry medics had decided to pick up weapons.

In truth, Dino had felt just a little naked in only his uniform and the white mark with the red-cross banding his arm as he'd slogged up Omaha Beach and dragged to cover countless soldiers, their bodies burned and torn. However, not once had he been tempted to pick up one of their Brownings.

Violence made him a man he didn't respect. Even for a good cause.

"Okay, what's next?" he said, finishing the last of the whipstitches to this private's chest. He checked his dog tags. Lund, David.

Vivian laid a dressing over the man's wound. "Next you take a break." She smiled at Dino, a gentleness inside it. He guessed her to be about twenty-four, not much older than he'd been when he'd shown up at the recruiter's office.

Two days after Sofia left him with his hat in hand, desperate to make things right.

Three years later, after the army conferred on him his medical degree, gave him surgical experience, and declared him a captain, they sent him to France.

"I have an entire courtyard of wounded soldiers out there. I can't—"

"You need a break. You've been on your feet for sixteen hours. Twenty minutes won't matter, sir." She raised an eyebrow, and he had the uncanny feeling she might be an incarnation of Elsie.

He did want to scrub the taste of sand and smoke from his teeth. Maybe get a drink of water, douse his face, and attempt to scour the grit from his eyes.

He washed his hands, removed his mask, his surgical apron. "I'll be back. Thanks, Vivian."

"Vivi. And you're welcome." She gave him a sweet smile that, in another time or place, might have made him pause. Made him wonder who she was, and if she liked to dance.

If she left behind someone she loved.

Behind him, Dr. Flash had inserted the tube, was now taping it in place. His nurse gave Dino a sour glance as he exited.

They'd shipped in sixteen nurses. He passed the five other surgical rooms in the Chateau, other doctors with their hands inside the chests or heads of soldiers. Too many of them were from the 101st Airborne, dropped four days ago behind enemy lines. Wounded paratroopers dribbled in from the countryside, on foot, in jeeps, with broken limbs, chest wounds, a few with head injuries—all grubbing for life with everything inside them, clinging to the salvation of the field clinic. Most hadn't even met up with their units. Triage turned into reunion.

The ambulatory gave blood or created billets while the dire rotated into surgery. Or elsewhere. Parachutes turned into blankets, became the webbing for cots.

At the end of the hall, patients crammed the post-op room, cot to cot, their IVs filled with plasma or blood, dangling from bottles over their heads. A continuous moaning echoed down the corridor, as if the chateau itself had been torn asunder.

The medics who came on the later wave of gliders, after the Normandy storm, set up rooms for blood transfusions, plasma delivery, shock, burns, and even general medicine.

Dino could just as well be at Halloran General Hospital on Staten Island. Well, except for the chipping of gunfire into the horizon.

Standing on the second floor, he stared out at the courtyard. Cows gobbled hay from a mangled stack, two grubby soldiers sat atop an ancient tractor, smoking cigarettes. Medics, the red cross banding their arms, trundled men on stretchers into the château. Soldiers cluttered the yard, some digging into K-rations, others checking their field gear.

Too many simply stared with stripped expressions across the ravaged countryside, littered with trampled hedgerows, burning tanks, bloated cows. Acrid smoke darkened the horizon.

A scratchy radio transmission played some sort of military encouragement.

Probably the BBC. Those Brits were always so jolly.

Dino descended to the main floor. Every room filled with groaning men, medics working over them, triaging them for the surgical rooms upstairs. Nurses crouched on the ground, adjusting plasma IVs, taking vitals—or listening to, oh, hopefully not—deathbed confessions.

Although, if he had been crushed on the beaches of Normandy, he might also be pouring out his confessions to some blue-eyed Betty from Detroit.

I fell in love with my brother's girl—slept with her.

Yeah, that's the first thing he would say, followed by, *I was so angry with my brother, I think I wished him dead.*

Until he was, of course.

Third might be something about Yannis, and Kostas, and the regret that he'd never written his mother, never returned to Zante.

But those sins seemed so far behind him now, he might not waste his breath to confess them. Just move on to—*please, God, take care of Sofia.*

He'd set up a bank account, had been pouring his military pay into it for the past three years. Someday he'd find her, and, if she wasn't already married, he'd hit his knees and beg.

And, if he pleaded well, perhaps she'd marry him. They might even have a child. He imagined a little girl with blue eyes, like Sofia. Or perhaps a boy—with Markos's dark bronzed skin, a shank of sooty hair shagged over his reddened nose, the keen eyes of a fisherman narrowed against the sun. He couldn't bear to bequeath upon a child his own narrow nose, his sometimes too-big mouth.

He hadn't a clue what traits, really, he might pass on to his child.

No, in his mind, the child always bore a mix of Sofia and Markos.

But first, he had to find her. He'd barraged the census bureau, but of course she'd never bothered to become a citizen either. Written to Elsie, but Sofia never returned to the boardinghouse.

He spent the past three years praying she'd simply—wander back into his life.

"Got a light, sir?"

The voice came from a sergeant sprawled by the door, his leg encased in a field dressing. He held up a Camel. Coughed.

"Sorry, no. But I'll track one down for you."

Thankfully, this morning's rain had diffused the scourge of war, but it created a swamp in the yard. No wonder they'd moved the patients inside.

The German 88s continued to batter the horizon. An acrid haze of smoke hung in the air, scratched his eyes. Burning rubber. Or—animal.

Dino picked his way over to the well, pumped it, bent his head down, and let the spray hit his neck. At least the knot between his shoulder blades eased. He hadn't realized his own exhaustion. He'd done sixteen hours on his feet before, but not after dodging land mines and scrabbling his way through smoke, chaos, and death to the operating room.

He counted his blessings, however, that he hadn't been assigned to the First Airborne Surgical team. He only recognized a handful of his fellow surgeons who had the fiber to drop in with the rest of the 101st as a part of the 326 Medical Company.

He'd come in on foot. The easy way.

The high rumble of a plane engine tremored in the sky. A few soldiers looked up, searching for it. Dino braced himself as, in the distance, a 105 anti-aircraft gun erupted, spitting at the bird from the ground. His entire body shook with the sound.

Yes, he could go deaf under the battering of the German guns.

Behind the cough, he made out the whining, mechanical roar of a tank. In a way, the metal beasts frightened him most of all. More than the 105s' flak guns with their thunder, or the MG42 machine guns with their ripping growl, a tank's clanky rumble could travel up his spine and crush him with its menace. He'd seen them rip apart the beaches, eviscerate the strongholds of the Germans. Crush a bunker filled with grimy soldiers.

With everything inside him, Dino wanted to flee the thunder of the tanks.

Still, he stayed by the pump, water saturating his collar, dripping down his spine as the tank cleared the road and rumbled into the courtyard.

A slew of American soldiers rode atop it as if it might be some sort of massive beast of burden. It argued itself to a stop, and they scrambled down, began shouting. One in particular—obviously a commander—gestured toward the back, and sure enough, from the tail appeared two men on stretchers, borne by their buddies. They jogged them to the triage area.

"We need some help over here!" the commander yelled, no question in his demeanor, with his wide shoulders, the stain of blood turning his fatigues black. He held his Tommy gun in one white-fisted hand.

Something about the voice, the faint soured tone of an accent, faltered Dino's step.

Still, Dino ran to the injured men. The first clutched his helmet across his chest, moaning—or singing? One look at his unfocused gray eyes told Dino they'd overdosed just a smidge on morphine. A field dressing, sopping with blood, draped his lower leg, and closer examination made Dino grimace. "We have a near amputation at the ankle." He nodded to the nurse who directed the litter inside. This one he might be able to save.

The next victim—he looked eighteen—or even sixteen—where did they get these kids?—lay white-faced, and miraculously, or perhaps pitifully, awake. A medic, probably with bullets chipping up dirt and pinging off his helmet, had made a crude but admirable attempt at stitching an abdominal wound. This one would need a resection of bowel, perhaps, maybe even a repair of the small intestine.

"Get this soldier upstairs, stat." Dino got up, shaking off his fatigue. Turned to follow the boy.

A hand grabbed his arm. "Save him, Doc. He's a keeper."

Dino stared at the commander, his helmet pushed back to reveal muddy dark hair, dark blue eyes. His face bore days of filth, grime embedded in his grizzle, and he reeked of swamp and blood and smoke. The battery only made him appear a bona fide hero.

As if he'd walked through Hades…and lived.

No, it couldn't be. Dino couldn't speak, his mouth opening, his chest imploding. No—

And then the commander saw it too, his face paling as he stepped back, blinking, holding up his hand as if pushing away the truth.

The disbelief.

"Markos…," Dino whispered.

A half laugh, half chortle, mostly a huff of joy— "Dino. *Dino!*" And then the commander slung his arm around Dino's neck, pulling him to himself. "Oh, God, thank You! Dino!"

Dino didn't know how to embrace this man, his brother. Instead, he just stood like an idiot as Markos thumped him on the back, nearly buckling his knees. "Dino!"

He set him back, and Dino drank him in. Wider. Taller. Darker. Strong hands, built for battle. Of course he'd have a troop of soldiers following him. "I—thought you were dead."

Oh, perfect. And the irony. He made a face—

Markos just stood there grinning, one side of his mouth tipping up, a different kind of mischief in his eyes. "I was." He clamped Dino around the neck, touched his forehead to his, eyes shining. "I was."

Then, as Dino scrambled for—well, any intelligible response—Markos leaned back, banging him on the shoulder. "I should have known you'd become a doc. Go—take care of my soldier, little brother."

* * * *

He should feel joy.

"Doctor, his pressure is dropping." Vivi stood beside Dino, her finger pressed to the pulse of Markos's soldier—Private Burke—while Dino's hands probed deep into the boy's gullet, searching for the last perforation, the one that kept filling the cavity with blood.

"I need more O neg."

Take care of my soldier, little brother.

Relief, perhaps. That's what he should be feeling.

"He's crashing, doc."

"I can't find the bleeding." He didn't mean the bite of his words, but he'd spent more than two hours repairing the damage done by the fragments of a land mine—a lacerated liver, one kidney destroyed, his stomach turned into chewed meat, his intestines tangled. "I'm missing something."

"Doctor—"

"I need five hundred milligrams of epinephrine."

Vivian pressed the drug into the soldier's IV. Checked for a pulse.

Anger. He definitely felt anger. "C'mon, Private!"

"Nothing yet, Doc."

"I need that blood, nurse."

"We're trying—"

"Try harder!"

Vivi shot him a look, and he ignored it. *C'mon, c'mon.* "I'm getting a pulse."

Dino pressed his stethoscope to the boy's chest, confirmed a thready rhythm.

"I've got to find that leak."

Vivi stood across from him, gauze in one hand, a suction tube in the other.

"Try to keep his chest clear. Here!" He grabbed her hand, directed the suction to the right location.

She jerked under his grip.

Okay, he knew exactly how she felt. And it had nothing to do with joy or relief or even anger.

"He's coding again."

Dino ran his arm across his forehead, his body trembling. Night slicked into the room, turning the operating room freakish under glaring bulb lights. For a moment, he was back in his rotation through the morgue, smelling the formaldehyde, the murky cold seeping into his bones.

"Private, you are *not* dying today!" Dino pounded on Burke's chest with a fist, began CPR again.

"Sir—he's gone. He's too wounded. You can't save him."

"I can—just give him another round of epinephrine."

"I've already given him three rounds. Sir, he came in beyond hope—you did more than anyone could have expect—"

"He's *not* beyond hope. I just have to stop the bleeding. I can fix this!"

"Doctor!" Vivian clamped her hand on his arm. "There's no pulse. He's gone. There's nothing more you can do."

"Go...take care of my soldier, little brother."

"Live, damn you!"

But Private Burke refused to live, of course.

Dino stood over him, Vivi's hand clamped on his arm, a tight grip that told him perhaps he'd lost a little—or perhaps too much—of himself on the table.

He backed away from the corpse, held his hands up, as if in surrender. Blood dripped onto the floor as he stared at the mess—the tubes, the bloodied gauze, the flesh torn beyond recognition. Beyond hope.

"Time of death." He glanced at the clock. "8:05 p.m."

Vivi wrote it down. "I'll clean up."

"No. I'll do it." He turned his back to her, began to close the man's wounds. *Sorry, Markos.*

So, so sorry.

The medics carted the private's body away, and Dino began collecting the bloodied clothes, pads, instruments. Vivi hadn't left, and silently she piled it all together in a sheet, dumping it into a hamper. The instruments she submerged in water for sterilization.

He caught her arm as she turned to leave, not looking at her. "Thank you."

"I'm sorry, sir."

He let go, but she didn't move away. In fact, she turned to him, pressed her hand on his arm. "Doc, you're a brilliant surgeon. You've put so many men back together and given them second chances. But you can't save everyone. You'll have plenty more opportunities tomorrow, unfortunately."

She had a pixie nose and green eyes, and if he didn't have so much scar tissue, he might have reached out to her. Instead, he stood there, feeling her warm hand on his arm, tasting the burn in his throat.

"I have to go find—my brother. And tell him I lost his man."

CHAPTER 19

"Please tell me Private Burke is alive." Markos sat propped against the rocky wall, away from the chaos of the courtyard, his fingers in a can of C-rations—what might be beef stew but looked just as appetizing as one of the muddy bogs indenting the French countryside. Smoke bit the air, the glow from burning houses or tires pulsing against the night. In the courtyard, men smoked cigarettes, coughing, slapping at mosquitoes. Firelight lit their faces, brutal shadows hollowing their eyes.

Dino stared at his clean hands, at the way they shook. Fisted them. "I'm sorry, Markos. He was in bad shape."

Markos winced. Looked back down at his dinner. "He was a fighter, that kid."

A fighter. Dino's exhaustion shuddered through him as his eyes traced his brother's form. He'd filled out—well, they both had, probably, but with Markos nearly thirty, he reminded him of their father, wide-shouldered, seaweed-tough hands. A square jaw, his face grizzled with whiskers, which parted at an open wound on his cheekbone. "Probably someone should take a look at that cut."

"It's fine. People are missing legs. I think I can handle a little scrape." Markos took a slug from his canteen, wiped his mouth with his sleeve. "I missed our drop zone by miles—had to walk through most of the night before I found anyone from the 101st. Dead troopers everywhere. I finally hooked up with a crew from Fox Company, and we bedded down in a farmhouse. Woke up to find a slew of Jerries parked outside, chowing down breakfast—apparently, they'd liberated a number of eggs from the remaining chickens. Burke decided that he was hungry—and before I could put together a plan, he lit out of our bunker, hosing them all down. Took out the entire group." He shook his head. "But not before they managed to tear him in half." He pulled out a tin, the lid partially opened. "We saved him some eggs."

Dino dug his thumbs into the palms of his clean hands, now chilling in the night. "I'm sorry, Markos."

"It's war." Markos put the tin away. Stared at him, as if seeing him for the first time. Dino stood under his scrutiny, wondering if he saw the boy who'd dived off the boat in search of a turtle. Or perhaps the teen who resented him on the voyage to America. Perhaps the young man who wrestled him up the stairs after Uncle Jimmy's beating.

He closed his eyes before Markos could see the man—whoever that was who had slept with the woman Markos loved.

"I never expected to see you here."

"Where did you suppose I'd be?" Dino didn't mean the sharp tone, but he let it remain, a knife between them in the dusky night, cutting away the images of the past.

Markos measured him, his eyes betraying nothing.

Dino looked away, his sins rising again to condemn him.

"Maybe it's just that I didn't want you here," Markos finally said, using his finger to wipe out the final contents of his dinner. He licked it off, closed up the tin, set it in the dirt next to him. "Did you eat?"

"Not hungry. Never am after surgery."

Markos unwrapped a piece of gum, stuck it in his mouth. He smoothed the wrapper between his finger and thumb. "How long have you been a doctor?"

"Four years. I had a year of internship in Minneapolis then joined up after Pearl. They gave me my training. I'm with the medical corps."

Markos folded the paper in half. "A doctor." He smoothed the crease. "Mama would be proud." He didn't look at Dino, but his mouth hitched up in a half-smile. "A doctor." He gave a sort of chuckle and Dino let himself feel it, a harrumph of surprise.

You will be someone great. For a second, a smile curled up inside him. *Leave your mark on the world.*

"So—you got a wife back home?"

Oh. The question sliced fast, a blade through his heart. Dino shook his head, leveling his voice. "I never found anyone who would have me."

Markos cut him a dark look. "No one?"

Dino heard the suggestion. *Not even Sofia?* He flattened his mouth into a line. Shook his head. "What about you?"

"I haven't been out long enough to find a wife." He caught the paper between his thumbs, pressed it to his mouth. A whistle leaked through.

"Out?"

Markos whistled again. "Of prison."

Dino stilled, watching his brother as he blew again, ever so gently, a trickle of air through his thumbs that emitted a high squeal. He put down the paper, nodded, glanced at Dino.

"Yes, I said prison."

Dino's mouth opened—

"How? Uncle Jimmy. I tried to get away from him—even drove my car into Lake Michigan. Managed to escape, but on foot I couldn't run from him for long. Luckily, the cops found me—and I use the term *lucky* lightly, because after the cops who were on the dole nearly finished me off, they routed up a bunch of charges, including arson and murder, and sent me off to prison." Markos's mouth flattened into a grim line. "I counted myself lucky I didn't get the chair."

A chill went through Dino. The chair?

"The army had a deal—they let you out on parole if you joined up. Seemed like the right thing to do, you know?" He brought the paper to his lips again. The whistle tickled the night, barely a sound.

Yes.

"So, see, there's a reason you thought I was dead. I should have been. Felt like it for a long time. But prison gave me a chance to catch my bearings. Hear the truth." He took the wrapper, crumpled it in his hand. "So—how's—Sofia?"

He looked away, and the staccato of bullets ripped through the screen of night.

Sofia. The way Markos said her name, more like breath than actual sound, brushed through Dino and he shivered.

Or perhaps trembled. Because even as Markos lifted his gaze to him, Dino knew he'd piled the truth right there in his eyes.

Markos frowned.

Dino looked away.

"What's wrong?" It wasn't a question, but more of a growl.

Dino turned his hands over, rubbing his thumb against his palm. "I—don't know."

Markos's gaze was an ember on his skin. "You don't know?"

"She wanted to wait for you, okay?" Dino winced at the desperation in his tone. "She stayed at the station."

"What? You left her at the train station? What about the doctor?"

Off in the distance, the 105s ripped the sky. "She didn't want to go—and she was fine, Markos. She did just fine. Got a job, and worked and—" Only even as he said it, he saw her again, short skirt, fishnet stockings, Reg pressing her into the snow. "I found her later."

He winced at that, and thanked the night.

"You—found her?"

Dino couldn't tell if Markos's voice held confusion or hope. "Yes—we saw each other again. While I was in medical school. She—she worked at a local theater."

"Singing." A little sigh, perhaps of despair, slipped from Markos.

"No—not singing. She checked coats. And cleaned. I don't think she ever sung—well, after Chicago."

Markos had drawn up his knees, hung his arms over them, drawn in a breath. "So where is she now?"

Dino ran his hand down his face. "Like I said, I don't know. We lost touch." He'd said it too lightly, though, because Markos, as if he'd seen him yesterday, as if he had sat with him in the window of their home in Zante, watching the storms roll in from the sea, feeling Dino's fear, simply sighed.

"What happened, Dino?"

Death stenched the air—smoke, rotting animal, the iodine embedded on his skin.

"What happened?" Markos asked, softer this time.

Dino picked up the discarded wrapper Markos had tossed into the grass. Smoothed it out.

"I loved her too, you know."

Markos didn't speak.

"She left without saying good-bye. Just—vanished. I tried to find her. But..."

"What does that mean—'she left'?" Dino heard the years of prison, the brutality of war in Markos's voice.

The words burned in his mouth. "It means that I should have stopped her. That I wish I'd stopped her. That she thought I was in love with someone else."

Markos drew in a quick breath. "And she was in love with you?"

Dino ran his fingers into his eyes. "I don't know. I—maybe."

Markos said nothing.

"It's complicated."

"Simplify."

Dino watched the fires burn. "We were lonely. And for a long time, it felt—right. Like we were supposed to be together." Dino shook his head, looked away. "I never meant to hurt her."

In the distance, explosions tore into the night.

"What did you do to her?"

Markos didn't have to ball his fist and swing for Dino to feel the blow, although perhaps it would have been easier.

In fact, please. *Yes.* Dino wanted Markos to hurt him, wound him, explode the ball of guilt so webbed inside his chest that sometimes he thought he might suffocate. He ached for the blow, really. He put his hand over his face.

"Tell me."

Dino let out a breath, hated the shudder in it. "I—I slept with her."

It was the first time, really, that he'd said that out loud, and it shucked the wind out of him. He'd slept with Sofia.

He deserved whatever Markos dished out. He didn't even brace himself.

Except…

"It seems we just can't get it right, doesn't it?"

Dino glanced at him, jolted. "What?"

"I don't want to know any more, Dino. I just—" He closed his eyes. "I failed her first. Don't forget that."

Dino just stared at him, unable to breathe. "What?"

Markos picked at the dirt embedded in his hands. "I—was so full of myself when we came to America. Angry. And afraid. I held so tightly to both of you." He pulled off his helmet. His hair had been buzzed short. "I felt like God abandoned me, but I was just trying to figure out how to not need Him."

"You were just trying to protect us."

But the words felt hollow, suddenly, as fire exploded in the distance.

"But Mamma was right—God does deliver—"

"Really? Where was He the night Kostas died? Or when Uncle Jimmy was beating you nearly to death?"

The words punched the night between him, but Markos didn't flinch. "He was there, Dino. See, we created this mess of our lives, and we think God abandoned us. But He didn't, He hasn't. He's the hope that we have out of our darkness."

Dino stared at Markos's dark profile, the one he remembered from when they'd watch the storms striding in over the sea. He leaned his head back against the stone. "I joined the army in hopes I could do something with my life. But sometimes it just feels so—twisted. I just can't seem to get it right."

Markos said nothing. Perhaps he hadn't even heard him. But then....

"Maybe you're not supposed to. Maybe that's the point. Maybe we're all supposed to be a little broken, a little afraid, a little overwhelmed by our own sweeping mistakes. Otherwise, we might believe we can save ourselves, instead of letting God deliver us. Maybe being on our knees is the only way we can ever be used by God." He looked up at Dino, emotion in his eyes. "Because without knowing what grace feels like, how will we ever really know how to give it away?"

The words cut through Dino, through his scars, piercing so deep it took his breath. "I'm sorry, Markos. I'm so sorry."

And then Dino became a child, right there, quiet sobs punctuating the chaos around him. If he'd been younger, he might have actually found himself with his arms over his head, his body curled tight.

Instead, he looked away, mortified.

Markos's arm went around his neck, hard, fast.

Pulled him tight to himself. Held him there.

Let him sob.

"Me too, brother. Me too."

* * * *

The 105s had stopped arguing with the night; the morning, a hand drawing a mist across the countryside. Dino lay next to his brother, listening to mosquitoes, his brother's solid breathing, smelling the earth in his nose. Dew slicked his skin, and he closed his arms over his chest, holding in heat. Probably he should push himself from the hard ground, check on his patients, prepare for today's onslaught.

No. For just a moment, he'd capture this moment, savor it.

Let himself travel back to Zante, to the lap of the ocean against the hull of his brother's boat, the skies so blue above him he could dive in, the sun licking his face.

"Thinking of fishing?"

His brother's voice jolted him, despite the husky, low tones. "How did you know?"

"I used to wake every morning in my cell, and I'd be back in Zante, watching you dive after Lucien, or on the dock with Papa, repairing the nets."

"Sometimes I'm in the kitchen with Mama, stealing bread. Or in the olive grove overlooking the village, watching the sun glide through the buildings, the jangle of goats' bells in the background."

"Remember how Lucien would sneak into our bedroom at night?"

"You know it was because he was running from his father."

"I know."

Sunlight began to burn away the mist, heat licking Dino's neck. He waved at the mosquitoes that harassed him.

"I'm going back there after the war." The words from Markos sounded more like hope than decision.

Dino said nothing. But maybe, yes. "Do you think Mama is still alive?"

"I hope so."

Dino smiled. "I can't imagine what she'd say to us—"

"I expect she'd tell us to stop lying around and get to work."

Dino let his own smile leak through. "He who laughs not in the morning, laughs not at noon."

"Add not fire to fire."

"Thinking evil is much the same as doing it."

"As long as you have the blessing of your parents it does not matter even if you live in the mountains."

Dino's smile died. "Do you think she'd give her blessing?"

"I think she already did. She told you to leave your mark on the world. I think she'd be proud of you," Markos said quietly.

Dino's stomach growled. Oh, he wished he could remembered her better. He strained to hear her soft voice, or had it been harsh? He reached back into his memory, dug around.

Markos hummed. Dino couldn't place the song.

Then, "We'll go back, someday," Markos said quietly.

"Yes." *Yes.*

"I'd better check on my men." Markos pushed up from the ground, and Dino realized how close they'd been when a chill slipped down his spine. He sat up, ran his hands over his face as Markos tromped across the field, his helmet and pack left behind.

Markos stopped at the pump, ran water over his head, then greeted soldiers who sprawled around the courtyard, some smoking, some still asleep, most cradling their .45 Tommys. It didn't surprise Dino that the men peered up at his brother with respect in their eyes, nor that Markos occasionally reached out, touched a man on the shoulder, banged him on the helmet.

A smile edged his mouth. Markos. Alive.

Yes, someday they'd return to Zante. Together.

Markos moved into the house, probably headed toward the surgical wing.

Mosquitoes. He thought he'd escaped them when he'd left Minnesota, but they seemed to have found him, zeroing in—he waved his hand again, shooing them—

Only, across the courtyard, men were getting to their feet, rousing others.

No—

The buzzing turned into a hum, then a rumble as Dino found his feet, propped his hand over his eyes.

Two Stukas dropped from the clouds, set on a course toward the hospital.

"Take cover!" Dino sprinted toward the hospital, screaming, even as the first fighter peppered the yard with bullets. Men shouted, some dropped behind sandbags, returned fire.

Dino zagged into the yard. "Markos!"

The Stuka dove, aimed toward the hospital, and unloaded his payload from under its wing.

No!

Dino threw himself into the bunker of sandbags as the hospital exploded. Fire punched the sky. Metal and cement in a cloud of debris rained down as he curled into a ball. Around him, men screamed, the shrapnel biting into their skin, severing limbs, burning—

"Medic!" The shouts pushed him to his feet. Black smoke billowed from the fractured chateau, the door now rubble.

"Markos!"

Fire torched the building, flames like forked tongues licking from the doorways.

Screams, the horror of the injured as they spilled from the building, too many on fire, jolted Dino to himself. He grabbed a sandbag, used it to put out the flames on a man—left him groaning in the dirt even as he raced around the end of the building.

The servants' entrance. Black smoke choked the hallways, blinding. He pushed in, but it punched him back. He fell to the earth, his lungs wracking. *Markos!*

Debris continued to spit from the fire, even as he scrabbled to his feet, fled to the backyard of the chateau.

Soldiers had pushed a ladder up to the third-story window, some carrying patients down, others managing on their own.

There. Of course Markos helmed the evac from the window, hauling men from the burning recovery rooms, gripping their arms as they slid down the ladder. Men at the bottom caught them to safety even as an explosion crumpled another section of building.

Dino ran to the ladder, braced a patient sliding down, then yoked his arm over his shoulder as he looked up. "Get out of there, Markos!"

Soot blackened Markos's face. "Right behind you!"

Dino stumbled away, toward a hedgerow where a cadre of soldiers was building a hasty barricade of vehicles and hay bales.

He eased the man to the grass, torn between checking his vitals or racing back for another victim when he heard it.

The high buzz of the second Stuka, on an attack run toward the chateau. He turned, spied Markos still in the window. *"Get out of there!"*

Markos threw a leg over the frame, then the other, then, as the morning sun glinted off the silver hull of the incoming bird, he balanced a man over his shoulder and stumbled down the ladder.

The Stuka strafed the yard.

Dirt chipped up. Dino ducked into the hay bales.

He watched with sickness as the bullets pinged the ladder. It crumpled, and Markos dropped like a brick.

"No!" He hit the ditch as the second fighter dropped its payload onto the hospital.

CHAPTER 20

Dino expected an explosion that would decimate the rest of the hospital, crush his brother under the rubble.

But…nothing.

He raised his head, his hands still over his face.

No phosphorous explosion, no rock and debris as the chateau collapsed. The entire yard turned eerily silent.

"Misfire!"

He heard the word, and it scooped out his breath. But the bomb could still go off—jostled by falling debris, or even a stray bullet.

Markos lay crumpled beside the crushed ladder, his leg clearly broken even as he pushed himself up, grabbed his gun.

He fisted the uniform of the hurt soldier, as if to pull him away, but the soldier came to life, crawling to safety under his own power.

The Stuka that had dropped its payload banked in the sky.

Dino's mouth opened as heat crawled up inside him. A heat like the night he saw Kostas, his eyes wild, tackle Theo to the stones. Back then, the hot rage propelled him into the fight. Now as he saw it replayed, he recognized the truth.

A part of him had…hated Markos. Hated him for being bigger, and better, and smarter. Hated him for owning the sea, and Sofia's beautiful love.

Hated him for being the brother who kept them safe, and endured Uncle Jimmy's rage…and fought to keep his promise.

A promise Dino couldn't quite wield.

He'd spent too much of his life with the specter of Markos telling him who he wasn't. Who he'd never be, caught inside his failures.

Thankfully, he'd left that hatred, that Dino behind.

But maybe…maybe he hadn't quite been healed from the wounds of that hatred. *Greater love hath no man than this, that a man lay down his life for his friends.*

What if he wasn't supposed to leave his mark on the world? Perhaps he was simply supposed to be a real friend. A real brother.

The Stuka's engine cut through him, galvanized him to his feet.

A hand reached out, grabbed him.

"Doc—no!"

Vivi crawled up beside him, her face bloodied, her uniform ripped. "It's going to go off!"

"He's my brother!"

"You can't save everyone!"

He pulled her hand away. "But I can save him."

God will deliver you.

The voice came now, soft, firm, and he recognized it.

Maybe I was meant to save him. Maybe in fact, for the first time, he could keep his promise. To Markos.

To Sofia.

Take care of her.

He wrenched away from Vivi. The Stuka devoured the yard, even as he fought his way to Markos. Dirt bit his face, his heart already outside his body.

Markos was struggling to his feet, shooting at the sky. He stumbled a step before he pitched into the dirt. "Go back! Go back!"

Then Dino had his hands on him, clenched into his uniform. He threw his arm over his shoulders. "Move it, brother!"

Markos had at least two inches, probably thirty pounds on him. Still, Dino lifted him to his feet without effort—

The Stuka chipped at the building.

Dino had taken three steps into the open when he felt it. The rumble of the earth, a convulsion.

He threw his brother to the ground and fell on top of him as the chateau exploded.

* * * *

"It's okay, Dino, I'm here, I'm here."

He was under the pier, the water chipping away bones, salting his mouth, choking him. He coughed, splattered out the sea. Still it seared his chest to breathe.

Cold, so cold.

"Markos." The starless sky blackened his eyes. Markos's arm bracketed his shoulders, holding him to his warmth.

"Don't try to talk." Markos's voice, husky and calm in his ear. "Oh, God, please."

"Don't let him find us," Dino said. "Yannis will kill us." The man's drunken rage still tremored through Dino's body.

Something about Markos's voice… "Oh, no, Dino. He won't find us. I won't let him find us." His words broke at the end. Maybe Markos was afraid too.

The waves. They tossed him, again filled his lungs. He coughed, and pain speared him in half. *I'm…*

Voices churned over him, screaming, and a rumble of a faraway explosion.

Light crackled across his vision, and it cleared.

Not Zante. Not the night of Theo's wedding under the docks.

Markos, blood dripping from the open wound on his face, leaning over him, his jaw set tight. Eyes that held Dino, so dark he could barely wrench away. Behind him, smoke churned through the sky, the sound of Tommy guns tearing it apart.

Cold, so cold.

"I'm hurt, aren't I?" His voice emerged roughened, even garbled.

A muscle pulled in Markos's jaw. His eyes told Dino the truth as he met his gaze. "You can't die on me, little brother. Please, don't die on me. I need you."

He couldn't feel his body, not really—amazing how the pain he'd remembered had simply vanished. Yet, with Markos's words, something unhinged inside him. A lightness, as if a fist around his chest had released. He sucked in a quick breath, let it fill him.

Smiled.

"Dino?"

If he'd had use of his hands, he would have cupped one around Markos's neck, maybe drawn him close, making sure Markos could see his eyes.

"We'll go back, won't we?"

Markos stared at him, nodded.

"We'll go back, and Mama will make us bread. We'll drink retsina from the cellar." The cold began to dissipate, become nothing.

"Medic!" Markos clutched the front of his fatigues. "I need help over here!" A tear raked down his face as he turned to Dino. "Don't you die on me!"

He wanted to crawl his fingers to Markos's hand, to pull out a new promise.

"I love her too, you know. Sofia. I love her too."

Markos shook his head, his face twisted. "Hang on, Dino. Please, hang on."

A medic appeared in his vision. He gave Markos a grim look, shook his head.

Markos lunged for the medic even as he vanished. He didn't quite mask the stricken look before he again met Dino's eyes.

"It's okay."

Greater love hath no man than this, that a man lay down his life for his friends. That is how you will discover the man you want to be.

"I love you, brother," Dino said softly, his eyes wet.

Markos bent over him. "*Dino!*"

Beyond him, the smoke parted. Dino glimpsed the faint, Ionian blue sky, cool and deep, beckoning him even as he spread his arms and dove.

SECTION THREE
Sofia

CHAPTER 21

Nights like this one, with the sky so black it poured through her and shook her to her bones, Sofia Frangos despised the day she'd moved to America.

Learned English.

Then returned to Zante with a skill the Greek resistance needed to communicate with the English OSS, their suppliers.

She leaned against the sea-washed stone wall of the fishery where, inside, Nikos copied the letters of the English phrase spelled out by Morse code. A phrase they would decipher using the phrase code—and then bring to her to translate.

It was bad enough that they required her to gobble up and pass on the tidbits of information dropped by the SS officers who ate at the taverna. She didn't count the colonel—especially since that was more about keeping Dino alive and safe than helping her countrymen escape the grip of the Nazis.

No thank you, this was the last time she stayed out past curfew to decipher a message. She didn't care how many German transports were leaving, when, or how.

Okay, that wasn't true. She could still feel the hungry eyes of the German officers on her, their gazes dogging her into the kitchen, their conversations feasting upon her as she cooked their suppers.

And the partisans she worked with didn't bother to hide their own ravenous appraisals. Apparently, she wore some sort of brand on her head.

She pressed her finger against the bruise on her upper arm, despising the memory of Colonel Kessler's touch. The more she did to push the Germans out of her country, the faster she and Dino might move away, perhaps start a new life. A life outside the landscape of shame.

The wind scraped from the wooden dock the briny odor of fish and seaweed, rustled the grove of calamus reeds along the shore. She pulled her knitted sweater tighter over her thin cotton dress, the air having turned cool with the desertion of the sun. Gooseflesh raised on her arms. Somewhere in the darkness, waves knocked against the bright red hulls of fishing boats tied up at the long piers in the bay. Farther out, the beady lights of a German transport peered into the starless night.

A spotlight sliced through the night from the hilltop overlooking the city, sliding over the faraway cliffs, the blue cupolas of the Greek Orthodox churches, the tall bell tower, the whitewashed homes that flowed up the mountainside, between whitewashed Cyprus, and willows, aspen, and poplar. What had been a village exploded into a small city over her ten-year absence, and she'd donned a black scarf and slipped back into her life, her scars folded neatly inside.

Now she pressed herself against the building, even as footsteps shuffled toward her.

"Sofia?"

She bristled, slipping into the shelter of the building. Nikos shoved a piece of paper into her hand. She scanned it with a penlight as she translated in her head. "They're sending in more supplies. And an agent. Meet at the drop zone tomorrow night to the north of the Blue Cave." She shoved the message back at Nikos.

"An agent? British?"

"They didn't say." She peered past him, down the boardwalk, her heartbeat swishing in her ears.

"Why?"

"I don't know, Nikos. Can I go?" She didn't mean the tone, but Dino needed his—

His hand on hers stilled her shaking. "Sofia, this war is going to be over some day, and we'll remember who helped us. Long after this war is over, we'll remember. I promise."

Perhaps he meant it. She glanced at him—the dark panes of his face, the earnest eyes. So young to live his life on the sharp edge of risk. His zeal reminded her of a young man who'd too quickly despised his life. A blade of pain made her edge away from him. "Thank you, Nikos. May God allow us all to live that long."

She slipped out, kept her feet light on the boardwalk, a whisper against the tumult of waves, and a faraway melody, probably from some taverna catering to a cadre of Germans.

Rules, apparently, didn't apply to the enemy.

She would label the taverna where she worked more of a café than a rousing eatery. Ava Stavros didn't have the manpower—or supplies—for more than a few offerings—egg sandwiches, eggplant salads, grilled octopus. But the German officers loved to drive their bare feet into the sand, to watch the dark Greek children splashing in the waves just beyond the portico, to tuck fresh basil behind their ears, twine together the white oleander that grew nearly from the rocks that spilled toward the sea.

One might think the invaders considered themselves on vacation.

Gathering up her skirt, she cut between two whitewashed stone homes, scuttling along the road toward the olive grove overlooking Zante. If she didn't return soon, Dino might cry.

Then the colonel would note her absence, make her answer his too-probing questions. *Please, Zoë, be there.* Zoë would hold Dino to her breast, sing to him. Zoë herself found a new birth when Dr. Alexio caught Dino from Sofia's body.

Her feet scattered pebbles against the stones. She stilled as they sprinkled out before her. Down the street, light trickled out from the overhang of a taverna, three Germans silhouetted, their laughter raucous as they raised glasses of Ouzo. Shrinking back, she swallowed around her heart in her throat.

Last time she'd been caught out past curfew, she'd had to appear before the new magistrate. Lucien's father had been just as cruel as she remembered, his years mourning Kostas sharpening his grief, turning his power dangerous. His sour threats rang in her ears as she pushed against her stomach.

Please.

She shuffled forward—

A hand pressed against her mouth.

Her scream caught in her throat. Then an arm dragged across her and clamped her tight, pinning her back against a hard body. A voice rasped into her ear. "Hush, Sofia."

She curled her hands up over his arms, sinewy from so many years working his nets, and shook her mouth free from his grip. "Lucien!"

"Shh." He shuffled her back, into the courtyard of a darkened home, under the archway of too-fragrant bougainvilleas, pushing her into the alcove and bracing one hand over her shoulder.

Voices, raucous laughter drifted down the street—louder until footsteps marched by. She held her breath, her heart lodged in her ribs.

In the dim light of the doorway, she made out a scar in the wood, a lighter rectangle pierced with two holes. She ran her finger over the mark of the mezuzah. "A Jewish family lived here."

"Jewish families lived all over the city. *Shh*, the soldiers are almost gone."

She pressed her hand on the mark, remembering the day the SS had demanded the list of the Jews in Zante from the mayor. He and the local orthodox bishop had heroically appeared in the square the next morning, only two names on their roster—the mayor's and the bishop's.

No wonder Lucien's father so quickly cooperated when he gobbled up the new position.

Truthfully, overnight, the Jews of Zante had vanished. They now lived in cellars and barns and secret rooms all over the island.

But not at her house.

Still, they'd left little black holes all over the city, darkened, vacant houses, shops left to decay in the salty wind. She missed Sarai Avramidis and her friend Ruth Ann Mizrahi, granddaughter of Dr. Alexio, The way they'd hovered around the taverna, watching her weave wedding bread and playing with baby Dino on the floor, reminded her of herself during her school-age years. She'd heard rumors of Ruth Ann's brother and father being drafted into the Greek army during Italy's invasion.

Too much war. It never ended.

"They're gone."

She turned under the umbrella of his arm and didn't need light to trace his face, to see the dark, tousled hair, the bristle of whiskers across his leathery skin. The hooded, almost black eyes that seemed ever watching, ever weighing. Lucien Pappos had turned into a rebel, a soldier, a hometown hero.

Probably only she truly remembered the scamp he'd left behind.

"You need to be more careful." His breath reeked of lamb and garlic. Beer.

Someone had been visiting his father's home tonight. The perks of politics—food. "Did you see the colonel?"

"He's still drinking with my father. You'll be home long before he will. I doubt he even makes it back by morning."

She could almost make out Lucien's smile, a wink. "Did you drug him....again?"

He caught a tendril of her long hair, pushed it behind her ear. "I didn't want you getting caught. I knew you had a late message. What did it say?"

She met his hand, pulled it away, despite the warmth in it. "There is a shipment tomorrow. And an agent coming in. I gave the information to Nikos."

Voices, then footsteps, and Lucien secreted her farther into the alcove, his black coat like the night over her own white blouse, even though she'd covered it with a shawl. He smelled of the sea, salty and wind-whipped, his skin weathered from the sun. Oh. It reminded her too much of—

"I think they're gone." Only, Lucien didn't move away. Instead, he caught her chin with his hand. "I will see you home."

"Lucien—"

But he touched his lips, whisper soft, against hers.

She should feel something sweet under his caress. Instead, her stomach burned, a very real ache that never quite vanished, flaring to life. "Lucien, you know I can't..."

"Won't." He ran a rough thumb down her face. "Won't. At least not for me..."

"That's not fair."

"Life isn't fair. C'mon." He turned and found her hand in the darkness. Then he pulled her through the courtyard, into the street, along the buildings, through the shadows, almost as if he'd planned the route that led her through the village and up into the olive grove overlooking Zante.

They ducked against a gnarled olive tree on the far edge of Zoë's property as the searchlight trickled across the grounds, then back across the scape of the city.

"I can find my way from here," Sofia said.

Lucien kneeled beside her, her hand still locked in his. He said nothing, his breath coming long and thick. Finally— "I could keep you safe, Sofia. You and Dino. You know I have connections. You don't have to—"

"Shh." She pressed her hand to his mouth, and he looked up at her. If only he didn't remind her— "I made my choices. Besides, you don't want to be with me, Lucien. I will only hurt you."

His jaw tightened.

She found something sweet, flavored it into her voice. "I'll see you tomorrow. At the taverna. Bring me some *bacalliaro*."

He shook his head. "I'll see you to the villa."

She didn't argue—he had the will of a Greek—and let him direct her through the olive grove, between the trees bent like arthritic fingers, the silvery flash of leaves under a ghost of moonlight. They caught their breath, hiding from the searchlight beside the stone wall, then he secreted her up to her house. No light from the second-story window suggested he'd been correct—no colonel tonight. Next to it, from her window, curtains blew out into the night.

She unlatched the front door, stepped onto the stone landing.

"I'd do anything for you, Sofia," Lucien said. He kissed her hand. "Anything."

"Be safe," she said softly, as she slipped into the house.

The whitewashed walls seemed to have collected the light of the day, even as the moonlight dipped into the windows, splashed on the stone floors. She noticed fresh oranges in the bowl—the tree over the house must be in fruit.

Nothing but darkness streamed from Ava's door on the main floor. She fooled herself into believing that Ava was ignorant of her activities, but the middle-aged woman never let on. Indeed, Sofia depended on her steady calm, her strong hands keeping the taverna running to keep her looking forward into hope. No, Ava might be nearing sixty, but she had the strength of her sons in her robust frame, and the wisdom of a woman who understood sacrifice. She could scare a drunken man speechless with a look, yet hold little Dino as if he might be her own child.

Or grandchild.

She climbed the stairs, breathing a full breath at the colonel's dark room, then eased her own door open.

Zoë sat in the soft glow of light, knitting, her rocking chair creaking, the wind chasing the curtains behind her. She seemed older than her years, her face framed in a black headscarf, as if she might still be in mourning.

Her Bible lay open on her lap. "He asked for you." She glanced at the child asleep in the wrought-iron double bed in the corner.

Sofia slipped off her sandals, dropped her shawl onto a chair. Pulled off her own headscarf, working her fingers into her hair. The sea air tangled it, turned it sticky, and she longed for a brush. Not tonight. She let out another long breath.

"Did he eat?"

"An orange and fried egg. And some goat's milk."

"Perhaps we will have fish tomorrow." She should probably clean up, wash the stress from her body, but she let herself sink onto the bed first, run her fingers across his tiny, soft cheek. She combed his inky hair from his face, his lips parted as if ready to say something. His tiny fingers curled around a sock she'd stuffed, drawn a face on, and turned into a monkey.

"You're late," Zoë finally said. She ran a finger under her eye. "One of these days—"

Sofia reached over, caught her hand. "No. That won't happen. God will deliver us, right?" She added a smile, but Zoë didn't match it.

She shook out of her grip. "Perhaps you might try really believing that."

Sofia turned back to her son, saw on his face the curve of a smile, as if he might be dreaming. She lay down alongside him, propping her head on her hand, settling her arm around him. He smelled clean—at least someone had a bath tonight. She imagined him splashing in the washtub—his laughter like sunshine, and her chest tightened. "I *am* trying to, Zoë."

Zoë sighed into the night, ran her finger down the open page of her frayed Bible. "'Bless the Lord, O my soul, and forget not all his benefits: who forgiveth all thine iniquities; who healeth all thy diseases; who redeemeth thy life from destruction; who crowneth thee with lovingkindness and tender mercies…"

The door down the hall closed, almost a slam, and Sofia jumped.

Zoë caught her eye even as footsteps echoed down the hall, past her room. The bedroom door next to hers opened.

Closed.

Catching her eye, Zoë shook her head. "Please—"

"If I don't go, he'll knock. Or worse." She steeled herself against a shudder. "Lucien said he drugged him."

Zoë got up, sat next to her on the bed, ran her hand down her arm. "Lucien says a lot of things."

"He wants to marry me."

"In the meantime, he's going to get you killed."

Sofia turned, met Zoë's flashing eyes. "I'm already dead. My only job is to keep my son alive. For him, I would give up everything."

"Including yourself."

Zoë's mouth tightened, and shame burned through Sofia. Well, she'd long ago made the choice to survive. "I have nothing of myself to keep anymore."

She sat up in the bed. "You will stay here with him?"

Zoë pursed her lips. "They take everything. The olives. My father. Our home—"

"*Your* home. Ava's home."

"Colonel Kessler's home."

Next door, they heard a crash, a curse. Dino stirred.

Sofia kissed him softly, got up, and moved to the bureau. She picked up the brush, drew it through her hair. Wincing, she hid the tears that slicked into her eyes as she worked through the long strands. Zoë watched her in the mirror without a word.

"Someday, this war will end. And when it does, Dino and I will start over. We will leave Zante, and I will no longer be the woman who—"

"Has no husband?" Zoë's eyes sharpened in hers. "You think you are the only who rises with grief in her breast every day? Ava burns for two husbands. And me. I want my dreams back. I want love, and the children that grief and war has so far denied me. But I believe, Sofia, that God does deliver."

"Will He give you a husband? A child?"

Zoë put her hand on Dino's body. "Perhaps he already has."

Sofia put down the brush. "I have never had dreams. Except, of course, what I have stolen from others."

From the bed, little Dino sighed.

"You did not steal what you didn't know you had."

Sofia skimmed on a layer of lipstick—something she used when she didn't want to recognize the woman in the mirror. "I stole enough."

She paused, sweeping her hair back up into its pins. *God will deliver....* She didn't even know what God's deliverance might look like. After so many years, she'd given up looking for it.

Zoë caught her hand on the way out. "You are not dead."

Sofia stilled, drew in a breath. "If he wakes, sing to him, please."

* * * *

Sometimes the colonel fell asleep with his arm clutching her waist. Other times he turned his back, and she snuck out with the sun bleeding over the western horizon and tucked herself beside Dino, his smell enough to heal her.

For Dino, everything. Food. A roof over his head. Safety.

She'd made that decision crossing the ocean, when he'd come alive inside her. When she realized she'd stolen him from his father.

Tonight, however, the colonel's hairy arm imprisoned her, and she stared out the window at the sky, slate grey with the invasion of morning.

Yes, possibly it gave her the smallest stir of satisfaction to know that the colonel couldn't keep his secrets, not in her arms. And those secrets she'd used to betray him. Thank you, Elsie, for teaching her German.

It didn't exactly redeem her, but she'd lost that privilege three years ago, when she'd seduced herself into a different Dino's arms, bartered his affections for honor.

She'd just been so—tired.

Alone.

Could she help that she fell for Dino's adoration? His attention? His ministrations. It felt so much like love that in his arms…

The colonel stirred. Moved his arm off her, turned over.

She eased off the bed, grabbed her dress, and pulled it over her as she moved to the window. Light splintered between the silvery trees, their shadows gnarled and long.

Shouldn't we talk?

Her own voice rattled through her, swept her back to that moment in her flat in snow-blanketed Minneapolis when she'd awakened, spied Dino staring into the sunrise, as if netted inside the misery of his sin, and a darkness seeped into her bones. She'd done this to him. She'd seen his eyes wanting her, wheedled herself into his arms, and slowly broken him.

Then she'd given him herself—or at least as much of her as she could—and ignored the sweep of shame inside.

Until morning.

Talk about—what? What a terrible man I am?

He'd kept his back to her, but she'd seen how he wiped his eyes, and she wanted to curl into a ball and wail.

Poison. *You're not a terrible man, Dino.*

Next door, a cry—one that curled out through the open window—jolted her. She glanced at the colonel then slipped through the door, back to her room.

Little Dino thrashed in his bed, in the fist of a nightmare. Zoë lay asleep in the opposite bed. Outside, a gate opened, the squeal of Ava treading out to gather the eggs or milk the goats before heading to the taverna.

Sofia wanted to drop onto the bed, curl into a ball. Instead she pulled Dino's tiny body into her arms, settled his head against her chest. "Shh, my little fisherman. Shh." His hair against her lips smelled like soap, silky and soft.

No, not a terrible man at all.

She leaned her head against the headboard as sunlight crept into the room, curling itself around Dino's tiny form.

Sofia held him tight, refusing the rescue of slumber.

CHAPTER 22

"I won't do it!" Sofia pushed the last of the leaves off the step. A few still scattered into the open door in the back of the kitchen, but she needed the breeze to skim the heat from the taverna.

"Keep your voice down!" Lucien used his arm to bar the door leading from the kitchen, nearly cutting Sofia off at the neck. She ducked and went under it, heading toward the oven. Grabbing a towel, she pulled out the baked bacalliaro—nearly slammed into Lucien—and placed it on the counter, the smell of roasted onions, olive oil, the tang of lemon and fresh parsley rising up to taunt her.

Lucien reached out to nip one of the roasted onions from the pot. "Why not? You know English."

"I also want to stay alive." She picked up a serrated knife. Gave Lucien a back-away look, then grabbed a thick loaf of bread. "Ava will be back soon. You'd better leave."

He barely hid a flinch at that, the past scouring through his eyes. He avoided Ava Stavros as if she might be his own personal ghost. Now he held his hands up in surrender. "What if it's a trick? What if it's one of those pirated transmissions and the Nazis are trying to embed one of their own into our group, figure out our organization?"

She tossed a piece of bread onto a plate, stepped up to him. "Exactly." She moved him aside, picked up another knife, and went at the fish. "The last thing I need is to bring some traitor into my life." She used a fork to slide a slab onto one plate, then the other, finishing it off with the carrots and juice drizzled over the top. "I do enough for this country."

"Too much."

She glared up at him. "What would you have me do? Choices aren't a luxury I can afford." She picked up the two plates.

His dark eyes flashed. "Or want."

If her hands weren't full, she would have slapped him. Her voice dropped, quivered there. "Is that what you think? That I want—this life?"

"I think you can't bring yourself to see anything different."

She blinked at him. Shook her head. "Stay away from me."

"Sofia—"

"No, Lucien. I can't bring danger into Dino's life."

He caught her elbow, put his ear close to hers, hissed into it. "You do every night."

She stared at his grip. "I keep him *safe* every night. Because of the colonel, we're fed. And safe. He promised."

"And he doesn't suspect that you're the one stealing his secrets?"

She ground her jaw, glanced at the open door. "Maybe you could say that louder."

"Sorry. It's just that we're trying to save lives here. Partisan lives. If this is a trick, we need to know."

"I'm not your girl."

"That's clear."

She narrowed her eyes at him. "Lucien—"

"I'm not a fool. I know you loved Markos, and frankly, your kid looks just like him."

Every cell in her body froze.

"C'mon, you can't seriously think that Ava hasn't noticed. That she doesn't see at least one of her sons in little Dino."

"You don't know anything." She made to shove past him, but he levered his arm in her path.

"I know that we need your help. And you won't give it."

"So, you're trying to blackmail me?"

He recoiled. "I didn't think so..." He raised his hand, freeing her to pass. "Does he know?"

She slowed, not looking at him. "Does who know?"

"Dino's father. Markos. Does he know about his son?"

She drew in a long breath. "Markos isn't his father."

Lucien's eyes flickered, something at the edges. "Then who..."

"Leave me alone, Lucien."

He came around the table. "No...is Dino the father?"

"I didn't say that. I don't know where his father is. He—joined the military." Oh, please, don't let the truth slide across her face, the fact that her only letter to the hospital in Minneapolis came back to her, the scrawled words of "gone to war" across the envelope. She could only guess it might be Europe—he might indeed be on a ship in the South Pacific.

Lucien reached out to touch her, but she recoiled. He dropped his voice. "What if this agent can help you find him?"

"That's not fair—"

"Sofia, we really need your help."

She stepped away from him, into the hallway. "Go."

Her skin bristled in the wake of his fuming as she stepped down into the portico. Two SS officers, their black hats propped on the table, leaned back in their chairs, smoking. She set the plates in front of them, grabbed their beer steins.

Beyond them, Zoë and Dino built a sandcastle in the honeyed sand. A twist went through her, even as she watched Zoë laugh, scoop Dino up in her arms, rush him out into the water.

She and Ava had been generous with a pregnant, unmarried Sofia. She owed them the truth. Perhaps someday.

If, as Lucien suggested, Ava hadn't already figured it out. Little Dino did look the image of—well, both of them. Markos *and* Dino.

But, when she stepped off the boat, she couldn't shame Dino's name with her own terrible sins.

And it seemed easier, somehow, to let Ava believe that he might be Markos's son. In her traitorous heart, even Sofia sometimes thought that and wished she could hate herself completely for it.

But he was Dino's flesh and blood, and the man *did* deserve to know he had a son. Lucien's words simmered in her head—what if this officer could help locate him? What if—what if she could—make it right? Perhaps she might be able to look into her son's luminous dark eyes—so much like his father's—without wincing.

When she returned to the kitchen, Lucien had vanished, half the loaf of bread with him.

She refilled the beers and returned to the portico. The colonel had joined the officers. He usually spent his afternoon at the taverna, eyes trained on her. In the light of day, she supposed he could be considered handsome, if one disregarded his pale blue eyes. Tall, brown hair, sturdy hands, a singing voice that could have made a willing woman weak. He loved his accordion and now strapped it on, glancing at her without a smile. "Retsina."

"Of course."

He sang a mournful song, something that should probably move her, but instead it turned the taste in her mouth sour as she poured the last of the barrel of retsina into a pitcher.

She banged it onto the colonel's table. He looked up at her, whined out a couple bars in her direction. Winked.

How, exactly, did Lucien think she might sneak away to meet this supposedly English contact, let alone determine if he was truly British? Ask him for tea? Perhaps make him sing "God save the King?"

A shot cracked the air, as if the blue sky had split in half.

Sofia jerked, the plate in her hand crashing to the stones.

Another.

The colonel put down his accordion, the last of the song eaten in the waves. Sofia turned, spied Dino in Zoë's arms.

Lucien flashed by her periphery, running down the boardwalk.

Towards the fishery.

No.

The Germans had risen, grabbed their caps.

The colonel shot her a glance, almost—was that a warning? It jolted her for a moment, that scant texture of concern in his eyes. She raised her chin and ducked into the kitchen.

Ava stood at the back door, her apron to her mouth. From the warehouses, a finger of black traced the sky.

"Stay here," Sofia said. She untied her apron, balled it into Ava's hands.

Please, God, don't let it be Ari and Nikos. She hadn't checked the time, but certainly they hadn't a scheduled transmission—unless—oh no!—unless last night the SS had triangulated their position.

She hustled down the cobbled street then picked up her pace to a run, skirting flower stands, women selling bags of walnuts, cigarette vendors. She dodged two bicyclists and nearly trampled a goat that ran from her in erratic terror, bell tinkling.

Above the harbor, smoke blackened the sky.

A chill swelled inside her as, from a half-block away, she saw the flames licking out of the fishery, windows shattering in the blaze. SS men, their *Sturmgewehr* rifles at their hips, dared anyone to extinguish the flames.

Of course, a crowd turned out, gasps as people pressed against each other, drew back when something inside—maybe the barrels of oil they used as a cover business—exploded.

Sofia pushed through the crowd, spotting Lucien on the other side, his hat low, standing away, arms folded. His gaze slipped off her and landed on—

No. Ari and Nikos, shackled, the radio in pieces at their feet. Nikos's nose bled, crooked at an ugly angle. Ari, no more than sixteen, hung his head, his shoulders rising and falling.

No.

The flames licked out of the building, reaching toward the crowd. The SS agents backed their captives onto the beach then turned and pushed them down, onto the sand.

Sofia began to tremble. She searched for Lucien. He had his head down, almost as if he didn't care.

Or couldn't.

No! She pushed to the front of the crowd, her voice webbed inside her chest. No!

God, please... She didn't know where the prayer emerged from, but she let it free, followed it with a moan.

An SS officer—she recognized him as a regular at the taverna—pressed the barrel of his pistol against Nikos's temple.

Nikos raised his eyes, and Sofia stood paralyzed as his gaze caught hers. A single tear tracked down his cheek. She cupped her hand over her mouth, crushing her lips to her teeth as she held in her scream.

God, please, if You are listening...!

It happened so fast, the click, the shot, almost like the popping of a cork. But in that second, right before her horrified eyes, Nikos crumpled to the ground. His blood wept into the sand.

Next to him, Ari began to sob. Beg.

Sofia felt hands on her arms and realized she was swaying.

She must have kept her feet, although the world whooshed up at her. She must have stumbled back to the taverna, although she had no recollection of the kitchen, of Ava gathering her into her arms. She had no idea how she made it home.

She woke in the double bed, sweat slicking her body despite the cold tremor wracking her. Dino played on the floor, as Zoë rocked in the chair beside him, her eyes on Sofia.

"How did—"

"The colonel. You collapsed at the taverna, and he'd returned for the accordion. He brought you home."

Zoë said it without rancor, a sort of relief in her eyes. "He doesn't suspect that you might be involved. He thinks you were overcome with heat, perhaps exhaustion. Ava told him that you'd been feeling ill."

Yes. For over a decade now.

"Lucien stopped by after the colonel left. The SS took Ari for questioning at the central offices. We don't know what will happen to him. They're trying to find out more information."

Sofia scrubbed her hand down her face. Right now, the English might be dropping their agent at the landing zone near the Blue Cave.

Dino got up and toddled to her. She pulled him onto the bed with her. He straddled her lap and she played patty-cake with him. Patty-cake, patty-cake—and put it in the oven for Dino and me… "I'm done, Zoë. No more."

Zoë just rocked, her eyes on Sofia's.

The breeze carried in the smells of the olive grove, the roses twining up the house, the sound of cicadas nestled in the trees. Behind it, night pressed into the room, dotted by a thousand pricks of traitorous, damning light.

* * * *

"We need new wine." Ava's voice echoed through the taverna, like a stone skipping into the sea. Sofia heard her footsteps slap across the portico but didn't turn from her place just inside the lap of the thatched roof.

It could be any day, the sky cloudless over the azure Ionian Sea, the waves barely lapping at the shore, the water so clear that if she were in a fishing boat, she could trace the schools of sardines and the gallop of an octopus as it ballooned the sand.

A day to deceive herself. Perhaps if she closed her eyes to the German transport ship in the harbor, the swastika flags hanging like cockroaches from the building in the central square, the black garb of the two SS officers sitting at a table in the portico, their smoke twining up to catch in the overhanging bursts of bougainvillea—yes, if she concentrated on the salty tang of the sea in the air, the cry of gulls, the tinkling of goat bells, the smells of the *mavro psomi* baking in the kitchen, she might cajole herself into believing that time hadn't passed.

That Markos would soon arrive, hauling in his fresh catch, steal a glance at her in the kitchen. She could always sense him, her ears tuned to his step, his soft voice. She loved to lure him with her song, capture his thoughts so completely it rendered him motionless, dripping seawater onto the stone floor, stolen by her muse. She could trace his outline even as he secreted himself behind her—his lean body tan, his shoulders sculpted by the sea, powerful hands, his eyes watching her—never intrusive, but with a sort of wonder.

Her throat filled. She hadn't sung since the day he disappeared. She'd simply lost the tune and had no desire to root for it in her heart.

Recently, however, when little Dino curled into her breast, she heard something, not unlike a song, echo deep inside. Someday, perhaps, she might find the tune, although she had no hope for words. Not with such sorrow stealing them away.

"Did you hear me?" Ava stepped up beside her, wiping her hands on her apron. "We need new wine. Can you help me haul it from the cellar?"

"Why should we give them our best wine?" Sofia didn't even try to scour the bitterness from her voice.

"Because…we have it to give. It is not the recipient who determines the value, daughter. It's the giver."

Daughter. Ava had called her that from the moment she stepped into the taverna off the boat, wearing Markos's coat, her stomach already filling out her dress. Sofia couldn't help but lean into the name, to swallow it down.

Let it salve her.

"I hate serving our best to those pigs."

Ava stepped out of the portico's shadow into the sun-baked sand. "We will make our bread, pour our best wine, and we will serve it to the Germans. Just because we serve it to swine doesn't make it slop."

The sunlight had chased the shadow from Ava's face. For a moment, the battles vanished, and instead, a young woman looked to the sky. Opened her mouth, as if she might be drinking it in.

"What are you doing?"

"Drinking the sun." She held out her hands, strong, lined, empty hands.

Sofia held up her own. Closed them against the resemblance.

"I stood here every morning after my sons left. Watching. Hoping that the ferry would return them. Sometimes I could even see Markos, his bag over his shoulder, his hair too long in his eyes, scraping up the beach to me. Or Dino, his face so full of mischief, arms open, flinging himself into mine." She turned to Sofia.

"Then one day, you appeared. Just stepped onto the pier, staring at Zante. And when your hands went to your belly, I tasted the sunlight pouring through me, heating my bones."

Ava had Markos's—and perhaps Dino's—eyes. She had the ability to pour them into Sofia, make her forget herself and believe in the person reflected there.

"You have never told me what happened to my boys." She drew in a breath. "I admit, I was afraid to ask."

"Ava—"

"No. I no longer need to know." She touched her fingers ever so lightly to Sofia's cheek. "When I look at little Dino, I feel as though I have my answers."

Sofia pressed her hands against her stomach. She'd awakened with it empty and angry, and now it spasmed.

"I know, if I am to see my boys again, it is because God wills it. And if He doesn't…"

Sofia looked away. "How can you believe in God's deliverance after everything that's happened, everything you've lost?"

Ava sighed, dropped her hand. Patted it on Sofia's. "Everyone thinks that believing in God means that He will deliver us from trouble. But this isn't true—God delivers us *through* trouble. It is in the middle of trouble that we truly discover what it means to live, who we truly are. Our God says that He has overcome everything the world throws at us—but we are stubborn, we want to handle it ourselves. Or we believe that because of our sins He won't help us. Or even, because of what has happened to us, that God has turned His back."

Sofia drew in a sharp breath.

"But when we try and deliver ourselves, our strength will give out. We have to open our angry, stubborn fists and let it go. That's when we find our deliverance."

She held her hands out again. "God *will* deliver us, daughter. One day at a time."

Sofia closed her eyes in a slow wince. Turned to fetch the wine. Ava caught her arm, nudged her back to the hot sunlight.

"Drink the sun with me, Sofia. You will need it for the cloudy days."

Drink the sun. Sofia instead stared out at the waves, saw Markos on his tiny red fishing boat, standing with his hand on the mast, waving to her. Dino beside him, hands behind his head, his legs lazy over the side as his feet trailed in the water. A warmth stirred inside, and she longed to let escape the smile that nudged her. Then the sun caught her eyes, burning, and they watered.

"I'll fetch the wine."

After standing in the heat, her skin chilled against the clammy exhale of the wine cellar. She stood at the open door outside the taverna, the steps leading down to the grotto chipped out of the rock, and waited for her eyes to adjust to the shadows.

Water sweated down the walls, turning the stones black. An electric wire ran along the outside of the rock. At the bottom, a bulb dangled from a socket, and from it, a chain.

Running her hand along the side of the rock, she descended into the shadows.

Her hand brushed the chain. She caught it, tugged. Nothing. Blown, probably. From memory, she edged into the blackness, toward the next light.

Water puddled the floor, the breath of the damp cellar licking her skin. Around her rose casks of wine, stacked against the walls. The cellar had originally been a twisting cave until the Stavroses generations before hollowed it out, turned the tunnels into storage. She reached for the next dangling chain.

"Stop. Don't."

The voice shook her cold. Low, but with a warning tone to it that raked up a tremor.

Then someone stepped from behind a tall pallet of barrels, shining a flashlight onto the floor, chasing away the secrets. Taller than she remembered—although, yes, time would have done that. Broader too, and on his face an expression she couldn't read. Not with the layer of grizzle and dirt, a scrape across his jaw, a fisherman's cap pulled low over black—probably grimy—hair that skiffed his collar. He looked every inch a fisherman, tanned and ruddy and seasoned. The man he should have become.

No…it couldn't be.

But she met his eyes and recognized in them a teenager, a boy caught in a song, even as his mouth opened, his breath coiled, his eyes blinked at her.

Markos.

CHAPTER 23

"Sofia."

She thought he'd breathed her name, heard it whisper inside her someplace, or perhaps her heart heard it, because it stirred a long-dormant heat inside.

"Markos?" Part of her wanted to slap him. To harness the fury—or perhaps pain—that bolted through and center on his grizzled jaw. The other part—well, it simply wanted to fling herself into his arms, to run her hands down his face, drink in his eyes, his smile.

No, not a smile. He blinked at her, a sort of stripped, almost hungry expression in his eyes. "Yes, it's me. I can't believe—" He held up one hand, as if to calm her, the other to reach out to her.

She snapped away from him. "You're supposed to be dead." She didn't exactly hate her tone—she needed it to shore up the woman inside that suddenly wanted to curl into a fetal position, caught.

His eyes tightened, as if she'd struck him. "I know."

Steps behind her made her whirl around, and the light Markos carried went dark. She heard Markos—whisper-quiet, but when had she not heard his movements?—as he slipped back behind the casks.

She couldn't very well be caught standing here in the dark. She found the pull chain that dangled from a bulb, and a weak spotlight illumined the center of the room.

If it had been the colonel, or any of the SS, she would have betrayed them all with the shaking of her body, her quick intake of breath. Instead, Lucien blocked the light as he paused on the stairs, his expression flint, his lips knotted into a grim look. "I see you found our agent. I told you it might be a trick. I just didn't realize what kind."

He squeezed her arm as he brushed past her, as he moved in front of her, possession in his posture.

"It's no trick." Markos moved back out into the dim light. He stared at Lucien, apparently nonplussed by the sight of his former best friend.

Sofia's gaze stuck for a second on the Nagant revolver jutting from the back of Lucien's waistband.

Lucien and Markos. She'd never truly understood what transpired between them that day on the docks when they'd escaped Zante. Lucien's stricken expression. Markos's sharp rejection.

Now she stood between them, measuring.

"I asked to be assigned here." Markos's eyes fixed on Sofia. "I didn't know what I'd find."

She heard ringing in her ears, a sort of high-pitched scream she couldn't shake. Markos, alive. Why hadn't he come for her? Had he found Dino?

"Like we should believe you." Lucien handed him a bag. "We found this near your drop-point. It looks like a shoeshine box. What is it?"

"A portable Morse-code radio. We feared you'd lost yours when your contact didn't radio in confirmation of the drop last night."

Lucien didn't spare her a glance when he said, "Our radio was discovered yesterday morning."

Markos took the box then slung his rucksack from his shoulders. "I tried to find it in the dark, but I lost it in the drop."

"You dropped? As in…parachuted?" Sofia asked.

"Yeah. From five hundred feet because it was so light out. Nearly didn't get my chute open. Thought I broke my ankle too." He glanced at Lucien. "Sorry about your radio—"

"A good man died. The other will."

Sofia closed her eyes.

Markos drew in a breath. "And your men. I guess that explains why no one met me." He shoved the radio into the rucksack. "And why I had to hide out in my family's cellar." He shot a look at Sofia.

"Your mother is upstairs. In the taverna."

It seemed a blow to him. His mouth opened, his face paled, as if the blood or wind had flushed from him. His closed his mouth, and a muscle pulled in his jaw. "You can't tell her I'm here. It'll only put her in danger."

His words sucked the breath from her. What kind of man didn't rush back into the arms of his mother?

Probably the kind without a heart. Perhaps Uncle Jimmy had beaten that out of him after all.

She studied him. A white scar traced his cheekbone, and his face seemed leaner, chiseled almost. The image of her closed in his arms while they hid in Uncle Jimmy's restaurant flashed behind her eyes, and she could nearly hear his heartbeat. Or perhaps that was the far-off staccato of old bullets.

"We didn't know if it was a trick or the real thing." Lucien went to stand by the cellar door, glanced up. Probably one of his men stood guard at the top of the stairs.

"I promise, it's no trick. British command sent me here." Markos glanced again at Sofia. "If I'd known you—"

"What are you doing here?" Lucien came back across the room, striding hard. "You left. You left us all."

"Lucien," Markos said quietly.

Sofia touched Lucien's arm, digging her fingers into his shirt. Still—"He's right, Markos. What *are* you doing here? You…vanished. You left. You…" The truth punched her then—she saw it in his eyes and heard his words—*You can't tell her I'm here. It'll only put her in danger.*

He hadn't even intended to follow her to Minneapolis. Hadn't intended to keep his promise. He'd—just abandoned her. She drew in a sharp breath. "You lied to me."

He shook his head. "I never lied to you, Sofia. I just—I couldn't follow you. Not with Uncle Jimmy after me. But I never stopped thinking about you." His eyes flicked to Lucien, back to her. "Never."

She stiffened. Willed herself to ignore the flicker of emotion on his face. "Your mother deserves to know you're alive."

He let her words fall between them, his chest rising and falling without response. Finally, "I will. When it's time. You'll have to trust me."

The smallest laugh—or perhaps a gasp escaped her lips. And yes, he cringed.

Good.

"Anyone who knows I'm here is in danger."

"That much is true," Lucien growled.

"I don't understand why you didn't at least tell us you were alive. Dino and I—we thought…." She held up her hand as he sucked in a breath.

Another flicker of emotion, this time different, creased his face. Something almost—angry.

Or—oh no. She knew that look. She'd seen it in the mirror too many times. Disgust.

Everything inside her closed like a fist. Her breath, her heart, it all simply seized.

The truth found her then, sank into her core.

He knew. Somehow, Markos *knew* she'd been with Dino. Knew she'd given herself to him, betrayed their unspoken promises. Only—and anger sparked the thought inside her—if he didn't love her, if he hadn't returned for her, then she hadn't *really* betrayed him, had she? Except, that was the problem—it wasn't so much *his* heart she betrayed—but hers. With Dino, she'd betrayed herself.

And she hadn't stopped there.

Her hand cupped her mouth, fighting the burn in her throat, her eyes. Her gaze flickered to Lucien, fell off him, to the dank floor. What if Lucien had told him about the col— "Get him out of my cellar, Lucien. Right now. I can't—I won't be a part of this."

"Sofia!" The tone in Markos's voice would have stripped another woman, one who had something left to wound. But she turned her back to him, walked to the stairs. "Get him out of here, Lucien. Before the SS shows up."

"I'm on a mission, Sofia—Lucien, I need your help."

"What mission?" Lucien hadn't moved, although Sofia did see him drop his hand to his side, as if he might reach for his revolver.

She might just do it for him.

"We intercepted a message from the German post here. They're leaving the island, and they're taking some sort of cargo with them."

"What kind of cargo?"

Sofia stopped on the bottom step. Looked up. Sure enough, Cosmos stood sentry at the top of the steps, his shadow long as it cascaded into the earth.

"We don't know. Germans have been raiding Greek museums, ransacking homes, and secreting out of the country millions of drachma's worth of Greek treasures as they flee. The OSS has been working with the partisans to stop them. Our intel, and the German communications we've intercepted, lead us to believe this cargo is something priceless—some Greek religious artifacts, something they've hidden right here in Zante. Maybe at a church, or a monastery, even an old fort. Wherever it is, we plan on finding it, before they steal it."

His tone made her turn back. Something about it spoke of a different Markos, one who knew the taste of honor.

Lucien's eyes narrowed. "A cache of priceless religious artifacts? Here in Zante? I doubt that."

Markos took a breath, his gaze settling on Sofia. She turned away, began climbing the steps.

"Maybe not artifacts. Maybe something even more valuable. But it's here, Lucien. And I promise you that I'm not leaving without it."

Sofia put out her hand, braced it against the sweaty wall of the cave. The moisture seeped into her pores. From deep inside the cavern, water dripped into the silence between them.

Leaving. She'd been so webbed into the shock of seeing him, the truth had raced right by her.

Leaving. Markos hadn't come here to stay, let alone to find her.

Leaving. *Of course.*

Flee. The urge welled inside her, poured into her bones. She should find little Dino, snatch him up, pull him so tight to her that his smell might embed into her pores, remind her, cool her grief.

But she didn't run. Instead, she glanced at Lucien. "I need a new cask of wine. Can you help me hook it up to the block and tackle?" Somewhere back in time, an ingenious Stavros had rigged a pulley system that transported the wine from the cave to the taverna. Now Markos moved to intercept Lucien's movements.

"I'll do it." As if he'd worked in the taverna every day for the last fifteen years, Markos rolled one of the wine barrels down from the pile, rolled it over to the dolly.

Markos, alive. And he knew about Dino. She closed her eyes, pressed a hand to her mouth.

He couldn't know about little Dino. Not yet. Not until she could explain…

Lucien moved in to help. Markos pushed him away. "I can handle this."

"She asked *me* for help."

For a second, she saw them—two boys fighting for the rudder. Lucien, standing whipped as Markos helmed the boat. He'd always stood in Markos's shadow, and suddenly, there he was again, out-muscled by the boy he wanted to be.

"Thank you, Lucien," Sofia said softly even as he stepped away.

"Sofia, are you down there? Do you need help with the wine?"

Sofia could see the yearning on Markos's face for a split second before he stepped away, back into the shadows, as if closing in on himself.

She dashed halfway up the stairs. Ava stood at the opening. Clearly, Lucien's guard had opted for secrecy. "I'm just hooking up the pulley now. I'll be there shortly."

"I'll help—"

No. "No!" Sofia took another step, held up her hand. Yes, she deserved to see her son. She'd made enough sacrifices.

But should the SS catch him, Ava *was* safer not knowing.

Perhaps they'd all been safer not knowing. Her eyes burned. "Stay there. You can unhook it from the top."

Ava gathered her skirt, moved away.

Sofia slipped back into the cave. Lucien had already hooked up the pulley and now began to maneuver the bucket.

It rolled up the steep incline.

"Do you know what treasure he's talking about?" Lucien's voice cut low, for her ears only.

"I don't—I haven't ever heard of such a thing." *I'm not leaving without it.* She longed to knock those words from her brain, just tilt her head to one side and let them fall out.

They had the power to make her fall to her knees, fists to her eyes.

"What if…" Lucien bent his head close to hers, his face so close she could smell last night's beer on his breath. In this resemblance to his father, he scared her sometimes. "What if there *are* some sort of valuables—maybe from the Jewish houses they ransacked? Or the churches—"

"What do we have on Zante that could be that important? Nothing. We are an island of fishermen."

"You heard what Markos said. They're hiding it here—that doesn't mean it came from Zante. The Germans have plundered our people, our land, our homes. If we let them steal our heritage, what will we have left? Think of—"

"Shh!" She pushed a hand to his mouth.

He shook it away. "We have to find the cargo, Sofia. For Greece. What if…" He paused, as if chewing on his words. Then, quickly, "What if the colonel knows where it is?"

Sofia caught his eye, sucked her breath at the suggestion she saw in it. "I don't—Lucien. I can't—"

"He takes his briefcase home every night. You told me that."

"Yes, but—I—can't. It's too dangerous."

"You even told me he'd stopped sleeping with it beside his bed. He trusts you. He knows you won't betray him."

"Because he'll *kill* me, or…" She met his gaze, the truth of her words in her eyes.

The wine barrel reached the top of the stairs. "I have it!" Ava called from the top.

"I'll be right there!" Sofia called back, her eyes still fixed in Lucien's. She cut her voice to a whisper. "We're safe because he thinks I'm afraid of him. But if he knows I've betrayed him—"

"He is in love with you."

"No. He's in love with what I—what I give him."

Lucien drew in a breath. Tightened his jaw.

"What do you give him, Sofia?" Markos edged into the light, his eyes hard in hers, something akin to the old Markos she'd known—brazen and foolish. Angry.

Or perhaps guilty. She'd never been able to separate the difference.

"What do you give him, Sofia?" His voice softened, and he drew in a breath, as if steeling himself, as if asking the question again scooped something from inside him.

Yes, well, perhaps he should know how that felt.

"Nothing. I give him nothing. Nothing that matters." Then she turned and followed the wine barrel from the cellar.

* * * *

"You seem upset tonight."

Sofia let the words drift out, with a tone of care, rather than defense, or more accurately, fear. Because either of those might elicit a response that included accusations, assumptions…and, on occasion, threats.

The colonel stood at the window in his black trousers, a white, sleeveless undershirt, arms folded, the muscles in his back taut.

He stared into midnight, and from far away, inside the grasp of night, thunder rumbled. Indeed, the breath of storm threatened the air, and the olive trees shivered under it. Sofia sat up on the bed, her back against the wooden headboard, drew her legs up to her chest, and covered herself with the sheet.

"I killed a man today."

She held her breath, secreted any response.

"I am tired of these partisans who can't accept that they have been beaten."

She tucked her chin into her knees, holding back a quiver. *Oh, Ari.*

"And now that we've found two, we'll have to find them all. We can't leave with a rebel group in control of the island."

Leave?

He turned, braced himself against the window. "Do you want me to leave?"

Had she spoken aloud? She looked away from him, not sure what her face might betray. "Why would I want you to leave?"

He sighed, strode over to her, sat on the bed beside her. She made no movement when he reached up and ran his hand down her face, cupped her chin in his hand. "Haven't I kept you safe? Fed? And your fatherless son—haven't I been good to him?"

She pulled in a breath, found the courage to nod.

He leaned close, kissed her, his lips nudging hers open. She had learned not to resist, to place herself someplace else—perhaps in the square before Zoë's wedding, walking in the sunlight to meet Markos. Or dancing with Dino in the kitchen at Elsie's. Yes, those moments held her even as the colonel pulled her hairpins from her hair, let it tumble down her back, pressed her into the bed linens.

Not tonight. Tonight, Markos's dark eyes, his tone found her, pulled her away from the colonel's attentions. *"What do you give him, Sofia?"* She blinked back tears and turned her mind to little Dino. The way he dove into her arms tonight as they'd played hide-and-seek in the olive grove.

Markos couldn't—wouldn't know about her son. Who knew what he'd do? The Greeks had threatened to shave the heads of women—even to stone those who conspired with the Germans. But she'd conspired with no one but herself.

And, they couldn't kill someone already dead.

Still, if Markos knew about Dino, he might steal him from the arms of his harlot mother.

She wrapped her arm around the colonel's neck and wiped away the wetness below her eyes.

"What is it?" The colonel raised his head, frowned.

She found a smile—something leftover from her playtime with Dino—and shook her head. "I'm just—thinking of you leaving. It makes me sad."

The words turned her chest sour, even as his expression softened. He kissed a tear. "That makes me quite happy to hear."

Probably it also made him more gentle.

He held her longer than usual. "Maybe I should bring you with me." He ran his fingers into her hair. "Would you like that?"

She closed her eyes, made herself nod.

He was silent for a moment, then, "I knew that someday I could make you mine."

She thumbed away another tear before it fell upon his chest.

He pushed her away, sat up. "I need something to eat." He dressed and didn't even glance at her as he slipped from the room.

Mine.

She swallowed back bile at the word, sat up, her hands shaking. In the dim light of his bedside lamp, she caught her reflection in the mirror above the bureau. Her long black hair frayed and messy around her gaunt face. Her lipstick smeared, her arm still bearing a bruise.

Mine.

She wasn't even her own.

And she certainly didn't recognize the woman before her.

Her gaze caught on his briefcase, now on the table by the window.

What do you give him, Sofia?

She slipped out of bed, padded to the briefcase. Or, perhaps she'd call it more of a satchel, with an arm strap and a flap that closed, with a locked clasp.

She pressed it.

Yes, locked, but Uncle Jimmy's desk had been locked too.

She swept up her hairpins, returned to the satchel. Refused to look at the door, listen to her heartbeat banging, threatening, screaming in her ears as she bent out one end of the two-pronged pin and inserted it into the lock.

Don't look, don't—there. The lock snapped open.

Just like Uncle Jimmy's desk.

She dropped the pin on the floor, didn't bother to retrieve it as she pulled open the case.

Papers, communiqués, memos, a map…she studied it—shipping routes from the mainland to Zante.

Footsteps. She shoved the papers back into the satchel, closed it with a too-loud snap, dove back for the bed just as the door creaked open.

She swallowed hard, sure that he could see her pulse betray her at her neck. Or her flushed face.

Idiot, idiot…what if she'd been caught.

She shouldn't let her regrets destroy her fragile hold on the future. Markos and his fictitious "treasure" could get her—and her son—killed.

Never again. Never…

The colonel slipped back into bed, garlic on his breath. He wove his arm around her. "You are so warm."

She willed her heart to slow.

He ran his hand down her hair. "I have decided that you will come with me when I leave."

She nodded. "And Dino?"

He sighed. "If he must."

She splayed her hand over his chest. "I've heard the partisans will—hurt women like me."

His chest rose and fell. "I, too, have heard the threats." He nudged her chin up, her eyes to his, and she blinked at the concern—or perhaps possession—in them. "If something should happen, you must go to the monastery. I will tell my men to protect you. There you will be safe."

She didn't know what to think as he rolled over onto one elbow, above her. "I won't let anything happen to you."

Outside, lightning flashed against the window, behind it again the soft rumble of thunder. Rain wept upon the olive grove.

CHAPTER 24

Ari's beaten body hung from the bell tower in the city square, swinging with the nudge of the wind in the soggy air.

A few women threw stones at the seagulls and crows that settled on his head, his shoulders. More knelt in the square, covered in black, their faces scarred with the rending of their own nails, their wailing echoing against the stones.

Gestapo set up a perimeter below him, their presence probably designed to thwart attempts to cut him down.

Even Sofia could feel the tremor of hatred, more than fear, pulsing through the crowd. She cupped her hand over Dino's eyes and pushed his head into her shoulder as she hustled him past the square, toward the olive grove. Behind her, the late afternoon sun dipped into the sea, crimson fingers reaching across the waves.

"You're hurting me, Mama."

"*Shh*, Dino, it'll be okay." *God will deliver us.*

She pushed the words from her head. Ava, again, trying to beguile her into faith.

His little legs clamped around her, his arms sweaty on her neck even as the sun scraped up Ari's odor and lashed it into the crowd. Her eyes watered and she set off at a run.

Dino struggled in her arms, and her hand ached where she'd drawn a blade across it today. She'd wrapped it in a towel, but it still burned.

"I want to see Auntie Zoë."

"She'll have some goat's milk and currants waiting for you when we get home." Please, don't let Zoë have seen Ari's body today. Sometimes she seemed so fragile, and Ari's death—

"Sofia!"

Lucien's voice emerged, and she startled at the sight of him, his hair tucked under a fisherman's cap, his knit sweater warmer than necessary for such a hot day. He shoved his hands into his pockets, hunched his shoulders, fell into step beside her. "What did you find out?"

"Go away, Lucien." She strode out ahead of him, her breath coming hard. Of course, the colonel had to show up for lunch today, catch her hand, remind her of their conversation.

And her foolishness.

Every eye had simmered on her as the colonel pulled her onto his lap, threaded his hand into her hair.

Mine.

"Did you do it?"

"Please, Lucien. Leave me alone."

He clamped her arm, yanked her to a stop. "It's important, Sofia."

"So is my son!" She gulped back her words, thankful they'd left the town. Her voice lowered to a hiss. "Did you not see Ari…?" her eyes burned.

He had the decency to duck his head.

"I need to get Dino home for his nap."

She met his eyes, too much hope in them.

"I will come by tonight—late."

"You'll get us all killed."

"Tomorrow night then—come to the feast. Certainly the colonel will allow you to honor the Feast of the Cross. Please—"

She shook off his hand and continued up the hill. Lucien disappeared somewhere along the way. She drew in a breath.

She hadn't asked about Markos. Hadn't wondered where he was. Hadn't uttered his name.

See, he could die to her again. She would live through it.

She ground her jaw against the burn in her throat. At least he was taking her at her word to leave her alone.

Little Dino's body slumped against her, sleep nearly upon him as she reached the house. The stone walls had stored the cool breezes from the sea, and Zoë had baked fish, cut up cucumbers and feta cheese to add to the currants. Sofia sat on the bench at the table as Zoë took Dino from her arms, roused him awake enough to drink the milk.

"I'll settle him into bed." She hummed into his ear as she carried him down the hall.

Sofia unwrapped the cloth from her hand. The cut had opened, and now blood trickled down her palm. A foolish wound from cleaning fish.

And not paying attention.

And seeing Ari's body swinging in the breeze.

And listening to the colonel in her head. *Mine.*

She hung her head, sickened. Not his. She belonged to no one…

But Lucien's words had blinded her, turned her into something she wasn't. She couldn't believe she'd risked herself for nothing. Where exactly had her brain been in that moment? Worse, she stared at herself in the mirror this morning, pinning up her hair, and realized she'd left a hairpin in the colonel's room.

On the floor under the table. Bent in a betraying position.

And it had been those corrosive thoughts that had caused her to slip, plunge the filet knife into her skin.

She rewrapped the wound, took the knife, and cut the cucumber left on the table. Taking a slice, she put it to her forehead, letting the cool juice seep into her pores.

His voice plowed through her. *I will tell my men to protect you. You must go to the monastery. There you will be safe.*

The monastery.

Maybe at a church or a monastery, Markos had said. Sure—if the colonel had some sort of valuable cache, he'd hide it at his own personal fortress.

Maybe she *did* have information for Lucien.

She'd find him tomorrow. But what if that was too late? What if Markos's treasure *was* at the monastery, and the Germans planned on taking it out tonight?

Besides, the sooner Markos got what he came for and left, the sooner they could all breathe. The faster the fresh wounds might heal.

But what if—what if he were caught?

She opened the cloth, dabbed again at her cut. She'd rather die herself than live through his death again.

She could go to the monastery herself. Certainly, with the hunt for the partisans, it couldn't be safe for any of them. But Sofia—she could go on the pretense of the colonel's protection…

There she went again, thinking she might be some kind of heroine. Save her country or something. She could barely save herself.

She examined the wound. When she'd first opened the skin it burned, flashed tears into her eyes. Now it throbbed, a dull pain she might be able to ignore.

If not for the blood stain on her shirt. She should probably change.

"You still do that? The cucumber trick? I remember my mother wearing cucumbers when she worked in the kitchen."

The voice pressed her eyes closed. Just for one second she simply gulped down his low tones, like cool water against her parched throat.

And then her head snapped up and she found her feet. "You shouldn't be here."

Markos skulked into the house, looking every inch like a rebel. He'd shaved and probably bathed, because his hair hung in waves below his wool cap. Anyone else looking at him might see a fisherman, although he seemed under-baked by the sun, his hands strong but not weathered. His eyes flashed, so blue she'd forgotten how they always reminded her of the sea. Yes, he'd grown taller, his shoulders broader. His grim look, however, seemed darker. "You're hurt."

His face didn't move, as veiled as the shadows.

Still, just his presence moved her into the past. She saw her own frailties in his eyes, the girl who had believed in him, loved him with more of herself than she should, who had clung to his promises.

That girl had died so long ago, Sofia had forgotten that she existed. She tied up the wound on her hand again—the last thing she needed was him examining her scars—as she walked over to him. "You shouldn't be here."

Please, Dino, don't wake. Don't cry. "Zoë will be back any second. She shouldn't see you."

He nodded, followed her outside, down the path behind the well, the goat corral, into the olive grove.

He stopped her with a hand to her arm, but she shook out of it. "Sofia—"

She folded her arms. From here, she had a view of the entire city, the azure domes of the Greek Orthodox church, the creamy white houses vined with pink explosions of bougainvillea, their pomegranate roofs caressed by orange trees pregnant with fruit. The fishing boats, red and green, tied to the long piers, filled up the crescent bay, and a burnished beach rimmed the Ionian blue sea. Zante had nearly tripled in size during her time in America—she wondered if Markos recognized it now. She drew in a breath, let the thick, salty air brace her. "I think they're hiding something at the monastery of the Virgin Anafonitria."

Oh—why had she said that? But perhaps it was for the best. Let Markos accomplish the mission he'd come here for...

"How do you know?"

She let her words be as brutal as possible. "An SS colonel told me last night that if I wanted to leave with him, he'd keep me safe. I just needed to go to the monastery. I'm guessing that if he has something of value, he'd probably keep it there."

Markos drew in a long breath. Silence pulsed between them, and she didn't know who she'd wounded more.

Finally, "Do you want to go with him?" His voice so soft, it shouldn't have hurt, really.

She fiddled with the knot that tied her bandage. "No. But—I should. Start over."

"Do you love him—"

"Of course I don't love him!" She whirled, the power of her words shaking her. "*Love him*? He gave me an ultimatum. He would live in my house, eat my food, and—" She closed her eyes, longing to chase away the memory of him standing at the door to Dino's room, his voice a whisper as he told her what he could do to Dino. Starting with sending him to an orphanage.

"No. I don't love him." She whisked a tear from her cheek. Raised her chin. She hadn't a clue as to how to sort out her sins.

Markos's jaw was so tight she thought it might shatter. His eyes glistened. "I really want to walk in that house and kill him."

"Of course you do. Because that's how you solve your problems, isn't it? Anger. Violence."

He flinched. "I deserve that. But I'm not that man anymore, Sofia. Even if that is exactly what this colonel deserves."

He turned away, wiped a finger across his cheekbone, and that undid her, stripped the tension from her voice.

"I had to make a choice, Markos."

"I am not stupid. I understand war. But—I want you to come with me when I leave, Sofia. I—I'm so sorry that I didn't come back to you. But I had a good reason."

She held up her hand. "Really, I don't care—"

"I couldn't. I was in *jail*. And then—"

"I don't care!" She pushed against his chest, slapped it hard with both hands. "*I don't care*!"

He grabbed her wrists, even as his face crumpled. "But I do! I never left you, Sofia. Not in my heart. I thought of you every single day, and if I had known you were here, on Zante, I would have returned the second I found out. I swear to you—" His voice shook, and he scraped it out barely above a whisper. "I never left you."

She drew in a breath at the red in his eyes, but she couldn't bear to let his words in. No. Wrenching her wrists from his grip, she stepped back. "But I left *you*."

His eyes narrowed, ever so briefly.

She stepped away from him, steeled her voice. "I left you. You were dead to me. You still are. I don't…" She made a fist, punched her chest. "There's nothing left in here for you, Markos. Nothing."

"I don't believe that—"

"Why would I wait for a man who is dead?" She spat on the ground. "I moved on. Found someone else."

"The colonel?" His eyes flashed. "He means nothing."

"How about your brother. Dino. *Does he mean anything*?"

She couldn't have hit him with more crippling effect. He sucked in a breath, recoiled. And then his face buttoned down hard.

There. See. She knew he'd be horrified—

"I know. I know about you and Dino, Sofia. And I understand."

Nothing. No words came to her even as his swept in and scooped out her breath. She held in her gasp, however—prided herself on that.

"And, you should know—the last thing he ever said to me was that he loved you."

The...*last thing*...

"What do you mean...?"

But she saw it on his face, every nuance of his phrase.

Oh.

"Oh!" She cupped her hand to her mouth. "*Oh!*"

She bent over, wanting to retch—if she'd had anything in her stomach, she might have. Markos touched her shoulders, but she backed away, her arm out. "Don't touch me."

"Sof—"

"Don't touch me!" Dino. *Oh*— She saw his smile as he met her outside the theater, the way he'd tackled Reg, in her honor. Tasted his breath on her skin as he'd held her. Yes, she'd loved him too, as she could.

Oh. Turning, she stalked away, her legs shaking. She stared at Zante, the cool blue of the sea that he loved to swim in, the taverna and little house where he'd sat in the window and sometimes watched her. The fishing boat he loved to helm, when Markos wasn't looking.

She finally slid to the ground, her back to the wall, and clasped her knees to her body, rocking. Markos hovered, finally sinking beside her. "I'm sorry. I should have told you better. I should have prepared you." He winced, took off his hat. "This isn't going how I'd hoped."

"How you hoped?" She had no strength to her voice. "What did you hope, Markos?"

"I don't know. I guess—I'm a fool—"

"What? Did you think that you'd come here, tell me you're sorry you never showed up, and I'd fall into your arms, that finally we'd have that happy ending you promised me?" She didn't care how her tone might cut him. "I'm not that girl—I don't believe in dreams anymore, Markos. I—I can't afford them."

Markos met her eyes, his hard. "Dreams are all I have."

She shook her head. "Then you're a fool."

"Why? Because I never gave up on you, on the hope of seeing you again, on loving you?"

"No. Because you believed I was worth that."

His eyes absorbed her words, and he recoiled, but she held him fast with her eyes.

"I am not the naïve girl who dressed up like a flapper to make you jealous. I am—a woman who's bartered her body for safety, more than once. The Sofia that you rescued on the boat, the one you tried to save—she died with you, Markos. You don't want this one."

He reached up, and his thumb cast aside a tear she didn't know she'd leaked. "Yes, I do. I want the Sofia who does what she has to in order to survive. The woman who could save the world with her song—"

"I don't have any songs inside me, Markos."

"Who risks her life to save her people. This Sofia is beautiful and brave and—"

"Broken."

He cupped her cheek. "So am I. Can't we help each other heal?" He smiled, and her gaze went to the scar on his cheek, whitened against the scrub of the sun. Oh—no. Still, her hand went to her cheek, her fingers folding into his, and for a moment, she let his words linger.

No. This she could not survive.

"Don't love me, Markos. It's too late for us."

She got up, but he caught her hand. "It's not too late. It's our second chance—"

"You should know that the colonel is hunting the partisans. If you go to the monastery—well, he might just find you. I'm going to go and see what I can find out."

"What? No! You're already in way over your head." He found his feet, caught her other arm. She winced as his thumb dug into her bruise.

He let her go as if she might be aflame. Then he took her arm, raised her sleeve, examined the bruise. His tone came out lethal. "Who did this to you?"

"It doesn't matter."

The terrible expression on his face made her turn away. She didn't want this Markos, the one who could stir dead feelings to life, who could make her feel as if she—as if she mattered.

"Go away from me, Markos."

"No."

"You always have to be the hero, Markos. Well, maybe I'm tired of watching you try and rescue me."

"But this is what I do—let me do it. Besides, I know God will deliver us."

Poor, naïve Markos. Still holding on to his mother's hope.

"Let me handle this myself. Please—I can't watch you die again." And there it was. The past, in ugly shards between them. Markos drew in a breath—her own felt racked over shattered glass.

"I'm not afraid of dying. I think that might be preferable to living without you, Sof." Only the words sounded angry, even ferocious, and in the wake of them, he put his hand over his eyes, shook his head.

She didn't—couldn't—give him a chance to soften his tone.

"Well, you're going to have to. Because you being here is just—a reminder of everything we went through. So I want you to leave. Please, if you care about me, you'll stay far, far away."

Her words must have sunk in because, as she stumbled away, he didn't come after her.

* * * *

Are you sure this is a good idea, Sofia?

Zoë's words barged into her head even as Sofia leaned her bicycle against a poplar tree, for a moment letting the shadow from the mountain enclose her. The monastery nestled into a foothill and overlooked the ocean, the golden sands of Navagio Beach. Through the archway of the fifteenth-century stone tower that guarded the entrance, she could make out the domed basilica of the cathedral, a long building with a stone-tiled roof. And in front of a smaller chapel, the ominous outline of a black two-door coupe.

Just like the colonel's scout car. She remembered when she'd stood on the hill overlooking the city and watched the Germans unload their ships, little beetles invading their island.

Now she curled her hands around her waist. Please, let this work.

Yes, she could agree it was brazen. But for the first time in three years, she wondered if maybe she could use her, well, relationship with the colonel to really—help.

Maybe even save herself from being stoned on the streets, Dino in her frail arms, when the Germans left them with nothing but crumbs.

Perhaps she would even save Markos's life in the process. That should count for something too.

She rubbed her hands on her arms, pulled in a breath. Smoothed her navy dress, one she'd purchased in Minneapolis. She'd even tied up her long hair, rouged her face, tidied her lips.

Stupid, so stupid…

She walked up to the guard at the gate, armed with the colonel's spoken invitation. The guard seemed younger than her, ruddy, shaven face, reddish hair. Nothing in his gaze bespoke anything but curiosity.

And yes, she let him drag his attention over her.

"I'm here to see Colonel Kessler," she said. "I'm—a friend. He told me I could come here if—if I was afraid."

His eyebrow tweaked up, and he drew in a breath. "I don't know if he is here, but you can check in." He nodded to the smaller chapel, with the scout car at the entrance. "There."

She had to dig deep past her quivering body to find the strength to walk under the archway and into the courtyard of the monastery.

In the early evening, the cedar and spruce trees dragged shaggy shadows across the yard. At the door to the office, she glanced back at the guard, gave him a flick of her hand when she found his eyes fixed on her.

A fan blew in the empty office. The Third Reich had swept away any vestige of faith—a swastika hung from between two windows where there might have been a cross. And where saints' faces had hung on the walls, pictures of the fuehrer and his henchmen.

A tribute to evil. The thought pulsed in her even as she listened for presence. "Hello?"

She expected someone to appear in the doorway leading to an anteroom—intended for a priest perhaps, but now turned office. No one answered her call.

She glanced back outside. The guard had turned away, and perhaps in that move she found the boldness that had been simmering inside her since her argument with Markos.

She slipped outside, and before he could turn, before she could stop herself, she secreted herself between the chapel and an outbuilding. She slipped inside the outbuilding, listening to her breath echo off the cement floor. It seemed a bathing room of sorts, with a drain in the center, a trough for water.

Evening crept into the yard, over a long building with an overhang and porch. A row of tiny windows stared at her without life, with one large door on the end bolted shut. Probably the monastic cells.

From a two-story stone building next to it, a German officer stepped out of a door, pulled it shut behind him, and crossed the yard.

Sofia's heart thrummed in her mouth. She didn't breathe until she heard the thump of his feet in the chapel.

The guard at the entrance had apparently forgotten her. Oh, she hoped, even as she eased out, found the shadows, then darted across the yard. She pocketed herself against the far wall of the building that housed the brothers' cells.

She needed to get into the two-story—

Crying. Or something that sounded like it. She held her breath, willed herself to listen. Yes, something soft, or perhaps just the walls muffled it. Still, it sounded…

She peered out—nothing stirred in the courtyard. Her hands slick, she scurried to the first window.

Raised up on her toes to peer inside.

No… Her breath caught even as she tried to get a fix on what she saw—

People. Maybe four of them, huddled together in the tiny cell. Dirty, yet they seemed healthy; however, they wouldn't be for long, if she were to believe the rumors of the German brutalities. A woman, a boy, a girl—and what looked like an old man.

Why—

She lowered herself before they could spot her, cry out—or perhaps before she could retch.

Jews.

How had they been caught? She'd heard the rumors—over two hundred Jews hidden in dark nooks and crannies across the island of Zante.

Not as well as they'd hoped.

She fled back into the shadows, pressing both hands to her mouth. It didn't matter anymore *what* Markos's treasure might be. They couldn't leave these people to be murdered.

Now what? She couldn't leave. What if they decided to move them tonight? But—

From the entrance, the German guard shouted. Sofia dared a look and her heart sank. The officer on duty had exited his office.

She translated his German perfectly…

Where is the woman?

CHAPTER 25

Where is the woman?

The guard called again to the officer, who shut the door of his car, stood up to scan the yard.

She flattened herself against the building. *Where is the woman?*

Out of her mind, obviously, but of course Sofia couldn't scream. Although screaming seemed exactly the right thing to do. Scream at her own stupidity.

Scream that Markos had been right. At least about her being in over her head.

The crying inside the building had stopped. A breeze hissed in the trees, the tang of cedar laden the air.

She pressed her hands against her chest, trying to silence her beating heart.

She'd come here because the colonel invited her....

And if she ran, simply vanished, they'd know—and he'd go straight to Dino.

She stepped out into the shadows, fixed an angry look on her face. "Where is Colonel Kessler?"

She even surprised herself with the way she marched up to the officer, spouting the colonel's name without a quiver.

She placed the officer in his midthirties, clean shaven, dirty blond hair, the scrub of a late-afternoon beard, and yes, he looked familiar.

Perhaps she'd seen him at the taverna, hopefully one of those times when the colonel had forced her down to perch on his knee.

The man hesitated a moment, glanced past her as if she might have in her wake a cadre of partisans. No, not yet. But the second she returned to the villa, she planned on tracking down Lucien.

She'd found Markos's so-called treasure. Or at least the one he *should* be rescuing. She raised an eyebrow, budded her lips in annoyance. Ignored the screaming in her head.

"The colonel's not here. But I will take you to him." The man opened the door to his car—and what choice did she have?

She slid into the backseat, knotted her hands on her lap to keep them from shaking.

The vehicle reminded her of the days she'd ridden with Uncle Jimmy, Markos at the wheel, and she imagined him now, climbing inside, glancing back at her to tell her he'd take care of her. That she didn't need to be afraid.

Then, she'd believed him too much, but now, she let the memory cajole her out of the reality of being driven along the winding roads, through the skinny, cobbled streets to the Zante city square where Ari hung in the breeze and the *Wehrmacht*—the Waffen SS—prowled like rats, on the hunt for partisans.

Like her.

Her hands lost their circulation.

"Stay here," the officer said as he pulled up to the municipal building. In the center courtyard, the sharp fronds of the palm trees cut the twilight like knives. Armored cars—two of them—rumbled by.

Mercifully, they had cut Ari's body down.

"Come with me." The officer reappeared at her door—why hadn't she run?—and she pried her frozen legs from the car.

A crisp wind curled around her, raised gooseflesh on her arms as she followed the officer up the steps, past the two guards, and inside the building. He took her by the arm—never mind the ache of her bruise—and guided her none-too-gently down the hall and to a tiny room, the high window allowing only the barest of light to spider through.

"The colonel isn't here. You will wait for him here."

She rubbed her arm as the door shut.

Darkness enclosed her like dust. Placing her hands on the wall, she slid down, letting the cold seep into her back.

Perhaps this was how those poor people in the monastery felt—afraid. Alone. Helpless.

God will deliver us. Ava's words rushed at her, filled her head, burned her eyes. She closed them, trying to remember. *Everyone thinks that believing in God means that He will deliver us from trouble. But God delivers us* through *trouble.*

It is in the middle of trouble that we truly discover what it means to live.

Live? Hardly. She'd survived. Okay, perhaps there were times, with Markos, when she felt like she lived. Even the day she'd buried her grandfather into the lap of the sea. That night Markos had given her a glimpse of his dream, and somehow that image—of him as a fisherman—allowed her to cling to Zante. To hold on to hope, all the way into her life with Dino. He'd made her laugh—in Chicago and even Minneapolis. Made her believe that she could someday return home. And yes, she had felt safe—even alive, however briefly—in his arms.

Perhaps, yes, the challenges of life made those moments sweeter. Richer.

We discover who we are.

She wasn't so sure she really wanted to know. She wiped her cheeks. But yes, she wanted to live. Because out of the rubble, well…

God had given her little Dino. She saw his pudgy face, the lopsided smile—the very image of his father. And his uncle.

She sucked a breath. She'd survive. She didn't care what it took, how the colonel might punish her. She'd—

The door pushed open, light cutting like a blade into the room. She jumped.

A guard stood in the outline, his features hidden under an officer's hat. "Let's go."

She froze.

He extended a hand. "Sofia—now, let's go. We don't have much time."

Somehow she moved, somehow she put her hand in Markos's. Somehow she let him rescue her off the floor.

And then she let him lead her out of the room like a prisoner, right out the front door, and back into the officer's car.

Which he neatly stole and drove out of the square as if he owned it.

She let herself exhale, ever so briefly. "What are you doing?"

"Getting you out of there." And he didn't sound happy about it. No, his tone could reach out and strangle her. "What were you *doing*? Trying to get yourself shot, maybe hung from the square?"

She recoiled into the plush velvet seat. "Yes. That's exactly what I had in mind. What are *you* doing? Where did you get this uniform—have you lost your mind? The colonel is going to come looking for me." She unloaded a harsh laugh. "I was safer with him."

In front, Markos's hands whitened on the steering wheel. "You're going to say that one of the officers told you to go home. They'll spend days looking for the man who should be wearing this uniform."

"And…where is *he*?" She leaned up, grabbed Markos's arm. "You didn't—"

"No. He's actually a sympathizer. There are a few, you know. Now that the Nazis are pulling out, some of the Germans have come forward, handing over their uniforms, asking to be smuggled out of the country, or even joining forces with the partisans. The ones that don't want to fight will barter information in exchange for the guarantee that when the British and Americans invade, they'll be taken prisoner. Apparently they're afraid of the Russian front."

They cut down streets, turned back, made more turns.

Finally he wove his fingers into hers, still clutching to his arm. His anger seemed flushed out. "You scared me."

He drew in a long breath, cut down another street, slowing for a man on a bicycle. "What were you doing at the monastery? I thought we made an agreement."

She unhinged her hand from his, sat back, stared out the window. "No. You made an ultimatum."

He finally pulled the car into the open courtyard of a house, U-shaped, with an overhanging porch and a red-tiled roof.

Just like that, the gate shut behind them.

Three young men appeared from the colonnade; one opened her door to help her out, another ducked in behind the vacated driver's seat.

Markos stood in the headlights, stripping off the uniform—handing over the jacket, the hat, the weapon.

Then he rounded the car, slipped her hand into his, and pulled her toward the house.

She realized immediately he'd taken her to the partisan safe house. An apartment complex turned renegade hangout, judging by the supply of angry, dark-eyed young men lounging around the main room. A group sat at a long wooden table playing cards; a man sat in the window and played mournful tunes on an accordion. From the kitchen, the smell of baked bread and some sort of meat stirred her empty stomach.

"What's going on?"

"We're honoring our fallen—Ari and Nikos." Lucien stepped out from the kitchen, rolling a keg of beer.

She eyed it. "Do I want to ask where you got that?"

He didn't smile as he shook his head. He set the keg upright, tapped it, and then left it for the card players. He walked over to her, glancing fast at Markos. "What happened?"

"She went to the monastery, that's what. Just like I told her not to." Markos narrowed his eyes at her a second before he disappeared into an adjacent room.

Lucien filled a beer stein, brought it to her. She shook her head, her gaze darting to Markos's closed door.

"You went to the monastery? Why?"

"The colonel told me that if I was ever scared, I could go there—that I'd be safe there. So—I thought maybe...."

"She thought he might be hiding something there, and that she'd walk right in, maybe ask for a map and a key." Markos emerged, pulling a shirt over his chest, having changed into green army trousers. She noticed that yes, his shoulders had widened, his body leaned over the years.

A blush pressed her face, and she hid it behind a biting glare before she turned back to Lucien. "No, that's not what I thought, although, if they'd asked I planned on using Ari's"—she winced as a couple of the men at the table lifted their eyes to her—"death as a reason why I might be afraid. I thought maybe I could ask the colonel for protection. Only, he wasn't there."

Markos poured himself a glass of water. Drank it fast. "I nearly died when I saw you at the gate."

"You were spying on me?"

He frowned at her. "No. I was watching the monastery for any suspicious activity. Like a beautiful young woman trying to sneak in." He raised an eyebrow. "You know that if they have anything there, right now they're moving it."

His words caught her breath. "No—" She turned to Lucien, the only one able to listen apparently. "I found something."

In Lucien's eyes flashed too much hope. "A treasure? What—artwork? Maybe gold icons from one of the churches?"

"Jews. They're hiding Jews there. Four of them, at least—maybe more, I couldn't tell. It doesn't matter why Markos is here—we need to help—"

"No."

Lucien's words stripped the room of movement, noise—the men playing cards, the accordion in the corner—all stilled. Markos wore a terrible look, dashing it between Sofia and Lucien.

Lucien took his hat off and banged it against his knee. "I'm sorry, but that's not Markos's mission. We have to keep looking for the treasure."

"Lucien—we have to rescue them!"

Two men got up from the table, walked to the window. The accordion began to sigh.

"We can't leave them there. The Nazis will kill them before they leave—we all know it."

Two more players threw down their cards, pushed away from the table.

"What? Don't you remember the stories from Thessalonica? They lined them up, put them onto ships..."

"You forget, Sofia, Zante does protect its people," Lucien said, his tone schooled. "I was in the square the day the bishop's and the mayor's blood spilled into the stones. I know the price. And I too helped hide—friends."

"So how did this family get caught?"

Lucien shook his head.

"You read the papers. You listen to the radio. You know what will happen to this family—"

"We also know what happens to the villages who rile the Germans." The voice came from Cosmos. She'd only met him twice; both times he was guarding the radio shack. A taller man, with a scar down his jaw, wounds in his eyes. "Have you forgotten the massacres at Kos, and Cephallonia, at Kommeno and Kalavryta? Women and children, burning in a school. The entire male population—massacred. All reprisals against partisan attacks."

"Why do we fight, if not for these people?"

"Haven't we done enough? Are these people worth our lives? The lives of our families?"

She didn't know who said it, but she put as much horror into her expression as she could. "And Ari and Nikos were murdered for a *radio*. These are *people*, not money. Aren't they a thousand times more valuable?"

Lucien's mouth tightened into a knot. He glanced around the room. "No one is arguing that. But that's the problem, isn't it? If there *is* a real treasure out there, we have to find it, and soon. The Gestapo is hunting us, and the truth is, we need the money. We're not the only partisan group, you know. And some of them are siding with the communists. We just may have another war here, Sofia, and we need to be ready."

She didn't know this man. The boy whose antics had made her laugh.

The boy who had grieved his best friend. The one who understood suffering better than any of them. "You make me sick."

"Sofia." Markos stepped up to her. "Of course we'll free them." He glanced at Lucien. "Of course."

Lucien spit on the floor. "How? They're hunting us all over the city. If they don't move them tonight, they'll move them tomorrow, or maybe the day after. But we can't possibly rescue them and find—"

"We strike tomorrow night," Markos said.

"And the colonel?" Lucien said, his tone equally lethal.

Sofia had the sense of two dogs, their nape's burred. "I'll distract the colonel—"

"What? No!" Markos rounded on her. "Have you lost your mind?"

"I—I—" Maybe she had—or at least her heart, although his tone left her strangely raw.

"No." His eyes stopped her, held her, a look in them she hadn't seen since—well, since he was back-dropped by the dark frothy ocean. An expression that preceded promises.

She turned away before the wounds opened.

Lucien, however, nodded. "It's a great idea."

"It's suicide—he'll suspect her!"

"No, he won't—he's in love with her." Lucien kept his eyes on Markos, an odd smirk on his face.

"He's not in love with me," Sofia said softly. "But I can distract him." She looked away from Markos when she said it.

But from her periphery, she saw Markos close his eyes, as if unable, also, to look at her. "No. Absolutely not. I'm not letting you risk your life—"

"She risks her life every day. Besides, it's not your decision," Lucien said tightly. "It's Sofia's."

She stared at the partisans, the way they regarded her. Some with cool eyes, others something more like zeal. "Of course I'll do it."

Markos held her a long time with his gaze. Finally he walked over to the window. Stared outside, his chest rising and falling.

Two men filled carafes with retsina, carried them around the room, filling glasses. A bouzouki player joined the musician in the corner.

Sofia turned down the wine but sank into a chair as the men brought out food, filled plates.

Markos leaned against the wall, arms folded, his expression so familiar, it could take her apart if she looked too close.

As if she'd reached into the past and plucked the moment he'd seen her singing, her hair bobbed, Uncle Jimmy crowing in the front row, right before the raid on Tony's. He looked then, and now, as if he didn't recognize her.

Perhaps he didn't.

Too bad. She'd told him the truth from the beginning. Poison.

Around her, the men broke out into song. Greeks. She'd missed the celebration, even in the face of grief. They found life in the middle of tragedy.

Round one, two. They toasted to Ari, then Nikos, toasted to freedom and women—she blushed at that.

Then they hooked arms and began to dance the kaslamantiano.

Still Markos stood, away from the drinking, the party, his arms folded.

"C'mon, Sofia!" Cosmos grabbed her up, inserted her into the dance line. She allowed herself to laugh—after all, she bled Greek too—and even reached out for a glass of proffered retsina from the bottles they'd scrounged up from—well, probably her own wine cave. It bit her throat going down but warmed her through, shook loose the claws of despair.

Slowly she ceased to care how the night crept in through the open window, how the stars pricked the canopy above, the smell of midnight in the air. She danced, letting herself go, laughing, round and round and—

She lost her balance, tripped, fell.

Cosmos caught her. Nearly as big as Markos, he swooped her into his arms, twirled her around. She hooked an arm around his neck.

He laughed then, and before she could stop him, pressed a beer-seasoned kiss to her mouth.

She stilled under his touch, even as he kissed her again. "Cosmos—"

But the music played and he danced with her in his arms. She pushed against him. "Put me down."

"No, dance with me, *moro mou.*" He bent his head for another kiss.

She wasn't his baby. "Put me down—" But she didn't have to finish her sentence, because an arm curled around her and another pushed Cosmos back.

"Let her go."

She swayed ever so slightly against Markos even as his arm curled around her. Cosmos backed off, hand up, eyes suddenly sharp. "Calm down, Markos. She's not your girl anymore, you know. She's"—he glanced at her, winked, something ugly in it—"she's a partisan. *Serving* her country."

It was the laugh at the end, so clearly not humor, that dried her mouth.

Beside her, every muscle in Markos's body turned rigid as he stepped back, still holding her. A kind of danger sparked, simmered in his quiet voice. "You will never know courage like Sofia's. Be glad I don't rip you apart for your words."

Cosmos, however, laughed again, glanced at Lucien. "Go ahead.

Isn't that what you Stavroses do best? Steal women then kill anyone who gets in your way?"

The music stopped, and only Markos's heavy breathing filled the silence.

Markos—please... She saw it then, the explosion, the way his fist had connected with Uncle Jimmy's, shattered his nose. And right behind it, heard his moans.

She closed a hand over his arm.

But Markos didn't explode, didn't even step forward. "Yes. Once, perhaps. But I'm not that person anymore. I left him—back in prison."

Prison. He'd said that before, but now the word sank into her bones. *Prison.*

"But I guarantee you that if you talk about her that way again, I'll find him. Just for you."

Cosmos flinched even as he picked up a beer stein, raising it to Sofia. "You're not worth it."

This much she knew.

Cosmos spit on the floor at her feet, turned away, sloshing his beer.

Lucien, however, hadn't moved, his eyes red, his fists white, his eyes on Markos. "You're a liar. You've been back twenty-four hours, and look who you have in your arms."

Sofia jerked.

"Leave her out of this, Lucien. You hate me—I get that. But this is not about Sofia."

"No. It was about you, and how you always had to be the hero."

Lucien acted so fast, Sofia nearly didn't see it, but suddenly she'd jarred her hip hard on the stone floor, and Lucien had a knife pressed to Markos's neck.

Markos didn't move, despite the beads of blood at his throat. His chest rose and fell…rose…fell.

Sweat trailed down Lucien's face. "Tell me why I shouldn't have my revenge right now."

Markos didn't even blink. "Go ahead, Lucien. I'm not going to fight you."

Sofia closed her eyes, a scream burning her lungs. Of course it would come to this—it had to—

The switchblade clicked. Sofia opened her eyes to Lucien stepping back. He glanced at Sofia, a cold look that reached into her and told her exactly what she already knew. Poison, and she might now get them all killed. Then he turned his back and stalked out of the house.

Markos pulled her from the floor, his hand hot in hers as he enclosed it. "I'll walk you home."

He brushed past Cosmos as he left. Sofia didn't look at him.

But his cold voice snaked out behind them. "You might want to find out who the father is to the little mongrel she's hiding up there in her villa, Captain, before you start hearing wedding bells."

CHAPTER 26

"I don't want to know."

Apparently Markos had let his steps distance him from his disgust, because she heard not a trace of it lingering in his voice.

Mongrel. She clenched her teeth against the bite of Cosmos's word.

She rubbed her arms, exhaustion buzzing through her as she followed him toward the villa, rocks spilling under her feet. He reached back for her, but she ignored his help.

Behind them, the city lights pricked the nightscape. The breeze reaped the scent of bougainvillea twining up the stone walls, the sea-salt air mixed with a touch of brine. Above it all filtered the fragrance of the sea daffodils. So delicate, and yet she could smell the lily woven through all the others.

"Tell me about him, though." Markos slowed his step, fell in beside her.

"My son?"

Markos nodded, his arms swinging. For a second, she felt them again around her, pulling her away from Cosmos. Back into his embrace. She shook it away.

"He's…everything. My life."

"I would imagine he has your eyes." He tried a smile, something tender in it as he glanced at her.

She looked away, offering nothing more.

"How old is he?"

"Old enough to miss me tonight. I am just hoping I can offer the colonel a story—"

"We can rescue these people without your help, Sofia." Markos's tone shifted, back into something harder, although it lacked the bite from before.

"Perhaps. But maybe I can buy you time."

Markos reached over then and took her hand. And, heaven help her, she let him. Relished his strong grip around hers.

He walked with her in silence.

The silvery leaves of the olive grove shimmered under the moonlight. All around them, cicadas buzzed, a nearly deafening chorus.

"Were you really in prison?"

"Don't you think I deserved to be? I did kill Kostas."

She had no words for that.

"Yes. I got ten years—well, almost. I was lucky, after everything Uncle Jimmy did to get me convicted, that I didn't get the chair. But it gave me lots of time to think." He hadn't released her hand, and now directed her away from the barns, the gate, and toward the stone wall. He sat on it, turned his back to the glittering city, almost eye level with her.

The wind tickled his hair against his neck, his eyes so luminous that she could fall inside. She kept herself away, too tempted to step near for her own good.

"I came back here because, well, somehow I hoped that maybe I could make it right. It felt like a second chance. I wasn't even sure Lucien would be here. I—never thought I'd find you."

He reached up, combed her hair from her face, his eyes so tender she had to look away.

"Lucien still hates me, that much is clear."

"His father is the magistrate. He took over after the mayor was killed. He—has allied himself with the Germans and—well, you know as well as I that Lucien's had a rough life."

"Lucien is caught inside his hatred. I know how that feels. It only turns you bitter."

She looked past him. "This view always reminds me of crossing the ocean—watching the lights glisten on the water." She wasn't sure why she'd let that memory drift out, but only he could share that with her.

"I remember." He took her hair, twined it between his fingers. "I like it long better."

Oh, yes. The last time he'd seen her, it had been cut just below her jaw line. "Me too."

"Cosmos is a liar, you know."

She backed away from him, but still he held her hand.

"Listen to me—"

"No—see, that's the problem. You don't get it. No, he's not. He's absolutely right."

"I do get it, Sofia. I really get it."

Oh. She tugged on her hand, but he had it. He eased her to himself, his hand under her chin, guiding her eyes back to him.

"Oh, why don't you see what I see?" He shook his head. "Hear me. When Cosmos said you weren't worth it—he was dead wrong."

He ran his hand to her face, and yes, she leaned into it. Let it bathe her, if only for this moment.

She met his eyes—definitely a mistake, because he had such amazing eyes, and this time she let herself explore the emotion in them.

"I should have known there was more to God's plan. I shouldn't have let my fear of disappointment keep me from trusting Him."

"I don't understand."

"I begged God for another chance to keep my promise. But when Dino died...I let myself believe that God didn't give people like me a second chance—"

"He doesn't."

"He does. He does, Sofia. That's the point. Don't you see? He doesn't give us a second chance because we *deserve* it. He does it because that's who He is, what He is about."

Sofia shook her head, but Markos didn't seem to care about her rejection. His hand wrapped around the back of her neck, eased her close. His breath fell against her lips.

"Let me kiss you. Please let me kiss you."

She'd lost her mind, probably back there in Gestapo headquarters, or maybe she'd never had it with Markos. Maybe just being with him made her stop thinking and just feel because, yes, she nodded.

And then he kissed her.

She thought she'd remember his touch, but this Markos tasted different—the desperation absent. Instead, he touched her with a sweetness that could make her weep, a gentleness that moved her into his arms, made her wrap hers around his shoulders, lean into him, and forget.

She was again seventeen, tasting her future on the lips of the man she loved.

She ran her fingertips into the stubble on his cheek even as he deepened his kiss. His hand moved down to her jaw, and finally he made the softest of noises, as if something had broken loose inside him—almost a whimper—"Sofia."

He backed away from her, a look so fragile on his face that she didn't even have to see the glisten of his eyes to know he was crying. Then his breath caught—a harsh tumble of emotions from his chest—

and he pulled her to him, burying his face in her shoulder. "Oh, Sofia—I've missed you. I've missed you so much."

She let herself sink onto his lap, let him wrap his arms around her waist, and held him.

Perhaps she wasn't the only one who'd spent the last fifteen years lost.

* * * *

"Wake up, Sofia."

She knew the voice, but to find it just above a whisper, in her ear—she lifted her head and it took a moment....

Rose-gold brushed the mandarin roofs of the city, and higher up the mountainside the green spears of cyprus trees poked through the gauze of the early morning. A cool breeze shivered the cedars, shook the olive grove awake.

"Wake up."

She turned, rooted for a moment by Markos's stricken look.

"What?"

"I fell asleep—*we*—fell asleep." His appearance matched the emotion inside her—his hair sweetly tousled, a dark etch of doom to his mouth, eyes that drank her in. Oh, please, she just wanted to lay her head back onto his chest, to sink back into the warm cradle of his embrace.

He pulled her to her feet. "I should go with you—what if—"

"It will be okay." She pushed on his chest, swayed, and he caught her arm. She let him pull her to himself. Kiss the top of her head.

"Come with me, Sofia. Please." He held her away from him and put everything he had, it seemed, into his eyes. "I'll wait for you. Go get your son, your things. We can leave right now. I'll call for an evac—"

"No!" She cut her tone to a whisper. "No. We can't—I can't leave Zoë—and your mother. Your *mother*, Markos."

He closed his mouth, his eyes darting to the house. Nodded. "Her too. Get her and we'll leave—"

"Stop, Markos. Stop thinking with your heart and use your head. If I leave, the colonel will hunt for me. No one will be safe. He'll find the partisans. I can't leave."

"But—you didn't come home last night. He'll..." Markos shook his head. "I can't believe I'm not going in there and simply killing him."

"You're not that man anymore."

He closed his eyes. "Sometimes I want to be. It *is* war."

"This isn't war. This is Kostas speaking."

A muscle pulled in his jaw.

"I will take care of the colonel. And—and—" She couldn't help it. Everything inside her leaped at his words, and hers tumbled out before common sense yanked them back. "I *will* leave with you, Markos." She palmed his chest, felt his heart banging under it. "As soon as we free this family, come to me. I'll be ready, with my son. And your mother. Maybe she won't come, but I will try—and at least you can see her. Or—she can see you."

He drew in a breath.

"I know you're afraid of what she might say, but, to use your words, 'I wish you could see what I see.' " She ran her hand down his cheek. Rose up on her toes. Kissed him, lingering there.

He cupped his hands around her upper arms, held her. "I will get you—all of you—out of here. I'll come up with a plan."

Of course he would. "Come for me tonight. I'll be here."

Then she left him there—and ducked through the gnarled trees to the house.

Only a few chickens bobbed in the yard, a goat bell jingling faintly on the breeze as she went into the house. A bowl of figs sat in the center of the table. She took one, let it pinch off the hunger inside.

Ava's door was shut—although, most likely, she'd be up soon.

Sofia climbed the stairs and tiptoed down the hall, glancing at the colonel's door. It too remained closed. Her breath leaked out, just a smidge. She put her hand on her door latch, eased it open. She'd answer his questions later, after seeing Dino, after packing her bag and secreting it under her bed—

Something tumbled to the floor at her feet, bounced into the room, a tiny footstep against the wood. It vanished inside the shadows of the floorboards.

Dino lay curled under his wool blanket. Zoë too, in the opposite bed, her dark hair in a braided rope to her waist. She didn't move even as the sunlight now crept to the windowsill.

Maybe Sofia could simply slide into bed next to Dino, curl around him, pretend she hadn't tugged them all into this nightmare.

She kicked the object as she shuffled into the room. It pinged against the floorboards and she bent to pick it up.

Everything turned to ice inside her.

Her hairpin. The one she'd dropped beneath the colonel's briefcase.

Still bent, like a finger pressing out to accuse her.

She closed her eyes, pressing her hand to her stomach. *Run.*

How much did he know? Did he suspect that she'd been after information? *Run.*

Did he think her a conspirator with the partisans?

Run.

She turned to Dino, her pulse in her ears. She could simply scoop him up, run with him and his bedclothes to Markos—he was probably halfway to town, or—or—she knew the partisan hideout. She could go there…

And what? Wait for the Gestapo to find her? To kill them all?

Think. She caught her image in the tarnished mirror. Disheveled, her hair in knots, her dress soiled. She looked like a harlot who had been dragged through the streets.

Up until a few moments ago, she'd felt young again.

Untouched.

Now her hand shook as she dropped the hairpin to her bureau. She unbuttoned the dress, let it puddle at her feet, grabbed up her silk dressing gown, and knotted the sash hard at her waist. Her bones pushed at the silk. Then she picked up the brush, worked it through her hair, her eyes big in the mirror.

Maybe Zoë had found the hairpin—didn't she sometimes clean his room? Only, hadn't it been lodged in the door?

She stared at it, as if it might be a grenade and at any moment would explode, devastating the fragile hope she'd knit together.

"Sofia?"

She dropped the brush onto the bureau, jumped. It bounced off, clattered to the floor.

The colonel stood just outside her door, fully dressed in his gray field jacket, with the black shoulder boards, the two oak leaves of the *Oberführer* shiny on his black collar. His oily boots emitted a shine. His low-brimmed hat hid his eyes.

Her gaze dinged off the Mauser pistol clasped onto his wide belt.

"You're up early," he said, his voice low.

"I, uh…I'm sorry I didn't come to you last night. I was very tired."

He drew in a breath, let it out. Her hand settled on the bureau; the hairpin pricked her finger.

"I understand." He nodded, made to turn.

"Colonel—"

She wasn't sure where the voice came from, or why, but it seemed she couldn't stop it. "Will you—be home tonight?" She didn't even try to scrape away the fear—it gave her request the flavor of hope.

He smiled, his lips thin. "Yes, of course I will." He drew his finger down the slope of her face.

She nodded, manufactured a smile.

She could feel Zoë watching her in the darkness.

The colonel dipped his hat, moved away from the door.

"What are you doing?" Zoë hissed, sitting up, holding the covers to herself.

Sofia walked to the door, closed it, leaning against it, even as her breath fled her body. She shook her head, looked at Zoë.

"I—I don't know. Hoping, I guess."

Zoë said nothing as Sofia climbed into bed with Dino and pulled his limp body against her trembling bones.

She slept too long, too hard, and awoke with creases on her face. Dino and Zoë were nowhere in sight. The sun played greedy with its light, hid behind the clouds, and swathed the room in gloom as she pulled out a bag and threw into it Dino's pants, a sweater, two dresses—Markos's black fishing coat.

Probably she should give it back to Ava. Yes—it belonged to Ava. She took it from the bag, hung it back in the closet. Added instead a sweater, her hairbrush.

Then she rolled it all into a blanket and hid it under the bed.

Not unlike how Markos had done with Uncle Jimmy's money.

She'd barely bathed, bundled up her hair by the time she heard the colonel's foot on the door.

Dinner—perhaps she could distract him with—

"Sofia!"

She closed her eyes, pressed her hand to her stomach. Opened the door to his knock. Darkness etched the lines in his face, and with everything inside her, she longed to shrink back, close the door.

Hide. The hairpin lay secreted under her mattress.

"We will go out tonight. Be pretty for me."

She nodded, her throat scorched. She closed the door, leaned against it. Yes. The colonel liked that—parading her on his arm. And in a gown he'd provided.

She picked the blue one, with dark blue embroidery on the bodice. It had probably belonged to a lovely Jewish woman now in hiding somewhere on the island. It made her skin itch. But she pasted on a smile when he knocked on her door.

She slipped her arm through the colonel's as she stepped out of the car. *I hoped that maybe I could right what I did.* Markos's words strummed in her head. Right what *she* did.

She smiled up at the colonel, then at the dark cover of heaven, wanting to pray.

But the thought seemed brazen. She didn't have the right to pray. Although, desperation seemed a good reason to try—and if Lucien and Markos truly planned on going through with the rescue…

The central square outside the basilica was jammed with people—leathery men wearing their black wool fisherman hats, eating currants, drinking retsina. Women with babies on their hips, others garbed in black or embroidered shawls with gifts to offer before the tall cross the priest had brought out from the church.

The Festival of the Cross. She'd forgotten this day—although, really, she attended Mass about as often as she went fishing.

"Let's stop," she said, moving toward the line. "Please." The colonel's mouth tightened on the sides, but she ignored him, pulling her shawl up over her head even as she joined the line to venerate.

"What are you doing?" The colonel's Greek had improved, and he used it now, probably to stave off attention.

Not like the entire city wouldn't notice her dangerous company.

"It's the Feast of the Cross," she said. "I'm honoring the sacrifice of our Lord." Although her words sounded tinny to her own ears. Still, something about the fervor of the crowd drew her.

Desperation demanded a savior.

However, she noticed, already through the line, dressed in a black shawl—Ava. The woman stood back from the cross, serenity on her face.

Almost like, hope.

Sofia knelt before the cross, made the sign.

Beside her, the colonel did the same. Sofia closed her eyes to it and stayed on her knees a moment longer, clinging to Ava's words. *Deliver us, O God. Please.*

The colonel took her arm. "I'm hungry."

The tavernas stayed open later on feast nights—mostly due to the twenty-four hours of fasting preceding, and the colonel dragged her to the café Zeus.

A company of his SS compatriots sat at a table, finishing bottles of ouzo. The colonel pulled up two chairs and ordered a plate of moussaka for her, a lamb kebob for himself. A bouzouki player walked the perimeter, a weathered man who hid his derision for his audience with a gap-toothed smile. Bougainvillea twined up the outside of the wooden portico, the wind reaped the scent, and she turned into it, even as the colonel drew her close. He handed her a glass of the white liquor. She smiled, let it burn her lips. Dumped the rest in a climbing rose.

The moussaka roiled in her already sour stomach, and she watched the moon rise over the water, part the ocean in a luminous trail, and despised it for its betrayal. Markos needed the darkness if he hoped to rescue the Jews.

The colonel moved his hand to her knee as the ouzo warmed him. He laughed loud, spoke German so quickly she couldn't follow. A couple of his fellow officers glanced at her, gave her a reptilian look.

Her gaze landed on a couple at another table, their smiles easy in each others' eyes. She remembered when she and Markos had been that way—and hid a smile at the future, so close.

Tonight. Tonight she'd steal away with him, put Dino into his arms, introduce him to his uncle. Perhaps, someday—stepfather.

An SS scout car pulled up, its round lights blinding the patrons. Waffen officers emerged.

She ducked her head away before the leader recognized her.

But he went straight to the colonel. Whispered into his ear.

Emotion flickered across Kessler's face, but she couldn't place it before he turned to her. "They need me at headquarters. I'll ask my man to drive you home."

"I can walk—"

"I insist." He nearly yanked her up by her elbow, and she bit back the sting of his grip as he forced her outside. He nodded to his compatriots and pushed her into the car.

"What's the matter? You seem upset."

He glanced at her, and she suddenly had the sense that she sat next to Uncle Jimmy, that same sort of dark liquid syruping through her. But the colonel smiled at her, something that never met his eyes, reached back, and pulled the hairpin from her hair. "I like it down so much better."

Then he grabbed her jaw in his gloved hand and kissed her. "Be waiting for me when I return."

He got out and she knitted her hands together to stop the shaking.

The officer said nothing as he drove her home. Without her directions.

She fled into the dark house.

"Zoë!" She banged up the stairs, slammed open her door.

Skidded to a stop.

Lucien stood in the room, his face dirty, his clothes bloodied. Zoë held Dino to herself, and he saw Sofia. "*Matera*!"

She scooped him to herself, holding onto his heat as she scoured Lucien's terrible expression.

"No..." She shook her head, squeezing Dino's body tight against hers. *No, God—* "Please—Lucien."

"He's alive. But he's been captured. And—we need your help."

CHAPTER 27

Four people huddled in the barn, in the hayloft, flinching as Sofia scanned her flashlight across their dirty faces. She ducked back down the ladder, landed with a soft thud beside Lucien. She handed him the flashlight. "Why did you bring them here?"

"We had nowhere else to go. The Germans were after us, and we figured that the last place they'd look would be under the nose of the colonel."

Sofia pressed her hands to her head, trying to keep herself from unraveling. "Are you sure Markos was captured?"

"Yes. He and two others—we were ambushed, Sofia." He wanted blood. She could nearly taste it in his tone.

She whirled to face him, studied him in the dim glow of the flashlight puddling out at his feet. In the dark, she wouldn't have recognized him, his face rubbed black with char, a stocking cap over his head, even his hands covered in black wool gloves. She had closed the door behind them after Lucien led her across the yard to the barn, but at any moment the colonel might return, a fact evidenced by his tight grip on his revolver.

"What do you mean—ambushed?" She shot a look toward the window, where Zoë hid right behind the curtains.

Lucien stepped close, a hiss in his voice. "They knew we were coming—the Germans waited until we'd freed the Jews, and then they simply descended. We got them out but—" He walked over to the ladder, stared up. "Cosmos is dead."

"And Markos was captured." She had to stop shaking. For Dino.

Perhaps that's where the colonel had rushed off to—to torture the man she loved.

She gripped the side of a stall before her knees buckled. "How did they know?"

He considered her, as if debating his words.

"Lucien."

"We think the colonel played you, Sofia. He probably even sent out decoy messages to lure Markos—any OSS agent here. The Germans would love to know the British plans for invasion. If they could trick an agent into embedding with the partisans, they'd have the perfect catch. You know the colonel's been hunting us partisans for months, and I'll bet he knew that you were a part of us—"

"No."

"They planted the bait with Markos—leading the British to believe there was valuable cargo on the island, and then used the Jews to bait us to the monastery. They knew that after we'd been hiding them for two years, we weren't going to let the Germans have them." He glanced out the window toward the house. "Did he ever catch you doing anything—anything that would connect you to us?"

"No, of course n— oh." She pressed her hand to her roiling stomach. It was probably no use—she felt like losing it right there in the hay and muck.

"What?" Lucien's hand closed around her arm as he steadied her. "What?"

She closed her eyes, moaned out her words. "He found my hairpin. In his room. I thought maybe Zoë found it, but…" She covered her face. "Oh, Lucien, what have I done?"

"It's not your fault." But his tone said he didn't believe his own words.

"We have to rescue him."

"We?"

She rounded on Lucien. "Don't you see? The colonel used me—it's my fault Markos is being tortured—probably going to be..." Her breath caught, and she forced it out through clenched teeth. "Killed. *Killed.* Because I thought I could do something..." She held up her hands, backed away from him. "I'm going to go find the colonel. There has to be something I can do. I'll beg for Markos's life..."

"Markos? Markos is here?"

Oh. No. The voice trickled over her, so full of disbelief it shook Sofia to the core. She turned and wanted to cry at Ava's expression.

"My son has returned to Zante?"

The woman stood in the doorway, her dark eyes alight, a lamp smoothing out the creases in her face. "When? How?"

No, it couldn't end like this. Not with so much hope in Ava's eyes. Sofia advanced on her, caught her strong, wrinkled hands. "He—*is* here. But..." Oh, she didn't want to say it—looked away, in fact, even as Ava's hand came up to rest on her cheek.

"Tell me, daughter."

Oh, she was no daughter. Didn't deserve to be. "The Gestapo caught him when he was freeing"—she glanced up—"a Jewish family."

"The Germans found a Jewish family?"

"Yes. The colonel used me—he told me where to find them, and then used me to lure the partisans. Markos—he was captured."

Ava stared at him as if she might be speaking Russian. "Markos—is a partisan? How long has he been here?" Her face darkened as she turned to Lucien. "How long?"

"Two days. He is with the OSS and came in on a mission."

Ava drew that information in on a long breath. Then finally nodded, even as she moved away. "Of course he didn't want me to know. He was worried for me."

Sofia caught her hand. "He wanted to see you. But he didn't want you hurt."

Lucien turned away under Ava's eyes.

"And now the Gestapo have him."

She said it so calmly, just as she had faced every other catastrophe in her life. *My husband and eldest son are dead. My remaining sons have moved to America. I married a widower, watched him die of cancer.*

Sofia refused to add the future—*I watched my son's body hang from the town square.*

"We have to rescue him."

Lucien came to life, now striding past Ava, who stood at the bottom of the ladder, looking up at the haymow. "How? How do you suppose we'll break into Gestapo HQ and rescue Markos?"

Sofia moved to the door, an eye on the house. Please, don't let the colonel return home—but what if he was torturing Markos—oh! "I don't know, Lucien! Maybe—maybe you can ask your father. He's the magistrate—can't he help?"

"My father would like to see all the partisans shot at dawn. You forget the German army pays him to turn over his people, to keep the so-called peace." He shook his head. "He won't help."

"Wait—Markos told me there were Germans friendly to our cause. Perhaps they would help us?"

Lucien considered her. "Go on."

"There were uniforms, right? Markos wore one when he helped me escape last night. Maybe our people could wear them, and the guards—what if they could be persuaded to—"

"How? With what? Retsina? I might remind you that Markos hasn't found anything of value—and he has nothing to barter with."

"What will you do with these people?" Ava's voice broke through his harsh tone.

Sofia ran her teeth over her lip, then, "We'll take them with us. Markos had a plan to escape…" She looked away when she added, "And Dino and I were going to go with him. Our bag is packed, under the bed. I—wanted to start over."

Ava didn't move, her face still. Finally, "Of course you did."

"Matera, I wanted you to come with us." She let the endearment trickle out, afraid of the rush of emotions behind it.

Ava glanced at Lucien. "Give me the flashlight."

He obeyed as if she had a sort of hypnosis over him. "Now—go to the house. Get Dino, and Zoë, tell her to pack, to come to us."

Lucien met Ava's eyes as Ava touched his cheek, her fingers running into all that char. "Then, you go and free my son, Lucien Pappos."

Her touch held him a moment, and he seemed to breathe it in. Then he nodded, not unlike a small boy told to fetch the wine, and disappeared out the door.

"Sofia." Ava caught her face in her hands. "Of course I will go with you. You are my family now. You and Dino and Zoë."

Taking both hands, "I know where to hide these people. And then, I have an idea. Perhaps for such a time as this, Sofia, you have carried my most valuable possession across the sea and back. We will use it to save the life of my beloved son."

"Your most valuable possession?"

She drew her shawl up over her head. "My topaz ring. I wore it last on the day my oldest son was murdered. I sewed it into Galen's coat and gave it to Markos. I told him to never part with it. He obviously gave it to you."

Sofia shook her head. "Dino gave it to me. Markos gave it to him."

Ava smiled. "Of course he did. And you brought it home to Zante. The ring is sewn into the hem at the bottom. After we deliver our friends to safety, you will fetch it and give it to Lucien. He will use it to pay for Markos's escape."

"You trust Lucien after what his family did to yours?"

"I believe in Lucien's heart. And I trust in God's deliverance. Now, we must hurry. Every moment we delay brings more danger." She stepped up the ladder, gathering her skirt as she climbed.

"You will be safe with us—come."

She hopped back down, helping an elderly man down the ladder and to the floor.

He smiled at Sofia, patted her cheek. "I always knew you came back for a reason."

"Dr. Alexio." She'd expected him to be more gaunt, perhaps, but their host Greek family had harbored them well. Beneath the grime of his prison cell, he still bore the robust spirit she remembered from the day he delivered Dino.

"I didn't know it was you—"

"And yet you came for us." He kissed her on one cheek, then the other. Then reached out for a little girl who looked about seven. "This is my granddaughter, Ruth Ann."

"Yes, I remember Ruth Ann, the baker." She exchanged a smile with the girl—had it already been two years since she played with baby Dino on the floor of the taverna?

Sofia reached up for the next person—a woman she recognized as Ruth Ann's mother.

The last down the ladder was an adolescent boy that Sofia vaguely remembered as a scoundrel who had tried to steal baklava from her taverna. Now all four refugees stood in the barn, radiating danger.

"Where are we taking them?" Sofia asked, fetching a horse blanket and tucking it over Alexio.

"To the caves—they're below the olive grove." Ava picked up a rope from one of the stalls. "We'll tie ourselves together when we get to the caves. It's dark, and we don't want to get lost."

She flashed the light out into the yard, farther, into the grove. The olive trees beckoned like gnarled fingers. "The caves lead to the sea. The Germans don't know they even exist. Our friends will be safe there. As will Dino and Zoë and I while we wait for you and Markos to join us."

She opened the door, gestured to the group, their pale faces, eyes glued to her light. "Follow me, and…hold on to each other." She reached out her hand and took Alexio's, flashing him a smile.

Alexio had probably delivered Markos and Dino also.

Ava stepped out into the darkness, clicked off the light.

Dots sprayed into Sofia's vision, even as her eyes adjusted to the pitch. A hand reached out for hers, and she clasped it, fell in line with the others.

Please let Ava know where she's going, what she's doing.

"Wait! Wait for us!"

Footsteps thumped across the dirt, and Sofia made out Zoë, Dino plastered to her body, a blanket in her hand. "Where are you going?"

Lucien ran up behind them, clutching Sofia's satchel.

"We're leaving—tonight." Sofia pulled Dino into her arms. Caught his chin in her hand, "Are you okay, *xryso mou*?"

He nodded, his eyes so big in his face she could be lost in them forever. Yes, truly he was her treasure.

"That's my brave boy." She kissed Dino on the forehead, handed him back to Zoë. "You be good and stay with Auntie Zoë, and Mama will be right behind you. I promise."

Zoë hiked him onto her hip. "Where are we going?"

"The caves below the olive grove—follow Ava."

Zoë took the satchel from Lucien, slipping into the night.

"What's going on?" His gaze followed Zoë.

"I have the money."

His dark eyes pinned hers, searched them. "What?"

"Or, I'll have the money. For the bribe. Just—go back and get help." She turned, tracking the group into the night—yes, she could still see them, Dino's big eyes trained on her over Zoë's shoulder.

"What are you doing, Sofia?"

"I'm going to free Markos."

"No, I mean how do you think this is all going to end, Sofia?" Lucien grabbed her arm, yanked her back around to face him. "You and Markos are just going to run off together into the night, like you did before, only this time it's going to end happily?" His expression made her feel stripped to her undergarments. "Don't tell me you're still living in that dream."

She shook out of his grip. "It's not a dream. He came back for me."

"He came back for a *treasure*." He held up his fingers, snapped them close to her head. "Wake up. He didn't even know you were here."

"He—would have come back for me."

"He *says*. But he didn't, did he? For ten years, or more. You waited for him, and he didn't show up."

"He was in prison!"

"Again—so he says! How do you know that?" He gave her a terrible, scorching look that turned her raw. "And even if he is telling the truth—tell me, how's he going to feel after you tell him about Dino?"

Everything inside her hollowed.

"It's one thing to accept a son by another man. It's completely another to accept *your brother's son.* And—I'll bet that Dino doesn't even know he has a kid, does he?"

He moved closer, his voice lethal. "That's why you haven't told him, or anyone else, isn't it, Sofia? Did you seduce him?"

Oh, she wanted to slap him, but her muscles wouldn't work.

"I thought so. You seduced *both* of them, didn't you? But Markos still hasn't shaken free of you, has he? What happened—did Dino see you for what you are?"

She hated him. Hated him clear through—hated him more than the colonel, who hadn't pretended to love her. "I *loved* both of them. And I hurt both of them—yes, I..." She turned away, Lucien's words burning. Yes, what would Markos say when he found out about Dino? Her...betrayal?

"But you know what, Sofia?" Lucien stepped away from her, just enough for her to see his smirk. "I don't care. See, here's the difference between me and Markos. I still want you. I don't know why—maybe it's because I know you must have *some* charms. But the fact is—yes, I'll go and bribe the German guards. I'll even risk my neck for your Markos. On one condition."

She let the hatred spiral through her, consume her.

"You have to marry me. Once Markos is free, you come to me. I'll hide you, and even Dino and Zoë, if I have to. I'll hide you from the colonel until the Germans leave. It can't be long now anyway. And then, you'll marry *me.*"

"Why?" Her voice emerged stripped, raw. "Why would you want to marry me?"

He ran a hand down her arm, clasped her hand. "Because you *are* truly beautiful."

She stared at his sea dark eyes.

"And, because Markos wants you."

Then he yanked on her hand, clamping his other around her neck, pulling her hard toward him. His lips banged on hers, crushing hers to her teeth. She tasted the tinny acid of fresh blood, even as his mouth devoured hers. She froze.

He leaned back, considered her. "Do we have an agreement?"

"Why, Lucien?"

He shook his head. "Meet me at the taverna, at dawn."

"Markos won't leave here without me—"

"Yes, he will. Once he sees what you really are, and that he returned to Zante for nothing."

CHAPTER 28

Of all the places for Ava to hide her valuables, Markos's ratty old sea jacket seemed the most ridiculous. Or, perhaps, ideal. After all, it took Sofia running her hands down all the seams—twice—before she found the lump in the bottom edge hem, near the knee. She closed the door to her closet, and by the wan morning light spilling through the window, used a knife to open the seam.

The topaz ring tumbled out into her hand. Yes, now she remembered it. Ava wore it the day Theo married Zoë—the sun turning it the color of the sea on a cool day.

To a German officer staring at a chilly Russian front, it would be worth a fortune.

Definitely Markos's life. She closed her hand around it. Held it against her chest.

Perhaps for such a time as this, Sofia, you have carried my most valuable possession across the sea and back.

For such a time as this.

Sofia slipped the ring onto her finger. Saw herself again in the square that hot day, ivy and orange blossoms twined in her hair, her gaze on Markos as he stood tall beside his father and Theo.

His eyes never strayed off her, beckoning, a sweet hope in them that curled warmth inside her. Somehow, last night, that hope stirred to life.

Secured in his arms as the cool of the morning stole in, she'd felt, for the first time in years, yes—warm. Safe, even.

That same warmth had kept her alive on the frothy waters of the Atlantic, right after she released her grandfather to the sea. Sometimes—probably too often—she went back to that kiss on the boat, and the promise Markos made.

"You won't leave me, right?"

"Never. I promise. Because you are not poison, Sofia Frango."

Not poison.

Maybe, but then again, she *felt* like poison.

She ran her thumb over the ring. Slipped it off and into her sweater pocket.

God will deliver us, daughter. One day at a time.

Could it be that God had sent her across the ocean, to learn English, a smattering of German, used little Dino to drive her home, and then plunked her down in the middle of a war so that—so that He could deliver them all…

Through—her?

Just because we serve it to swine doesn't make it slop. Ava's quiet voice spilled inside, like a drink. No, not slop.

And not even a survivor. A rescuer.

She swept over to the open window—one last view of the city before she fled the house. The moon had already crested the sky, the stars dying into the morning. A few sturdy lights twinkled in the milky darkness, like fireflies. The wind shivered the olive leaves and she breathed deep, drew in the mix of roses and bougainvillea, and the orange tree loping over the house, the tang of the olive grove, the salty lick of the sea.

She loved this view of the city—so different than the one from the taverna. There, with the sea at her back, the city crouching over her, she suffocated.

It depended on where she stood.

Headlights flashed across the courtyard, and she ducked back. The colonel. She watched as he climbed out, closed the door. His gaze slid up to her window and she ducked back.

She could still sneak out. After he came inside, she'd simply—

"Colonel."

Everything inside her seized. No—

"What are you doing here? She'll see you."

"No, she won't—she's helping hide those Jews."

No…*no*…why hadn't she seen it?

"So it worked then."

"We'll recover them. But the important part is—I got him, just like you asked. Everyone thinks it was an ambush."

She saw him, in her mind, skulking outside the burning warehouse.

"Is he alive?"

She hazarded a glance.

"For now."

He stood in the yard, his black cap and sweater eclipsing him in the night. But she knew the trace of his body, knew the way he leaned against the colonel's car, arms folded, as if he mocked the world.

Knew even the hatred in his voice when he said, "We have an agreement then? I'll deliver Markos—and you will leave behind the weapons and armament for our partisans."

Weapons—for Markos's life. He truly had become a man of violence, so much like his father.

The colonel nodded as Lucien stuck out his hand.

A juvenile shard of satisfaction sliced through her when the colonel ignored it. "When?"

"Dawn. Sofia's taverna. And, I might have another surprise for you."

"I don't like surprises."

"This one you will."

Sofia put her hand to her mouth, clamped down on a cry. *Of course.* Lucien never intended to marry her. The slick of relief should have made her feel better. Instead, he meant to hand her over to Markos's enemy—to use her as leverage against Markos? Yes, that made sense.

Apparently, she *did* have value—Markos would spill everything if he knew Sofia's life hung in the balance.

No.

Lucien slipped into the shadows as the colonel stepped into the house.

Sofia shucked off her sweater, securing the ring in her pocket, then tying it tight and shoving it on the windowsill. Then she stepped to the mirror, grabbed her brush, and tugged out the snarls.

The colonel climbed the stairs, his steps thundering down the hall.

She held her breath as he stopped before her door.

His knock nearly sent her through her skin.

She opened the door before he had a chance to notice little Dino missing. Stuck her head through. "I'll be right over."

He nodded, his eyes without expression.

She closed the door, turned her back to it, and let it brace her for a moment. Plan—she needed a plan. But she'd never been a person who figured things out—that was Markos's job. And Dino—or perhaps Dino had simply tried to keep up with life. She seemed to be the one who flung herself into tomorrow without a thought, hoping life might catch up.

Outside, with the dent of light into the steel gray morning, the birds began to chirp.

She opened the door, smoothed her dress, padded out into the hall, her heart in her throat. She wouldn't do this. Not after giving her heart back to Markos.

But—

The colonel opened the door. He'd removed his officer's jacket, draped it on a straight-backed chair at the desk. His satchel sat on the floor beside it.

"I didn't expect you to be awake," he said, taking her hand, pulling her into the room. She ignored the pistol at his waist but noted where it landed when he slipped it off his belt, took it out of its holster, and hid it under his pillow.

Smart. Be smart, Sofia.

He pulled her close, but even as he stared down at her, a new look edged into his eyes. Triumph. More than before, when he'd taken her into his arms and reminded her that she had no power, this victory seemed…

Evil.

She backed away, drew her palms down his arms, lifted his hands. The skin had opened around his knuckles, and she stared at it, trying not to be repulsed. "Are you hurt?"

"We caught some partisans tonight." He lifted a shoulder. "Perhaps my anger overwhelmed me." He kept his gaze on her as he said it, and she kept her hands loose, her face without expression. "Perhaps I should bandage them—"

"No bandage is necessary." He traced his finger down her décolletage. Her skin prickled. "You can take the sting away."

She stiffened. "I…" No. Not anymore. She had tried resisting him in the early days, thinking he wouldn't want an unwilling partner.

Clearly, he hadn't minded so much.

She'd stopped fighting him long ago. But Markos wasn't dead anymore, was he?

Still, she didn't have to forget the lessons she'd learned…

Turning, she ran her hand down his shirt, catching the buttons. "You've had a long night, you must be tired." She pushed him onto the bed, sitting beside him. "I will fetch some water—"

He grabbed her wrist. "Don't try and leave me, Sofia." A strange tinge of what sounded like desperation in his tone shook her. "I—need you." He pulled her close to him and, oddly, put his arm around her. "Stay with me."

She ran her hand down his face. "Close your eyes. I will stay."

His hand shackled her wrist across his chest, even as he closed his eyes.

The gun lay under his pillow.

She lay there, her heart outside her body, watching the dawn slick into the room, over the bed, across the wooden floor.

His chest rose and fell, his breathing even.

She slipped her hand under herself, scooted it toward the pillow.

He opened his eyes, and she found a smile for him. Then he rolled over, toward her.

Her hand closed around the gun.

He pressed one hand above her head, leaned into her.

Now. She snaked out the pistol—jammed the barrel against his head. Screamed—no, more shrieked in a voice that didn't sound remotely like her own— "Back away."

He didn't move, just showed his teeth in a reptilian smile. "You really think you're going to shoot me?"

She nodded, or thought she did, but he gave a harsh laugh and slammed his hand against her arm.

The gun flew across the room.

It triggered as it landed, a sound that rocked her through to her bones as she slammed the palm of her hand into his chin. His head jerked back.

She kicked him and rolled out of his arms.

Landed on the floor beside the bed.

With a roar, he leaped at her. She managed to fling herself away from his fist, and he cursed as his knuckles exploded against the wooden floor. She hoped every one of those wounds opened, bled hard.

"Get away from me!" She scrambled to her knees, but he shackled her ankle. "No!" She kicked at his face. Blood spurted from his nose.

"You little—"

He dragged her toward him, but she caught the edge of the bed, gripped it. "No!" She needed a weapon—a stick or—the pistol! She spied it under the bed—on the other side.

The colonel rose above her, but she turned, kicking at him. She managed another kick that doubled him over.

She rolled and scrambled to her feet.

He caught her hair, pulled her back.

She covered her face with her hands as he picked her up by her arms and flung her onto the bed.

She hadn't even landed before she sprang off.

Crashed onto the floor.

Swooped up the gun. "Stop!"

He froze, his eyes narrowing at the barrel, now shaking, pointed at his naked chest. "What are you going to do, Sofia, shoot me?"

"Stay back."

"You can't pull the trigger. I know you. You don't have it in you."

"Are you kidding me? It's *all* I have in me. You took the rest." The gun shook in her grip.

He leaped at her then, and she screamed.

The pistol recoiled in her hands as the shot cracked the morning air.

The colonel howled, pitching onto the floor, holding his leg. Blood surged from his knee and he rolled in agony. "You—you—!"

She didn't have to know the nuances of German to understand that word.

"Poison is the word you're looking for," she said as she backed out of the room.

* * * *

Sofia had watched Markos enough during the days when he drove for Uncle Jimmy to know how to put the colonel's scout car into drive, how to maneuver it out of the courtyard onto the dusty road to town. Without a telephone, without a vehicle, he hadn't a prayer of getting to the taverna before dawn.

Please let her arrive before Lucien.

The pistol lay in the well of her lap. She picked it up and placed it on the seat next to her, her thoughts scandalous.

Did she think she'd just hold Lucien at gunpoint and make him give her Markos?

Maybe.

Adrenaline prickled her—her stomach, arms, legs—even out to her fingertips. She saw the colonel, clutching his leg—she thought the shot had hit his knee, but she couldn't be sure. Did she want him to die?

She shook the thought from her head. She hadn't killed him. That should count for something.

The faintest hint of morning nudged the shadows in the alleys she wound toward the taverna. Grapevine hung from wooden porticos. Now and again she passed a goat wandering the streets, chased a dog from the road.

She parked the scout above the taverna. If Lucien saw it, he'd assume the colonel had kept his part of the bargain.

Swiping the pistol from the seat, she tucked it into her sweater—the one she'd retrieved from the windowsill of her room on her dash from the house. The colonel's voice had chased her down the stairs, into the cool morning.

Now she held her breath as she tiptoed into the dark taverna. Ava had covered the remaining bread and cheeses from the day before in pots on the wooden chopping block. The smell of olive oil, fresh basil, and dill embedded the stone walls. She crept out of the kitchen, onto the portico, half expecting to see Markos and Lucien—perhaps one of them bleeding on the stone floor.

Odd that Lucien would pick this place to betray Markos—or perhaps not odd. She stood on the cold porch and memory caught her.

Markos, watching her from the table until he had the courage to get up, reach out his hand to ask her to dance. The band, the taste of celebration in the air as they danced. Markos's hand in hers, roughened by the sea, his eyes shining.

Lucien stood in the shadows. She'd spotted him as they danced, seen fear in his eyes. Then Kostas—angry. Loud. His fury exploding.

She pressed her hand to her stomach, shuffled out into the sunlight.

A fiery sun simmered on the horizon, crimson upon the gray waters. Frothy waves gulped at the shore. The golden sand seemed almost black even as the light clawed at it. And, on a lick of wind, she could taste a storm.

Still, the coming sunrise heated the air, and she lifted her face to it, let it soak her bones. For a second, she held her hand out, opened her mouth to it. Drank it in.

"You came."

She closed one hand over the ring in her pocket.

The other over the pistol.

She half-turned. "Of course."

Lucien stood just outside the portico—where he'd stood so many years ago, only this time without a trace of fear in his dark eyes. He still wore the garb of partisan—or, perhaps, now traitor.

"Did you bring the money?"

"It's a ring—a topaz ring. You can—sell it. Or give it away. Did it work—did you free Markos?"

All those years playing the vamp for Uncle Jimmy, the sparrow to the colonel, paid off. Not a quiver in her voice.

He entered the portico, his boots scuffing on the stone. "Of course."

"I want to see him."

Lucien's eyes narrowed.

"Please. To say good-bye." She looked away, as if embarrassed. Slipped the pistol from her pocket.

She'd made up her mind on the way down the mountain. Saw it in her head.

She'd already shot one man. Certainly—

"Sofia."

Markos appeared in the corridor of the taverna. She winced at a bruise on his cheek, the way he held the wall as he eased down the steps.

Still, seeing him here, in the taverna, standing across from Lucien, it brought tears to her eyes.

She wiped them away with more violence than it merited.

"I'm okay. Lucien and his men did some sort of miracle—I'm not sure how—"

"I know how." She took a breath, listened to her heart pound in her head—and lifted the gun from behind her. "The SS never had you, Markos."

She expected Lucien to flinch, but his lips tightened into a knot of anger.

Markos, however, came at her. "Sofia, what are you doing?"

Lucien raised his hands, glanced at the door where Markos had appeared.

"He's not coming," Sofia said on a sliver of breath.

Markos stopped. "What are you talking about? Who's not coming?" He reached out for her but she slipped away.

"Tell him, Lucien. Tell him how you betrayed us all." The weapon shook. She put both hands on it. This time she wouldn't miss. Beyond her, the waves roared onto the shore, seagulls cried.

Lucien shot a look at Markos, then back, shook his head, as if to say *this crazy woman—*

Fine. She glanced at Markos. "He was going to sell you to the Germans. To the colonel."

Markos gave no indication that he comprehended her words.

"She's lying, Markos. She just doesn't want me to tell you the truth."

"What truth?"

Now. She should shoot the traitor now. "I am telling the truth—Lucien has betrayed us!"

"Her son belongs to your brother—she seduced him."

She couldn't look—not with Lucien so close to the entrance of the taverna—but she heard it, in the swept breath, in the strange sound Markos emitted.

Oh—see…

"You betrayed us, Lucien?" Markos voice cut through her, even as he stood beside her.

Lucien recoiled, one eye closing as if he'd been slapped. She saw it then, the years of anger, stewing for this moment, as Lucien's face twisted.

"Why?"

She wouldn't look at him—oh. Her gaze went to his—out of her peripheral, she just had to know—had he even heard Lucien?

Lucien kicked a table. It barreled toward her and she jerked. A shot ripped through the thatch in the ceiling.

Lucien speared the sky, frozen in his escape.

"Lucien."

"I'm finally giving you what you should have had years ago—justice. You don't just get to come back here, steal Sofia away, leave us with your mess again." This Lucien she recognized—the one who'd come running to the end of the dock so many years ago.

Markos didn't move, his body so tight she thought he might snap. Sofia waited for him to explode, perhaps dive at Lucien. But he just stood there, breathing Lucien's words in and out.

She tightened her grip on the pistol. *Shoot!*

"You're right. I don't."

Markos's calm words shook her. "I *don't* deserve to make it right. But I learned long ago that God doesn't give us what we deserve. If that were the case, we'd all be in prison. We'd all be—dead."

Markos wore an expression like she'd never seen—almost as if he'd been turned inside out, shaken, put back fresh and new. "But see, I learned that God is also the giver of second chances, and third and fourth—not because we deserve it, but because that's who He is. We are that valuable to Him."

Redemption. So that's what it looked like.

"As you are to me, brother."

Lucien drew in a breath, his eyes black. He shook his head.

"Let him go, Sofia."

What? "No! He is just going to betray us—"

"Give me the gun. I'm not going to let you shoot him. You're not this person." His calm voice threaded through her, reached deep.

"No! You don't understand. He was going to hand me over to the Nazis too!"

Lucien jerked.

"Is that true?" Markos's voice, low, lethal, scared even her.

"You love her," Lucien said simply.

"Give me the gun, Sofia. If anyone should kill him, it should be me. I already have my hands bloody in this taverna."

She glanced at him, the dark slice of fury on his face, and something inside her died. So much for the possibility, the miracle of redemption.

Her throat filled as she handed the pistol to Markos. She turned away, her hand closing around the ring, waiting for the shot to echo against the stones. Perhaps it would be fitting for it to end here.

The gun clattered on the stone floor.

"Go, Lucien."

She turned in time to see Lucien's face, whitened even in the gold of the dawn. Then he turned and fled the taverna.

CHAPTER 29

She didn't know this Markos—the one who had lost his mind.

"Why did you let Lucien go? He'll run straight to the colonel—and they'll find us!" Sofia chased Markos through the kitchen of the taverna.

"Maybe. But hopefully we'll be gone by then." He grabbed her hand, pulled her out into the street. The sun had just begun to boil away the moisture from the morning.

"By then? What's happening—where are we going?"

"You're coming with me."

She had no words for that. "You still want me to go with you—after—Markos, didn't you hear Lucien?" She hated the terrible burning in her throat, but— "I *seduced* your brother, Markos. *I have his son.*"

Markos stopped then, looked at her, and she knew. Oh—his gaze went right through her.

She knew it. He could no longer see her, really.

Just her crimes.

The sun cleared the house, burned the back of her neck, sweat driving down her spine. For a second she longed to slip back into the cool shadow of the taverna. She started to pull away, but he reached up and touched her face, ran his thumb down her cheek.

"Zante is about to be liberated by the British. I received a message from the OSS before the rescue mission, and they're commencing liberation at 0600. We have to get off this island."

"Not without my son." She stepped away from his touch. "And Zoë. And your mother."

She couldn't read his eyes.

"We'll take them *all* with us. Where are they?"

"Your mother hid them in the caves beneath the olive grove. They're waiting for me—us."

He turned, started up the gravel path.

"Wait—we don't have time." She pulled him up the hill to the colonel's scout, gleaming in the sunlight. "Drive."

Markos stared after her then caught up quick, jumping into the driver's seat. "Do I want to know where you got this?"

"No." She slid into the passenger seat.

"Hold on."

She pressed one hand to the ceiling, the other to the dashboard as they crashed through the streets, toward the olive grove. The silvery green leaves shone like knives as they careened into the courtyard. Sofia held her breath—please don't let the colonel be waiting with a cadre of guards to mow them down.

The house remained silent.

Maybe she *had* killed him.

She glanced up at his darkened window, sucking in a breath as Markos broke through the gate and bumped into the field. A couple of goats skittered out of their way as Markos muscled the car down the lane between trees. "Where to?"

"It's at the end of the property. Near the cliffs."

His expression bespoke some sort of memory. "Right. Of course." In the distance, thunder rumbled.

"British Mosquito bombers. The fleet can't be far behind."

The caves looked different in the revelation of dawn. She remembered a tumble of rocks that led into a hollow of earth, the musty smell clawing out to chill her. If Ava hadn't pointed out the grotto, she would have never identified the lip of rock that hid the mouth of the cave. Now, light spilled in, revealing veins of gold and silver that twined deep into the cliff.

She got out of the car and scrambled into the mouth, slipped, nearly fell as pebbles tumbled into the darkness.

Markos caught her. "I'm right behind you."

"Your mother had a light. Now it's so—black."

He held out his hand.

She took it. One last time.

Because, well, she couldn't go anywhere with a man who despised her son, right?

Or did he despise her?

"How far does this go?" he asked, as she followed him into the maw of the cave.

"I don't know—it opens into a huge cavern. I think the sea spills into it; there's a sort of lake—"

"Shh—"

She stilled, even as she brailled her way deeper, testing each footstep twice. Were those voices? "Ava!"

The darkness ate her voice. If it weren't for Markos's grip, she might have let it swallow her, paralyze her.

A light flickered, caught her. Then it scraped against the wall and puddled at her feet. "Over here."

The hand holding hers spasmed. She tightened her grip around it. *Yes, Markos...*

The tunnel opened into the gullet of the cave, and in the wan glow she made out Ava, panning the flashlight across her eyes.

Settling on the man behind her.

"Oh." Ava sucked in a breath, her hand clasped over her mouth.

"*Matera.*" Markos's low voice might have been for himself, but Ava let out a cry.

Sofia stepped away as Ava pulled her son to her bosom, her hands pressing at his back as if she might actually draw him into herself.

Yes, she understood that feeling. Dino scrabbled across the rock toward her and leaped into her arms. She swept him up. His legs clamped around her waist, his entire body shivering. She breathed him in. "We're going to be okay. I promise."

Behind him, Zoë rose to her feet, shuffled near, her eyes on Markos. She glanced at Sofia, then back to Markos, still holding his mother. "Theo."

For a second, Markos whitened, as if the name stripped something from him.

But Zoë came back to herself and rescued him. "Markos."

Markos stepped away from his mother, her hand still in his. "Zoë." He reached for her, but as he did, the ground trembled.

Zoë caught his forearm as Sofia rocked on her footing. "What was that?"

"The British are bombing the port. It's probably aftershocks. We need to get out of here." Markos took Zoë's hand as, from some cleft in the darkness, the Mizrahi family moved forward.

"Markos Stavros. I remember you hauling in fish." Dr. Alexio extended his hand, the same one that had cradled him at birth.

Markos stared at him as if he might be a specter from the past. "Dr. Alexio."

The elderly man smiled. "And my family. Your Sofia found us."

His Sofia. She glanced at Markos and found his eyes on her, something like pride in them. She kissed Dino's head, tried to swallow.

"I have a ship meeting me on the other side of the island. We'll get there—you'll all be safe. The British will give you asylum."

Another tremor. Sofia fell to her knees, bracing herself with her hand.

"Mama!" Dino's arms vised her neck.

"It's okay, Dino," Sofia said, her hand stinging. She climbed back to her feet.

Markos had stilled. *Dino.* "You named your son after his father."

Sofia glanced past him to Ava.

Her gaze flickered over Sofia. "He's *Dino's* child?"

Oh, how she thanked the shadows. "He never knew. I'm—so sorry. I didn't know how to tell…"

"What do you mean, he never knew…?"

Sofia had no words. She looked at Markos, and he took his mother's hands.

"Mama, Dino died in the war in Europe. But you would have been so proud—he became a doctor. He saved hundreds of lives including mine."

"He became a doctor." Ava closed her eyes, as if trying to picture it.

Sofia saw him then, in his lab coat, his stethoscope around his neck. Remembered his stories from the hospital. Yes, his mother would have been proud of him.

The cavern floor convulsed.

Sofia pitched forward, her arms clutching Dino.

Markos caught her, cushioning her as they smacked into the rock.

Boulders broke free, bombing the viscera of the cavern, and pebbles rained on them as she lay in Markos's shelter.

Dust boiled out from the entrance, burning her eyes, salting her throat. Sofia coughed, her body wracking.

She wasn't the only one.

"Are you okay?" Markos said between bouts. He had one hand cradled behind Dino's head.

"Yes," she finally managed. "What happened?"

"Mama—can I borrow your flashlight?" Markos untangled himself from Sofia and retrieved the light. He disappeared through the cloud of dust into the gullet of the tunnel.

Without the flashlight, darkness bled into her eyes, her mouth, her pores. She clutched Dino and fought to breathe. Markos's footsteps slapped against the stone as he returned, a phantom out of the murky gloom.

"Bad news." Markos splashed the light across the cavern, as if searching for something. It panned across the dark waters, on the foamy spittle floating on top. "An aftershock—maybe a direct hit, who knows? It crumbled the mouth of the cave. We're trapped."

* * * *

Trapped.

The word hurtled around her brain as she watched Markos stalk the length of the cave and back.

Trapped.

"Are you sure?" Sofia tried to keep the tang of fear from her voice. "Did you check—"

"I'm sure."

She recognized this Markos. The same Markos who had stood in the train station and handed her over to Dino, ready for his own demise.

Yes, in the glow of the light, he looked every inch the rebel she'd met in the wine cellar, an angry, almost nail-bitten look on his face. He stalked out to the edge of the inky water.

Then he stripped off his shirt.

She tried, oh, she tried to keep her gaze away, but it arrested on the blooming red bruises across his chest where a boot had met his ribs.

She hoped she'd hit the colonel's femoral artery.

Sofia tumbled Dino to Zoë's arms, launched herself at Markos. "No. No—you are *not* going in there."

He rounded, and his strong hands caught her arms. She expected that same unbridled passion—the kind that could shake right through her bones to sweep away her words of protest. Instead, his voice lowered, something in it she didn't recognize.

"Listen, when I was a boy, I used to swim on the other side of these cliffs. There were caves there called Whistler's Drink. I knew about them, and I always knew they tracked back into the mountain. But I was always afraid to go in them." He glanced at the water, back to her. "We have no choice, Sofia. There's a tunnel somewhere under this water—and I'm going to find it."

"You're going to drown—"

"No—listen, I'll find the current. There has to be a waterway to the sea." He flashed his light onto the water. "See—look. The water is moving, in and out of the tunnel. Which means there are waves pulling at it. I just need to find them, follow them through—"

"And what if it's too tight? What if you get stuck?"

He glanced up, behind her, to Alexio's family, his mother, Zoë, and Dino. Then he gave her a hard look. She knew it too well. "We don't have a choice."

"Use the rope, Markos." Ava held out the rope from the barn. "We'll hold one end."

Yes. The rope they'd used to tie themselves together as they stumbled down into the cave.

Markos grabbed it, looped it around his waist. He handed Sofia the other end. "Don't let go."

She glared at him. "I hate this—this is a terrible idea. Please, Markos, there has to be another way—"

"Shh, Sofia. We're going to be fine. God will deliver—"

"Don't you dare say that to me, Markos Stavros!"

"God will—"

She couldn't help herself. With everything inside her, she slapped him.

The sound ricocheted off the cave, a thousand times sharper than she'd imagined, and it knifed right into her soul. "Don't you say that," she whispered.

He tightened his jaw, his eyes in hers wet. Then nodded. "Of course you can't believe. I guess it's too much to expect."

He gave her a long look.

She hadn't a hope of reading it.

Then he kissed her on the forehead, walked to the edge of the pond, and dove into the cauldron.

CHAPTER 30

"Markos!" Oh, she hated herself for letting her fears bubble free, hated the way she called him back. "Markos!"

Of course. She stared at the oily water, every word slicked out of her. What did she expect from one of the Stavros brothers?

Ava cast her light upon the pond, dark as ink, edged in foam. Sofia couldn't make out anything, let alone the bottom. The rope bit into her hands.

Her heartbeat thundered in her ears. *Please...*

How long could he stay down there—had it been a minute? Two? She gulped in her own breath—maybe if she held hers...

But the air shuffled out of her.

She should pull him—

"Pull him back," Zoë said.

"Wait," Ava said. "Wait. My son knows the sea."

Sofia's pulse thundered against the gulp of water rumbling deep inside the cave. And in the veins below the cliff floated Markos, maybe trapped, maybe even drowning. Sofia ran her thumb over the hemp. *Please—*

Ava stepped over to her, the light searching the depths. "Pull, Sofia."

Sofia gave a tug—but the rope tightened in her grip, threatened to yank from her hands. She yanked back. "No!"

It nearly ripped out of her grip. "Markos!"

Ava's mouth set in a dark, pinched line, her light scanning the surface.

"Markos!"

A splash, then gulping of air.

Ava stripped her light across the waves, uncovered Markos in the corner, clutching a ledge. Blood dripped from his shoulder, a raw scrape from the teeth of the rocks.

He kicked over to her, clung to the edge, his hair back, his face suddenly, strangely boyish. It seemed, in the passage through the darkness, he'd discovered more than just a tunnel. "I knew it— I always knew it." He leaned back into the water, ducked his face, came up, shaking his head fast. "Whistler's Drink is just on the other side. I tied the rope to some coral. We're going to be okay."

She didn't even know where to start to protest. *Okay...?* "You can't be serious. What about your mother—"

"I can swim." Ava had already stripped off her shawl.

"And Dr. Alexio—"

"Child, I was swimming before—"

"What about Dino?" Her voice shrilled, and in her arms, Dino began to cry.

"I'll carry him. We'll go one by one. We can hide in the cave on the other side while I contact help." Markos pulled himself out of the water.

"It's the only way out of here." He stood and put his wet hands on her. "Listen, I tied the rope—you can stay here and hold it. They'll go through one by one. I'll be right there with them. It's not that far—I promise."

"Go into a dark cave without a clue where it leads? I don't think so."

"Sofia, you can hang on to me. I won't leave you."

She jerked away from him then. "Dino will drown."

"I'll take care of him."

"How? What are you going to do—*breathe for him*?"

"If I have to." He cupped her face with his hands, his warm breath on her face, now his lips moving to her ears. "And I will breathe for you too, Sofia. To my very last breath."

She wanted to believe him—the way he skimmed his lips against her cheeks, then everything in his voice as he began to describe his plan to Ava and the rest of them.

But she just stared into the blackness and imagined the water swallowing her.

She could do just about anything. Travel across the sea, bury her grandfather on the way, croon like a flapper, chop her hair off at her ears, learn German, and play the maid for the highbrows in Minneapolis. She could bear a child and even barter herself to keep him alive. Yes, she could—and had done just about anything.

Not this.

She placed it now, that deep, engulfing, deafening thunder.

It wasn't coming from the cave.

* * * *

"After Mother, you're next, Sofia. You and Dino. You'll go together." Markos reached out for his mother's hand.

Next. No— A sort of hysterical moan emerged from her even as Ava handed Dino into her lap and eased into the water.

Markos caught her in his arms. "We'll just follow the rope, Mother. There's nothing to be afraid of."

"Oh, I know, Markos." Her dark hair, streaked in with gray, shone against the black milk of the water. Markos gave one last look to Sofia. "I'll be right back, I promise."

She clenched her teeth, digging deep to find a nod.

But he didn't swim away. Instead, he met her eyes. "God *will* deliver us, Sofia."

She hadn't the strength to argue. Horror had scraped her thin by watching, one by one, the Mizrahi family sink into the blackness. She'd long since begun ignoring the screaming inside. Now Dino turned into her, and she tucked his head under her chin.

Markos reached for his mother's hands—put them on the rope. "Deep breath now..."

They slipped under the surface. Sofia clung to the rope, feeling their handholds traverse it until they slipped into the claws of the tunnel.

God will deliver us.

Oh, how she *wanted* to devour his words, let them nourish her, like Ava. And, apparently, Markos.

Even Zoë. Her words whispered inside Sofia. *Bless the* L*ORD, O my soul, and forget not all his benefits: who forgiveth all thine iniquities; who healeth all thy diseases; who redeemeth thy life from destruction; who crowneth thee with lovingkindness and tender mercies....*

Beyond the cave, the waves drummed the walls, as if trying to beat them down.

Forgiveness. Healing. Lovingkindness—mercy?

Why couldn't she see it, believe like...

The cave convulsed around her. Boulders splashed into the pool. Water crested into her lap, ripping at her grip. Dino screamed, clenching her neck in a hold that swiped out her breath.

The rope ripped from her hands.

She hung on to Dino even as she dove for it, but it sank too fast—*No!*

The darkness sucked it under.

She splashed the water but touched nothing. "No!" Her voice echoed against the walls, bounced back to her, raising gooseflesh.

No—no— She wrapped her arms around Dino, staring at the waters, listening to rocks plunge into the sea.

It started faintly, more a feeling, a murmur more than a tune, but something stirred inside, a humming, notes. She let it bubble out, gave it strength.

A different song than the one she'd forgotten, but she knew it all the same. The song filled the cavern, a soft thrum of noise that rebounded to her, settled in her chest.

She stroked Dino's head and let herself return to the taverna, to that moment when she believed life would be as simple as dancing with Markos.

She slipped into Dino's embrace in the kitchen of Elsie's boarding-house, his soft voice in her ear.

She found the tune, heard inside it Dino's laughter, Markos's whispers.

Little Dino's smile.

She rocked as she hummed away the burning inside, raising the volume, sinking into it.

Letting it overwhelm her.

A splash, then gulping of air.

She picked up the flashlight, panned it across the room. Markos clung to the rocks, working his way back to her. "The rope—I pulled it and it came back to me. What happened?"

"I don't know—it just ripped out of my hands—"

"I thought maybe the cave had collapsed." He rested his head in his forearms, his shoulders rising and falling. He shivered. "I thought I heard—were you singing?"

She couldn't answer him.

"We need to go, Sofia. The British are still bombing the shore, and already the tunnel is collapsing. Another nearby hit, and I'm afraid we're going to get trapped—"

As if cosmically heeding his words, a shock wave rumbled through the cavern. Markos reached for Dino.

"No!" Dino clung to her with all his toddler strength.

She held him, her eyes searching Markos's. "He's three. He can't—he'll drown."

Markos met her gaze, in his a sort of sadness, or perhaps simply the truth. He said nothing as he hauled himself out of the water.

"What are you doing?"

"I'm staying here. With you."

"What—*No!* You can't do that."

"Yes, I can. I should have done this long ago."

She cast her eyes over him, the way he drew up his legs to himself, shivered in the clammy air. "You really mean to stay."

"Where else would I go? My life changed the moment I saw you, Sofia. Everything simply clicked into place. You are the reason I came back to Zante. I didn't know it—but God did. Do you really think that I'd turn my back on you?"

He brushed the dust from her face, running his hand across her cheek. "I'd die for you, Sofia."

"You already did, once."

"No, I *lived* for you."

Something told her that perhaps that's exactly what it took to survive. Hope. *Her?*

Oh, Markos. To have pinned so much on so little.

"And my son, Markos? Would you die for him?"

Markos met her eyes, his face crumpling.

Oh. Please, no, she didn't need his answer—

"Of *course* I would." He lifted his head, let frustration show in those beautiful eyes. "Sofia, Dino would have been *thrilled* to have a son. He *loved* you."

"I loved him too." She let the words be as brutal as she could. Maybe it would make Markos see the truth, slip back into the black water to freedom.

"How could you not? I'm *glad* you had each other."

She didn't recognize this man, truly.

"I'm not a fool who thinks I deserved you then. I don't deserve you even now."

"I'm no good for you—"

"Don't tell me you still think you're poison!"

She looked away.

"Oh—you do. Oh, Sof." He pulled her hard to himself, wrapped his arms around her and Dino. "Don't you know you're the cure, baby? You're what healed Dino—and *me.* You saw us both for what we hoped to be. You believed in us. You made us both better men."

She closed her eyes, letting his words find her scars, breathing them in.

"I will love your son, Sofia. Inside this cave—or out. Please—out?"

It was the please, of course, and the "I love you" that followed it that made her nod. He took the flashlight from her hands and eased into the water.

She kissed her son. "Go with Markos, Dino. I'll be right behind you. Markos won't let you go, I promise."

Markos met her eyes, nodded. She unlatched Dino from her neck, handed him to Markos. Dino's eyes widened, his lip quivering.

"Shh," Markos said, as he took the boy into his arms.

She sank into the brackish water, the chill prickling her skin, cooler than she would have guessed. No wonder he'd shivered.

Her skirt ballooned around her waist.

"Listen. Once we go in the tunnel, we can't turn around. There's no room, and we'll get stuck. We just have to keep moving. There's no rope, so hang on to me. Don't let me go."

And perhaps that had been her problem all along. Letting them go without a fight. Or perhaps—letting *herself* go without a fight.

"We'll go with the current, but it could turn against us, and if it does, we'll have to kick hard. Use the rocks to pull yourself through—there are lots of little nooks and crannies you can hang on to. Whatever you do, don't let the current push you backward."

Oh—she couldn't—

He gripped her hard around the neck, and before she could brace herself, he kissed her. She tasted desperation—or perhaps boldness—and for a second she was on the boat, in his arms, their future in his touch.

Then he turned to Dino. "Take a big, deep breath for me, champ, and don't breathe until we get to the other side."

Dino nodded. Markos opened his mouth, and they breathed in together.

Then he dove below the surface.

Sofia gobbled up a breath…

The current grabbed her, just as Markos warned, and she let it propel her into the throat of the tunnel. She opened her eyes, desperate, but she saw nothing as she held Markos's pant leg. She fought a scream, panic burning her lungs, and tried not to let her imagination take her.

The passageway narrowed, the walls nipping at her even as she kicked with the flow. *Hurry!*

Then it stopped. The flow died and the sea gathered itself to spit her back into the depths.

Markos twisted in the water, as if torn between kicking hard and dislodging her. She clung to his pant leg, the fabric squeezing out from her grip.

Then the current rushed back at her. It ripped at her skirt, tangling her legs.

They weren't going to make it.

Markos's hand found hers in the blackness, a vise grip, as if he feared she'd let go. He kicked again, but they floated backward in the current.

They were headed back into the cave.

Dino needed the air.

But Markos's would die before he'd let her go.

Forgive me, Markos. She pushed him away.

Markos foot caught her in the jaw as he kicked forward.

Light flashed in her eyes as the pain splashed through her.

Keep swimming. Keep…

She scrabbled for purchase on the ridges and grooves of the tunnel, fighting the current, her fingertips ripping. She should turn back—the cavern, with its murky air—lay right behind her, didn't it? She put her hand up to turn around—

Her knees scraped the bottom. No, she'd get stuck—or wait, had she already turned around?

Her lungs turned to fire. She turned the other way, lunged for a handhold, anything—

She slammed into a wall. Her head burned, as if cut. How had she turned around—where—

Her breath hiccoughed out.

She lashed out, hitting the wall. No. It wouldn't end like this. She wasn't going to die here in this tunnel, like some sea urchin. She had a son, a man she loved—*God—deliver me!*

Beneath her, in the bowels of the cave, she heard a rumble, or a growl, as if the earth opened to swallow her.

The current stilled, whirlpooling around her as the tunnel shuddered. Under her hands, the rock convulsed.

Then something pushed her—water, frothing forth in a wave, tumbling her, ripping her skin, knocking her against the walls.

Something brushed her hand. She fought to find it again, twisting, clawing at the water, black dotting her eyes.

Light. It strobed against the blackness. She reached for it. Kicked.

A hand found hers. She put everything into clenching it.

The water warmed, and even as she began to burp out the last of her air, she cleared the darkness.

Hands around her waist pushed her to the surface.

She broke into the light, gulped in cool, fresh, salty air.

"Just breathe—you'll be okay." Markos's voice in her ear. He secured his arm around her waist, pulled her against his chest. "Why did you let go?"

She gasped, gulped in more air. It razored her lungs.

"I—what…?" She couldn't catch her breath as she peered through the teeth of a cavern to the pewter blues of the morning sky.

He shook, even as he held her to himself.

"Dino—where—"

"I think the cavern collapsed? The shock wave must have pushed you out. I would have never seen you but for the cave-in. Half this cave also came down. I barely got Dino out—"

She wanted to collapse there but—

"Where..."—she coughed water from her lungs—"where's Dino?"

"He's with Dr. Alexio—" He started to pull her to the opening.

"What the matter?"

Markos pushed her to the edge of the cave, helped her out. On the other side, the sea crashed against a tumble of rocks. "Hurry, Sofia. He wasn't breathing."

* * * *

Breathe, Dino, breathe!

The voice propelled Sofia as she dove into the water, long strokes taking her out into the blue of the sea.

Breaking the surface, she gulped in a hot, watery breath. Markos surfaced behind her.

"Where is he?"

"I don't—wait—there." Markos grabbed her shoulder, turned her.

Out beyond the reef of the shore, a cutter coughed black smoke. A *German* cutter. And men in uniform pulling Ava aboard from a dingy tethered to the boat.

No!

She kicked out ahead of him, but he grabbed her leg. "Wait—what are you doing?"

"My son is on that boat!"

"Yes, I know, I just..." He stared back at the ship. "I can't believe Lucien betrayed us."

"I can." She turned in the water, took a breath. Met his eyes. "God will deliver us, right?"

Water clung to his eyelashes as he stared at her, as if drinking in her words. "Right."

Right.

Then she swam for the ship in quick strokes, eating the waves, coughing out the foamy water that burned her throat, her eyes.

Markos swept past her.

She waited to see the colonel appear at the stern, robed in his grey uniform, and knew that she'd never let him hurt her again. No matter what it took.

Yet, as she swam closer, she saw the men reaching over the side of the boat to haul Ruth Ann Mizrahi aboard wore sweaters, fisherman caps…

Partisans?

They'd already swept Markos aboard when she reached the boat. Indeed, partisans whom she recognized rescued her, and she shook the water from her face, her gaze skimming over the sodden Mizrahi family, across a shivering Ava and Zoë, to Dino.

His tiny body lay on the deck, grey, sodden. She had a scream in her somewhere, but it webbed in her chest as she dropped to her knees, crawling toward him. *Breathe!*

Markos—probably Markos—grabbed her from behind. "Wait!"

Alexio knelt at Dino's head, and now lifted the boy, bending him forward at the waist. Pounded his back. "Dino, breathe."

He raised Dino's arms. Pounded him again. Zoë began to moan. Ava turned her, pulled her into her breast.

Alexio hit Dino's back again.

Water spat from Dino's mouth. He hiccoughed, then his body wracked with coughs.

Sofia lurched toward him, again, but Markos gripped her arm. "Let him breathe."

Let him breathe. Let them *all* breathe. She watched her little boy writhe with the intake of air, her own body curling in with his pain.

Then he began to cry. Sweet sounds that rent the air, made them all, suddenly, shake to life.

Markos let her go, and she swallowed Dino into her arms, inhaling his sodden body.

Breathe, just breathe.

Beside her, Ava broke into weeping.

Zoë knelt beside them, her arms around Sofia and Dino. Ava too, her hands on Dino's head. "Dino. My sweet Dino. Of course, I knew it."

Sofia met her gaze, let herself feel the forgiveness.

"My son has come back to me, Sofia." Ava reached out, touched her hand. "Thank you."

"I'm sorry I didn't tell you."

Ava nodded, her hand going to Sofia's face, then to Markos's. "It's enough that you delivered my boys home."

Behind them, smoke blackened the harbor, the German transport ship in flames. The skyline turned bright orange. A flock of spitfires buzzed over them.

"Let's get out of here." Markos unhanded her, and she lifted her head to watch him find his feet. Backlit by the sunlight, his body filled out to manhood, his black hair glistening and wild in his face, freshly baptized by the sea—yes, this was the Markos she'd imagined.

Longed for.

Loved.

Alexio reached out his hand. "Galen would be proud of his fisherman son."

Sofia didn't have to see Markos's face to see his smile.

"Let's pull up anchor before the Germans find out we stole their boat."

The voice jerked her attention to the wheelhouse. Lucien, his black sweater pushed up at the elbows, came down the stairs onto the belly of the boat.

"You stole their boat? You came out to rescue us?" Sofia couldn't help the surprise in her voice.

He glanced at her then, wearing the inklings of the scoundrel smile she'd missed too long. Lifted his shoulder in a shrug.

Markos reached out to Lucien. "Friends?"

Sofia watched them, the two men, ruddy, zealous.

"No, Markos," Lucien said quietly, reaching out with a groan to grasp it. "Brothers. Always."

Markos smiled, and she could have sung a song to it.

She buried her face in Dino's hair, relishing his tiny body in her arms, now heaving. "Shh."

As the boat lurched, Markos slipped into the shadow beside her, his body warm against hers. He looped his arm around her, around Dino.

Dino looked up at him, his tears dying to hiccoughs.

Markos ran a hand down his cheek. "You're a brave kid, Dino. I'm proud of you. I think you get that from your papa."

Dino stared at him, his eyes as blue as Markos's, almost drinking him in. Suddenly he disentangled himself from Sofia and climbed onto Markos's lap.

Markos opened his arms, a tenderness on his face that shook her through. He kissed the boy's head as little Dino nestled into his strong arms.

Then, like two fisherman they stared out into the horizon.

She should have known her son would fit so well into Markos's embrace. But she didn't expect the mercy of it, the way it reached inside and filled her. Made her whole.

"Any room for me in there?" she asked softly, nudging herself into the knot of his arms.

"It's where you belong," Markos said, and he drew her in, wrapping his arm around her waist, the tang of the sea in his skin.

Beside her, Ava sat, her hands upturned, her face to the sun.

"Do you think you could find a song for me, Sofia?" Markos said in her ear. "Something of home?"

Sofia closed her eyes and let the sunshine bathe her as the boat parted the Ionian Sea. "For you, Markos, I could even find the words."

And then, to the sound of the motor spilling thunder out in its wake, Sofia loosed the song too long tangled in her heart and delivered it up to the hazy golden morning.

summerside
PRESS